BITTERFROST

Bryan Gruley

SEVERN
HOUSE

First world edition published in Great Britain and the USA in 2025
by Severn House, an imprint of Canongate Books Ltd,
14 High Street, Edinburgh EH1 1TE.

severnhouse.com

British Library Cataloguing-in-Publication Data
A CIP catalogue record for this title is available from the British Library.

ISBN-13: 978-1-4483-1540-6 (cased)
ISBN-13: 978-1-4483-1541-3 (e-book)

Typeset by Palimpsest Book Production Ltd.,
Falkirk, Stirlingshire, Scotland.

Praise for *Bitterfrost*

"Visceral, vivid, and suspenseful, *Bitterfrost* immerses readers in a chilly – and chilling – world of lost dreams and deadly feuds. I was instantly and completely engrossed. Masterfully done"
Meg Gardiner, #1 *New York Times* bestselling author

"*Bitterfrost* is my kind of crime novel . . . propelled by a razor-sharp plot that swirls around things we can all relate to: getting older, opportunities missed, and the uniting power of sports. Gruley's at the top of his game"
Alex Segura, bestselling and acclaimed author of *Secret Identity* and *Alter Ego*

"Intense, insular, stunning, Bryan Gruley's *Bitterfrost* exposes the blood and violence churning beneath the ice surface of a tiny northern Michigan town"
Reed Farrel Coleman, *New York Times* bestselling author of *Blind to Midnight*

"A riveting mix of small-town mystery, legal drama, and high-stakes crime thriller. With crisp prose and a vivid portrayal of Michigan hockey culture, *Bitterfrost* is slick as ice and just as chilling"
Tessa Wegert, author of *The Coldest Case*

"Haunting, atmospheric, and absolutely gut-wrenching, *Bitterfrost* shows the oh-so-talented Bryan Gruley perfecting the chilling grit of Midwestern noir. With rivetingly authentic settings and brilliantly genuine dialogue, this beautifully written, hockey-centric mystery shows how it is more than a game – it's a lifestyle . . ."
Hank Phillippi Ryan, *USA Today* bestselling author

"*Bitterfrost* reads like a terrific seven-game NHL playoff series. The ebbs and flows in the tense courtroom scenes mirror the drama of a game you can't stop watching, with lead changes and potential heartbreak up against a game clock that is winding down"
Dave Poulin, National Hockey League executive and retired NHL player

About the author

Bryan Gruley is the Edgar-nominated author of six novels and one award-winning work of nonfiction. A lifelong journalist, he shared in *The Wall Street Journal*'s Pulitzer Prize for coverage of the September 11 terrorist attacks. He lives in northern lower Michigan with his wife, Pamela.

www.bryangruley.com

For Pam
Forever

ONE

Jimmy wakes to a pinging sound in his head.

And the smell of blood.

He sits up, too quickly, and pain blazes up from the base of his neck and wells inside his skull like a fist forcing its way out. He shuts his eyes, trying to squeeze it away. The high-pitched pinging ebbs but the throb persists.

He opens his eyes. He's sitting on his kitchen floor in the dark. He checks the clock on the microwave: three fifty-three. He's still wearing the black-and-silver IceKings jacket he wore to the hockey rink and then to the Lost Loon Tavern. A draft of winter air cascades over his face. He sees his back door is open six inches and trembling on its hinges. He gets up to close it and notices he's wearing only one boot. He hobbles outside on his booted leg. The security light blinks on. Jimmy's other boot is lying on its side on the porch step. As he squats to pull it on, he spies a ragged path of packed-down snow leading away from the porch. As if someone dragged in an animal.

He goes back inside, closes the door, and flicks on the lamp hanging over the kitchen table. Still smelling blood, he lifts his left hand to his face. 'Jesus,' he says. The hand is spackled with dried blood, the knuckles a hash of shredded skin and exposed bone a shade of rust. Blood spatters the silver sleeve of his jacket from wrist to elbow. As he stares at it, the hand begins to ache like it would after pounding some guy's forehead and cheekbones in the middle of a hockey game. What did he do to himself? Or, God forbid, to someone else? He's seen his hand like this before, but it's been a long time, when he was still playing in the minors.

The thrum in his skull is deafening. He can't think straight. He goes to the sink, splashes water on his face and neck. It doesn't help. He gazes out the window over the sink. Outside is black all the way to the tree line several hundred yards away. All Jimmy can see is his reflection in the glimmer from the overhead lamp. A strawberry of a lump has risen on his right cheek. He touches two fingertips to it. It stings.

He turns the water on hot, squirts dishwashing liquid on the hand, and washes the blood off as best he can, the soap tingling in the spots where the knuckle skin is shorn. The hand comes clean enough, but he'll have to put his jacket in the wash and wear something else to work. That's not ideal because it's a game day and everyone, especially Jimmy, driver of the Zamboni, is expected to be in IceKings gear.

He checks his back pocket for his wallet – it's there – but, patting himself, finds no cellphone. Maybe in the truck. He goes to the garage. It's empty. He hits the garage-door opener. As it rattles upward, he sees his truck parked at an odd angle across the two-tire drive that bends through a span of sparse woods to his house.

Why is the truck outside? Did his garage-door opener malfunction earlier? He can't recall. Did his one drink keep him from parking properly? Or was someone else driving? None of this is right. But he can't remember how it got wrong. His stomach clenches. He feels afraid but doesn't know what he feels afraid of. Which frightens him even more. And, man, it's cold. Must be twenty below. He wraps his arms around himself and walks to the truck, shivering.

Whenever Jimmy's driving, he stuffs his phone in one of the coffee cup holders on the center console. It's not in either of those. He leans across the driver seat to check the passenger side, grabbing the steering wheel for balance. The wheel is tacky on his palm. More blood? Holy shit, he thinks. Somebody got hurt.

His breath billows white around his head. He checks the glove box, searches under the seats, rummages through the back seat. No phone. Goddamn. His boss will start texting him at seven and won't stop till opening puck drop twelve hours later. He sits in the back seat, hands gripping his knees, trying to think: Did he leave the phone at the Loon? He doesn't remember using it there; he usually turns it off before he goes in.

Memory loss is an occupational hazard for a former hockey fighter who took a slew of blows to the head while delivering more than his share to other heads. If a doctor opened up his skull, Jimmy suspects they'd find tangles of that CTE stuff that supposedly blots out memory and drags its bearers to an early death. Still, this morning's full-blown blackout is peculiar, more like the sort that plagued Jimmy when he was heavy into the booze, after the lawsuits and the publicity and the divorce and the child custody fight. Basically, the whole damn night from the time he left the Loon is missing.

He tries to picture the Loon, where he was sitting, Ronnie behind the bar. He recalls having words, though nothing too bad, with a couple of guys who might have been giving Ronnie a hard time. For some reason he remembers thinking they must have been from downstate, probably Detroit or thereabouts. There was a woman in an orange hoodie. Not much else is coming. He figures he'll call Ronnie as soon as she might be awake, she'll clear things up. But then he thinks, no, dumb shit, you have no phone.

He twists himself around and digs in the crack between the seat and the seat back. Nothing there. He clambers back into the front and tries those seats. Nothing in the driver's side, but his fingertips brush something solid on the passenger side. He pulls his arm out and yanks his coat and shirtsleeves up, then plunges back in and comes out with his phone. 'Son of a bitch,' he says, feeling something he hopes isn't blood caked on the casing. He tries to turn the phone on, but it's out of juice. Why would it have been jammed into the seat like that? Jimmy can't believe he would've put it there on his own. Unless he was trying to hide it. But why? From whom?

His right ring finger has gone numb from the cold. He starts the truck and pulls it into the garage. The stuff on the steering wheel feels like tar. Jimmy puts a palm to his face and sniffs. He used to think when he fought two or three times a week that he could smell the difference between his own blood and another guy's. That was bullshit, just like it was bullshit that beating people up would propel him to the National Hockey League.

He needs to clean the steering wheel and check the rest of the truck for blood, but he doesn't want to freeze to death, so he goes inside and rubs his gluey hands warm then plugs the cell into the outlet next to the fridge. He goes back to the sink to rinse his hands and checks his reflection in the kitchen window. He's gotta get some ice on that swollen cheek. People are going to ask about it. Which makes him wonder if he ought to call the cops.

For what, though? What's he gonna tell them? There's blood in my truck but I don't know why? I have no idea how I got this shiner? Or why my knuckles look like spaghetti? I had one drink and can't remember much else because my brain is a sieve?

No.

He takes an ice pack from the freezer and presses it onto his cheek. He decides he'll give the truck a onceover later, before heading to the rink. A little snooze, some cleaning up, and everything will be fine. He tells himself he must have gotten into it with somebody, they got the jump on him somehow, and now, here he is.

He goes to the front room and sits on the sofa, holding the ice pack to his face beneath the framed photos of Avery when she was three, six, eight, eleven. His favorite is eight, where she's standing in unruly pigtails at the end of the Bitterfrost pier at sundown, showing off a steelhead she pulled from Lake Michigan that's almost as big as her. The house is dark and quiet but for the tocking of an old grandfather clock across the room. Jimmy has to be up and rolling in less than two hours.

In his head he says his nightly prayers. For Mama, long gone. For Avery, of course, extra prayers for her, and even for Noelle. For the Richards family, especially Cory. And, tonight, a prayer for his bud Ronnie, who may have had a rough go at the Loon. It's still too early to call her, but maybe a text. He gets off the couch and goes into the kitchen for his phone, now at thirty-one percent power. There's a text from his pal Devyn that arrived at one fifty-three: **Tell me you're not in trouble.**

Jimmy swallows hard. 'Shit, Dev,' he says aloud.

He calls up his regular text string with Ronnie. He's about to start typing when he sees a text he does not recall sending. It left his phone at two forty-two: **those two jagoff's won't be bothering you again.**

TWO

Eight hours earlier

Devyn doesn't see the guy right away, but she can feel him sneaking up from behind. It's Thursday night at the Bitterfrost hockey rink and Butch is at it again.

Devyn churns along the half-wall, puck cradled on her stick, as Butch angles at her from a face-off dot near the blue line. She probably stole the puck from him or bumped into him a little harder than he liked. Or, more likely, he's pissed off again that he has to share the ice with a girl – a woman, actually – even if she has faster feet and softer hands and better vision than him or most of the other guys out here. Or maybe *because* she does. Devyn is always dealing with this bullshit because she's always the only chick on the ice. She's also a Payne, something else that rankles Butch Dulaney.

She notices his stick first. He has it thrust in front of him for balance so he can lower his shoulder and drive his hip into her outer leg just above her knee. About as cheap as a cheap shot can get. Devyn wishes he wouldn't. But OK, Butchie, she thinks. Have it your way.

He catches up just as she stops on a heartbeat, draws the puck back between her skates, then jabs her stick blade through Butch's knees, using his momentum to catapult him into the boards like a rag doll. It's hard not to laugh. Butch springs to his feet and starts after her, fuming, 'You fucking tripped me, bitch.'

'Bitch is an upgrade from girlie,' Devyn says, turning to face him. 'Thanks, Butchie.'

'Fuck you.'

Every hockey rink in the world has a Butch, and everybody knows Butch Dulaney is an asshole on the ice, a wait-till-you're-not-looking shithead kicked out of half a dozen Detroit leagues before he moved 318 miles north, back to his family's 500 acres near Bitterfrost. He and his brothers Junior and DonDon own the busiest scrapyard north of Michigan's thumb and nearly all the land south of the Jako River that runs through the middle of town to Lake Michigan.

For years the Paynes and the Dulaneys have been sniping at each other over things trivial and, on occasion, important. Devyn, personally, doesn't give a damn, at least not until Butch pulls something like he is now. She backpedals as he lunges and misses, the other guys trying to wedge themselves between them.

'I'll kill you, bitch,' Butch says.

Devyn chirps back something about his dinky dick, something she'll regret later but that translates well to Butch and the other sweaty males crowding around, pretending to fend for her when, really, they wouldn't mind if Butch got one nice whack in, wouldn't mind if Devyn chose to play in someone else's rental. They half-heartedly snatch at Butch as he flings his gloves off and grabs her jersey collar and twists it with both hands, lifting her off the ice and pinning her against the glass.

Butch keeps repeating his vow to kill her and she yaps back, 'You're a sissy, Butch, and you know it.' Not quite the sort of verbal joust that Devyn Payne, Esquire, deploys before Bitterfrost judges and juries. But boys hate it when girls call them sissies. She grabs Butch's jersey and tugs herself in tight, where she's too close for him to throw a haymaker. She stands atop his skates, grinding her blades on his laces as she smells the sickly-sweet tang of tobacco dip on his breath.

Right where she wants him.

'That's enough, Butch,' comes a voice from behind her. She screws her head around to see Jimmy Baker skating over in his black-and-white referee get-up. Jimmy's six-four, two-thirty-five, just ten pounds over his minor-league playing weight, usually enough to dissuade dickheads. Though not Butch, who says, 'Eat shit, Bakes.'

'Get out of here, Jimmy,' Devyn says. 'I got this.'

Jimmy snags them both by the collars and with one grunting heave pulls them apart. That's enough of an opening for Butch to throw a sucker punch that grazes Devyn's chin, snapping her head back. 'Damn,' she says, struggling to keep her blades on Butch's skates.

Jimmy grabs Butch by the throat and slams his helmeted head into the glass. Butch is struggling to breathe, but manages a choked-off gasp, 'Go ahead, Jimmy. Gonna put *me* in a wheelchair too?'

Jimmy lets go.

'Come on, Bakes,' someone says. Now it's Jimmy they're pulling away. They mean well. They know him and, like most Bitterfrosters, they like him well enough. They also know what he's capable of. Butch can throw down with just about anybody, but Jimmy's bigger, punches lefty, and, most important, knows exactly what he's doing.

'Let's go, bud,' Devyn says, clutching Jimmy's elbow. 'Come on, get out of here.'

He glances around the circle of skaters and backs away one step. 'Don't be pulling this shit again, Butch.'

Butch, unfazed, lurches at Jimmy and falls flat on his face. He struggles to his feet and immediately collapses again. Poor Butchie, Devyn thinks, grinning.

'What the hell?' Butch says as he struggles up again and peers down at his skates. The laces are sliced down the middle. The other players start laughing. Butch says, 'You got one coming, girl.'

'Noted,' Devyn says, and skates away, hearing the guys taunting Butch as she catches up with Jimmy retreating to the bench.

'Jimmy,' she says. 'I don't need you coming to my rescue.'

'I know.'

'You know I love you, but I don't need your help. Not out here. OK?'

He's looking across the ice toward Butch. She can tell Jimmy doesn't entirely believe what she just said. Which she understands. Had Butch tagged her clean, she might be on her way to the hospital.

'Sorry,' he says. 'Where'd you learn that trick anyway?'

'The laces thing? Some Canuck pulled it on me during a tournament in Buffalo.'

'Nice.'

'But Jimmy, are you hearing me? You can't be stepping in like that, for me or anybody else. I saw that look on your face for a second there. A little scary.'

'Right. You can fight your own battles.'

'It's not me you need to worry about, Jimmy. Every day's a penance, right? Isn't that what you say?'

He looks toward the far end of the rink. 'Gotta get with Zelda now. Then maybe have one at the Loon.'

She watches him collect his sticks and stump away toward the Zamboni shed. What a player he once was, maybe the best Bitterfrost has ever seen. Devyn remembers watching him play for the IceKings, the biggest, fastest, smartest player on the ice. At heart, he's a good guy. But that was close tonight. It could have been worse. A lot worse.

THREE

Jimmy makes his nightly rounds. He has only one puddle of spat dip to wipe up, not bad for twenty-three players in two hockey dressing rooms. Plus the usual balled-up wads of tape scattered around the black rubber floors.

The Thursday night pickup session shut down early tonight, not because of Butch's antics but because a stripper was due at the rink at ten and the boys wanted to shower before they surprised their betrothed bachelor bud – Jimmy can't recall his name – with the young lady from Elk Rapids. Jimmy stayed busy in the Zamboni shed till the boys went spilling out to the limos waiting outside. They tried to get him to join – 'Come on, Bakes, come on out for once' – and he told them he might, but they knew that was a lie. He did notice Butch leaving without them, probably good for everyone.

He carries the plastic waste bucket back to the Zamboni shed and dumps the tape wads, empty beer cans, and a sparkly pink-and-purple garter into a waste bin. As on most nights, Jimmy Baker is the last person at the Calvin & Eleanor Payne Memorial Ice Arena, a place he's considered a home for most of his forty-four years. He especially likes this time of night, the 2,198 seats empty, the championship banners hanging in darkness, the only sounds the drone of the compressors and the occasional ticking of a fluorescent lamp.

The last he checked, hours ago, the temperature outside was six degrees. By now it must be zero or below, worse with that heartless wind slicing through every layer you wear. But that could also mean the Jako River will be frozen thick enough soon that he'll be able to get out for some early-morning skate runs before it's time to punch in at the rink. Sometimes the river is solid enough that he can make it all the way to the tiny town of Bliss. Skating the Jako makes him think of his father chugging along beside him in his racer skates with the ridiculously long blades, like machetes strapped to his feet. They're the last fond memories Jimmy has of his dad. Maybe the only ones.

He goes back out to the ice for a last look. He knows it's not exactly right, not as smooth as it could be, not as fast as it ought to be for the IceKings, the junior team that plays here to standing-room-only crowds. Jimmy's been telling management since the season started that Zelda – his Zamboni – needs new blades. But he and Zelda are still making do with the same seven-foot-long scythes of steel they had at the end of last season. Jimmy has sharpened them a few times, but they're worn and uneven and Zelda needs new.

He squats and slides his right palm across the ice surface, knowing he shouldn't be feeling so much debris. 'Blade's too damn dull,' he says, making a mental note to send his boss another email in the morning.

Walking back to the shed, he thinks it's been a good day, mostly. That morning, he brought pancakes and sausage from Big Henry's Café for the office staff. He went for a solo skate on the rink before Zelda's first spin of the day and had a pleasant phone chat with his older brother in Alpena. The encounter with Butch wasn't a highlight, but Jimmy is glad he escaped without inflicting damage. He knew, watching Devyn and Butch, that he ought to just stand back, calm down, it wasn't his battle, the Dulaneys and Paynes were always in each others' faces. But the next thing he knew, he was rushing over, trying to fix things, even though he knew it could get him into trouble, even if it was the right thing to do.

Devyn said she saw that look on his face. He knows how that feels inside, how fast it can get ugly. He usually just leaves the ice if he feels himself getting riled up about some idiot knocking people around. He wanted to tell Butch, Come on, man, she's a girl, but he knew that would really tick Devyn off, and he liked her way more than Butch.

He crosses the concourse beneath the neon sign that reads COLD BEER'S. For the thousandth time, he winces at the apostrophe, remembering how Sister Mary Cordelia at St Henry's would make him stand at his desk through an entire class for such a grammatical crime. Though dead for many years, Cordelia remains quite alive in Jimmy's head. Some nights, he still diagrams sentences in his dreams. He knows he annoys friends with his grammatical observations, but he can't help himself, even on the ice. He once was awarded a two-minute misconduct penalty by a referee whose grammar he corrected; the zebra kept saying 'I seen' instead of 'I saw.' Jimmy didn't understand; weren't refs supposed to revere rules?

He secures the wide double doors where Zelda makes her grand entrances to a crowd that will shriek as loudly for her as for the IceKings. The team has a big game tomorrow night against the Bombers of Minot, North Dakota. The IceKings trail the Bombers by a point in the division standings and could leapfrog them with a win. The Dakota squad is sizable and ornery, but the IceKings have a step on them speed-wise. Which means the better that he and Zelda do their jobs, the smoother and quicker the ice, the better chance of a win for the boys. It's not cheating when everyone's skating on the same sheet.

The shed where Zelda lives is tucked beneath the upper-level seats in the south-east corner of the arena, a popular place to sit because it's near restrooms and a beer stand, things that go together like a puck and stick. For years, Zelda and her retired brother, Xavier, hunkered in a butt-cold, corrugated steel garage outside, until Jimmy persuaded the bosses to move the operation inside so the Zam didn't have to navigate snow drifts to get to the job. Now Zelda dwells in a high-ceilinged, rectangular room redolent with motor oil and refrigerant, the concrete floor slick with snowmelt, the gray walls lined with shovels, hoses, squeegees, brushes, pick-axes, and other tools Jimmy uses to manicure the ice. Zelda is still dripping water from the last run of the night. Jimmy claps her softly on her flat metal side, just beneath the painted-on ad for Big Henry's. 'Good job today, sweetheart,' he says. 'Working on that blade, promise.'

Outside, he climbs into his '98 Ram and cranks the heat, wishing yet again he could afford one of those pickups that start remotely so they warm up before you get in. He squints through trapezoids of frozen sleet glazing his windshield, switches the heat to defrost, and hits the windshield wipers for solvent, hoping that doesn't freeze too.

He takes out his cellphone and taps the first name on his speed dial. The call goes straight to voicemail. 'You've almost reached Avery,' the fifteen-year-old voice says. 'Unfortunately, I'm not much of a voicemail person.' He knows the message well, but he listens anyway so he can hear his daughter's sweet voice, five-and-a-half hours' drive from Bitterfrost. The beep comes. 'I love you, Ave,' he says, knowing she probably won't hear it.

He hits speed dial number two. 'Sorry, Jimmy,' his ex-wife tells him. She knows he's calling for Avery, not her. 'You're too late.'

'Come on, Noelle, put her on.'

'You know the rules. No phone after ten on weeknights.'

Noelle's a stickler for rules that suit her schedule, even as her schedule as a real estate agent constantly changes. But she's the rule-maker. Jimmy surrendered that privilege, however unwillingly.

'I got caught up in rink stuff.'

'Uh-huh,' Noelle says. 'Try tomorrow.'

'Listen,' he says, trying not to sound upset. 'I know I'm not on the calendar, but I thought I might come down this weekend, see Ave. The Kings are off Sunday and I—'

'This is not a good weekend, Jimmy. We talked about this.'

'Not good for who?'

'For Avery. She'll be in Pittsburgh for volleyball. I told you.'

'No.'

Noelle sighs. 'Yes, the other day. You have her schedule. Did you look at it?'

He strains to conjure an image of a magnet on his fridge next to a photo that shows Avery Baker, number twenty-two for Northville High. No, he didn't memorize her schedule. 'OK, sorry,' he says. 'Maybe next week.'

'I have to work all weekend. Sunday matinee.'

'I don't make your schedule, Jimmy,' Noelle says. 'Is everything OK? Everything under control?'

She's speaking in code they both understand. 'Everything's fine,' he says. 'Why do you have to do this, Noe?'

She doesn't answer right away and he pictures her shaking her head. 'Jimmy,' she says, 'I got two bills today from your lawyers. *Your* lawyers.'

He has yet to outrun his past. 'Why?' he says.

'Good question. Why do I still keep getting these bills? Addressed to me, as if I owe them all this money?'

'Mail them here. I'll deal with it.'

'Just do it, will you? Jesus. OK, I'm going to go to bed. Got a five thirty wake-up. Take care of yourself, OK?'

'Wait. Noelle.'

But she's gone.

The windshield still isn't quite clear. But Jimmy figures, hell, he can see enough to manage the two miles to the Lost Loon. Sheets of snow are curling along the rink walls and up the road snaking out of the parking lot. It's only the beginning of a storm the weather people expect to persist well into the night. Why anyone would live in Bitterfrost in December is beyond Jimmy. But he does it anyway. Maybe because he feels safe here, most of the time. People know him and what he's done and they're willing to forgive, mostly. The cheers that shake the arena when he pulls Zelda onto the ice three times each night – pregame, end of first period, end of second – sustain him, even if he knows they're more for Zelda than for him. The truck winds up the rink exit to County Road 901. Jimmy stops and glances both ways, the pines lining the road in either direction invisible in the night. He hesitates; right or left? Then it comes to him like a ray of sun breaking through a bank of nimbus. Left to the Loon, right to Lake Michigan. He's driven the route hundreds of times, but sometimes his head doesn't work right. That can happen to someone who made a sort of living fighting other hockey players. He tells himself he'll remember next time. He picks up his phone and texts Ronnie at the bar: On my way, lucky you!!

He grips the top of the steering wheel with his left hand and squeezes. Hard, then harder still. The familiar sting sizzles down from his knuckles through the back of his hand and into his wrist. He endeavors to savor the pain, to imagine the shapes of the tiny screws pinched between his knuckles.

Like Devyn said, like he says, every day is a penance. He loosens his fingers. The neon sign for the Loon blinks white and blue in the roadside distance. Time for his one cocktail before he heads home, eats a hard-boiled egg at the kitchen sink, maybe a cookie, then sacks out. That's all he can ask for, all he really believes he deserves.

FOUR

The flat musical chime of the phone rouses Devyn. 'Ain't Too Proud to Beg.' She loves the lyric more than the riff, though the riff is pretty cool, especially in the Stones version. She's on the couch, in the sweats and Red Wings fleece she wore to the rink, half a can of Bell's Amber warm between her knees. She had to tape two fingers together after jamming one of them into the goalie's chest protector as she crashed the net earlier. She apologized to the goaltender, but he yapped at her for the rest of the session anyway. Goalies.

Her day was long even before she went to hockey and had to deal with Butch Dulaney. Preliminary examinations back-to-back-to-back, a bail hearing, two hours at the jail listening to clients, a Zoom call with a rich Harbor Springs guy accused of bitcoin fraud. She could've used subtitles for that. She bolted the rink before the boys had their sophomoric bachelor fun. Devyn had no desire to see that stripper, whom she'd gotten acquitted, barely, on a cocaine possession charge three years ago. That was a win that almost got away, and it still lingers for Devyn, as losses tend to do. In the courtroom and on the rink, she hates to lose even more than she loves to win. For Devyn, triumph is a more fleeting feeling than regret.

She should be re-reading an order a judge entered late in the afternoon in one of her cases, but she left it in her office. The Wings are on the TV, somehow ahead of the Avalanche, 3–1, with under two minutes to go. She picks up her phone, fumbles it, picks it up again, then blinks once, hard, before reading the screen: PRIVATE 6. A client. This afternoon's client.

'Devyn Payne,' she answers.

'What the fuck was all that?' the caller says. Devyn knows immediately that the client has had plenty to drink, probably whisky, maybe tequila, who knows? 'I'll take that judge out and bitch-slap her all the way to the Mackinac Bridge.'

'Settle down, Jordan,' Devyn says. They had a version of this conversation earlier, but apparently the client wants to re-litigate.

They often do, even after cases are long over and the culprits are in prison. 'She telling me I gotta keep my mouth shut, well, I know my rights, bee-otch. I—'

'Jordan,' Devyn says. 'Shut the hell up.'

She shuts up. Devyn has learned in her three months as Jordan Fawcett's defense attorney that speaking her language gets her attention. 'How much have you had to drink?'

'Two, three Bud Lights, a shot or two of Fireball.'

Translation: eight Bud Lights, half a bottle of Fireball, an edible or two. This woman will be dead before the decade is out. Ten years in prison would be good for her health.

'Are you out somewhere?' Devyn says.

'At my old man's kitchen table.'

Devyn really doesn't want to be hauling her butt out in this weather to post bail because Jordan got in yet another snit with a bartender or a pool player or anybody else who looked at her without 'respect.' She's thirty-six with the empathy of a bawling infant. Tough broad, as Devyn's father would have said. But tough and stupid can be a toxic mix.

That's why Jordan was in front of a judge that afternoon, waiving her right to a preliminary examination so she could accept a plea agreement Devyn arranged with the prosecutor. Six months ago, Jordan got into it with a woman at the county fair over a stuffed animal they both claimed to have won at the toy duck squirting booth. The woman took a swing at Jordan and Jordan slipped the punch and grabbed the gauges in the woman's earlobes, pulling until the ears exploded with blood and fatty tissue. Jordan was charged with felony assault. Devyn and the prosecutor agreed she'd plead to a lesser charge with a lesser sentence of one year in state prison.

For whatever reason – probably some small-p, small-town politics that complicate Devyn's job on a daily basis – the judge balked. Jordan leapt up from the defense bench to call the judge a 'meddlesome cunt.' The judge took offense, no surprise, and Devyn had to scramble to keep her from revoking Jordan's bail.

'Who does that bitch think she is?' Jordan says.

'You wanna go to prison on the original charge? By the time you get outta there, you can go straight into a nursing home.'

'Fuck me,' Jordan says. Then she pauses. Devyn pictures her swigging or smoking. Devyn actually likes Jordan in the woman's clearer, sober moments. She's had a rough life, not all of it her fault.

'What is it I got to do then?'

'Be at the cop shop Monday morning, eight sharp. Wear what you want to be wearing when you get out of prison a year from now.'

'Shit.'

'Do not even think of disappearing, Jordan. I got you the weekend to get your stuff together before you go in, not to go out and get ham-boned and re-arrested. Understood?'

'You are one bad-ass lawyer, ain't you?'

Maybe, Devyn thinks. Maybe not. She's been voted one of the top twenty-five criminal defense attorneys north of Lansing for four years running by the Criminal Defense Lawyers Association of Michigan. It has a lot to do with a murder case she won that she almost wishes she hadn't.

'I'm *your* lawyer, that's all that matters,' Devyn says. Then she overhears a male voice echoing in the background.

'Fawcett. I'm looking at your cards if you don't get your ass here pronto.'

Jordan ends the call. She's out, all right. Playing cards. Getting smashed. Devyn has done what she can. What happens next in Jordan's life is up to her.

Devyn jumps off the couch, feeling tightness in her calves from standing on Butch's skates and digging her blades into his laces. It was kind of funny, but at the same time, it ticks her off. She's glad she dispatched the douchebag, but why should she have to? Why can't she just play with the boys and score a couple of goals and have a beer without having to be hassled? All because she doesn't have a dick. And, she guesses, because she's a Payne and Butch is a Dulaney.

On the TV, the Wings have blown the two-goal lead and are going to overtime. Devyn clicks the tube off. She makes a last check of her phone. The guys she skated with earlier have filled their beer-hockey app with pictures of that stripper straddling some guy in the locker room. In the rink named for Devyn's parents. Dear God, she thinks.

In her bedroom she undresses while reviewing tomorrow's plan: Skate with a different pickup group early. Meet with an assistant prosecutor. Prelim at ten fifteen. Lunch with Mom, unless she cancels again. Interview a potential client – marijuana possession, resisting arrest – in Pellston, half an hour away, at two. Paperwork until practice with the Little Kings at four, Little Queens at five, the best part of her day.

She'll be busy. Good. The guy on Tinder wants to have a drink way the hell down in Charlevoix. She's thinking about it. He does have a shapely sort of body. Or at least his Tinder photo does.

She's about to shut her phone down when a text pops up. It's her soul sister, Ronnie, messaging from the Lost Loon. **Shitshow aborning**, the text says. Aborning? Ronnie must be reading Gillian Flynn novels again. She starts to reply, then stops herself. You never know when an ill-considered text could show up in a courtroom. Devyn knows Ronnie sees shitshows everywhere, all the time. She shuts the phone off and slides into bed, listening to the night, resisting the urge to pray for quiet, because she knows it'll just jinx things.

FIVE

Jimmy takes his usual stool at the horseshoe-shaped bar. Above his head, an overstuffed bird bears the legend: 'Lonnie the Loon Says Free Beer Tomorrow.'

The place smells of week-old grease and spilled beer. Normal, in other words. The two-gallon jar of pickled eggs stands where it always does, as if glued to the bar, eggs floating in the same hazy greenish ooze they have for months if not years. Pat Benatar, Ronnie's favorite, sings on a rattling ceiling speaker behind Jimmy's head: 'Hit Me with Your Best Shot.' It reminds him again of his little clash with Butch. 'Evening, Ronnie,' he says.

She's wearing a black down vest over her favorite Michigan Tech sweatshirt. She attended the university for a year before her mother died and she came home to make sure her father ate real food and got more than three hours of sleep a night. A wool Red Wings headband wraps her shiny mane of silver-streaked black hair. She's shoving glass beer mugs, one after another, onto a soap-soaked brush jutting up from the bottom of a sink. Above her head the Wings play on a soundless TV.

'Giraffe?' Ronnie says, looking at Jimmy in the Miller Lite mirror on the far facing wall.

'High balls on me,' he says, quoting the punchline he uses every night. The old joke made Ronnie laugh the first couple of times. 'And don't be juicing it up like you do.'

'It's one little drink, Jimbo.'

'That's right. One. Don't try to fit two in.'

He and Ronnie have a past. They gave up on a future so they could have a peaceable present. And she does make a tasty highball.

The horseshoe Jimmy's sitting at is empty but for a woman sitting to his left at the top of the shoe. She's in an orange hunting hoodie, nursing a fat shot of something brown and a longneck Busch Light. Two twenty-somethings he doesn't recognize are making a racket playing shuffleboard on the other side of the bar, and a table of guys, maybe one woman, are drinking and playing cards in a far corner. The Loon is about as crowded as it gets on a weeknight.

Ronnie sets the highball down in front of Jimmy along with three one-dollar bills. He slaps a ten-spot on the bar: four fifty for the drink, plus a two fifty tip. 'Thank you, darling,' she says, flashing a smile, her pretty dimples deepening.

'The Kings gonna handle them Dakota Bombers tomorrow?'

'You mean *those* Dakota Bombers, right?'

Ronnie ignores him. She doesn't care a whit about Jimmy's grammatical obsessions. He sips the highball and raises an eyebrow at Ronnie, who's doing something on her phone.

'What'd you put in here?' Jimmy says.

She answers without looking up. 'Whiskey and Sprite, same as ever.'

'I like my highball with 7Up, dear.'

'You told me a hundred times. And I told you, find a distributor around here carries 7Up. We got less distributors around than we did before.'

'Fewer,' Jimmy says, picturing Sister Cordelia's fat red face.

'Huh?'

'Fewer. You have *fewer* distributors, not less.'

'And you'll have *less* drinks in here if you keep that shit up.'

Jimmy laughs. 'So how's the love life?'

He asks her this question most nights. Like most nights, she gives him a none-of-your-business look, but really he thinks she wants him to ask, either to make him jealous or to convince herself that she's doing all right. Her latest squeeze at least has a decent job at the hardware, so that's progress from the guy before, who appeared to live off Loon popcorn and disability checks. She leans her arms on the bar and looks up into Jimmy's face.

'How'd today go, honey?'

'Fine, Mom.'

'You ref tonight?'

'Yep. Boring game.'

'Ain't what Dev told me.' Dev is Ronnie's bud, so Ronnie probably knows about the Butch thing. 'Keep your head up, darling.' She nods toward the card game in the corner. 'Butchie boy's here with his crew.'

Jimmy shrugs, picturing Butch pinning Devyn to the glass. Ronnie returns to the sink, still fingering the phone in one hand. 'What about tomorrow night?' she says. 'Those Bombers gonna knock our boys around?'

One of the shuffleboard players approaches Ronnie. He's in a flannel button-down that looks pressed. He must be from downstate, probably some Detroit suburb with in-ground pools and lawns that get mowed every week. Guys like him show up in Bitterfrost on occasion, usually in the summer, or deer season, invariably shit-faced. They usually order Stella and settle for PBR.

The flannel guy's buddy starts yelling from the shuffleboard table. 'You know you suck at this, right?'

'Blow me,' Flannel says, then to Ronnie, 'I'll settle up, young lady.'

The other guy starts over to the bar. He's wearing a pleated jacket with lots of hunting and fishing patches sewn on. Jimmy wonders if he bought it that way or he ordered the patches online and had his mother sew them on.

'Wait,' the guy in patches shouts. 'Dude, you are not paying the bill, I am.'

Flannel chuckles and slides a few bills toward Ronnie. She's about to take them when the patches guy steps up. 'I'm paying,' he yells, too loud, obviously hammered. 'Missy, you pick that money up and I'll smack you.'

Shit, Jimmy thinks. 'Missy' isn't something you want to call a woman who worships Pat Benatar. He considers getting out of his chair. No, he decides, he's done his good deed for the night. Ronnie's got this. She once opened a quarter-sized gouge over some drunk's eye with a shot glass. Then again, Ronnie's jerk boss told her any confrontation with a customer will be considered her fault, no questions asked. She's a single mom who needs this job to keep her kids fed and in hockey gear. The boy plays for the Little Kings, the girl for the Little Queens.

'Hey there, guys,' Jimmy says across the bar. 'Welcome to Bitterfrost. Your server's name is Ronnie. She's the best.'

'I don't want trouble,' Ronnie says. 'Whoever wants to pay can pay.'

'Got it,' the patches guy says. 'Ronnie.' Then he angles his head to look at Jimmy. 'You can chill, cowboy.'

Jimmy takes a sip of his highball, steadying his stare on the drunk in patches. The guy has a snake of a scar on his upper lip that suggests he's been in a scrape or three before. Jimmy wants nothing to do with him. The guy can't be serious about smacking Ronnie. But he still shouldn't be making unfunny threats.

'Not a cowboy,' Jimmy says, trying on a smile. 'But thank you. Maybe you should just pay and leave things be.'

Flannel guffaws. 'Get the cowboy a shot on me,' he says. 'Anything you want, pardner.' He says this in what he must imagine to be a cowboy-like drawl. Jimmy notices the woman in the orange hoodie shaking her head.

'One-and-done here, no thanks,' Jimmy says. Ronnie starts to pick up the cash on the bar and the guy in patches smacks his hand down on hers.

'Asshole,' Ronnie says.

'Sorry, Rhonda,' Patches says, 'but I'm paying.'

Flannel speaks up. 'Listen, honey, maybe you can give us directions to your hockey rink?'

'Shut up about that,' Patches says. 'Tomorrow.'

'Hey! We're trying to play euchre over here.'

Great, Jimmy thinks. Sounds like Butch. Patches and Flannel spin around. 'Might as well get those dipwads a drink too, eh?' Flannel says.

'Me too,' Patches says.

'Not a chance,' Ronnie says. 'You're cut off.'

Patches twists his face into something like a fist. Jimmy can see this could get nasty fast. He wants to finish his highball and go home and email the boss about those Zamboni blades. 'Tell you what, guys,' he says. 'I'll throw down for that last round you had.'

Flannel says, 'Who the hell are you, dude?'

'No,' comes another voice. 'Who are you?'

Everyone turns as the voice from the dark corner emerges into the light. Butch Dulaney. And Jimmy can see his brothers rising from their table.

'Well, if it isn't Paul Bunyan,' Flannel says. 'We would've brought your drinks over ourselves, but Rowena won't give us any.'

'Ronnie,' Jimmy says. 'I think she asked you politely to leave.'

Butch gives Jimmy a sidelong glance and says, 'I ain't asking politely. You boys been spoiling the vibe in here.'

Flannel laughs in Butch's face. 'I'm sorry, Mayor Bunyan, but I was going to buy you and your pals a drink and this is how you thank me?'

Jimmy slides off his stool, reluctant, and meanders around the bar, thinking, What is this, some kind of cosmic test? Twice in one night? As he rounds the horseshoe, Flannel smirks at Butch and says, 'By the way, you guys actually playing euchre?'

'Got something against it?' Butch says.

'Euchre is – how should I say this? – a little more difficult than the game of War.'

Flannel waits for an answer, but Butch doesn't say a word. 'Anyway,' Flannel says, 'why you gotta be such a twat?'

Patches starts laughing as if he just heard the funniest joke of his life. Jimmy's watching Butch for twitches, for the slightest sign he's about to go off, which will cause his brothers to go off. One of them – nobody ever determined which – once fractured the skull of the son of a Bitterfrost police sergeant with a steel fence post. No charges were filed. Everyone in town knew you could get away with a lot if you owned as much of Bitterfrost as the Dulaneys.

'"Twat?"' Butch says. His brothers have moved closer to the bar. 'You don't have the first fucking idea who I am, do you, son?'

'Nor do we fucking care,' Patches says.

'Let it go, Butch,' Jimmy says. 'I can take care of these gentlemen.'

'Baker,' Butch says. 'You keep sticking your nose into other people's affairs and you might get it knocked off. What's your plan? Cripple these jokers up good, too?' He reaches into a pocket and pulls out two twenties he sets on the bar. He nods at Ronnie then says to Flannel and Patches, 'Be careful. This Jimmy Baker dude is one bad mofo.'

Butch flashes Jimmy an angry grin, then lets his gaze float past Jimmy before he turns and walks back to the table in the corner. Within thirty seconds, he and the others are in their coats and out the door. Jimmy gives Flannel and Patches another half-assed smile and says, 'You heard the man. Time to go?'

'Yeah,' Ronnie says. 'Take your bullshit back downstate where it belongs.'

Patches has his phone out. He's looking at it, then at Jimmy, then the phone again. 'Holy shit, man,' he says. 'Jimmy Baker. You're the hockey guy who almost killed that guy.' He looks at Flannel. 'We better get the hell out of here, eh?' Then he starts laughing again. 'Naw. You ain't on skates in here, cowboy.' He turns back to Ronnie. 'How about those cocktails, gorgeous?'

'You really don't want to do this,' Ronnie says.

'Fuck this fucking hick,' Flannel says. 'Cocktails, please.'

Fucking hick? Jimmy steps toward the two, hands balled into fists. Ronnie thrusts an arm over the bar, blocking him.

'It's OK,' she says.

An image materializes in Jimmy's head, how his fist would splatter the cartilage of Flannel's nose across his cheek, then how he'd grab Patches by the lapels of his silly jacket and slam his head into the bar rail. He has to get out. Now.

'Go on,' Ronnie says, reading his face. 'I'll be at the game tomorrow. Wave from Zelda, OK? Section one-eleven.'

He walks back to his stool.

''Night, cowboy,' Flannel calls out.

Patches adds, 'Maybe Zelda'll give you a hummer.' They convulse with laughter.

Jimmy ignores the dregs of his highball and pulls his coat on. As he walks past the woman in the hoodie, she peers out from under the hood and says, 'Punks deserve to get their asses kicked.'

Jimmy nods in agreement. Going out the door, he decides he might not head home just yet.

SIX

Devyn jolts awake in her bed. A police siren blares in the distance. She hopes to hell it has nothing to do with Jordan Fawcett.

She rolls out from under the covers and looks through the third-floor window. Outside, the Jako River bisecting downtown Bitterfrost lies white and silent beneath the faux gas lamps along the parallel sidewalks. No one is about, all the businesses dark except for Schmatta's Fine Dining, which must be clearing out regulars after last call.

She finally got to sleep about twenty minutes ago. Now she's wide awake again. She grabs her phone off the nightstand and turns it on. Nothing from Jordan. But more texts from Ronnie. **Jimmy almost got into it with a couple fudgies.** Meaning downstaters. **Hope he got home ok.**

Jesus, Jimmy, Devyn thinks. Two times in one night. That siren better not be about you, either. Again, she decides it's wise to leave the texts unanswered. Jimmy will be fine, Ronnie will be fine, the fudgies will be gone in the morning. But she knows as she mashes the back of her head into her pillow that those texts are going to keep her up. Jimmy almost got into it? She impulsively grabs her phone and dials his number. No answer. She doesn't leave a message. Instead, despite her better judgment, she texts him: **Tell me you're not in trouble.**

She lies in bed, waiting. Two minutes, five minutes, ten minutes, twenty. He must be asleep. She squeezes her eyes closed and folds her hands together under the quilt, thinking, Dammit, Jimmy, dammit, Ronnie, how the hell am I ever going to get to sleep?

SEVEN

Of course the siren that roused Devyn in the middle of the night involved Jordan Fawcett.

Devyn's client left a voicemail at three-sixteen, two hours after Devyn turned her phone off. She listens to it at six thirty-three. Jordan called from the police station. From her scratchy warble, Devyn divines something about her getting pulled over for driving drunk, how the cops forced her to take a breath test even though she refused, how they hassled her, assaulted her, wouldn't let her make her one call.

Never mind that she was making her one call.

'Dammit, Jordan,' Devyn says to nobody as she sits up in her bed. 'You need hearing aids or something?' There's undoubtedly some truth to what Jordan said about the police. They throw their weight around freely up north, feeling none of the pressure big-city cops do from protesters and liberal politicians and groups like Black Lives Matter. None of those things exist in Bitterfrost, population 3,347. Everybody's white, unless you count the Hispanic gentleman who occasionally brings his taco truck to town from Cadillac in the summer. The defining line in Bitterfrost is drawn not between white and black, but rich and poor, and in Devyn's experience as a criminal defense lawyer, the rich have nothing to worry about from the poor. She represents her share of both. The rich clients pay her bills. The poor ones keep her skills sharp, because their cases are often so hopeless.

Devyn can easily imagine Jordan telling a cop to go fuck himself when all he's done is ask for her license and registration, but she can also picture the cop going off on Jordan with a full-on frisk, tossing her against the car, the whole pathetic I'm-a-bad-ass-with-a-gun routine.

Devyn showers and dresses and stuffs two bananas and a granola bar in her briefcase. She takes the stairs down three floors instead of the elevator while psyching herself up for what awaits in the predawn dark. She steps through the door to the parking lot and the cold slams into her like a defenseman with his stick and elbows up.

'Christ on an iceberg,' she says, shutting her eyes against a gust that pelts her face with frozen needles and shoves her sideways. She forgot to start her car before she came down. She has to check on Jordan before she goes to the rink for a quick pickup skate, then make her nine forty-five with the assistant prosecutor, who won't be pleased about Jordan's DUI, if she's heard. Devyn scrapes the windshield while her vehicle warms up, guessing in the dark as to whether it's clear enough to drive.

Her rent-free office is in a building her mother owns next door to the condo building where Devyn lives rent-free. The cop shop is only six blocks away, which will seem like ten miles in cold like this, so no chance she's walking. She has lived in Bitterfrost for her entire thirty-seven years, except for the six at school in Ann Arbor, and each winter seems grayer than the last. And every year, it seems, she starts thinking a little earlier in winter about moving somewhere brighter and warmer. But then summer shows up and the river sparkles with boats and jet skis streaming out to Lake Michigan, the beaches and dunes turn golden, and Devyn forgets about the six long months of icy gray hell that will descend come November. The Finns who emigrated here to cut pine in the 1800s didn't call the place Bitterfrost for nothing. But at least they brought hockey.

She pulls into the police station lot and parks as close as she can to the entrance without taking one of the spots reserved for the chief, his deputy, and the head detective. The chief and deputy spots are vacant but Devyn sees Garth Klimmek's Ford Bronco in the detective spot. He's the hardest working cop in Bitterfrost but even he's never in this early. He wouldn't be here for something as routine as Jordan's drunk driving. Something else must be going on, and if Klimmek's involved, Devyn might soon be, too.

'Good morning, Skip,' she tells the woman ensconced behind bulletproof plastic at the front counter. 'I need to see my client.'

'Morning, Dev. Name?'

'Jordan Fawcett.'

'You know,' Skip says, 'you might want to tell that young lady this isn't a nail salon.'

'And you might want to come up with a new line. Paperwork?'

Jordan waits at a solid gray table bolted to a gray concrete floor in a room of gray walls with a single window the size of a postcard installed in the door. She looks like shit, her face the color of dirty snow except for flecks of yesterday's makeup, eyes sunken into puffy cheeks. Devyn doubts she's been crying, because Jordan never cries. Devyn lowers her briefcase to the floor, sits in the hard-backed chair across from Jordan, and sets the single page of the preliminary police report on the table.

'Good morning, Jordan,' she says. 'Why don't you tell me exactly what happened?'

Jordan just sits there for a minute, staring past Devyn, probably craving a cigarette. Finally, she says, 'OK, OK, I wasn't at my old man's place. I lied. Sorry. A girl's gotta—'

'Don't worry about it. Where were you really?'

Jordan tells her tale of woe. She had a drink, maybe two, with some guys at the Loon. The place 'got weird,' she says, and they all left around midnight, maybe a little later, best she can remember. They smoked a joint in the parking lot, then headed for home.

'What time would that have been?' Devyn says.

Jordan shrugs, still not looking at her attorney. 'I don't fucking know,' she says. 'One? One thirty?'

'That was some joint if it took an hour to smoke.'

'Whatever. We were shooting the shit, you know.'

'So you left the bar around midnight, spent an hour smoking a joint and then went home, or at least tried to. Yes?'

'Something like that.'

'Please look at me, Jordan.'

Jordan keeps her gaze steady on the wall behind Devyn.

'Jordan?'

Jordan finally faces Devyn, saying, 'This is bullshit.'

'I understand. But I need you to help me so I can help you. It's good that you told the police you wouldn't take a breathalyzer—'

'They fucking forced me, about stuck the goddamn thing down my throat, like they probably do to their wives.'

'They should not have done that. Do I have your timeline essentially right?'

Jordan looks away again. 'Yeah. So what are we gonna do? You gonna get me outta here?'

'So, the police report,' Devyn says, laying a finger on the page, 'says they pulled you over on Picard Road near 901 at two-fifteen.'

'So?'

'So you left the Loon at one thirty and it took you forty-five minutes to get to Picard and 901? Like, five or six miles from the Loon?'

'I had a buzz on. I was driving slow. I know, I know, I shouldn't drive slow, the goddamn cops are watching for that.'

No, Devyn thinks, there's something you're not telling me. But it might be better not to know, at least for now. 'They rough you up?'

'Yeah, the usual bullshit.'

Jordan describes the arrest. Devyn scribbles notes. Beating the drunk-driving charge shouldn't be too hard. She's more worried about the pending plea deal on the felony assault. Judges don't look kindly on defendants who get accused of new crimes while awaiting judgment on old ones.

'All right,' Devyn says when Jordan finishes. 'I think I can get these guys to let you go pretty quick.' Like, before the judge hears about the drunk-driving charge. 'Then I need you to lay low, OK?'

'Meaning what?'

'Meaning I don't want to have to come see you again in this room.'

Devyn steps out into the hallway and almost runs smack into Klimmek. 'Whoa, what's the hurry, detective?' she says. 'Extra sprinkles on the doughnuts today?'

Klimmek usually would shake his head at a crack like that, maybe inform Devyn yet again that she's a smart ass. Today, all he says is, 'Counselor,' as he brushes past.

'You got a minute?' He doesn't answer, just keeps going. She trots after him while pulling out a business card. 'Hey,' she says.

He stops and turns to face her. 'Make it fast,' he says.

'What's going on?'

'Have a good morning, counselor.'

'Wait. Here.' She shoves the business card at him. She's given it to him before but he's never used it. 'Call the six-one-six number. It's old-school, with an answering machine I clean out every day.'

'Uh-huh.'

He crumples the card into a pocket and lumbers away.

EIGHT

Detective Garth Klimmek is dying for a coffee – and sure, a doughnut – but there's no time. His phone is vomiting texts. A state trooper is holding on his landline. He can't remember when he's been this busy this early on a morning that's not one of the crazy summer weekends. He blew past that Payne lawyer without a thought.

'Sorry, trooper,' he says, clicking back into the call on hold. 'Tell me again what you can see.'

He listens, not liking what he's hearing. An anonymous caller alerted state police to a pickup truck sitting unoccupied in a forest clearing three miles east of downtown Bitterfrost, just inside the city's border. The seats front and back are spattered with what appears to be blood. Someone apparently tried to set the truck on fire, without much success.

'Got a read yet on the plates?' Klimmek says.

'Plates are gone,' the trooper tells him.

'Got a VIN?'

'Working on it.'

'You sure it's blood?'

'Pretty sure.'

'How bad is it exactly?'

'Like someone cleaned a deer in there.'

'No bodies?'

'Not so far. But we've only searched the immediate scene. Checking the woods.'

Klimmek checks a clock on the wall, then glances at a picture of his son on his desk. He was supposed to be heading north by now for a weekend of snowmobiling in the UP.

'All right,' he says. 'I'll be out there in fifteen.'

'There is one item, detective. Could be nothing.'

'Yeah?'

'A glove.'

'What kind of glove?'

'Basic winter. Brown leather with fake fur inside. Thinking a male's.'

'Which hand?'

'Left.'

'Got blood on it?'

'If I had to bet twenty bucks, yes.'

'You find it inside the vehicle or out?'

A deputy chief appears at the office door, gesturing for Klimmek's attention. The detective turns away.

'Outside,' the trooper says.

So the glove could have been there before whatever happened happened. 'And we have no clue who called this in?'

'Nope. Anonymous. All they said was something about an abandoned truck, said it looked fugly.'

'That's the word they used, "fugly?"'

'Fucking ugly. Believe so, sir. Not in my vocabulary. Although the snow out here is pretty much that, fugly.'

Klimmek turns to the deputy chief and raises a forefinger. 'See you shortly, trooper.' He ends the call. 'What's up?'

'We got a body,' the deputy says.

'By the truck?'

'No. Not far, but far enough.'

'Shit.'

'Yeah. Shit is right, sir.'

NINE

The morning wind is a howl of blinding white. Jimmy will have to feel his way down the two-track to the road. Not for the first time. As he climbs into his truck, he catches a whiff of something like smoke, and he stops, but then it's gone, on the wind.

As always, the IceKings general manager is texting with the questions he asks every pregame morning: Ice good? Zam good? Any issues with the turnstiles? Concession vendors able to get in? Other team's morning skate all set? Yes, yep, nope, for sure, all is well, Jimmy replies. Luckily, he got Zelda recharged and finished some routine clean-up while the boys were having their jollies with the stripper last night. Which is good because, at the moment, he's not thinking all that straight.

He pulls his truck out into the fury of snow. The defrost and wipers are going all out as he peeks through a patch of cleared windshield not much wider than a hockey puck. Whatever was sticky on the steering wheel earlier is gone now that he rinsed it with warm water and Windex. But the wheel's an icicle because Jimmy must have left his gloves at the Loon again.

So far his boss is the only one to text or call this morning, though it's barely eight o'clock. He dozed on the living-room sofa for about forty-five minutes but still can't remember much about what happened or didn't happen last night. He sure as hell doesn't recall texting Ronnie.

He winds onto Elm Street and passes the ancient train depot some developer is trying to convert to retail, then the feed store and next the Bitterfrost County Courthouse, three stories of eighty-four-year-old red-brick, limestone, and arched windows rising to a clock tower on a gabled roof. It's the most beautiful thing in Bitterfrost, short of Lake Michigan. But now it's a barely visible ghost rising from the hoary clouds of snow tumbling over its enormous lawn.

He's not moving too fast but still he slows to veer onto Main Street along the north bank of the river that splits Bitterfrost in two. Main Street proceeds past the not-that-old condo development, a couple of newer bars, and the town's fanciest restaurant, Schmatta's.

Jimmy hooks a left at the Division Street Bridge, crosses the semi-frozen river, and turns right onto Jaata Street, the original thoroughfare in Bitterfrost, named for the Finnish word for ice. Jaata is where most of the town's older establishments reside, or once did: a pharmacy that barely survived the pandemic; a dry cleaner that did not; a hardware store that opens only three days a week; a party store. The windows at Big Henry's Café glow with welcoming light. Jimmy can see Big Henry in his triangular blue-and-white cap shuffling around, sliding his girth between the nine tables, four booths, and six stools at what he likes to call the omelet bar. Jimmy would love an egg-cheese-sausage-and-potato pasty but he's already late to work. And if anybody's talking about something that did or didn't happen at the Loon last night, they'll be talking about it at Big Henry's.

The Calvin & Eleanor Payne Memorial Arena squats at the far end of the street overlooking the lake shore. It's more home to Jimmy than his two-bedroom house outside of town. He parks in his usual spot in the lot, dreading the window scraping and door-lock unfreezing he'll have to do when he calls it a night.

Zelda slumbers in the Zamboni shed. Jimmy likes to think she notices when he flicks on the overheads and gives her a friendly slap on the big black-and-silver Z painted on her nose. Even that hurts his hand.

'Yo there, girl,' he says. 'Sleep OK?'

He looks out at the ice surface shimmering beneath the dimmed fluorescent lamps. He'll turn them up in a few minutes, in time for the locals who call themselves the Drunken Clammers to start their Friday morning pickup skate. He opens the tablet on his work bench facing the rink and taps out an email inquiring as politely as he can about those new blades for Zelda. He's hitting send when he hears a familiar voice at the shed door.

'Hey, Bakes. Already at it?'

It's Devyn poking her smiling face into Jimmy's workspace. He doesn't usually like having guests, but for her he always makes an exception. Sometimes he thinks she might love Zelda as much as he does.

'Hell,' he says, 'I'm an hour late. And listen, sorry about last night. I should've let you handle Butch yourself.'

'Did you see my text? It was a little late.'

He has to think about it. 'Oh, yeah, saw it. I thought you were just joking around.'

'No trouble?'

'None that I know of.'

'Then what happened to your face?'

She means the knot on his right cheek. He slapped a bandage on and forgot about it. 'Oh, yeah. Slipped on black ice on my porch, whacked myself on the doorknob. Stupid. Getting old.'

'Icing it?'

'Of course.'

He can see she's not buying. But she doesn't press it. 'You don't have to apologize about Butch. Thanks for sticking up for me.'

'You skating with the Clammers this morning?' he says.

'Yup. Why don't you come out? You'd bring the pace up.'

Jimmy hasn't played much hockey since walking off the ice in the middle of a minor-league game in Erie, Pennsylvania, thirteen years ago. But his heart skips a bit to hear Devyn encourage him. He likes just about everything about her, especially how she handles herself on the ice, her edge work, her vision, her generosity with the puck. And that Red Wings logo tattooed behind her right ear. Sexy, at least to Jimmy.

He has even slipped into the courthouse a few times to watch her perform her day job, and she's just as deft and relentless there as on the ice. Sometimes Jimmy wishes he could finagle himself a little closer to her. She's in her mid-thirties, he guesses, not too much his junior. But her parents' names adorn the arena, her twin brother is Jimmy's boss, and the Zamboni driver who wants to keep his job probably would be wise to keep a polite distance from Eleanor Payne's daughter. Especially when it's a guy with a past like Jimmy's, and a woman who doesn't always get along with her family.

'One of these days,' Jimmy tells her.

'You get to the Loon last night?'

Jimmy hesitates, hoping Devyn doesn't notice. 'Did. Had my drink. Why? What did Ronnie say?'

Devyn chuckles. 'Who cares what Ronnie says? You watch the Wings?'

'Not sure they were on.'

'Come on, they're always on. The Wings and Pat Benatar.'

'They win?'

Devyn gives Jimmy a longer look than he expects. 'Lost in OT, 4–3. Everything OK today, Jimmy?'

'Everything's fine. Why are you always asking me that?'

Jimmy knows why, but he wants Devyn to know he knows.

'Can I ask you something?' she says.

'You just did.'

She shakes her head. 'You know a woman named Jordan Fawcett?'

Jimmy walks over to his work bench and starts fiddling with a motorized edger he uses to scrape the rink boards where Zelda can't reach. 'This some sort of entrapment?' he says. 'Is she actually your sister? Did I sleep with her and forget or something?'

'I hope not, for your sake. Do you know her?'

'Would I ask who she is if I knew her, Ms Attorney?'

'She's an acquaintance of mine.'

'Ah. So she's in some kind of trouble.'

'You didn't see her at the Loon, did you?'

'What does she look like?'

Devyn describes her: Skinny as a goalpost, pale as pre-Zamboni'd ice, fidgety as a goalie with a broken stick. The only woman Jimmy remembers besides Ronnie is the one in the orange hoodie at the bar rail.

'I don't think I saw your girl,' he says. 'She in trouble?'

'Not yet. You notice anything unusual going on there last night?'

'Seemed pretty normal to me.'

Devyn must know something he doesn't. Like maybe Ronnie told her about that text he doesn't recall sending about jagoffs never bothering her again. Were they the ones he just barely remembers in the bar last night?

'You know what?' he says, stepping back from the bench, 'I gotta get the beer cooler down to the Clammers dressing room or they'll have my ass. Good luck with your client – I mean acquaintance.'

'Nothing like the taste of beer in the morning.'

'Not like victory.'

'What's up with your hand?'

He was hoping she wouldn't notice. He shrugs. 'I guess I got a bigger piece of Butch last night than I thought.'

'Uh-huh. See you later.'

She disappears into the concourse. Jimmy waits a good minute to make sure she's gone before he picks up his phone. Ronnie read his text about those two guys six minutes ago. She replied: Jimmy wtf did you do?

As he rereads the text a second and third and fourth time, he struggles to picture Ronnie standing behind the bar, handing him his highball, jawing with those two guys, and everything and anything that followed. But almost nothing comes. Then out of nowhere he starts hearing that pinging sound again, the one that roused him hours earlier on his kitchen floor, sharp and unbidden now in the hollows of his skull.

TEN

Klimmek creeps down the bluff in half steps, grasping at tree trunks for balance, wind lashing his face with pebbles of ice. He's too damn old for this, he thinks. The snow is so deep that it's spilling into the tops of his knee-high boots. It will melt inside and soak the detective's thermal socks, rendering them useless. But he'd rather deal with that than what's becoming apparent in the clearing below.

Magnesium lamps illuminate a ring of snow tamped down by boot prints. Two state troopers and a Bitterfrost city cop stand on the outer edges of the ring, waiting along the yellow restraining tape zigzagging through the trees, steaming wraiths of their breath spiraling sideways in the squall. One trooper snaps photos while keeping enough distance so as not to intrude on the scene. In the middle of the ring is a circle of mottled darkness that Klimmek assumes is blood. A great deal of blood. At the center of the circle is what appears to be the body of a man. The arms are flung to either side like the dead man was making snow angels. He's wearing a jacket that looks to be covered with bloodied fishing and hunting patches.

Klimmek loses his grip and slides the last six feet of his descent, catching himself just before he bucks forward to the ground. Surveying the scene up close, he thinks, Holy Jesus, but doesn't say it because he doesn't want to add to anyone's instinctive horror at what is splayed at their feet. Instead, he nods at the cops, a woman and two men, and says, 'Garth Klimmek, detective with Bitterfrost. What do we have here?'

'We got a goddamn mess is what we got,' one of the troopers says. The brass nameplate on his navy-and-gold jacket glints in the lamp light: SCHMIDT.

'That I can see, Trooper Schmidt. Do we have any ID? Driver's license? Anything?'

The woman, also a state trooper, lowers her camera. 'We searched him best we could without disturbing things, detective,' she says. 'No wallet, no phone, no keys, no nothing.'

And no face to speak of, Klimmek thinks. The eyes are indistinguishable but for the sockets. The cheeks are pulverized into a red-and-brown slurry, as if the victim was beaten with a meat mallet. Or an especially brute fist. Twenty-nine years with the Bitterfrost force and Klimmek has never seen a face this destroyed, unless you counted a certain head-on car crash on M-119, which he did not. Auto accidents are tragic, but murder leaves a reek like Klimmek imagines a sneering Satan would trail behind him on his rounds of hell.

'What is that smell?' he says. 'Or is it just me?'

'The body?' the troopers say at once.

'Looks too fresh. And the cold would mitigate it anyway. No chance an animal did this?'

The Bitterfrost officer crouches at the edge of the snowy circle. His name is Sylvester. He's been on the force less than a year and has asked Klimmek enough questions for ten. He wonders how the kid's stomach is feeling about now. 'It's possible a bear or some wolves paid a visit,' Sylvester says. 'Though I'm not sure they'd spend much time on the face. I grew up on a farm and—'

'This guy got the living shit beat out of him,' Schmidt interrupts. 'Plain and simple. You can see the dent in his head from here. Animals are way more gentle than the average human shitbag.'

Lights start striping the bare trees as a siren howls from atop the bluff. An ambulance. 'Do you folks know how we found out about this?' Klimmek says. 'Please tell me it wasn't another anonymous call.'

'Another?' says the woman, whose nameplate reads: ARSENAULT.

Sylvester says, 'We got an anonymous tip earlier about an abandoned truck with blood all over it. Not too far from here. No plates. We're running down the VIN.'

'Oh, boy,' Arsenault says. 'This one was called in by someone walking his dog.'

'In this weather?' Klimmek says. 'You mean someone who *said* he was walking his dog. Do we have a name or number?'

'I don't think so, detective, but we should have a recording.'

Klimmek hears something behind him and turns to see paramedics struggling down the hill with a stretcher and other gear. The locals almost never have to deal with disasters like this. If it is indeed a homicide, it would be Bitterfrost's first since the claw-hammer matter. That did not turn out well for Klimmek. He survived, but it cost him. Is still costing him.

As he watches the paramedics situate themselves around the body, he has the eerie, maybe irrational feeling that something, or someone, is manipulating the scene, the call-ins, even him. As if the anonymous call and the dog walker weren't merely coincidence. He steps closer to the body and leans into one of the paramedics. 'First take?'

The paramedic answers without looking at the detective. 'Blunt force trauma to the head. Probable skull fracture. Obviously, heavy blood loss. If he was lucky, he died before most of the blows were inflicted.'

'Blunt force trauma from what?' Klimmek says. 'An object? A gun? A fist?'

'Any. All of the above.'

Klimmek looks up and sees Schmidt and Arsenault tromping around beyond the yellow tape, methodically searching as best they can in the whipping snow. He addresses the paramedic again. 'Do you know about the bloodied truck that was called in? Did we send any of your guys there?'

'I think I heard something on the scanner. Listen, I gotta—'

'Yeah, sorry, do your job.' Klimmek turns to Sylvester. 'You said that truck isn't far? I rushed out here and didn't get the coordinates.'

Sylvester gets out of his crouch and gives the detective a rough idea of where to go. 'Should I come with?' he says.

'No,' Klimmek says, 'this is our territory, you stay here.'

'Yes, sir.'

Klimmek peers up the bluff at the climb ahead. It reminds him of high school football in Grand Haven, running sprints on the towering dunes along Lake Michigan. He latches one hand onto a tree trunk and pulls himself up the first stride, his boot slipping back in the snow. 'Dammit,' he says.

'Detective.'

The shout comes from behind him. He turns to face Arsenault. 'We found something,' she says. He follows her past the paramedics and the body, ducks under the yellow tape, and scrambles up a slight rise behind her. Schmidt is waiting a few yards up, his face barely visible in the swirling white, pointing at something.

'Here,' Arsenault says.

Klimmek squints through the sidewinding snow. Dangling from a broken-off pine branch is a winter glove. Looks like brown leather. Klimmek steps closer to see the glove's inner lining. Synthetic fur. For a right hand.

'I'll be damned,' he says. He turns and starts running back toward the bluff, again snatching at trees to keep from tumbling. A glove here, a glove there, a body here, and, if the body here is connected to that truck, why would the body be here and not there? Unless there's yet another body somewhere? 'Bag that glove and mark it,' Klimmek shouts over a shoulder. 'I gotta get to that truck.'

ELEVEN

'Dare-You-To-Finnish-It Pasty?'

Big Henry is leaning over his so-called omelet bar, his zeppelin gut squeezed against the edge of the pinkish Formica top.

'You read my mind,' Jimmy tells him.

'Fast read,' Big Henry says, grinning. 'You loving this weather, Mister Jimmy? Huh? Huh?' His favorite expression is a double-huh. And it's no more than an expression; he never really expects an answer. ''Merican cheese?'

'Sure. To go, please.'

Jimmy slipped out of the rink after the Clammer skate got started. He has to get back before it ends. Now he watches Big Henry spin to his griddle, dip a spatula into a slab of butter, and flop a hunk down, sending a funnel of sizzling steam up and around the cook's melon of a head. As always, a powder blue KN95 surgical mask is snapped around his left bicep, a reminder of how he almost lost his diner. He survived the government shutdowns by offering takeout, but angered many customers later when he required masks on people who weren't actually chewing. The pickets outside his entrance didn't help business much. 'People see what they decide they want to see, then they can't see anything else,' Henry tells anyone who listens. 'Especially people who feel helpless.'

The diner is scrumptious with the aromas of bacon and onions and butter and maple syrup. That's what Jimmy came for. That and the sense that this is just another morning, he can go about his life with nothing to worry about besides the well-being of Zelda and the rink. But Henry quickly dispenses with that notion. 'That's one heck of a shiner you got there, Jimmy,' he says. 'Get that at Looney Tunes?'

'If you're asking if Ronnie hit me with a beer mug,' Jimmy says, 'the answer is, "No comment."'

Does Henry know he was at the Loon? He does seem to ask about the joint whenever Jimmy stops in. Sometimes Jimmy thinks Henry sweats over his griddle seven days a week, eight hours a day, less for the splendid food he makes than for the gossip that flows from table to booth to stool from six in the morning till two in the afternoon.

'So what was it?' Henry says. 'A puck? Or a person?'

'My porch. Slip-and-fall.'

By noon, Jimmy realizes, half the town will know he took a header.

'Sounds like a lawsuit to me. Huh, huh?'

'Yessir. Baker versus Baker. Maybe I can get the insurance company to settle? Excellent idea, Henry.'

He stashes his bad hand in a pocket and turns on his stool so that the knot on his cheek faces Big Henry rather than the rest of the diner. The booths and tables aren't as occupied as usual, maybe because of the storm. A couple of folks nod Jimmy's way and he nods back without making too much eye contact, hoping they won't ask about his face or the weather. Grow up in Bitterfrost and you'll wind up either hating or loving weather talk, no in between. Jimmy's a hater. Talking about shitty weather just makes it shittier.

He pretends to scan the wall over the booths where two rows of framed IceKings team photos hang between used sticks signed by dozens of players, ancient black tape fraying off the blades. Jimmy's a smiling face in three pictures and a signatory on one of the sticks, wielded by the IceKings goalie in a US Elite Hockey League championship. The goalie was tall and gangly and so flexible that the team nicknamed him Gumby. Jimmy wishes he could remember the guy's real name.

'Jimmy,' a woman shouts from a back booth. He's pretty sure he knows her, though that, too, eludes him. 'We got this tonight?'

'Think so. The boys want first place back.'

'As long as you're there on Zelda,' she says, 'we got a shot, right?'

'Absolutely.'

The door clatters open with the tinkle of Christmas bells Big Henry hung there Thanksgiving morning. Mayor Cox strolls in, slapping his mittened hands together. 'Good morning,' he announces. 'Armageddon appears to be nigh, so I better have my final pasty before it's too late.'

The door's about to swing shut behind him when someone else pushes through, head bowed inside the dull green hood of a body-length down jacket. The hood gets thrown back to reveal a second hood. When Jimmy sees its orange hue, he spins back and checks the mirror hanging behind the cash register. The customer looks like the woman who sat at the end of the horseshoe last night at the Loon, the one who suggested those two guys deserved an ass-kicking. He can't remember whether he agreed or disagreed. She appears to be approaching. He'd rather not engage, but there's nowhere to go. Does she remember him?

Big Henry sets Jimmy's food down in a plastic foam tray. The Finns who brought their doughy pasty dish to Michigan would laugh, or maybe cringe, at Henry's version, about the size of a football. 'One Dare-You-To-Finnish-It Pasty for Mr Jimmy Baker,' he says. 'Hope you like.'

'Oh, I will.' Jimmy picks up the tray and, as he's getting off his stool, hears the woman's voice at his back.

'Are you OK, sir?'

He turns to her. Her hair, the color of an old nickel, straggles limply out of the orange hood. She remembers him, all right. But does she know something he doesn't? That he should know? His phone is going off in his pocket, but he can't look now. The woman purses her lips as she surveys the damage beneath his eye.

'I'm fine,' Jimmy says. 'Took a spill on my porch. How are you? Did you get home all right?'

'Yes. Got home OK.' She swallows. 'Mr Baker, that your name?'

'Jimmy. Yes. What's yours?'

She looks past Jimmy at Big Henry, then over her shoulder at the rest of the room, then at Jimmy again. Her lower lip has begun to tremble. For an uncomfortable second, Jimmy thinks the woman might cry. He leans toward her. 'Are you all right?'

She jumps back, as if Jimmy frightened her. He hopes no one else notices, although Big Henry must be riveted.

'I have to go,' she says. 'I'm sorry.'

Before Jimmy can say anything more, the Christmas bells are jangling again and she's hustling out the door, hunching her shoulders against the wind and snow. Jimmy watches until she turns off Jaata onto South Street, disappearing around the corner.

'What in holy heck was that?' Big Henry says.

Jimmy moves closer to him so the eavesdroppers can't hear. 'Do you know her?' he says.

'Yeah. Anya. Comes in every morning for a coffee, heavy cream, three sugars.'

'That's it? That's all you know?'

'Why? What's the big deal? You two have a little something going? Huh? Huh?'

'No, it's just . . .' Jimmy glances in the mirror to see if other customers are listening. Of course they are. 'She's here every day? I've never seen her.'

'She usually comes in the second I open. Picks up her coffee and goes. Maybe she slept in today. You know, with the storm and all.'

'Anya,' Jimmy says. 'Finnish?'

'Polish, I think.'

'Huh.' Anya what? Jimmy doesn't want to ask in earshot of the busybodies. He touches his swollen cheek with an exaggerated wince. 'I gotta get some ice on this. Thanks for the pasty.'

Outside the snow has let up a little. Walking down Jaata toward the lake, Jimmy checks his phone. It was Ronnie who called a few minutes ago. He'll call her back from the Zam shed. He passes South Street then glances over his shoulder before hanging a left on Suomi and doubling back around to South. The street is a typical Bitterfrost neighborhood, lined on both sides with houses, some of brick, some of plankboard, all built decades before, trees suspended over the sidewalks and front yards. No one is out. Somewhere a dog barks.

Jimmy looks up and down the street for Anya in the orange hoodie. He wants to ask her why she was sorry, why she had to go, how he almost made her cry, and what any of it had to do with whatever the hell happened last night.

TWELVE

Devyn bursts into the locker room still wearing her skates, shin guards, baggy hockey pants, and sweat-damp sports bra.

Unwritten rink rules dictate that the stray girl skating with guys dresses in the referee room down the hall. Devyn doesn't mind because the boys' room stinks. She's also happy to do without the endless alpha-male bullshit. Almost every one of them can imagine themselves playing in the NHL, even if the only girl they skate with can blow their blades off in a race, with or without the puck.

'Whoa, whoa, whoa,' Curly shouts. 'Payner! The stripper was last night, babe. We're fresh out of dollar bills.'

Devyn doesn't know his real name, just that he's Curly because his head is shiny bald. She ignores him, surveys the room, then stomps across the black rubber floor until she's knee-to-knee with the mound of man sitting in a corner, a can of beer in each of his hands, naked but for his skates and protective cup. She doubts he's flummoxed by her presence; hell, he probably likes it.

'Butchie,' she says.

Butch Dulaney takes a pull on one beer can, then the other, without acknowledging Devyn.

'You still banging Jordan Fawcett?'

Butch gives her a bearded smirk that suggests the answer is yes. But he says, 'You owe me a pair of skate laces, bee-otch.'

'Got some in my bag. What about Jordan?'

'How is who I sleep with any of your business?'

'Don't get all sensitive on me now. It's a simple question.'

Butch and some others guffaw. 'You wanna talk sensitive?' he says. He extends his right arm, displaying a raised, purplish blotch on the skin above his wrist. 'What's that?'

During this morning's session, Devyn two-handed him good after he flung an errant elbow past her head as they were about to collide behind a net. 'That's called hockey,' Devyn tells him. 'What about Jordan?'

'What about her?'

'I think what he means is,' Curly interjects, 'old Jordy can suck the chrome off a bumper hitch.'

Butch shoots Curly a nasty glance and takes another pull on the beer in his left hand. Then he tells Devyn, 'You ain't supposed to be in here. I don't need you ogling my privates.' He sets his beers on the floor and pushes himself up. Devyn angles her head back and looks up into a pale scar that zigzags through Butch's neck stubble.

'Keep your privates private, then,' she says. Butch puts a glare on, apparently thinking he can intimidate her. Not a chance. Her father, when he was mayor, and Butch's dad had a few run-ins over local property matters and Devyn is just as happy to go toe-to-toe with a Dulaney as her dad was. 'You with Jordan last night?'

'You deaf? What business—?'

'Then you don't know about the DUI?'

This stops him. 'I didn't get no DUI.'

'Not you. Jordan.'

He considers this, then says, 'Maybe you ought to talk to her ass, huh?'

He sits back down and takes alternate swigs off each of his beers, then sets the cans back on the floor and belches. Naked men in flipflops are filing past to the showers, some with towels clutched about their waists, some not. This is what Devyn tolerates to play the game she loves. 'If you know anything that might get her a break from the authorities,' she says, 'I'd be happy to know. So would she.'

Butch stares at the floor, then starts to pull off one of his skates. 'She get pulled over?' he says.

'Yeah. Late. Like one thirty, two.'

'Last night?'

'Seven, eight hours ago.'

'You sure?'

'Just saw her at the jail.'

'She's at the jail?'

'She oughta be getting frequent flier points,' Curly says.

Butch grunts his other skate off, thinking. Sometimes people let on more by not talking than talking.

'Can't help you,' he finally says.

'You didn't see her?'

'Said I can't help you.'

'She's in trouble, Butch, and I'd think a guy who's tapping her might have enough decency to give her a hand. You weren't in the Loon with her? You couldn't testify that she laid off the drinks?'

'Jesus, woman.'

From his sitting position, Butch flicks the heel of a hand into Devyn's sternum, knocking her back half a step. Surprised, she catches her balance before toppling, but then Butch is on his feet again, towering over her. The punch wasn't much more than a love tap, but the other guys look on, not stupid enough to risk any commentary. After all, it's just a Payne and a Dulaney messing with each other again.

'What is your fucking problem, woman?' Butch says. 'This ain't no damn courtroom. Get out of here. Now.'

Devyn could drop him with a skate to the crotch but instead she eases back a step, picturing his name typed on a subpoena. Butch sure as hell knows more. Dulaneys always know more than they'll admit. She's guessing Butch saw Jordan last night at the Loon, maybe afterward too. She wants to know what Jordan was doing between the time she left the Loon and the time the cops picked her up. Maybe there's an alibi there, or part of one, something that'll get the charges knocked down and keep her out of jail for longer than she's already scheduled. Devyn smiles and says, 'Thanks, Butchie. I can arrange for a real courtroom, no problem.'

'You know what?' Butch says, suddenly grinning. 'Sometimes I think we oughta just bulldoze this piece-of-shit rink and put up a damn Walmart. Or something else that would hack off you and your mommy. What would you think about that?'

'Where the hell would you get the money for that?'

'Ah, so your mommy's got a price?'

The Dulaneys have coveted the waterfront lot where the rink sits since Devyn's father won it away from Butch's daddy in front of the local zoning commission forty years ago. It didn't help that Calvin was secretly bedding Butch's daddy's ex, who chaired the board. Devyn learned years later about her father's occasional indiscretions, but willed herself to love him anyway for his support and unstinting loyalty. She still hasn't fully recovered from his death from cancer fourteen years ago.

'Please, Butch. You don't have the money and never will,' Devyn says. 'You're just pissed that you can't get your hands on the one piece of land you don't own on this side of the river. You're lucky we even let you skate here.'

Butch takes a healthy swig from his left-hand beer and belches. 'And you're lucky your mommy pays all your bills, ain't you? Couldn't cut it in the big city so you ran home to momma, ain't that it?'

Even the best defense lawyer can have a challenge scratching out a living on DUIs, child neglect, and bowling alley brawls. Eleanor Payne, via the IceKings and a real estate portfolio, keeps her daughter on a monthly retainer for which Devyn does almost nothing. Other lawyers have found ways to have the payments disclosed in court, trying to make Devyn look bad to a jury, or just to tick her off, maybe get her off her game. Every now and then, some jerk like Butch throws it in her face. Sometimes she thinks they have a point, she ought to get off the dole. She's working on it.

'Whatever, Butch,' Devyn says. 'You don't wanna help your girlfriend, let her rot in jail then.'

'Why don't you talk to your boy Jimmy?'

Jimmy Baker, he means. 'What about him?'

'He was in the Loon last night, too.'

Too? Devyn thinks.

'Why ain't you asking about him?'

'Why would I?'

'I don't know. He's your buddy, ain't he?'

'Have another beer, Butch.'

She walks out, thinking Jimmy isn't her 'boy' or 'buddy' the way Butch probably meant it, then breaks into a trot as she hears her phone ring in the referee room down the hall.

She misses the call, which of course was from Jordan.

Devyn dials her back and gets instantly dispatched to Jordan's voicemail. Goddamn Jordan. Devyn feels a responsibility – not quite an obligation, strictly, but something like it, given her family's status in town – to stand up for Jordan and the other lost sheep of Bitterfrost. She honestly doesn't care that their cases don't pay well, if at all. She *does* care that the clients themselves often don't seem to care as much about their defense as she does. She does care that the cases are often so rote and routine, benumbing procedurals as banal as filling your gas tank rather than grand battles for justice, not the sorts of challenges that will make her a better lawyer, that will propel her to the next level of her competence and imagination. She does care that these cases eat up time she could be spending on bigger ones. She won the biggest case she ever took on, defending a guy charged with killing a couple with a gun and a claw hammer. It made her semi-famous for good reasons until the reasons turned bad. She'd love a new case that would let her make up for that one. But it's not going to be hapless, helpless Jordan Fawcett.

Now, though, she has to get her butt in gear. Butch kept her longer than she expected, and she has that nine forty-five with the assistant prosecutor, who can be prickly. She peels off her gear and stuffs it in a locker – she'll take it home for a wash this weekend – then grabs a sixty-second shower, dresses, and hustles out to her car, hair still damp, heart still thumping a bit from her toe-to-toe with Butch. The weather isn't as bad as it was when she set out this morning, but it's far from good. About five months far.

As she's plugging her phone into her car charger, she sees a voicemail alert. Jordan called again while Devyn was showering. 'Shit,' she says as she presses play on the message from Jordan, expecting the worst.

Which is pretty much what it is.

'I'm sorry, Dev,' comes Jordan's voice. 'Really . . . I'm . . . I just can't do this. Not – not right now. I just . . . I have to get out of here for a while. Listen . . . shit.' Devyn hears a car horn in the background. 'Fuck you, asshole – sorry, that wasn't for you, Dev. I'll call you when . . . when . . . when I'm, you know, when I get my shit together. And don't worry, I'll pay you. Promise. I will. But, you know, just figure things out until I get back, OK? I'm sorry. Really, I am, really, really sorry.'

Please don't, Devyn thinks. The call dead, she pulls her car onto Jaata, flicks her brights for the benefit of any cars coming her way through the fog of snow, and heads toward the courthouse. She got the cops to release Jordan for the DUI on Devyn's promise that her client wouldn't run. She ran anyway. Some gratitude.

In the courthouse lot, Devyn spies the assistant prosecutor staring out her office window. Devyn is only three minutes late, but that's too much. She starts up the twelve stone steps to the double-door entrance, then stops on the landing, gazing into the building without seeing it.

She touches a hand to her breastbone where Butch shoved her. Something about that whole thing nags at her. He definitely didn't know about Jordan's DUI. And he definitely wasn't pleased. Then, out of nowhere, he asked about Jimmy. What was that about? Butch doesn't give a damn about Jimmy Baker. Devyn steps inside the courthouse and stomps the snow off her boots, thinking about Jordan and how far from Bitterfrost she might be by now.

'Ms Payne? Are we meeting?'

The assistant prosecutor, clearly annoyed, is calling down the corridor to Devyn's right. 'Be right there,' Devyn says. But she's rooted to the damp boot mat she's standing on, thinking: Is Jordan running from jail? Or from something even worse?

THIRTEEN

Klimmek's climbing again. Up a shallow rise, into the toothy wind, one step forward that slides half a step backward in the thigh-deep snow. A haze of black and gray drapes the precipice of the hill before him. He's ascending into a cloud that reeks of smoke from a car fire.

His arthritic left hip starts to betray him as he crests the ridge. He sees the pickup truck fifty yards away, half a dozen cops and paramedics surrounding it. It sits in a clearing larger than the one a mile away where the corpse lies. The truck's doors are swung open and the rear half of the flatbed is partially blackened and smoldering. Klimmek spots two openings in the trees where the truck could have come from. He walks a little closer, cautious. These things don't warn you before they explode.

A cop trudges over, her boots crunching. 'Detective,' she says. 'We've secured the area. No signs of human life at the moment.'

'How about human death?'

'Not that we've seen so far. I mean, somebody obviously drove that truck up here. But other than that, no. You ought to take a look inside. Pretty bloody mess in there.'

'Any tire tracks? Like over there?' He points. 'Or there?'

'Lots of them. But not easy to read. Assuming this thing arrived here hours ago, the snow has covered a lot.'

Klimmek surveys the edge of the clearing from one end to the other. Through the trees to the northeast, he sees a low-slung house, maybe a quarter of a mile away.

'Anyone check in at that house over there?'

'Not yet,' the officer says. 'We've been working in concentric circles around the truck, moving toward the woods.'

'Good. You found a glove?'

'Yes, sir. Brown leather. Nothing special. You can probably get a pair for eight bucks at Glen's.'

'Left, correct?'

'Yes.'

'Uh-huh. Let's look in the truck.' He starts walking. 'Chevy, right?'

'Yeah. Silverado. You OK, detective? You're limping.'

'Hip's out of warranty.'

'My dad got a new one. Best thing ever.'

Klimmek stops at the open driver's door. The first thing he notices is the stain on the headrest above the gray leather passenger seat. It's shaped like the narrow end of a kidney, with the rest of the organ stretched onto the seatback below. The color is a flat brown, less like chocolate than plain old shit. But he knows it's blood. A lot of blood, like he saw around the body. Blood on the seat itself, on the console, the windows, the doors.

'Back seat the same?' he says.

'Pretty much.'

Though it's his job, he has no desire to look. He knows enough for now. The lab geeks will tell him what's what, whether the blood is from one person or more, the type, the manner of its projection across the truck interior. Yet he can feel himself getting worked up about the case unfolding before him. Not excited, no, that wouldn't be good. When he was a rookie, he got excited about the rare murder he was charged with helping to solve. Now it has more to do with the past cases he failed to bring to a just resolution. One in particular.

'Does it look like accelerants were used?' Klimmek asks.

'We found an empty gasoline can just inside the woods over there.' She points toward the forest beyond the truck. Klimmek looks and through the trees notices the chimney of the house he saw a moment ago. 'So maybe yes?'

'Maybe. Certainly mark the can as evidence. But it doesn't look like it worked that well, does it?'

'Not really. Maybe because of the wind and snow?'

'Maybe. Maybe not.'

'Should we assume the victim nearby is connected?'

Klimmek has had the same thought and banished it for now. Too many things – the glove, the other glove, the gas can – already line up a bit too conveniently. Then again, there could be a simple, chilling reason they all align. What's that rule – something about a razor – about the most obvious answer being the correct one?

'All we know for sure right now is we have a dead body in the woods,' he says. He flexes the fingers inside his gloves to get the blood going. 'I'm gonna go check out that house.'

FOURTEEN

Jimmy's in the Zam shed preparing to take Zelda out for a spin when his phone rings. Ronnie again. He still hasn't answered her 'wtf' text because he's not sure yet how to answer. But he can't blow her off anymore or her imagination will go into overdrive. And there's something he wants to ask after his stop at Big Henry's.

'Yo, Ronnie. How are you?'

'How am I?' she says. 'How are you?'

'Fine except for a little bump on the head. Went ass over tea kettle on my porch last night.' Jimmy's not much for lies, but he's getting comfortable with this one. Besides, for all he knows, he did slip on his porch.

'Maybe that explains the text you sent at, I don't know, two thirty? Kinda spooked me, dude. What did you mean those guys won't be bothering me?'

Jimmy can see the North Dakota team filing into the rink for their morning skate. 'Yeah, I saw your reply. I think I meant to say I *hope* those guys wouldn't be in again. Did they leave OK?'

'They left fine, actually gave me a pretty nice tip. They were talking about heading north, so I don't think we'll see them again.'

'Good.'

'Thanks for having my back, Jimmy, but I'm glad you didn't get into it with them. You really don't need to be going there.'

'I know, you're right. They had me worked up. So I left. I don't think I even finished my drink.' He sees his boss descending the steps from the upper arena boxes in his purposeful morning stride, undoubtedly on his way to Jimmy. 'I only had that one drink, right?'

'Yeah, no worries.'

'What about that woman?'

'What woman?'

'The one in the orange hoodie.' Anya, Jimmy thinks, but doesn't say. 'At the top of the bar.'

'What about her?'

'She get out OK?'

Ronnie pauses. Jimmy wishes he didn't ask. 'Um, I guess,' she says. 'Why?'

'I don't know. Sorry. Just . . . strange night. Anyway, my boss is gonna be here any second. Gotta go.'

'Take care of yourself, Jimmy.'

He hangs up just as the door to the shed swings open and IceKings general manager Evan Payne walks in. 'Good morning, Mr Baker,' he says, plucking an audio bud from his right ear. 'You *are* going to do the ice for our guests from North Dakota, yes?'

'Nope.'

'Well then, I guess you're fired.'

'OK, but I'm taking Zelda with me.'

Evan fakes a horrified look. 'All right, you win. But please do the ice, OK?'

'I'll think about it. How are you, boss?'

Evan is a squat man who still bears the ropy shoulders and bull neck of his power-lifting days, along with a more recently acquired pot belly straining against his black-and-silver IceKings pullover. He looks nothing like his twin sister, Devyn, and was never as good at hockey. But he inherited the running of the team after his father got sick while Devyn was off at law school. He gazes around the shed as if sizing it up for the first time.

'Got your email,' he says. 'About the blades.'

'Great.'

'Where's your jacket?'

At least he didn't ask about Jimmy's face.

'In the laundry. I'll grab it at lunch.'

'Good. On the blades, gimme a day or two and I'll get back to you.'

Lately, a day or two has meant a week, sometimes more, but at least Jimmy got Evan's attention. A decent Zam blade costs only a few hundred bucks. The Paynes generally aren't penny-pinchers, but Evan has grown a little picky about spending lately, even as he raised ticket prices and, less obviously, the prices of beer and brats and nachos at the concession stands. Just last week, Evan asked if Jimmy could find cheaper toilet paper for the locker rooms. Jimmy said, Sure, irritated butts might make the boys even faster on the ice. Evan said he was still trying to dig out from the half-season the team couldn't play during the 'plague,' as he and his mother referred to the Covid epidemic. Seems like ancient history to Jimmy, but then he's not the boss.

'Zelda appreciates it,' Jimmy says.

'How is the old girl?'

'Same as yesterday. Best in the league.'

'Man, you hear about the shit that went down last night?'

'What shit is that?' Jimmy says.

Evan keeps a police scanner in his office. He says he likes to keep abreast of local doings that might affect IceKings attendance, even though the team is the only real entertainment within a hundred miles and most games sell out. Jimmy suspects Evan is just a crime groupie.

'The cops found some guy beat to hell out in the woods north of town, can't even identify him yet.'

Jimmy swallows hard. 'No way.'

'Yeah. It'd be the first homicide here in a while. Not good.'

Jimmy wants to ask where it happened and do the cops have a suspect, but instead he changes the subject. 'What are you thinking for tonight?'

'Every seat sold,' Evan says.

'I mean the hockey.'

'Oh. You know, outskate them, play keep-away with the puck. The Bombers get impatient, take some penalties, we get a few power plays, get out with a win. We're faster. No need to start going toe-to-toe with their big boys.'

That sounds about right, but the IceKings, like the Bombers, are kids, mostly eighteen and nineteen, easily goaded into stupid stuff. Jimmy knows this all too well. He climbs on Zelda then, glancing up, sees Butch standing in the doorway to the shed in gym shorts, flipflops, and a sweat-stained long-sleeve shirt, swigging from a beer.

'Hey,' Evan says, 'keep the booze in the dressing room, will you?'

Butch ignores him. 'How you feeling today, Jimbo? Big night at the old Loon, eh?'

'You need a shower, Butch.'

Butch grins. 'You close 'er up?'

'Nope.'

'Take care of business?'

Jimmy sees Evan listening. 'I had my drink and went home, if that's what you mean.'

'Uh-huh.' Butch turns to Evan, guffaws, and takes another gulp of beer. 'I guess I should let you guys get back to jerking each other off, eh?'

'You really shouldn't be drinking in here,' Evan says.

Butch points his beer at Jimmy and says, 'I can see why he's gotta kiss your ass, you keep him in hot dogs and beer. But why does everybody else around here gotta suck up?'

Evan folds his arms, saying nothing. Which isn't like Evan, but he's probably preoccupied with his morning duties. Jimmy starts Zelda and pulls her toward the rink. 'Have a good day, Butchie.'

'Drive your Zamboni, loser. I drive a Corvette.' Butch flips his empty beer can across the shed and it bounces off the rim of a garbage pail and onto the concrete floor.

'Come on,' Evan says, hurrying over to pick the can up. Butch goes out the door chuckling. 'What is his problem?'

'Got me.'

'What did he mean about last night?' Evan squints up at Jimmy. 'That how you got that thing under your eye?'

So he did notice. 'Nah,' Jimmy says. 'Just took a little spill.'

'I'd get some ice on it.' Evan lingers for a moment longer, staring without a word. It makes Jimmy uncomfortable. 'Talk later.'

Jimmy swings Zelda out of the shed, across the concrete apron, and onto the ice. He starts to think about the body the cops supposedly found but forces the image out of his head and focuses on what he's doing, a moment he loves, as ordinary as it might seem to someone who's never played hockey. Gliding onto the ice with Zelda reminds him of the days when he would leap out between the benches before the start of an IceKings game, his skates slashing, the packed arena blasting with noise, the ice aglitter. Everything outside the frozen oval disappeared when his first skate blade – always the left, always – touched the ice. He always made sure to peek up at the league championship banners hanging in the rafters.

He looks now, using his good hand to steer Zelda to the right, then veering left up the half-wall. Most Zam drivers take the clockwise route around the ice. Jimmy likes the counterclockwise. It's the direction players take when they jump onto the ice; why shouldn't it be the Zamboni's? It's part of the luck he and Zelda try to bring the IceKings, luck commemorated by those banners marking eight league championships in Jimmy's tenure as Zam driver, including three in Zelda's four seasons.

Past the banners, at the far end of the rink, sits the clutch of upper-deck seats reserved each night for 'Zelda's Zealots,' a few dozen fans of Zelda and, to some extent, Jimmy. They show up in white jerseys emblazoned with big black-and-silver Zs and cheer more raucously while Zelda and Jimmy are making their rounds than they sometimes do during the games. One Saturday morning each month, Jimmy takes their children for rides on the Zam: *Zaturdays with Zelda.*

Curling around, Jimmy glances at Evan's windowed office just above the highest row of seats in the arena. He sees Evan pacing, waving his arms, talking to someone hands-free on his phone. He can't help but wonder what the police are saying on Evan's scanner. Someone's really dead? Murdered? Whoever died was probably from somewhere else and killed by someone from somewhere else. These things almost never happen in Bitterfrost. That's what Jimmy tells himself.

He remembers his back porch door being open the night before and tries to remember whether he locked it before he left this morning. He usually secures it when he leaves, if only so it doesn't blow open in a storm. But today, he was a little distracted. He'll check when he goes back for the jacket. He'll just have to scrub that sleeve and let it air dry, then hustle back to the rink for pregame prep.

As he rolls past the penalty box and the benches, he touches his face. It stings even worse now. Evan's right, time for some ice. Then again, he tells himself, the pain is good for him.

FIFTEEN

As he pulls into the driveway, Klimmek feels certain he's been in this place before. The house is a bungalow wrapped in dull green aluminum siding, with no more than three bedrooms, maybe only two, a brick chimney attached to one side, a one-car garage to the other. It's like a lot of houses in the woody hills outside Bitterfrost proper but within the city's legal limits.

A bare-branched oak stands in the middle of the front yard, and what appear to be garden stakes jut up from snowdrifts next to the garage. Klimmek leans out of his Bronco and takes a few photos with his phone, including one of the steel mailbox with the address tacked to its side. Maybe for nothing. He steers around the single trail of vehicle tracks that lead through the snow from County Road 816 to the house. The tracks are fluffy at the edges, so whoever made them probably did so earlier that morning.

He parks and steps down into the snow. He studies the tire tracks. Now that he's closer to the garage, he notices a few things. Again, maybe nothing, but Klimmek has been a detective for twenty-nine years, a cop for thirty-six, and he can't help himself. Sometimes, waiting for breakfast at Big Henry's, he catches himself squinting at salt and pepper shakers to see if he can tell one fingerprint from another. Or his wife catches him doing it and tells him to just stop.

There are two, maybe even three sets of tracks. The first, which Klimmek saw from the road, proceed toward the house, then appear to stop at approximately a forty-five-degree angle twenty or so feet from the garage, as if the vehicle might have parked there. Then the tracks veer toward the garage and end at the door, presumably because the vehicle went inside. Those tracks, Klimmek sees, aren't as filled with fresh snow as the ones that preceded it. So a vehicle – or maybe more than one, he can't tell for sure – must have stopped in the driveway, and for more than just a few minutes.

He steps closer to the spot where the vehicle's driver-side door seems to have been. There he sees a scatter of what appear to be boot prints. Not terribly fresh, but not covered over yet, either. In one of the prints is a smattering of faint blue spots. Klimmek crouches down. Is it vehicle solvent? Fruity booze? Smurf piss? His phone buzzes. Kris is calling. He stands and answers, 'Hey, honey,' his voice softer than normal, as if someone might be listening in.

'I thought you were going to call when you made the bridge.'

Klimmek sighs. 'I'm still here.'

'Here where?'

'Bitterfrost. We have a situation.'

'Nobody else can handle it? You're supposed to be with Kenneth.'

Kenneth, their twenty-eight-year-old son, is a schoolteacher in Escanaba in the UP. Each year, he and his dad take snowmobiles on a three-day tour of the peninsula, one year to the west, the next to the east. This year was to be an eastern foray, from St Ignace to Sault Sainte Marie to Paradise then down through the peninsula back to the Mackinac Bridge.

'I know where I'm supposed to be, Kris,' Klimmek says. 'I'm not gonna get there. We have a—'

'You haven't seen your son since Labor Day, but you have to be the hero.'

'Not fair, K.'

'What happened?'

Klimmek gives her the short version, which is ugly enough. She doesn't sound all that impressed. 'It'll still be here when you get back, Garth.'

'I know that, but this is—'

'Yes, yes, this is when the evidence is fresh and the bad guys haven't gotten their stories straight. I know all about it. Your son will be disappointed.'

'He understands.'

'Call me later.'

She had to live through the claw-hammer case and, worse, its aftermath of self-doubt and recrimination. But he doesn't want something like that to happen again. So, he's here, in Bitterfrost. He'll make it up to Kenneth.

Klimmek turns toward the woods where the officers are tending to the truck with the blood in it. If they'd found another body or part of one, he assumes he'd have heard by now.

He moves toward the house, steering clear of the tire tracks. Yet another set of tracks, seemingly fresher than the other two, leads from the garage back out to the road, criss-crossing the others in places. It's conceivable that that driver was struggling to find his or her way in the storm, perhaps within the last several hours.

Klimmek steps up onto the front porch. The porch light is off. The outline of a welcome mat is visible beneath a scrim of new snow. Klimmek pushes a doorbell button, hears a chime inside, and waits. Nothing happens. He opens the unlocked screen door and knuckles the inside door with four knocks. Again, nothing. He puts an ear to the door and hears only the faint ticking of a clock. If anyone's home, they're not answering. But it doesn't feel as though anyone is home. No sign of a dog, either, if this happens to be the house of whoever called in the body.

He shuffles to his left and peers in through the front window. The front room is simple: a sofa, a recliner, a fireplace on one wall, TV on another, four framed photographs of a young girl hanging over the sofa. Klimmek hops off the porch and trudges clockwise around the house. The brick chimney, he notices, could use some tuck-pointing. Beyond that is a window on the kitchen. Klimmek gets up on his toes and looks inside. Across the kitchen, stuck to the fridge, he sees something that might explain why this place seems familiar.

He continues around the corner of the house to a short set of steps leading up to a small deck. He can tell that some of the snow piled on the steps is fresher than the rest. Someone went up or down and back, probably in the dead of night. Klimmek climbs the steps and looks into the kitchen through the window on the door.

The side of the fridge is pocked with magnets shaped like the machines that go around at IceKings games. 'Hockey Gives Me a ZamBoner,' reads one. Ah, he thinks, the guy who lives here must drive the Zamboni at those games. Jimmy something. He's actually kind of famous around town, people think he's good luck for the team.

Klimmek recalls being in this house once, for about an hour, for a gathering Kris dragged him to. She had a co-worker whose kid played for the team, and he knew a guy who knew a guy, and there Klimmek was, in this Jimmy guy's kitchen, drinking a Stroh's and asking how did a Zamboni work anyway? He remembers Jimmy getting excited talking about it, long after Klimmek lost interest. Now here he is standing on the guy's back porch, pondering patterns of tire tracks and boot prints in snow.

He knocks again. No response. Nothing seems amiss in the kitchen, except for that stupid magnet. For the hell of it, Klimmek tries the door. The knob turns. Unlocked. He could slip in and look around. But he has no probable cause, no warrant. If he found something, he could compromise the investigation. If he found nothing, he's a jerk invading someone's privacy. His wife tells him he needs sometimes to ignore his 'puckering butthole' and walk away. Every single thing people do is not always a felony, she says. Which he agrees is correct, technically.

Klimmek backs away from the door. That's when he sees the stains. Two tiny ones, brownish red, shaped like teardrops, on the brass outer knob. He must have missed them before. He squats for a closer look. No, he tells himself. Those stains could be a lot of things. Paint maybe. Or maybe they've been there for years. He reminds himself that all he has now, all he has for sure, is a dead guy in the woods. A dead, grotesquely mutilated guy.

Klimmek takes his phone out and snaps pictures of the doorknob from different angles. He calls up his voice-memo app and narrates everything he has seen since arriving at the house. He emails the audio file to himself, then hits speed dial for the Bitterfrost Police. Werges answers. 'Rich,' Klimmek says. 'I need some details on a property at 22625 County Road 816.'

SIXTEEN

Jordan Fawcett's mother sits at her kitchen table, a six-seat oval of chrome legs and chipped turquoise Formica. She fondles a coffee cup that Devyn suspects is filled with something other than coffee. Devyn perches on a wobbly chair to Shirlee Fawcett's left. A TV blares from the living room, one of those morning talk shows for which Devyn has zero patience.

'Haven't heard from J-Bird since last weekend,' Shirlee says. 'Of course she needed money. That's usually why she calls.'

'Nothing from her in the last twenty-four hours?'

'Well. I'd be surprised, but I can't say for certain because my phone's dead and I left my charging cord somewhere.' She lifts her cup. It shakes a little as she takes a long drink.

Devyn digs in her briefcase and produces a cord. 'Use mine.'

'Oh, dandy, awful nice of you, sweetie.'

While Shirlee fetches her phone, Devyn looks around. Even from here she can see mold festering around the base of the sink faucet. Three empty handles of Smirnoff and a crumpled Cheetos bag peek out of an overflowing trash can. Devyn tells herself not to judge. She grew up in a different sort of house, where the disarray was more effectively concealed. She might not even be here now if her mother hadn't canceled their lunch date for the third time in the past month.

Shirlee returns and plugs her phone in near the kitchen sink. She collects her coffee cup and reaches inside the fridge. Her girth blocks Devyn from seeing, but she can hear the gurgle of something being poured. Shirlee takes a swallow as the fridge door swings shut behind her.

'How's the girl's case going?' she says.

'It was going all right until last night. She got picked up for drunk driving. To be honest, I'm worried about her, Shirlee.'

'I gave up worrying about that girl a while back. Don't do any good. She got a mind of her own, just not a brain.'

'I get that. But she's always happy to get on the phone and tell me whatever's on her mind, if you take my drift. Now she isn't picking up or texting back. I worry she might be on the run.'

'Been on the run her whole damn life. From school. From jobs. From anything like that old forgotten word: responsibility.'

She takes another sip from her cup.

'You don't know if she's been dating one of the Dulaneys, do you?'

Shirlee guffaws. '"Dating?" Ain't you a romantic.'

Her phone starts chirping just as a stentorian male voice interrupts the TV program: 'This is a breaking news alert. The News North I-team has learned exclusively that authorities are investigating the brutal murder of an unidentified male –' Devyn excuses herself and hurries into the living room – 'who was found in a forest outside Bitterfrost early this morning.'

A blurry image on the screen shows officers in parkas and earflap caps trudging around in trees ringed by crime-scene tape. Devyn scans the scene for a body but, seeing none, figures it already has been removed. No wonder Detective Klimmek was preoccupied earlier.

'Police aren't commenting,' the voice continues, 'but the I-team has learned the victim may have been bludgeoned to death. If confirmed, it would be the first homicide in Bitterfrost since the chilling claw-hammer case five years ago. Stay right here, we'll have more details as they become available.'

Bludgeoned, Devyn thinks. Please, not with a claw hammer.

'Holy jeez,' says Shirlee, now standing next to Devyn. 'Looks like the constables have more important things to worry about than J-Bird's driving.'

The talk show resumes. Devyn hands Shirlee a business card. 'If you hear from Jordan, could you please let me know? I don't want her getting into any more trouble than she's already in. I'm gonna get my cord and be on my way.'

'I will definitely keep you in mind.' Shirlee nods at the TV. 'Can you believe that? Beaten to death? I'd rather just get shot in the head.'

Devyn is almost to her car when she hears Shirlee shouting from her front door. 'Hey, Miss Lawyer. Looks like the girl texted me when my phone wasn't working.'

Devyn trots back. Shirlee is shaking her head. 'What in God's name are you talking about, girl?' she asks her phone.

'Can I see it?' Devyn says.

Shirlee presses the phone against her chest. 'Why?'

'Why what?'

'Why do you care?'

'Why do I care?' Devyn says, surprised by Shirlee's sudden defensiveness. Maybe she cares more about her daughter than she likes to let on. 'Jordan's my client. It's my job. And I did loan you my charging cord, didn't I?'

'Shit,' Shirlee says. 'Lots of people got jobs. Lots of people don't do 'em very well. They're just punching the clock.'

Perceptive for someone who's drinking before noon. 'You're right,' Devyn says. 'But yesterday, when your daughter stood up in court and called the judge a meddlesome cunt, I jumped up and took the hit and calmed the judge down and kept Jordan out of jail. It would've been easier to just let the judge toss her back in. I'd be at lunch now.'

'"Meddlesome cunt?"' Shirlee laughs. 'Big word for J-Bird. Nice job, Miss Lawyer.'

'Now can I see what Jordan sent?'

Shirlee hands over the phone. Devyn reads the truncated text three times, memorizing the bulk of it: **If something bad happens, check my phone. Don't let them feed mxjsfi!2s((**

'Thank you,' Devyn says, handing the phone back. 'Please give me a call if you hear from your daughter.'

On the way back to town, Devyn records a voice-memo of what she remembers of Jordan's text, wondering why the last few words were garbled, running the letters through her head, trying to discern the message Jordan was trying to send.

SEVENTEEN

The back door to Jimmy's house is, as he feared, unlocked. But what really startles him are the fresh boot prints on the back porch. The tread marks tell him they aren't his.

He pushes the door open for a closer look. He checks the kitchen floor for similar markings. He doesn't see any, but that's little relief. Who was traipsing around on his back porch this morning? Did he or she come inside?

He thinks back again on last night. He recalls recovering his right boot from the porch steps. He remembers the packed-down snow that made it look as though someone or something was hauled through it. The snowstorm has covered that over. The mailman isn't due till late afternoon.

Couldn't be police, could it?

He locks the door and throws the deadbolt. He can't stay long. He has to clean his IceKings jacket and get back to the rink before Evan misses him. He retrieves the jacket from his bedroom and brings it to the kitchen sink. He douses a steel-wool pad with dish soap and starts scrubbing the bloodstains on the silver sleeve. But he's just smearing the blood deeper and wider. He wishes like hell he hadn't stupidly forgotten to throw it in the washer before leaving for work.

Through the window over the sink, a flashing light catches Jimmy's eye. A police car is flying through the forest in the direction of town. If the siren is going, Jimmy can't hear it.

But he does hear the knocking at his front door.

He looks at the jacket. The sleeve is a damp, bloody mess. He stuffs the jacket into the cupboard below the sink.

He hears two more raps at the front door. He walks to the front hallway and freezes. Through the living-room window, he sees a black-and-gold Bitterfrost police cruiser parked outside, exhaust spooling into the frigid air. He considers retreating into his bedroom, pulling the shades, and ignoring the knocks, but he can see an officer sitting behind the police car's steering wheel who has probably already seen him.

Jimmy goes to the door and opens it. He thinks he's seen the guy standing on the porch before, but doesn't think he knows him. He's dressed in street clothes beneath a parka with a fur-lined hood. Jimmy leans out into the cold. 'Hello,' he says. 'Can I help you?' The man smiles. 'Mr Baker? James Baker?'

'Jimmy.' He extends his hand. The man shakes it and, with his other hand, displays a black leather wallet bearing a brass badge. 'I'm Detective Garth Klimmek,' he says. 'With the Bitterfrost Police.'

EIGHTEEN

The first thing Klimmek notices is Jimmy Baker's face. His right cheek is the color of a rotting plum and swollen to half the size of one. The bandage is doing a poor job of covering it. Baker's self-conscious about it, too, because when he sees the detective looking, he says, 'Had a little slip-and-fall on the porch here last night.'

'Ouch,' Klimmek says. 'I hope you're icing it.'

'Yes, sir. But that's not why you're here.'

'I need to ask you a few questions, Mr Baker.'

Jimmy Baker keeps glancing in the direction of the cruiser waiting in the yard.

'Any chance we could step inside?'

'Of course. And call me Jimmy.'

'Will do, Jimmy.'

Jimmy leads him into the living room Klimmek glimpsed through the front window that morning. Jimmy motions him toward an armchair while taking the sofa beneath the photos Klimmek saw earlier.

'That your daughter?' he says.

'Yes. Avery.'

'Very nice.'

'Thank you. She lives with her mother downstate.'

Klimmek finds it odd that Jimmy would volunteer that. Does he feel defensive about it? 'Do you get to see her much?'

'Not enough, you know?'

'I do,' the detective says, thinking of his son. 'You're the Zamboni driver for the hockey team, is that right?'

'Yep. Thirteen years.'

Jimmy is a big man, taller than Klimmek by about three inches and beefier by maybe twenty pounds. His strawberry blond hair is cut short and flecked with silver around the ears. He doesn't seem to remember Klimmek from that years-ago party.

'That looks like an interesting job,' Klimmek says. 'I have no idea how one of those things works.'

'It's not all that complicated. I'd be happy to take you for a ride if you're interested.'

'I might take you up on that.'

'Are you a fan?'

'Of hockey? Not huge. Too many rules.'

'I wouldn't guess rules would bother a guy like you.'

'You'd think, right? Anyway, I need to ask you about last night.'

'Sure. But can I ask whether this has anything to do with that thing I heard about this morning?'

Damn TV reporters, Klimmek thinks. He zips his parka open halfway. 'What thing is that, Jimmy?'

'A murder? We don't have a lot of those around here.'

'No, we don't. I'm not really at liberty to say much, but – between us?'

'OK.'

'We do have a potential homicide on our hands. Which is why I'm hoping you can help us on some things that transpired overnight.'

'Shoot.'

Klimmek shows Jimmy his cellphone. 'Mind if I record?'

'Go ahead.'

Klimmek sets the cellphone on a bookshelf next to him and pulls a notebook from inside his jacket. Jimmy unfolds his legs. 'Can you tell me,' the detective says, 'where you were last night, say, between midnight and four o'clock?'

Jimmy thinks for a moment, then says, 'Pretty much I was here. I mean, I had a drink at the Lost Loon after leaving the rink—'

'I'm sorry, approximately when did you leave the rink?'

'Uh, a little after ten thirty?'

'And you went directly from the rink to the bar?'

'Yes.'

'I'm sure someone could corroborate? As a matter of routine.'

'Ronnie the bartender. She served me.'

Earlier, after confirming who owns the house he's now sitting in, Klimmek did a little research. Were he a hockey buff, he probably would remember Jimmy as a popular left wing for the IceKings twenty-four years ago. According to what Klimmek saw on fan sites, Jimmy 'Bakes' Baker was drafted by the NHL's Chicago Blackhawks and spent most of seven seasons in the minor leagues, gradually gaining a reputation for using his fists to punish opponents who dared menace the stars on Jimmy's teams. He retired abruptly in the middle of a season – in the middle of a game – and moved back to Bitterfrost. There was more to the story that Klimmek was surprised he didn't already know. In his line of work, he'd encountered plenty of people – nearly all of them male – capable of inflicting lethal violence using nothing but their hands. But he had to wonder how this hometown hero, the second child in a seemingly normal Bitterfrost family, had become such a brute.

'How long were you at the bar, Jim?'

'An hour? Maybe a little less.'

As he talks, Klimmek scans the room for clues about who Jimmy is. Besides the photos of the girl, there aren't many. Three girls' volleyball trophies stand on the bookshelf, though nothing related to hockey. Maybe Jimmy keeps his mementoes elsewhere. Maybe he doesn't keep them at all.

'Did you have much to drink?'

'One highball. My limit.'

'Highball, eh? Old-school. Then you came straight home?'

Now Jimmy pauses just long enough for a sliver of doubt to wedge itself into Klimmek's brain. 'Yeah,' Jimmy says. 'Excuse me, though.' He's looking past Klimmek out the window. 'I think that officer wants a word.'

Klimmek turns and sees Sylvester trotting up. 'Pardon me a second.'

He steps out to the porch. Sylvester looks excited. 'Sorry to interrupt,' the officer says. 'Few things. State post in Gaylord got a call from a woman downstate trying to locate her husband, one –' Sylvester peers at a notebook in his left hand – 'Jerome Hardy. Hardy and the woman's brother, name of Aaron Diggs, were supposed to be in Mackinac City last night but apparently didn't make it.'

'Got it. Other thing?'

'We got a call—'

'Don't tell me.'

'Yeah. Anonymous. Woman saw something about the murder on TV. Said she heard a couple of Detroit guys were raising hell at the Lost Loon last night, might have run into trouble.'

'But she didn't give her name?'

'Nope. Dispatcher said she thought she had a bit of an accent. Couldn't place it, though.'

Klimmek's memory goes to a case he read about some time ago. Two guys from Detroit got shit-faced in a bar in some little up-north town and wound up dead at the hands of some locals. Took a state police detective eighteen years to solve it. Klimmek doesn't have eighteen years. He'd be seventy-frigging-seven.

'Great,' he tells Sylvester. 'That all?'

'No. The VIN on that truck with all the blood? It checks out as Jerome Hardy's.'

'Do we know whether the body we brought in was one of these gentlemen, Hardy and . . . who again?'

'Diggs. Not yet, but we're on it.'

Klimmek looks down at the porch. Where, he asks himself, is any trace of the blood from Jimmy Baker's slip-and-fall? Maybe Jimmy cleaned it up. Or maybe there was nothing to clean. In Klimmek's years as a detective, he has determined for himself that a single fib – a misspoken phrase, a misremembered moment, a mistaken conclusion – does not necessarily constitute a lie. Two fibs, however, usually qualifies. Did Jimmy really come straight home from the Loon? Did he really slip on his porch? As earlier, Klimmek thinks the evidence so far – the tire tracks, the gloves, the blood on the doorknob – is at once suspicious and convenient. He's trying not to get ahead of himself. But why would Jimmy lie if he has nothing to hide?

'Officer,' he says, 'do you have your phone? Mine's inside.'

'Sure thing, detective.'

'Take a couple of pictures of that, will you?'

'Of what?'

'That.' Klimmek points. Curled in the corner of Jimmy's front porch is a half-used, ten-pound bag of rock salt.

NINETEEN

Jimmy wants to get off the couch and go into the kitchen and do something with that jacket. Even though he can't fathom how the blood wound up on the sleeve. But there's been a murder and here's Jimmy with a bloody jacket stuffed under a sink and a detective asking questions.

'Jimmy? You OK?'

The detective is back in his living room, kicking snow off his boots on the throw rug by the door. Are those the boots that made the prints outside Jimmy's back door? The detective appears to know things Jimmy does not. It's making him even more nervous than he was before.

'I'm fine,' Jimmy says, getting off the sofa. 'I have to get back to work.' He pulls out his phone and waggles it. 'My boss is looking for me. Big game tonight.'

'No problem,' the detective says. 'I just have one or two more questions.' He steps over to the bookshelf. 'Almost forgot my phone,' he says, picking it up. 'You don't mind if I keep recording?'

'Actually,' Jimmy says, 'I think I do.'

'Your prerogative.'

'I mean, should I have a lawyer here?'

The detective looks at him for an unnerving couple of seconds, then says, 'That's up to you, Jimmy.'

'So I should?'

'You can, of course, but I'm really just hoping to find out what you might have seen last night –' he gestures toward the wall to his left – 'out that way.'

Jimmy's heart is suddenly pounding like it used to after a two-minute shift on the ice. 'I don't remember seeing anything.'

The detective points toward the kitchen. 'Could we take a look—?'

'I don't think so,' Jimmy says. A quiver runs through his hamstrings so hard that he almost has to sit down again. 'Do you have a specific question?'

The detective stares at his notebook for a few seconds. Then he says, 'You were here, in this house, around one o'clock this morning?'

'I believe so.'

'Do you *know* so, Mr Baker?'

'I told you. I punched out at the rink, had one drink, and came home.'

'Did you hear or see anything out your kitchen window after, say, one o'clock? Any noise? Anything?'

'How do you know I have a kitchen window?'

The detective gives him a look that makes Jimmy think asking the question was foolish. 'We appreciate your time, Mr Baker. I'll be in touch.'

'You know where to find me.'

The detective turns to go, then stops and says, 'One last thing. Is it true that during your hockey playing days you bit an opposing player's finger off in a fight?'

The memory floods back. Jimmy feels his face flush. It wasn't his best moment, but unfortunately, not his worst either. The guy tried to jab his finger into one of Jimmy's eyes and missed. Jimmy reacted.

'Not quite, detective. What did you say your name was again?'

'Klimmek. Call me Garth.'

'Anything else?'

'Your little fall on the porch? Was that last night? Or before?'

'I . . . why does that matter?'

Klimmek slaps his notebook shut. 'Probably doesn't.'

TWENTY

Devyn sees the assistant prosecutor's face appear in the mirror as she's washing her hands in a restroom at the Bitterfrost courthouse.

'Dev,' the prosecutor says, 'have I ever told you I love your hair? The way it shines?'

'Um, no, but thanks.'

Out-of-towners assume Devyn colors her silver bob. Most Bitterfrosters know she's been going gray since her mid-twenties. Devyn likes to think the hairstyle goes nicely with the town's name.

'Did you hear about last night?' the prosecutor says.

'Last night? What about it?'

'Some guy apparently got the living hell beat out of him. Cops found him in the woods. Dead.' Devyn heard that much on Shirlee Fawcett's TV. 'Then there's some truck that might or might not be involved, drenched in blood, maybe torched. If my boss was a guy, she'd have a stiffy a yard long. Her first murder case in years. The Detroit stations are already calling.'

Truck? Devyn thinks. Detroit? She feels her phone vibrating in a pocket. 'Why do the Detroit stations give a hoot?'

'Not sure yet, but I hear the truck's registered to some guy from a hotshot family down there.'

Devyn figures 'hotshot' to mean rich or connected or both. 'Is the dead guy the truck's owner?' she says.

'Apparently not.'

'Do you know the truck owner's whereabouts?'

The prosecutor shrugs.

'So he's gotta be a suspect.'

'How do you know it's a "he?"'

'Isn't it always?'

'Pretty much. If we find him, or her, should I pass along your cell?'

'Funny.'

Devyn sneaks a look at her phone. Jimmy called. 'Gotta deal with this.'

TWENTY-ONE

Jimmy waits until the detective is gone for ten minutes to go to the kitchen. He pulls the jacket out from under the sink and flattens the bloodstained sleeve against the counter. Cleaning it is hopeless.

He reaches back under the sink, pulls out a trash bag, and stuffs the jacket inside. He doesn't want the thing in his house. Not so much because it's potentially incriminating, but because it's a reminder that something happened last night, something he may have been involved in, something he may be responsible for in some way. A telltale heart in his own home, asking whether he killed someone.

He almost did, once.

Jimmy felt the tap on his shoulder barely nine minutes into the game. Coach wanted him to go. 'Fourteen,' was all he said.

Jimmy jumped the boards and dug his blades into the ice, his first strides on his first shift of the night, late in the second period. He hadn't played much actual hockey of late, but he'd fought opposing players twice in the past four games, all at the coach's behest, while managing one off-balance shot that the other team's goaltender easily muffled against his chest protector.

The puck rattled around the boards behind the net to Jimmy's left, the howls of four thousand Erie fans shredding the arena air. The few who noticed him jumping onto the ice sensed what was coming. Fans who knew jack shit about the actual game of hockey worshipped fights.

Number Fourteen barreled into the far corner to collect the puck, Jimmy in pursuit. He was seven years Jimmy's junior, six-foot-four, probably two-twenty, with sudden speed and a reputation for being willing if not eager to drop the gloves. Probably would get a shot in the NHL. Jimmy didn't begrudge the kid, even knowing his own time to make the big league had passed.

Jimmy leapt off his skates four feet from the corner boards, catapulting into Fourteen's back with a resounding crunch. The kid's head snapped sideways, helmet smacking the glass with a whack that screamed concussion. The crowd roared its sick appreciation.

Jimmy lost his balance for a beat, tottering on one skate and nearly toppling before finding his feet and thrusting an arm around Fourteen's neck. Referee whistles shrieked. Fourteen wrenched himself away. 'Are you fucking kidding me?' he said as he shoved the palm of one of his gloved hands into Jimmy's face.

Jimmy didn't bother to reply. Hockey fights demand thirty to sixty seconds of concentrated energy, and he'd learned not to waste a bit telling the other guy he was an asshole. Instead, he slapped Fourteen across the nose. He wanted to get the youngster's eyes watering, make it harder for him to see before the slugging commenced. Unfazed, the guy grabbed a fistful of Jimmy's jersey, jerked him to one side, and threw a glove off. Jimmy let him cannon a barehanded right at his face. It, too, was part of his battle plan.

The punch slammed into Jimmy's left cheekbone and zapped a bolt of electric pain through his temporal cranium to the occipital at the base of his skull. Jimmy had a rough understanding of how the whole bone-brain-and-blood mechanism operated. Fourteen's punch worked as he expected. The buzzing started immediately, coursing from the apex of his spine through the backs of his eyeballs then straight down through his face, the heat bubbling like lava into his throat and chest and belly, radiating into his biceps and forearms and fists.

The physiology Jimmy understood, but its source eluded him. He was skeptical of what the shrinks and other doctors had opined when he was younger. What did they really know but what Jimmy told them? Now, when the anger arrived, Jimmy just let it. The rage was his tactical advantage, the thing that helped him keep his job in the minor leagues. It seemed to come naturally, even if he wished it didn't, even if he secretly hoped, even longed, for the day it would not.

The next twenty seconds were a furious blur of flying sweat and punches. Jimmy must have thrown a dozen while Fourteen crumpled beneath him, body limp, eyelids fluttering, spittle on his cheeks. The refs pulled at Jimmy's collar as he lifted Fourteen by the back of his jersey and slammed him back to the ice, once, twice, three times. One ref wedged an arm under Jimmy's shoulder and levered him away, rasping, 'Jesus, Bakes, it's over, you win, settle the hell down.'

The sounds of the arena had vanished, sucked into a vacuum in Jimmy's mind. Then, as the refs pulled him away, the screams and catcalls leached back, the know-nothings in the stands shrieking, '*Bakes Bakes Bakes.*' Two refs ushered him off the ice.

In the locker room, Jimmy sat on a padded table, still wearing his skates, shin guards, and a soaked undershirt. The trainer, a flabby kumquat of a man named Newberry, cradled Jimmy's left hand like it was a wounded kitten. 'Looks like you pretty much shattered a knuckle,' he said. 'You gotta be more careful, Bakes. How the hell you gonna play like that?'

Drying rivulets of blood snaked down the back of his hand to his wrist. His hands usually went numb during a fight and stayed that way for a while. Sometimes, after a fight, Jimmy imagined his hands weren't really his, but instead extensions of a stranger who took control of his body when he was in need. A stranger furious with the world. A stranger he didn't understand.

'Can you freeze it?' Jimmy said.

'You're done. The zebras gave you a game.'

'Why? Fourteen threw the first punch.'

'I thought you were gonna kill that guy,' Newberry said.

'He could've killed me, too.'

'No.' Newberry shook his head. 'They took him away.'

'Away where?'

'In an ambulance. On a stretcher.'

'Did I break his nose or something?'

'They don't send busted noses to the ER, Bakes. The guy swallowed his tongue. You might not want to watch the clips on that one. I'll be back in a few to clean things up.'

Jimmy hitched himself off the table. He was alone in the room with the odors of tape and disinfectant. ER? he thought. Shit, he'd tagged a bunch of guys harder than that. There was the one in Bismarck with the broken cheekbone, but he'd all but begged for it. Maybe Fourteen – name, Cory Richards – just had a concussion.

Jimmy hadn't watched a video of one of his fights since his early seasons in the minors, when the coaches decided he could be an effective goon who would intimidate the other teams' goons. Sometimes he overheard his teammates whooping and laughing on the team bus as they watched one of his fights on someone's cellphone. He tried to block it out.

He walked out of the training room, still in his skates, to a small office where the coaches deconstructed games. There were laptops scattered on desks and two widescreen TVs on the wall. Jimmy tried three different remotes before finding the right one.

He rewound the video to the eleven-minute mark, about when his coach dispatched him. The video focused. He fast-forwarded, let it play, then stopped it before the refs intervened, feeling something squirm in his belly. He didn't recognize the person wearing his jersey.

He turned it off and set the remote on the desk. He looked at his hands. When he was a boy, his mother told him they were those of a concert pianist. They would be like doves flitting up and down the keyboard. She arranged for lessons. But hockey took over. Now Jimmy's hands looked as though someone had stomped on them with spiked shoes, his left as gnarled and misshapen as a werewolf's, the skin pleated with scars hiding dead tendons and floating bone chips.

ER, he thought again. The guy swallowed his tongue.

He walked back to the training room, found his jersey on the floor, then went to the dressing room. He pulled his skates off, shoved his feet into plastic flipflops, and stuffed his clothes from the locker in a team duffel. He heard the drone of the horn signaling the end of the period. The guys would be filing into the room in thirty seconds.

He draped the jersey across his neck, threw the bag over a shoulder, and dropped his skates in a trash can at the locker room doorway. The day he had quietly longed for finally had come.

Jimmy considers taking the jacket out to the yard and burning it, but he doesn't know if the detective or the officer are watching.

He pulls on his parka and slides the trash bag inside, zipping the coat and using his palms to flatten the slight bulge the bag makes. He makes sure the front door, the kitchen door, and the door to the garage are all locked before he heads out to his truck in front of the house.

He's almost there when he sees the boot prints in the snow. They're relatively fresh, and they aren't his. They appear to encircle the truck. At some points they come near enough that whoever left them could have peered inside the truck. Was it the detective? What could he have seen? Jimmy had washed the blood away. So why would the detective be looking? Why would he care? Jimmy feels an urge to run around and kick snow across the boot prints to make them disappear.

Instead, he stands staring at the scatter of prints, feeling the bloodied jacket bunched against his belly. Could the blood on that sleeve be someone else's blood? He looks around the yard, the snowy fields beyond, the trees beyond the fields. Why didn't he just tell the detective what he could, and couldn't, remember about the night before? Why didn't he just confess to what he did or didn't know? He climbs into the truck and starts it. He puts it in gear. He puts it back in park. What happened to his gloves? His face? His hand? His memory?

He picks up his phone and calls Devyn Payne.

TWENTY-TWO

After Devyn leaves the restroom, she makes sure the prosecutor isn't following and walks to the courthouse entrance. She steps outside, phone at her ear, arms wrapped around herself against the cold. In the parking lot a plow shoves around sloppy mounds of snow. She feels her phone go off. Jimmy.

'Devyn?'

He doesn't sound right. 'Everything OK?'

She hears a long sigh, then: 'Jesus, Dev.'

'Jimmy. What's wrong?'

'I think I need to hire you.'

'Wait,' she says. She walks down the steps into the parking lot, peeking over her shoulders for eavesdroppers. She edges as close as she can to the plow. 'OK. Talk to me.'

She has to stop him every ten seconds to slow him down. She's never heard him like this, voice cracking, words tumbling over each other. A detective named Klimmek was just in his living room. He was asking about last night. Questions Jimmy couldn't answer. All Devyn can think is, why would Klimmek think Jimmy could know the answers to these questions?

Next Jimmy's spouting about two young men, drunk downstaters, who were in the Lost Loon last night stirring up trouble. Ronnie was there and Butch Dulaney was there with some other people and one of the downstaters threatened to smack Ronnie. Jimmy got himself out before anything bad happened. At least that's what he thinks. He really can't remember.

'What do you mean, you can't remember?' Devyn says. She has had clients whose memories failed them at convenient times. Judges and juries weren't sympathetic. She doubts Jimmy is outright lying, because then why would he have called her in the first place? 'You can't remember going home? Exactly how much of the night is a blur, Jimmy?'

'Pretty much from the time I left the bar till I woke up in my kitchen.'

'And when was that?'

'I don't know. Three-something?'

'Woke up in my kitchen at three in the morning' is not something a defense attorney wants to hear her client say out loud in a courtroom. Devyn reviews what she knows about last night at the Lost Loon: Ronnie's texts about a 'shitshow aborning' and how Jimmy 'almost got into it' with those guys; Jordan telling her things 'got weird;' Butch's presence, never good.

'Listen, Jimmy,' she says. 'Listen to me now.'

'OK.'

'Don't mess this up, Jimmy, do you hear me?'

'Tell me what to do.'

'Do nothing. Just go about your life as you would have if nothing happened last night. As if you came home at midnight and had cookies and milk and went to bed. Get to the rink, do your job, and talk to nobody – nobody – about the Loon and whatever went on there.'

'What if the detective—?'

'Tell him you have nothing to say.'

'Can I tell him—'

'Nothing.'

'—he should talk to you?'

Devyn hesitates. She wants to help her friend. But she already represents Jordan – albeit on unrelated matters – and Jordan apparently was in the Loon around the same time Jimmy was. The question is whether Jordan has direct, material knowledge of what happened at the Loon and, possibly, afterwards. If she does, then taking on Jimmy could constitute a conflict of interest that would disqualify Devyn from representing him. But Devyn doesn't know what Jordan knows, or whether Jordan knows anything.

'I need a little time, Jimmy,' Devyn says. 'Just do what I told you. I'll get back to you.'

'I wish I could tell you I didn't do it, but I can't be—'

'Jimmy, do not say anything like that to me or anybody else ever again. Do you understand?'

'Am I going to be all right?'

'Don't jump to any conclusions. And keep your mouth shut.'

She turns and faces the courthouse. How quickly the shit can hit the fan, even in little Bitterfrost, Michigan. Hearing the scrape of the snowplow blade, she realizes she's outside without a coat or hat or gloves. She hurries back indoors and glances around before dialing Klimmek. He's not picking up. Devyn can't afford to leave him a message and have someone else hear it. She and the detective have had run-ins – that claw-hammer case in particular – but she trusts him enough to let him know Jordan may have jumped bail. Devyn wouldn't normally help the cops in this way. She can't, technically, unless she fears for her client's well-being. Which she does, given that it's Jordan. Then there's Jimmy, who's in his own shit-bucket of trouble. Devyn has to figure out how she can help him, if she can help him at all.

TWENTY-THREE

Klimmek sits watching while Bitterfrost Police Chief Robert Quarton paces from one end of his conference room to the other, narrating in his clipped, precise diction what is about to happen. 'The man who will be calling in a few minutes is rightfully perceived in Detroit as a savior. And it's not even his hometown. He headquartered his company there, hired thousands of people, built dozens of buildings, and invested hundreds of millions of dollars in the restoration of a once great metropolis turned to a pile of garbage.'

'And?' Klimmek says.

He's sitting at a table in the room adjacent to Quarton's office at the Bitterfrost Police station. At forty-three minutes past noon, the detective sips the day's first coffee and wonders whether Chief Quarton has ever actually been to Detroit. Maybe for a Tigers or Wings game, a Coney dog at Lafayette, dinner at that overpriced joint in one of the hotels. Whether he's been or not, attention from the big city, even if the city isn't that big anymore, could translate into national attention, even interviews on the nightly news. Like those chiefs dealing with shootings at schools and churches and shopping malls. Klimmek suspects his chief covets that sort of attention.

Quarton stops pacing, clasps his hands behind his back, and faces Klimmek. 'And?' he says. 'Philip Hardy is a serious man who commands serious attention and one of his family may have been murdered in our community. This is huge. The world is watching.'

So when nobody's watching, it doesn't matter? 'I feel for him and his family,' Klimmek says. 'We need to go as fast as we can, but at the same time, we have to be careful.'

'Of course,' Quarton says. 'But we also – oh, there's the call.'

The conferencing device at the center of the table beeps and a voice with an echo says, 'Mr Hardy is on the line.'

Quarton squares up to the table, addressing the device. 'Mr Hardy, this is Bitterfrost Police Chief Robert Quarton. We're being joined by Detective Garth Klimmek, who is overseeing our investigation of this extremely important matter.'

It's unusual to take a call like this so early in an investigation. All Klimmek and the cops really have, still, is a dead body in the woods and a truck that appears to be owned by the son of the man on the phone. They have yet to determine if the body is Jerome Hardy or his brother-in-law, Aaron Diggs. Or someone else entirely. Young Hardy and Diggs could be anywhere. Maybe they came north to disappear into the Upper Peninsula. Or Wisconsin. Or Canada. Maybe they'd had enough of their life downstate. They wouldn't be the first, or the last.

'My family thanks you in advance,' Philip Hardy says. 'We understand you may have our son Jerome's Chevrolet Silverado in your possession.'

Quarton sits and looks to Klimmek, who nods. 'That is correct, Mr Hardy,' Quarton says. 'We have confirmed the truck's vehicle identification number is connected to your son. However, we haven't yet established that your son was in possession of the vehicle when it was deposited where we found it.'

'In other words, we don't know where my son is, is that correct, Chief Wharton?'

'Quarton, sir.'

'Sorry. Chief Quarton. Do you have any estimate of how long it might take to determine whether my son was in his truck and where he might be now? I mean . . .' Hardy stops, Klimmek assumes to gather himself before Hardy continues, 'Jerome means the world to his mother and me.'

'Understood, Mr Hardy.' Quarton's assistant appears in the conference room doorway. She's holding up a yellow legal pad etched in black felt pen with the words: DETROIT CHANNEL 7 ON HOLD. TWO-MINUTE WARNING! Quarton waves at her to wait. 'Sir, it would be difficult to say much at this moment, as we've only been investigating for a matter of hours, but please be assured that we have the full resources of this department – as well as assistance from the state police – focused on determining exactly what happened.'

'We're glad to hear that, chief.'

'I know you're hearing things on TV and online. We need to be considerably more circumspect than the media.'

'And that, too, we appreciate,' Hardy says. 'Jerome . . .' Again he pauses. 'Is a well-meaning young man. But he has a regrettable knack for being in the wrong place at the wrong time.'

Quarton leaves his chair and starts pacing again, his face pinched tight. Klimmek imagines the chief imagining what Detroit's TV reporters might say about the cops in the boonies trying to solve a major crime. 'We hope to have a clearer picture of what happened in a matter of hours.'

'Detective,' Hardy says. 'I'm sorry, what is your name again?'

'Klimmek, Mr Hardy. Garth Klimmek.'

'Detective Klimmek, what is your next step?'

A somewhat presumptuous question for a civilian, but Klimmek charitably supposes that people who save cities feel they can ask whatever they wish. 'My next step, Mr Hardy, is to get off this call and find out what happened. I sincerely hope it doesn't involve your family.'

'Thank you. Let me say that you shouldn't feel the need to be sitting here listening to me. By all means, go do your job. And if you need anything in the way of resources, do not hesitate to ask. We have people, we have money, and we have every form of vehicle, including helicopters. And we are prepared to do whatever is necessary to get this matter . . .' He hesitates. 'Resolved.'

'Thank you, sir.'

'Whatever is necessary. And, no, thank you, detective. And chief. May I ask – do you by chance have any suspects in mind yet?'

'It's a little early for that,' Quarton says. 'We have yet to determine if there's even been a definitive crime committed.'

Jesus, Klimmek thinks.

A predictable pause comes before Hardy says, 'You do have a man beaten to death and, I gather, our son's truck, which I understand has considerable blood in it. I'm no expert in law enforcement, but it sounds to me like a crime has been committed.'

This is why, Klimmek thinks, you don't agree to calls like this. Your heart breaks for people who have lost a child, a spouse, a sibling, and you want to do everything you can to help them proceed to what the shrinks call closure but Klimmek calls justice. Whatever you call it, it cannot be rushed. You can't be pushed to conclusions you will later regret, conclusions that may punish the innocent or allow the guilty to walk free. As in the claw-hammer case. The defense attorney – in that instance, Devyn Payne – will pounce on the slightest mistake. The people who started calling the detective 'Claw-Hammer Klimmek' thought he'd feel better when the acquitted culprit hung himself from an oak where tourists could see him. Really, it only made things worse.

As patient as Philip Hardy seems, people who run their kingdoms by fiat tend to have a hard time understanding why guys like Klimmek can't just wave a wand and have someone captured, fingerprinted, convicted, and imprisoned in a matter of days. Klimmek would love to tell Hardy he knows what happened or didn't happen, that his son is all right or we know why he isn't and who is responsible. He'd love to catch a break on Bitterfrost's first homicide in years, maybe put that claw-hammer thing behind him for good. But he also doesn't want another disaster.

'Yes, Mr Hardy,' Klimmek says, 'we have a crime to investigate.' He stands. 'Thanks for your offer.'

'Just one other thing, detective?'

'Of course.'

'I know it's early but, do you think this is likely a local matter? Or is something bigger at play?'

'Something bigger?' Quarton says.

'I don't know,' Hardy says. 'Something, you know, you can't quite fathom as yet. Something that might not have much to do with your town.'

Klimmek supposes this is how bosses of huge companies think. 'Hard to tell anything this early, sir,' he says. 'Thank you for calling.'

'Godspeed, detective. Jerome is our only child.'

Who may well have been in the wrong place at the wrong time.

Klimmek leaves Quarton with Hardy. As he steps out of the station into the cold, he wonders if the chief will go ahead with that TV interview, given that Hardy almost certainly will see it. He checks his phone and sees that the defense lawyer, Payne, tried to call. He'll get with her later. Now he has a date with a bartender at the Lost Loon.

TWENTY-FOUR

'**N**o. No freaking way. Jesus, Varga.'

'Sorry, Dev. I hope—'

'I knew this was going to happen. Goddamn Jordan.'

'You knew? Did you alert the authorities?'

'It's complicated.'

'I don't want to know. I'm sorry I had to tell you. I didn't want you to hear about it on the tube or Facebook.'

'Jordan Fawcett has been my client for what seems like forever. Her bad decisions were her life's work, and an annuity for me.'

'You mean she actually pays . . . paid?'

'Sometimes, Varga, she did.'

'I have clients like that. They've gone through life getting lied to, abused, betrayed, fucked over every which way. They don't know anything but to do the same right back.'

'Dammit.'

'Sorry, kiddo. Next time you're in Petoskey, a drink, eh?'

'Yeah. Thanks, Ron.'

If she had to hear it, she's relieved to have heard it from her old lawyer buddy Ron Varga. Jordan Fawcett made it to Mackinaw City at the southern foot of the Mackinac Bridge to the UP. Maybe she was going to Canada, maybe to Wisconsin, or maybe she didn't know what the hell she was doing. Good chance of that. Police found her in a dumpster behind a CBD shop on Marquette Street. She'd been bludgeoned and knifed. There were no signs of sexual assault. Whoever killed her made efficient work of it. And made sure she'd be found. But why? Unless Jordan's killer was sending a message to somebody else.

Jordan is the second client Devyn has lost, counting the claw-hammer killer, Barrett Sawtell. She might have served him better by persuading him to plead guilty. She can't know what drove him to that noose in the oak tree – guilt at being acquitted? – but she can't help but think that he, like Jordan, would have been better off in prison.

What did Jordan know that might have gotten her killed? Is that why she ran? Devyn has a similar worry about Jimmy. Like Jordan, he too was in the Loon last night. What is in Jimmy's head that he can't unpack? What might he have seen or heard that could get him killed too?

Devyn climbs out of her car, lifts her hockey bag out of the trunk, and throws it over her shoulder. Inside her parents' rink, she goes to the referees' room and dresses. Black nylon sweats bearing the IceKings logo, black-blue-and-silver gloves, a black IceKings cap. She's a little late for Little Kings practice, but the boys are already doing one-legged figure-eights, backwards and forwards on the face-off circles. The kids have their shit together, which is good because, at the moment, Devyn does not. She didn't love Jordan Fawcett, but neither did she do her job and stand between Jordan and the human scum who fed upon her.

Devyn is about to step onto the ice, stick in one hand, whistle taped to a glove, when she feels someone touch her shoulder. She turns around. Before Jimmy can speak, she says, 'Yes, I'll represent you.'

'Good, but I—'

'What did I tell you, Jimmy? Shut up. Just shut up and take care of Zelda and let me worry about what comes next.'

TWENTY-FIVE

The black-and-white video on the desktop screen is as fuzzy as an old porn flick. Klimmek expected that. Dives like the Lost Loon don't like spending on stuff that might rat out their regulars.

'So this is from a camera mounted outside, on the front of the bar?' he asks Ronnie, the bartender Jimmy Baker told him about. She's sitting with him at a table of two-by-fours and a plywood top that still bears bluish grade stamps. The walls in this office in the back of the Loon are stacked with toilet paper, hand sanitizer, and cases of well whiskey and gin. It reeks of old cigarette smoke, even though a sign in the barroom says No Smoking. Like so many people in Bitterfrost, Ronnie looks vaguely familiar.

'It looks across the road to the woods?' he asks.

'I suppose,' Ronnie says. 'My boss doesn't usually like me messing with this stuff.' She clicks a mouse that brightens the view a bit, but it's still hard to see clearly for the snow whipping past the camera lens. 'As you can see, the weather was crappy.'

Klimmek came into the Loon fifteen minutes ago, operating on the tip from the unnamed woman with the unnamed accent. Ronnie was loading a fridge with longneck bottles of Bud. Klimmek told her he was investigating a potential crime, hoping to pique her curiosity by being purposely vague, knowing she'd probably heard about the murder by now, as it was all over TV and the web. Predictably, she asked if he was looking into that case, and he said possibly, which seemed to give her a little thrill, and she ushered him back to the office.

'Did you happen to serve a couple of young men last night?' he says.

'I serve young men most nights.'

'These gentlemen would've been from the Detroit area.'

'There were a couple of guys here I hadn't seen before. They were pretty sloshed. I had to cut 'em off.'

'Bet they loved that, eh?'

'Not much.'

'Could you excuse me one second?'

Klimmek's phone is going off. He steps outside the back office into the bar. All his years in Bitterfrost, he doesn't believe he's ever been in this establishment before. 'What's up?' he asks the phone.

'Got an ID on that body,' Sylvester says. 'Aaron Diggs. Twenty-nine. St Clair Shores.'

'Brother-in-law of the other guy?'

'Apparently.'

'You're some Grim Reaper, officer. Thanks.'

Klimmek goes into his phone and finds the photograph of Jerome Hardy he googled earlier. He steps back into the office and shows the photo to Ronnie. In it, young Hardy is smiling behind the wheel of a vintage Ford Thunderbird ragtop. 'Might this be one of the guys who were here last night?'

Ronnie looks. 'Oh, yeah. Stiffest flannel shirt I ever seen. Did he get killed?'

'Can't say much yet. But he left without causing any disturbance?'

She shrugs. 'Not much.'

'OK, let's look at this.'

On the screen Klimmek sees the rear lights of an SUV. A Chevy. It eases eastward onto the highway in front of the Loon. 'Stop it there, would you, please?' he says. Ronnie obliges. The truck's rear license plate is visible in a jut of light thrown by a parking lot lamp. Klimmek stretches his phone out and clicks a photo.

'Hey,' she says, suddenly skittish. 'You can't do that.'

'I can't? I didn't know. Sorry.'

'No, you're not,' she says, and Klimmek remembers why she feels familiar. He observed her being questioned some years back in a case of arson that leveled a house near town. She wasn't helpful, as he recalls, except in ways she probably didn't intend.

'Just a little bit more,' he says.

She's irritated, but lets the video play on.

'Do you remember who else might have been in the bar while those two guys were here?' Klimmek says.

Her shoulders stiffen. She remembers, all right. But all she says is, 'That about enough?' As if she didn't hear his question.

'Wait.'

Twin lights flash on in the middle of the computer screen. Headlamps. They emerge from the forest across the road. Ronnie leans closer.

'Oh, shit,' she says.

Klimmek squints at the front license plate on the vehicle – a Dodge pickup – just before it turns in the direction the Chevy went. He makes out three numbers. Enough for now.

'Thanks,' he says. 'Can I ask why you reacted that way?'

'What way?'

'It's not important. I assume you also have cameras inside the bar?'

She folds her arms. 'You need a warrant, detective. Or talk to my boss.'

'All right. I'll get a warrant if I think I need it.'

'Good. I need to get back to work.'

'One last thing: You know Jimmy Baker, don't you?'

'Who doesn't?'

'Roger that. I understand he was in here last night. Did he by chance have any sort of encounter with those two gentlemen?'

'An encounter?'

'Yes. An encounter.'

She hesitates before saying, 'No, not really.'

'But he was in here.'

'I didn't say that.'

'Who else was in here during that encounter?'

'I wasn't really paying attention.' She scrunches up her face as if she's trying to remember. 'There was a woman sitting at the bar.'

'What woman, may I ask?'

'Don't know. Never saw her before.'

'Uh-huh. Anybody else?'

Ronnie gets up from her chair. 'You oughta call my boss,' she says. 'So, if you'll excuse me.'

Outside, Klimmek scratches in his notebook. He's pretty sure he'll be speaking with Ronnie again, most likely at the station. He calls in the Chevy plate and the partial on the other vehicle. He suspects they might tell a story the Zamboni driver won't like.

TWENTY-SIX

The stands at the rink are nearly filled. From the Zamboni shed where Zelda waits to perform, Jimmy can see the fans in their IceKings swag ascending to their seats. He absorbs the rabid hum, sucks in the smells of mustard and popcorn, feels the anticipation of a throng come to holler and hoot for their team.

How he loves it. Whenever he's feeling down, usually because he hasn't talked to Avery for a few days, he imagines himself steering Zelda onto the ice for the last resurfacing before the referees and linesmen emerge, followed by the players and coaches, and then the face-off to start the game. Off-seasons are longer for Jimmy because he has none of these moments, and he dearly missed them when the IceKings shut down during the pandemic. Now he dreams about them through humid July nights. It's during those minutes before a game that he feels most keenly that he's part of something larger, even if it's only a bunch of post-adolescent males playing a game he loved.

The best Zambonis and drivers spread the slickest, hardest sheets of ice, something deeply appreciated by the players, especially the fast ones, because hard ice means fast ice means players with exceptional speed will leave slower ones further behind. The young men who handle their sticks like magicians also love Zelda's ice, because it helps them cup and feather and lift and snap and saucer the puck as if it floats on an invisible plane of air millimeters off the surface.

There's so much more to it than simply spinning a steering wheel and dragging a steel blade across the ice. Over the years, Jimmy has schooled himself in dew points and brine water and auger speeds and the chemical compositions of freon and glycol and the perfect temperatures of the cold water he lays down to clean the ice and the hot water he deposits to restore its flat sheen. The buttons and levers and wheels he operates while sitting atop Zelda are second nature, prosthetic extensions of his own limbs. He knows it's silly – as silly as most people regard his preoccupation with grammar – but he thinks his odd communion with

Zelda and the ice, as with the grammar fixation, bring actual order to his everyday. He climbs into his seat, wearing an old IceKings sweatshirt, and pushes the button that starts Zelda's motor. They roll out of the shed and veer toward the arena. Led by Zelda's Zealots in the far upper deck, the crowd chants, '*Zel-DA! Zel-DA! Zel-DA!*' Jimmy wants to revel in it. He doesn't want to think about what might have happened over the past twenty hours or his knuckles or his cheek or his blood-smeared jacket, now locked inside a workbench in the Zam shed. Jimmy forces a smile and waves, trying to acknowledge every section he passes, winking at the gleeful children waggling handmade Zelda signs. But he's not really here, not really where he longs to be, and he has an unsettling feeling that he may be stolen away from it forever.

TWENTY-SEVEN

Klimmek waits in his Bronco on a ridge overlooking the rink, Lake Michigan slumbering in the dark a few hundred yards to his left. Fans in parkas and scarves emblazoned with IceKings logos hustle toward the warmth of the arena, the parking lot a stew of white breath coiling upward. A marquee glows with the announcement of tonight's game against the Minot Bombers. Beyond the lot, idled construction vehicles hunch behind orange fence surrounding a snow-ringed hole in the ground. Klimmek doesn't recall what's going up there or he never knew to begin with.

The Bronco's heat is on high and Klimmek is eating an onion cheeseburger Kris grilled in a skillet and wrapped in wax paper. It's greasy and sloppy and delicious. He's watching his phone for texts from an ex-Bitterfrost cop who works security inside the rink. Opening face-off is scheduled for seven-forty, so Jimmy Baker, whose Dodge pickup is parked in a private lot behind the arena, will take the Zamboni for its pregame run around seven twenty-five. Klimmek will have to be inside shortly after.

He's not convinced this is the right way to go about things. Klimmek would've preferred bringing Jimmy in as a so-called person of interest, and doing it as quietly as possible so as not to raise the community's expectations for a swift resolution. But it was Chief Quarton's call, not his, and the chief said he wanted to 'send a signal' that the department was on the case. In other words, he wants to make a splash noticed not just in Bitterfrost and northern lower Michigan but all the way down in the big city. Klimmek was dismayed but hardly surprised to see a TV reporter brushing her hair out in the parking lot before fans started arriving.

As he chews the burger, he ponders the local woman who was found dead in Mackinaw City. Klimmek doesn't believe he ever crossed paths with Jordan Fawcett. He asked Quarton about her that afternoon, and the chief said, 'Stay focused on the big fish.' In other words, the Fawcett woman didn't matter as much as the rich Detroiter's son and brother-in-law, even though she's just as dead as Aaron Diggs. He figures she's Mackinaw City's problem until or unless Quarton tells him otherwise.

His son tried to call earlier, but Klimmek was busy and he can't call back now. He did text Kenneth to say he'd cover hotel or other expenses they'd have to pay even though they canceled their snowmobiling trip. He imagines what they'd be doing that evening if they were on their machines in the UP. He pictures a plate of fried perch at that cozy place in St Ignace, then stops and tells himself to pay attention. He checks his phone. There's a minute-old text from the ex-cop security guard: Crowd going goofy 4 zelda. showtime soon.

Zelda? Klimmek pulls into the parking lot. He drives to the arena entrance and parks at a forty-five-degree angle to the span of identical glass doors. He marinates in the car heat for another minute while finishing his burger. Two police cruisers, both marked, glide up on either side. He gets out of the car and tosses the wadded-up wax paper into the nearest trash basket before walking inside to carry out his orders.

TWENTY-EIGHT

Jimmy is tracing his second-to-last oval around the rink when he feels his phone vibrating in a pocket. He never brings his phone on Zelda, but tonight he thought he needed it in case . . . He didn't want to think further than that. He takes a look. Avery. He presses the phone to an ear while steering with his other hand.

'Hi, honey.'

'Dad,' she says. 'I saw you called.'

He can barely hear his daughter over the din of the crowd. He pictures her sitting on her bed, twirling a curl behind an ear, stuffed toys piled on her pillows. 'Just wanted to say hi. Your mother said it was too late.'

'Poor Mom,' Avery says.

'She's just thinking about you, Ave.'

'What's all that noise?'

'We're doing the ice. Game starts in a few minutes.'

'Whoa,' Avery says. 'How's my girl Zelda?'

A sob bursts into Jimmy's throat before he can stop it. He chokes out a reply. 'She's fine. Thanks . . .' He can't finish.

'Dad, what's wrong?'

Jimmy swallows and swings Zelda right, starting the turn back toward the shed. 'Nothing, honey. Everything's fine.'

'Did Mom tell you about my recital?'

Zelda comes around. Jimmy sees the police and almost drops the phone. 'Honey,' he tells Avery, 'I'm sorry, but I have to go. Can you text me about your recital? I'll be there, promise.'

'It's tonight. I'm actually backstage.'

'Oh. I'm so . . . I screwed up again. I'm sorry. I love you, baby.'

'Me too.'

The crowd has gone almost dead quiet. Jimmy sees the refs standing at one of the benches. Their heads are turned toward the opening that leads to the Zamboni shed. Four uniformed officers wait there with someone who looks like the detective who came to Jimmy's house. Jimmy isn't shocked, but he feels a pit of fear stick in his gut anyway.

He crosses the red line and then the blue line, guiding Zelda between the face-off dots seventy-five feet from the police. He glances over at the stunned, suddenly quiet fans. They can't help him. There's nowhere to go, nowhere to hide, nowhere to escape. He starts to feel that rage rising in his gut, as if a punch just caught him flush on the jaw. He slams his foot on the acceleration pedal and pushes Zelda as fast as he can through the howling silence.

TWENTY-NINE

D evyn watches the officers file in from her season ticket Seat 6, Row 11, Section 108, at the blue line Jimmy just passed, with a view of the net the IceKings shoot at two of the three periods.

She can't process what she's watching. Are these boneheads really going to arrest Jimmy in front of all these people who've loved him as player and Zamboni driver for so long, their good luck charm who's been around for more league titles than any coach or player? He's one of them, born and raised in Bitterfrost, and these asshole cops are going to make him pay for it?

She shoves her cup of beer under her seat and bounds down the stairs to Row 1 along the glass. She pushes past a pear-shaped usher who tells her, 'You need to go back the other way, ma'am,' and jostles her way through spectators' knees and beers and nachos along the front row to the corner of the rink. She jumps a restraining chain into the damp concrete well where Zelda is heading at an unnerving rate of speed. Jesus, Jimmy doesn't really think he's going to blast past the cops, does he?

Devyn scrambles out to the edge of the ice, boots skimming along the damp tarmac. She waves her arms over her head as Jimmy and Zelda bear down. 'No, Jimmy!' she yells. 'Don't do this. Stop.' One of the uniforms tries to grab her, but Devyn squirms free. Zelda is barely twenty feet away and still moving. 'Jimmy, no,' she shouts.

Another cop tugs her backward, saying, 'You're going to get yourself killed.'

Zelda hums to a stop. The officer lets Devyn go as he and two other uniforms descend on Jimmy. He raises his hands over his head but the cops are having none of it after he almost ran them over. They yank him roughly away from Zelda and pin him against the glass behind the net. 'What kind of bullshit is this?' someone yells from the stands. Exactly what Devyn is thinking as she watches, helpless. Scattered boos echo from the seats. The police are going to regret this spectacle. She will see to that.

She moves to where Jimmy stands with his hands cuffed behind him, staring at his boots. 'Pick your head up, Jimmy,' she says. 'And say nothing.'

'Who are you?' asks a cop who looks as young as one of the frat punks Devyn used to out-chug at college keggers. He steps in her way. 'That's far enough, ma'am.'

'Don't be ma'aming me, junior,' she says. She sees Klimmek approaching and catches his eye.

'It's OK, officer,' he says. Then, to Devyn, 'Why are you here, Ms Payne?'

'I'm representing Mr Baker.'

'Mr Baker isn't even charged with a crime yet. Are you expecting something? Do you know something we don't?' Before Devyn can reply, Klimmek turns to Jimmy. 'Sir, you are under arrest for the murder of Aaron Diggs.'

Jimmy shakes his head. 'I don't know anyone by that name.'

'Jimmy,' Devyn says. 'Shut up.'

'You do have the right to remain silent,' Klimmek says.

'Hear the man, Jimmy? What did I tell you?' Jimmy looks at her, his eyes filled with pleading. Devyn says, 'It's going to be all right.'

Klimmek turns back to Devyn. 'We're taking your client in now, Ms Payne. Feel free to follow.'

'For the record, detective, my client just now was merely doing his job, getting Z– the Zamboni off the ice so the game could begin. Nothing more.'

'Did someone say there was something more, Ms Payne?'

She points at the lapel of his coat. 'You forgot some mustard there.'

Devyn watches the officers walk Jimmy away, a silhouette against the cascade of cop lights outside. Dammit, Jimmy, she thinks. How can this be happening? He's just a Zamboni driver who does his job and keeps to himself. And she is now his defender. She sees Klimmek stop in the rink lobby to scribble something in a notebook. *You and me again, eh, Garth? I look forward to it.* Even though she knows, if anybody in Bitterfrost is capable of . . . No, she tells herself, and expels the thought from her head.

PART TWO

THIRTY

'You can't say no, Elly.'

'Horsepucky, Devyn.' Eleanor Payne picks up half of her walleye sandwich, dips it in tartar sauce, and takes a bite without looking up at her daughter.

'No way,' Devyn says.

Eleanor shakes her head as she chews. Then she takes a concerted pull on the straw jutting from her double Bloody Mary and lifts her eyes to Devyn. 'Are you ever going to do something about your hair, dear?'

Her hair. Devyn is talking to her mother about Jimmy's future, and whether he'll have one, and Eleanor wants her to 'do something' – that is, color – her silver hair. 'Not today,' Devyn replies.

'Then may I just enjoy my lunch, please?'

Devyn knows not to push too hard, but she also knows it's important that Eleanor knows how much something matters because her mother can find it difficult to care as much about something as someone else does, even one of her twins. And certainly her late husband. There's a connection between these attitudes that Devyn hasn't quite figured out. How Eleanor and Calvin stayed together for nearly thirty years is a puzzle Devyn will never solve.

'Sorry,' she says. 'Go ahead.'

'The walleye here is the best,' Eleanor says.

'Yes, it is.'

'How's your salad?'

'Too many grapes.'

'Should've had the walleye.'

Devyn drove her mother an hour south to the Mitchell Street Pub in Petoskey so it was less likely they'd bump into anyone from Bitterfrost. They could have had this talk at the Payne spread along Lake Michigan north of downtown Bitterfrost, where Eleanor lives alone with her three goldens. But that would have been a home game for Eleanor. Devyn thought she'd be more receptive in the bustle of the popular tavern, which even in December attracts a healthy Friday afternoon clientele.

Devyn lets her mother eat, taking a breath as she gazes down the narrow tunnel of the tavern, its dark hardwood and low lighting, the Red Wings and Tigers mirrors gleaming on paneled walls, the snowflakes swirling into the front vestibule when patrons come in doffing hats and stomping snow from their boots.

'Tell me, dear,' Eleanor says. 'Do you think the Red Wings are really any better this year? I mean, a new coach, all those new players –' she scoops up a piece of wayward walleye –'are they actually making any difference, or is it too early to even know?'

Unless you're one of Eleanor's twins, you might think this is her way of steering clear of the issue on the table, which is posting bail for Jimmy Baker in the amount of $250,000. Really it's Elly's way of easing into a subject she prefers not to discuss but knows she can't avoid with her insistent daughter sitting across from her. Besides, Eleanor actually knows hockey. She never misses a home IceKings game and occasionally travels with her team to away matches. At home, she can sit in the owner's box with son Evan but opts to use the season tickets – ten rows behind the IceKings bench – that Calvin bought in the seventies before ultimately acquiring the team itself along with that precious corner of land. Sometimes during pregame warm-ups, she sits with Zelda's Zealots, joining their feverish cheers for Zelda and her driver, whom she also happens to be fond of. During the plague, as she called the pandemic, she despaired of the games missed because of shutdowns, not to mention the financial losses.

'Too soon to tell,' Devyn says. 'The offense looks like it'll be more productive. Hard to tell about the D. Kinda young, prone to mistakes. As you know, it's all about the defense.'

Eleanor allows herself a smile. At sixty-five, she's still fetching, with a lush head of chestnut hair – artificially colored – and many a hopeful suitor in whom she has little interest.

'Speaking of defense, how's your romantic life going?'

'Very funny,' Devyn says. The guy on Tinder actually sent an odd message that morning, saying if they couldn't connect for a date, maybe he could at least help her sell the rink. She knows he's in real estate, but she has no idea what he was talking about. 'It's going about like this salad.'

'All right,' her mother says. 'Where do things stand with Jimmy?'

Devyn's relieved to get back to why she's here. 'He's been arraigned. Meaning we went to court for about fifteen minutes and the prosecution surprised no one by alleging he committed a crime.'

'Murder. Only one, so far.'

'That's the charge. They asked the judge to deny bail and keep Jimmy in jail until trial. But the judge said no, he can go free if someone posts bail.'

'He might as well have just left him in jail.'

'I realize the bail is high.'

'"High" is right at two-fifty K,' Eleanor says, then flips her straw aside and takes a gulp of her cocktail. 'You know, Devyn, that's more than what your father paid for the team back in the day. Now I'm supposed to hand it over to a Zamboni driver?'

Eleanor doesn't have to bring up the condo she lets Devyn live in for nothing or the handy monthly retainer. They're on the table as clearly as the salt and pepper shakers. Nor does it help that Eleanor has never forgiven Devyn for forgiving her father for his marital wanderings. 'You're not giving Jimmy a penny,' Devyn says. 'You'll get it all back after he's – ' she hesitates – 'after his case is decided.'

'That's still real money, dear. The damn plague and our idiot governor just about wiped us out, you know.'

No, it didn't, Devyn thinks but doesn't say. The team qualified for an interest-free federal loan that her mother happily funneled into an interest-bearing savings account.

'It's more money than I have,' Devyn says, 'but I'd put it up if I could.'

'Let's just set that aside for a second, OK? I have the cops wanting to search my arena and string that ugly yellow tape all over. Our lawyers have held them off for now. It's a good thing I open up the checkbook for judges' re-election campaigns.'

'You could have asked me for help.'

Eleanor shoves her almost empty plate aside. 'Who are these two men from Detroit anyway? Why were they even here? Who in their right mind comes to Bitterfrost this time of year?'

Good questions, Devyn thinks. She's working on them, with limited success so far. Same with Jordan Fawcett's demise.

'Not as yet clear.'

'So what happens next? Because my ticket sales have turned to crap, honey. Your brother raised prices – without giving me a heads-up, by the way – and we're dealing with actual fights in the stands between people who like Jimmy and people who want to see him hung. The fights are supposed to be *on* the ice.'

Devyn has heard. She doesn't believe the fights are mainly about Jimmy. He's a convenient excuse for scrapping about every other damn thing people relish bickering over these days. 'Next up is the preliminary exam,' she says. 'The prosecution will lay out some of the evidence and unless they have squat, the judge will send Jimmy to trial.'

'They'll have more than squat, won't they?'

'I expect so.'

Eleanor twists her body around and signals the bar for another drink. 'Who's the judge for the preliminary thing?'

'Lindon.'

'Who thinks cops can do no wrong.'

'All the more reason to get Jimmy out of jail.'

'Because?'

'Because I can't put up as strong a defense without him. He can't help much from jail. Once we get to trial, we'll have Judge Esper. She's a curmudgeon, but she'll give us a chance. Jimmy also needs to be out and about, looking calm, looking like he knows he didn't do anything wrong.'

'Why did you even agree to represent him, Devyn?'

Why did she indeed? She'd admit, if asked, that she made a bit of a snap decision, prompted in part by what she'd heard about Jordan Fawcett's violent undoing. But all she says is, 'He's my friend.'

'Isn't it some sort of conflict of interest, because, I don't know, your brother signs his checks?'

'It doesn't look fantastic, but no.'

'He's my friend, too, and I'm sorry, but his past suggests at the very least that he has, you know, I don't have to tell you. People are talking.'

Devyn knows. She's even heard some parents are debating whether they want their kids to continue having her as their hockey coach. Which breaks her heart. But what has weighed on her just as much since Jimmy's arrest, what has kept her up at night, isn't only what Jimmy did or didn't do, but what happened with the claw-hammer guy Devyn successfully defended.

Lawyers aren't required to know whether their clients actually did what they're accused of doing, and often they're better off not knowing. But that was little salve for Devyn when she learned along with everyone else, after his acquittal, that Barrett Sawtell had done exactly what the authorities alleged he'd done. Even though it was police screw-ups, not her lawyering, that sprung him. Again and again she told herself, and Varga told her, and other lawyer pals told her, that she'd done the job she was sworn to do. None of it stuck. And she didn't want to go through anything like that again.

'Look, Mother, I'm not naïve. Jimmy certainly has the physical ability to do something like this. But he's my client now.'

'What if he gets out and does something bad again? It won't be just Bitterfrost screaming for our heads. It'll be the whole world of hockey, from the NHL on down.'

'Screw the hockey world, Mother. They encouraged Jimmy's behavior when he was playing – hell, they demanded it – and then they abandoned him. Now his life is at stake. I'm going to do whatever I can to help him. And I need you to help me help Jimmy.'

'And I need another drink,' Eleanor says, twisting around again to wave at the barkeep. 'If only the service here was as good as the walleye.'

'The service here is fine. Are you coming to the prelim?'

Eleanor has watched Devyn's closing arguments in a few of her more dramatic trials. Never a prelim. But this is different, the defendant being an IceKings employee. 'I don't know,' she says. 'I'd have to sit somewhere in the courtroom, pick a side, bride or groom.'

'Understood. What about the bail?'

A waitress brings another Bloody Mary. Eleanor dispenses with the straw. She doesn't usually have more than one this early in the day. 'Is Jimmy even paying you?' she says.

'He will.'

'How, exactly? He's not working and, even when he is, he's not exactly making a mint.'

'I'll be fine, Mother.'

'Seriously? I assume you're spending most of your time on Jimmy. So it's a risk financially as well as professionally, am I wrong? Have you spoken with Evan about this?'

'Not yet.'

'Maybe he could front you some of Jimmy's wages.'

'Please.'

'What is going on with your brother anyway? I had a look at the budget the other day and it looks like he's trying to cut his way to profits. Never works.'

'Have you asked him about it?'

'I've tried. He gives me the runaround, you know, he's doing what's necessary, times are different now. But really, Dev, they aren't that different. I mean, come on, it's just a hockey team.'

'You're the owner. Sit him down, find out what's up.'

'I should. But, you know, I want him to feel like it's his own show. I don't want to be a meddler. I feel the same way about you, dear.'

Devyn knows Evan isn't happy about what's going on with Jimmy. He texted her early the morning of the arraignment: Woulda been nice to get a headsup you're repping JB. Do I need to find a new zam jockey?

'I'm not asking for team money, or Evan's money,' she says. 'I'm asking for yours, Mother. And just for a little while.'

Eleanor twists a straw around a finger. 'Dammit, Jimmy,' she says. She looks up at Devyn. 'Have you seen the posters around town?'

'Hard to miss.'

'I've torn down a couple. I saw one of the Dulaney boys tacking one up at the party store. What's wrong with people?'

'Predictable,' Devyn says. 'People love to attack. But they aren't going to decide the case.'

'No, but still. What would it look like, the IceKings paying to free an accused murderer? The league wouldn't like it. The players—'

'The players worship Jimmy.'

They sit in silence for a while. Eleanor sips her drink. The waitress leaves the check. Eleanor shakes her head. 'I need to talk with your brother about this,' she says. 'You do, too.'

'I will.'

'Is this just about winning, Devyn? You always have to be the winner, don't you?'

'Well. I certainly don't want to lose.'

'If you lose,' Eleanor says, 'you might as well move somewhere else.'

'Not Detroit, right?' Devyn says, and they both laugh as Eleanor picks up the check.

THIRTY-ONE

Six years ago

I t was Devyn's big night, and it was in Detroit.

On a crisp late-winter Friday at the Bad Luck Bar, a table of cocktails, small plates, her two favorite girls.

'So,' Biz said, 'your name'll be on the firm, right? How cool is that?'

'So cool,' Adriana said. 'You've got to get T-shirts made.'

Devyn lifted her drink, something pricey called The Comet, and raised it in a toast. 'Probably not,' she said. 'In fact, certainly not. But, hey, someday, Eagan, MacDonald, Browne & Payne? I like it.'

'Eff that,' Biz said, lifting her martini. '*Payne*, Eagan, whoever.'

They all laughed.

Bad Luck didn't take formal reservations, but Biz knew a bartender who set aside a table for that Friday, when the partners at Eagan MacDonald & Browne would vote whether to elevate Devyn from associate to full partner. Assuming she received the nod, she would gain an equity share in the firm, a healthy annual bonus, and a little even-more-deserved swagger in her step. Only three other women had ever been named full partners at the firm; one was now a circuit judge.

Devyn's boss, an Eagan himself, had assured her that the vote was ninety-five-percent done deal. The law, he liked to say, invoking the grandfather who co-founded the firm, did not allow for a one-hundred-percent chance of anything, be it a verdict, a finding of fact, the chances of a case settling. But ninety-five percent, those were pretty good odds, and Devyn was counting on them, counting on Spencer Eagan to come through.

Devyn's work as a white-collar defense lawyer, fending for companies that peddled insurance and industrial chemicals and opioids, was admired at Eagan MacDonald for its detail and thoroughness. She had shined brightest in a product liability case on behalf of Superior Motors, an automobile manufacturer accused of making an SUV with a rear hatch that popped open for no apparent reason, endangering children sitting in the back seats. The case settled, with Superior paying a pittance of its revenues and admitting to no wrongdoing. The delighted CEO sent Devyn a bouquet of three dozen white roses and a bottle of thirty-six-year-old Macallan. All in all, the money was good, but the winning was the best.

When Biz texted her the Bad Luck dinner plan, Devyn felt grateful for her friend's thoughtfulness, then mildly apprehensive, as if a table at a bar dubbed Bad Luck could somehow jinx the partner tally. She'd been at Eagan MacDonald seven years and sometimes, she knew, these things didn't turn out as expected. Just one senior partner who felt threatened or insufficiently appreciated by a candidate could upend the vote. But her boss and mentor was a descendant of the firm's founder. Spencer Eagan was her ace in the hole, as he'd reminded her more than once.

'Six fifty-eight,' Biz said, brandishing her phone. 'Liftoff anytime now.'

'Shoot the puck then,' Devyn said. She was supposed to get a call around seven informing her that she'd made partner. If it didn't come by, say, eight o'clock, then things had gone sideways. Devyn didn't care if she heard it by email or text or telegram or carrier pigeon, she just wanted to know that she had done it, that she was valued, that she belonged, that she'd won.

Biz was beaming. Adriana was ordering chilled shots of Reyka vodka. Devyn slid her phone out face-up so everyone could see when it lit up with the call. The time signature clicked over to seven o'clock.

'Here we go, kiddos,' Biz said.

But no call came at seven, or seven oh-five, or seven fifteen. Devyn checked to make sure her ringer was working. She looked at her recent calls to see whether she'd missed one. She had not.

She sipped her drink, not wanting to even look at her pals, let alone speak. She almost wished she'd blown off the celebration and skated in her hockey game scheduled for that evening. Out on the ice, at least, she could have ignored her phone and the call that might not be coming after all.

When at seven thirty-four Biz reached to grasp her hand, Devyn knew something had gone wrong. 'Well, hell, he could be on a conference call on this one case that's worth a boatload of money,' she rationalized, knowing that was highly unlikely because Devyn herself was helping on that particular matter. 'I'll give him till eight.'

At seven forty-seven, she reached for one of the shots. 'We can't have these get warm,' she said, then snapped the frosty liquid back into her throat with her eyes closed. 'Well, well,' she gasped as Biz and Adriana looked on, speechless. Before they could swallow their own shots, Devyn snatched them up in each hand and slammed them back.

'Easy, girl,' Biz said.

Devyn stared at the tablecloth, willing the flat white plainness to wash the noxious noise away, the sounds of the bar now crashing all around her, the thrum of the electronica music a taunt, the laughter from the surrounding tables a torture. She felt two palms slide warm and unwavering onto the tops of her hands. 'Babe,' Biz said. 'I'd put a hundred bucks on you having a plan B.'

An early snowfall dusted downtown Detroit the next Monday morning. Devyn wore the dark business suit she usually reserved for court and funerals, accentuating it with a scarlet silk scarf secured with a gold ring.

She'd worn boots to walk over, taking a roundabout route to avoid passing the Bad Luck Bar. In her office she was about to change into heels, as she normally would have, but decided to leave the boots on before gliding past the empty desk of Spencer Eagan's assistant into his forty-first-floor office in Ally Detroit Center.

Devyn stood facing his desk. Eagan was on his landline, his back to her. He acknowledged her presence with a nod in a small hexagonal mirror he used to coif his hair before court appearances, then reached behind himself to gesture at the three chairs semi-circled before his desk.

Devyn remained standing, fixing her gaze on the mirror. Spencer Eagan was a handsome man of fifty-three, lean from yoga and triathlons, the kind who could just as easily charm a juror as repel one with a sureness that could come off as practiced. He liked younger women – at twenty-nine, his third wife was then two years younger than Devyn – and expensive cars. Because Superior Motors was a top client, Eagan was careful to keep his ownership of a Tesla Model X100D quiet. Sometimes Devyn joked to her non-lawyer pals that Eagan was a walking cliché. But clients usually were fine with clichés, because most of what they knew about lawyers came from books and movies and television. Eagan was, in fact, exceptionally skilled at bringing in new business.

So was Devyn.

'We'll reconvene tomorrow,' he told his phone. 'Have a quality day.'

He set the phone in its cradle and spun slowly around. 'Devyn,' he said, assessing her. 'Do you have court today?'

'I do not.'

'You're all dressed . . . wait. The Tancil meeting? I thought that wasn't until tomorrow.'

'It's not today,' Devyn said, choosing her words with care. She nodded at Eagan's credenza. 'I never noticed that picture of Noah before. Nice.'

She wanted him to feel relief that she didn't seem too upset about his failure to deliver the promised partnership. He turned to look at the framed photograph of his eleven-year-old son hugging a dog on a beach, probably at the family cottage on Torch Lake.

'Thanks,' he said. 'I miss summer.'

'What's the dog's name?'

'Ziff. But that's not why you busted in here, is it?'

'No.'

Eagan sneaked a glimpse at the laptop open to his left, then pressed his fingertips together and gently set his hands down on his blotter. 'I'm sorry about Friday night,' he told his hands. Then, looking up, 'I was preoccupied with a prospective client. I should have called you.'

She had learned officially of the partner vote in a six-word text from Eagan's assistant late Friday night.

'How'd it go with the prospect?'

Eagan hadn't expected that question. 'You know,' he said, 'fifty-fifty at this stage.'

Devyn knew he'd actually gone to dinner at Marrow with other partners because one had posted a drunken group picture on Facebook. But she said, 'You've got them on the hook?'

'Let's hope. Might be someone for you.'

Probably not, Devyn thought.

'So,' she said. 'Why am I not a partner today?'

Eagan loosed a drawn-out sigh. She'd seen him do it a thousand times in court, strictly for effect. 'Sit, will you?'

'No, thank you.'

Objection, rhetorical, Devyn imagined him thinking.

'I have arranged for you to get a twenty-percent bump in your compensation, effective immediately,' he said. 'And of course, there will be another partner vote next year and, well . . . I'm sorry this one didn't work out the way we'd hoped.'

'"We?"'

'Yes, "We,"' Eagan said, sounding a hair irritated.

'It is what it is, right?' Devyn loathed that vacuous expression but it was one of Eagan's favorites. 'I'd just like to hear where I came up short and how I can pick up my game.'

He chanced another sidewise look at his laptop. Unless you were a paying client, Eagan seldom had more than one foot in the room of a conversation. If you were talking with him on a phone, you knew he'd lost all interest when you heard the background tapping of his keyboard hunt-and-peck.

'I was one-hundred-and-ten percent in your corner,' he said. 'Unfortunately, there were questions about your ability to, how do I say it, split the baby?'

'King Solomon didn't think that was such a good idea.'

'But it forced the parties to settle, didn't it, Devyn?'

Devyn had come to her office the day before with a bottle of Pinot Grigio and three cardboard boxes. The boxes, crammed with her supplies and law books, now crowded the living-room floor in her downtown condo.

'Have you ever wondered,' Devyn said, 'if Solomon got paid?'

Eagan didn't find that funny. 'You and I have talked about this before. Sometimes you are less willing to compromise than a case demands.'

'You've told me many times: never accept defeat.'

'In the abstract, Devyn. In the abstract. But finally, in the real world, you have to compromise. Or at least demonstrate that you are willing to.'

'But you hate compromise. You fight like—'

'Yes,' he said, the pitch of his voice rising, 'but I'm already a full partner, aren't I? I can afford to be an absolutist.'

'"Absolutist,"' she repeated, thinking, Fuck off. 'So, is this what you told the other partners before the vote?'

'The other partners don't need me to tell them what to think.'

'But you told them they should vote me partner, correct?'

'Of course.'

'All right,' Devyn said, pasting on a smile. 'Aside from inability to compromise, do you think I would have improved my chances if I'd fucked Ransom? Or at least jerked him off?'

Carter Ransom was a partner Devyn had worked with on the Superior case. Late fifties, recently divorced, and enamored of Devyn for more than just her ability to wheedle key documents out of the opposition. He stayed at the office late on a number of occasions. Devyn had evaded the advances he probably imagined to be subtle and defensible.

'Excuse me?' Eagan said, sitting up in his chair. 'That is entirely inappropriate, Devyn, and—'

'You're right, never mind.'

Eagan looked out his window. Gray light was filtering in over downtown Detroit. 'Did you tell anyone?' he said without looking at Devyn.

'You're a good lawyer,' she said, 'asking a question you already know the answer to.'

He picked up a pen from his desk, then set it back down. 'So, today,' he said, ending the conversation about the partnership vote. 'Where are things with the Tancils? How did your meeting with Carla go? That was Thursday, yes?'

The Tancils of Lake Angelus were a couple that founded and still ran a company that manufactured a vital component for electric vehicles. Their smallish firm booked annual revenues in the hundreds of millions of dollars. But they'd recently been sued in a product liability case involving a number of vehicles that had ignited and burned passengers, some to death, allegedly because of their component. They were shopping for a defense lawyer. Eagan MacDonald was one of a handful they were considering.

Eagan had assigned Devyn to present the firm's strategy to the Tancils, partly because she was a hockey player and four of the five Tancil children played. Once Devyn softened them up, Eagan would close the deal, presumably at the meeting scheduled for Tuesday. Eagan expected a bonanza because the case was highly technical and would take months if not years. 'Like an annuity,' he'd told Devyn.

'Last Thursday,' Devyn said now, 'I met with Carla Tancil and her attorney. That went fine. Then we met again over the weekend.'

Eagan did that cocked-head thing he did in depositions when an opposing lawyer said something that took him unawares. 'Over the weekend?' he said. 'What do you mean "we"?'

'Carla and me.'

He swiveled to his left. Devyn was looking at the side of his face. He had sharp cheekbones that weren't terribly flattering from a certain angle. 'Carla?' he said. 'Her lawyer . . . what's his name, Toddy? He wasn't there?'

'Mr Toddy was not there, no. And then on Sunday I saw Tony.'

'Tony?'

'Mr Tancil.'

'Devyn, you know you're not supposed to meet with clients – and the Tancils aren't even clients yet – without notifying a partner. Especially . . .'

His voice trailed off. He was staring stone-faced out the window now, something beginning to dawn on him. He swung back hard to face Devyn.

She smiled.

'So, what about tomorrow's meeting?' he said. 'Are we getting the job?'

'I believe tomorrow's meeting is off.'

'Excuse me? When did you plan on telling me this?'

'I just did.'

'What the hell is going on, Devyn?'

'Well, first off, I'm never going to be a partner at Eagan MacDonald.'

'You will be a shoo-in next year.'

'As for the Tancils, they've decided to go with a smaller firm.'

'No frigging way.'

'I'm afraid so.'

'Which smaller firm?'

'You know,' Devyn said, 'I haven't decided on a name yet.'

It took Spencer Eagan only four days to persuade the Tancils to forget Devyn and hire Eagan MacDonald. Maybe he told the couple that Devyn was not skilled at compromise. She was a little relieved, actually, because the case was probably too much for her to handle on her own. But she'd made her point, or at least hoped she had.

That Friday evening, she took the unopened bottle of thirty-six-year-old Macallan down Grand Central Boulevard and across Michigan Avenue to Hart Plaza on the Detroit River. The lights of downtown Windsor gleamed on the water. She uncapped the bottle and held it high in a salute to the Canadian distillery and its glowing red sign across the river. 'Hey-ho, Hiram Walker,' she shouted, 'you won't be seeing me walking these streets no more.' She took a long guzzle of the Macallan, knowing how her father would shake his head at such a waste of good scotch. She let out a long sigh and screwed the cap back onto the bottle. Then she flung it as far as she could out over the river, listening for the splash.

She knew exactly what she was going to do. The next morning, she was going to pack her things in her Toyota Camry and drive the 301 miles to Bitterfrost. She would stay with her mother until she could find a place of her own. She would hang out a shingle, as small-town lawyers like to say, and offer herself as a defense attorney for people more in need than the wealthy CEOs of multinational corporations. She would fend for murderers and drug addicts and drunk drivers and wife beaters.

And she would fend for herself.

THIRTY-TWO

Jimmy's jailer is a Bitterfrost officer with the ashen cheeks of someone who's ready to retire, if not die. 'You have fifteen minutes,' he tells Jimmy with a phlegmy croak. He makes a display of tapping his wristwatch. 'Not a second more.'

'Understood.'

He opens the door and Jimmy sees his older brother, Alex, over from Alpena, sitting at a table bolted to the gray floor in the middle of the gray-walled room. Jimmy shuffles toward the table in his ankle shackles, his hands cuffed behind his back. Alex gets halfway out of his chair and starts toward Jimmy, saying, 'Hey, bud,' but the officer interrupts.

'No contact allowed.'

Alex stops. 'Sorry.'

'Got it,' Jimmy says.

'I'll be watching.'

'How about these cuffs?'

'How about them?' the officer says as he shuts the door.

Alex sits, Jimmy sits.

'Man,' Alex says. 'Every step might be that dude's last.'

'And how about those short sleeves?'

'Like someone else I know.'

He means their father, who even on the coldest days wore short-sleeved Kmart button-downs. Cheaper, more comfortable, no need to iron, he'd say.

'Thanks for coming,' Jimmy says. 'Did my lawyer—?'

'She got me in. Girl's a pistol. How long you been in?'

'A week?'

'Sorry. I would've been here earlier but I was busy putting the old man in the nursing home.'

'Sorry I couldn't help.'

'Better you weren't there. He'll get the treatment he deserves.'

Both statements are true, Jimmy thinks. 'He ever gonna kick?'

'He'll go when Hannity goes.'

They both smile. Jimmy hasn't seen Alex in months. His beard is freshly stippled with silver and gray. 'How's the fish business?'

'Slow,' Alex says. 'Ice isn't quite thick enough yet on the inland lakes, but when it is, another week or so, I'll be busy.'

'Sorry to take you away.'

'It's just work. How are Noelle and Avery?'

Jimmy looks at the table. 'About as you'd expect.'

He tells Alex he called Noelle yesterday. He had to try three times before she picked up. Their conversation wasn't much of one. He couldn't blame her. She told him Avery was staying home from school because of what kids were saying about her father. 'I hope the hell you're innocent, Jimmy, for my daughter's sake,' she said.

'Noelle will calm down,' Alex says. 'And Avery's not going anywhere.'

'I hope so.'

'So what happened?'

Jimmy says, 'To be honest—'

'Wait,' Alex says. 'They can't listen in, can they?'

'Doesn't matter,' Jimmy says. 'I don't remember much about that night. My lawyer's trying to drag it out of me.'

'You can't do this, Jim.'

As always, big brother won't let Jimmy off the hook. 'Do what?'

'Pretend like this isn't happening.'

'Pretend *as if* this isn't happening,' Jimmy says. A penciled grammatical diagram of the sentence appears in his head.

'Nobody talks that way, Jimmy.'

'They should. And I'm not pretending anything.'

'Something set you off that night, right? The usual?'

Jimmy tries to shimmy back in his chair, but his manacles won't let him. 'I pleaded *not* guilty, Alex.'

'Good. Are you not guilty?'

'As far as I know.'

'Now there's a defense the jury will love.' Alex looks to his right and stares as if there's a window or a painting on the empty wall. 'You know,' he says, 'you gotta let the old man go, Jimmy. He's just gonna keep getting you into trouble.'

The brothers and their father were once inseparable, at least for a time, after Mom died. When the boys weren't in school, they were in Dad's Jeep, going from rink to rink, from practices to games to tournaments all over Michigan, Illinois, Wisconsin, Minnesota, the

Soo, Alex for the sixteen-year-old IceKing midgets, Jimmy, three years younger, for the bantams. Alex didn't have what Jimmy had in his hands or his feet. Or his heart. Their father couldn't understand that and wouldn't tolerate it. Trips between rinks became loud, angry rants about Alex's lack of goals, lack of assists, lack of playing time, lack of grit. 'Your mother wasn't no pussy,' he'd tell his son. 'I'm no pussy. Your brother ain't. Where the fuck you'd get this?'

Alex had no answers. He'd sit in the front passenger seat staring at his lap, trying not to cry. It went on game after game, night after night, Jimmy hearing his father from the back seat. One night late in the season, he hurried out to the Jeep after one of Alex's games and took the front seat so Alex couldn't. His father, who'd left the arena early to nip at the flask he kept in the glove box, told Jimmy to get in the back. 'I gotta have a talk with your brother.'

Jimmy stared out the passenger window. 'No, you don't,' he said. 'You just want to yell at him. But you don't know what you're talking about.'

'What did you say?'

'You don't know shit about hockey.'

The knuckles on his father's right hand caught Jimmy just below his cheekbone. He kept looking out the window. 'You're an asshole,' Jimmy said. 'I'll kick your fat drunk ass.'

'You'll what?' His father leaned across the seat and laughed in Jimmy's face. Jimmy gagged on the stink of Seagram's as Alex appeared outside the window.

'What's going on?' he said. Their father shoved Jimmy toward the door. 'Get in the back now, boy.' Jimmy got in the back.

The rants kept up. Alex hung his head, absorbing the blows, while Jimmy sat in the back seat, speechless, helpless, fuming. Then, a week or so later, their father got so worked up at Alex for taking a tripping penalty late in a play-off game that, barely halfway home from Manistee, he pulled off the road and ordered his son out of the car. 'Just get your faggoty ass out,' he said. 'You don't deserve a ride.' Alex opened the door and started to step into the frozen dark.

'I'm going, too,' Jimmy said, pushing his door open.

His father reached over the seat and tried to grab him. 'You stay where you are, boy.'

'Fuck you, old man.'

The boys scrambled out onto the icy road shoulder, their father out of the car now and stumbling through the headlight beams in their direction. The way he was wobbling, he must have had more than just the flask that night. 'You little bastards,' he said. 'I ought to just run you over.'

He went first for Alex, but his left foot slid sideways on a patch of ice and he nearly toppled. As he struggled to regain his balance, Jimmy, bigger than most thirteen-year-olds, launched himself forward, driving the heel of his hand – he didn't want a broken knuckle keeping him off the ice – square into his father's nose. His father was unconscious before he hit the ground, blood spewing onto the snowy shoulder.

But Jimmy did not stop. He climbed atop his father's chest, squeezing him between his knees, and pounded his face with the undersides of his fists, screaming, 'Fuck you fuck you fuck you motherfucker.'

'Jesus, Jimmy,' Alex yelled, grabbing his brother around his neck and dragging him backward. 'Stop. Stop, you're gonna kill him. Stop.'

Jimmy backed away and stood up, panting. 'Who's the pussy now?'

They both looked up at the sound of their father's car crashing into the woods ahead of them. He'd left it without putting it in park.

He never attended another of their games.

'It's really not him,' Jimmy tells Alex from his chair at the table. 'It's me. All me.'

Alex starts to reach across the table, then appears to remember the guard's admonition. 'It's both of you, pal,' Alex says. 'Give yourself a break. Give him a break. Losing Mama about killed him.'

'About killed all of us, Al.'

'I know. But just try to think of the good times. There were some. Remember those nights on the river?'

Their dad would take Alex and Jimmy to the Jako after it froze hard and thick enough to skate on it. He bought used IceKings sticks for a buck each and cut them down to the boys' size, and they each got their own puck to shove around on the bumpy surface. He parked the car on the bank so the headlamps threw a haphazard oval of light across the stilled river. There was a bag of windmill cookies and a thermos of hot chocolate. They stayed until Dad thought the car battery might give out.

'Those were cool,' Jimmy says.

'Remember that time we skated all the way to Bliss?'

Jimmy chuckles. All the way to Bliss. If only. 'Yeah,' he says as he hears the door to the room click open. He turns in his seat, his shoulder blades pinching together, and an image appears in his head out of nowhere. Something from the Loon that night. He tells himself he needs to tell Devyn before it flees his memory.

'You said fifteen minutes,' Alex tells the officer.

'I know what I said,' the officer says. 'You're out of here.'

'What do you mean?'

The officer steps behind Jimmy and grabs his cuffed wrists, a little roughly. 'Some numb-nuts posted your bail. You're free to go.'

'Seriously?' Jimmy says, hands now free.

'Don't worry,' the cop says. 'You'll be back.'

THIRTY-THREE

Nobody in Bitterfrost gives a good goddamn about Jordan Fawcett. Those who knew her seem to think her particular end was inevitable; those who didn't are way more interested in the two strangers from Detroit, the dead man, Diggs, and the still-missing Jerome Hardy. Even the cops in Mackinaw City, where Jordan died a week ago, don't seem to care. Devyn has been calling and emailing and received nothing but a faxed, smudged, partially redacted police report and bureaucratic non-answers to her questions about Jordan's death. She doesn't understand why, although she has heard that the department up there doesn't employ a single female officer. Might that be the problem?

Now she's in her running car outside the Bitterfrost courthouse, on hold for a Detroit parole officer who once had Aaron Diggs as a client. Jimmy's preliminary exam begins in forty-five minutes, and she's hoping the guy on the phone can give her some insight into Diggs and his missing brother-in-law and why they would have been in Bitterfrost at all.

She's had almost no luck learning much about young Hardy. Every one of her emails and calls has been returned by a lawyer or a public-relations person employed by Hardy's father. Some googling revealed that Jerome Hardy grew up in well-to-do Bloomfield Hills, aced his way through the Cranbrook prep school, and won a lacrosse scholarship to Albion College near Ann Arbor. All was going as rich folks expected until he tore up a knee in preseason, never played a minute, and left the school after two semesters. He accepted a lowly position at his father's real estate development firm and worked his way up, showing a flair for writing that eventually landed him on the public relations staff, a staff that is now trying to make sure Devyn gets nowhere.

Diggs is another matter. He has an actual public trail, left in court and police records. It's not too lengthy, but it's impressive nonetheless: aggravated assault, selling illegal drugs, car theft. He served two years in prison on the assault charge, which was reduced after he pleaded guilty. He grew up in St Clair Shores north-east of Detroit and dropped out of Wayne State University after his father died. Assuming it's the same Aaron Diggs, after he got out of prison, he opened an auto body shop that specialized in dressing out 1960s muscle cars. Photos invariably show him glowering at the camera. No smiles for Diggs.

Diggs and Hardy became friends when Diggs was fixing up Hardy's 1970 Chevelle SS. They liked to fish and water ski and consume edibles and liquor. At least that's what Devyn could divine from the short phone interviews she'd managed with two of the men's buddies, neither of whom was eager to speak. Hardy fell in love with Diggs's younger sister and they married the year before the boys made their fateful trip.

Devyn's reading a ten-year-old *Detroit News* story on Diggs's assault case when a slap on her window startles her. 'What the hell?' she says, looking left to see her brother, Evan, grinning and staring at her through sunglasses that look jarringly out of place on this leaden-sky afternoon.

'Open up, I'm freezing my nuts off,' he says. She hits the unlock button while he scrambles around to the passenger side. 'Christ,' he says, dropping into the car. 'I thought I'd find you here some-where.'

'What are you doing?' Devyn says.

'Funny, that's what I was going to ask you.'

'I'm on hold for a call I have to take.'

'Involving our Zamboni driver?'

'Maybe.'

He stares through his tinted lenses at the frosted windshield. 'Just hang up now. Drop the case. Tell Jimmy to get another lawyer. Get us out of this mess. Get the goddamn media assholes out of my cellphone.'

'Get "us" out of this mess? Are you serious?'

'Us. The Paynes.' He starts shaking his head. 'It's not a good look, Dev. Not a good look at all, defending killers.'

'How can you say that, Evan?'

He's known Jimmy since he was a boy watching Jimmy play for the IceKings. Evan wanted to *be* Jimmy on the ice, but he couldn't handle having a sister who skated faster and shot the puck harder. He gave up the game, and while Devyn was gone to AAA tourna-ments then later skating for the University of Michigan women's club, Evan turned his attention to the business of hockey – the family business. He did some good things that grew the fan base and stitched the IceKings into the local fabric, including starting the kid programs – the Little Queens and Kings – that Devyn coaches.

Now he's sitting in her car, still shivering a little behind his shades as he tells her to give up on Jimmy. 'Look,' he says, 'I don't know what happened that night, but Jimmy obviously got himself into a spot. Again. You know the guy's got issues. That's how he wound up back here in the first place.'

'Issues don't equal evidence, Ev. But I'm glad you stopped by because –' she glances at her phone, still holding – 'I want you to give Jimmy his job back. It'll be good for the jury to hear his employer is behind him.'

Evan had suspended Jimmy from his duties at the rink pending the disposition of his case. 'Are you f . . . are you kidding me?' he says. 'No way. And Mom would agree, by the way, even if she did pony up all that cash – our family's cash – to bail him out of jail. Damn, Devyn. I'm proud of what you've become and how you step up for lost causes, even if you don't have two nickels to rub together. Every game this goes on, we're selling fewer tickets and losing fans. It's a threat to the value of the franchise.'

She hates it when her brother refers to the IceKings as a 'franchise,' as if it was a Cinnabon. 'Maybe you shouldn't have raised ticket prices,' she says. 'Maybe you shouldn't be so miserly with your customers. You never were before, Ev. Even Mom's wondering what's going on.'

'What exactly do you know about running a business?'

'Nothing. But until you – that is, Mom – sells the team, its *value* is just a number on some ledger nobody cares about.'

He finally turns to look at her. 'I saw Jimmy the morning after the murder. He was acting weird, Dev. I mean, like he had something to hide. His face looked like he'd been in a fight. Which means the other guy's face probably didn't look great either, right?'

Right, Devyn thinks, without saying it.

'Do you really want to put another killer back on the street, Dev? I know that bothers you.'

She's considering telling Evan to go to hell when her phone squawks, 'This is Raymond, how can I help you?'

'Hey, Mr Jones, thanks for picking up. Gimme one second?' She covers the phone and tells Evan, 'I should kick your ass for what you just said.'

'Sorry.'

'No, you're not, but we will get through this. I love you. Now get out of my car. And take off those goddamn sunglasses.'

'Mr Jones,' she says.

'Call me Raymond.'

'Raymond. Devyn Payne here. I'm an attorney in Bitterfrost.'

'That in the great state of Michigan?'

'Yeah. Way up north.'

'UP?'

'Not that far, but close.'

'Not sure I can help you, but shoot.'

She has about five minutes. Outside, townspeople are streaming past into the courthouse. It'll be full by the time Devyn goes in. She tells Raymond Jones she's trying to figure out why Diggs and Hardy came to Bitterfrost. Raymond seems vaguely aware of what befell his former parolee.

'Aaron loved trouble,' he says. 'It didn't have to find him. He went looking for it. And he usually found it.'

'I gather that. But it looked like he cleaned up his act after he got out of Jackson, with the body shop and all.'

'He was doing better, for sure. Still probably using, still drinking. But he was lying low, mostly. Waiting.'

'Waiting for what?'

Raymond chuckles. 'What we're all waiting for. The jackpot.'

'What do you mean?'

'We all have dreams, right? Aaron had one dream and it was very specific: Costa Rica. He saw some play about a guy who lived alone in the jungle in Costa Rica. That guy was his idol. He just needed that one big payoff so he could go to Costa Rica. The jackpot.'

'But he wasn't gonna get the jackpot at his body shop.'

'No. The jackpot would come from extracurriculars.'

'Like?'

'Excuse me,' Raymond says. Devyn hears his muffled voice say something to someone else. 'OK,' he says, coming back on. 'I have about thirty seconds.'

'Extracurriculars?'

'You know, side jobs.'

'Illegal side jobs?'

'He didn't tell me. Just said he was building his Costa Rica fund.'

'I noticed in one of the news stories I read about Aaron that he had a pretty prominent lawyer repping him in his assault case.'

'As I recall, yes.'

'How did he afford that?'

'He didn't.'

'Then who?'

'I'm gonna guess Rooney.'

'Rooney?'

'Mario Rooney. The Black Mario. Never heard of him?'

'Don't know. Bad guy?'

'Well. Never been convicted.' Raymond gets off the phone again, then comes back. 'I gotta go,' he says. 'That help?'

'Did Diggs work for Mario Rooney?'

But Raymond has ended the call. 'Shit,' Devyn says. She thinks about what he said: *We all have dreams, right?* It reminds her of that long-ago night on the Detroit River, the bottle of Macallan, and she almost laughs. She turns her car off, tugs her scarf tighter, and steps out into the cold while tapping 'Mario Rooney' into Google.

THIRTY-FOUR

Klimmek waits behind the prosecution bench in the Bitterfrost courtroom. Behind him he hears the rustle of people filing into the gallery. Some are family of the deceased, Diggs, some of his brother-in-law, Hardy, who remains missing.

Klimmek concentrates on the job at hand – offering just enough evidence to persuade a district judge to order a trial – without getting caught up in the emotion of a crime that has riveted media across the Midwest and sent shockwaves of disbelief and anger rippling through Bitterfrost. On Klimmek's cellphone is a voicemail he received this morning from a producer for Fox News in New York City. Chief Quarton has fielded similar calls from Chicago, Miami, and Los Angeles. It appears that Philip Hardy, father of the missing man, father-in-law of the dead one, has some pull. At this moment, the elder Hardy is sitting with his wife, Jerome's mother, two rows behind Klimmek.

The detective hasn't had a case that attracted such widespread interest – scrutiny is the word he prefers – since the one that saw the claw-hammer killer set free. He'd be lying if he claimed he wasn't nervous. He can't afford to be checking the gallery or scanning the people standing beneath the portraits of dead judges on the marble walls to his left and right. He chooses not to look in the direction of the defendant Baker and his attorney sitting at a table on the other side of the rail to his right. Instead he fingers the beads of a Rosary inside his jacket pocket, saying Hail Marys for each of the roses carved into the mahogany frontispiece of the judge's bench. He silently prays for clarity and calm as he counts the roses along with the beads, one by one, left to right, then right to left, then again, and again, until finally he hears the call.

'All rise.'

Klimmek stands and buttons his suit coat over his blue button-down and striped tie held in place by a gold Bitterfrost Police tie clasp. District Judge Matthias Lindon, a strapping sixty-two-year-old with a bushy white beard, takes the brown leather chair behind the bench. 'All righty,' he says, which strikes Klimmek as oddly casual for a case like this but also, perhaps, a subtle sign that Lindon is poised to move it quickly to the next stage. '*The State versus James Robert Baker.* The charge is murder in the second degree. Is the prosecution ready to proceed?'

The prosecutor, Genevieve Harris, stands at her table. 'Yes, your honor,' she says. 'The prosecution has only one witness to call, and we will introduce evidence as he testifies that will provide a sufficient basis for the defendant to be bound over for trial.'

'We shall see, shan't we? And the charge is second-degree murder, not first, correct?'

'Correct.'

'I'm merely guessing here, counselor, but as opposed to the condition of premeditation required for a first-degree charge, might this qualify under the law as "an impulsive killing with malice aforethought?"'

'Yes, your honor.'

'Please proceed.'

'The prosecution calls Bitterfrost Police Detective Garth Klimmek.'

Walking to the witness stand, Klimmek indulges a glance at Baker and his lawyer Payne. The swelling on Baker's face appears to be down. He's wearing khaki slacks and a sport jacket, white shirt, no tie. As Klimmek learned two days ago, someone posted Baker's bail. The record shows that someone to be DAP LLC. Payne's middle name is Abigail, so Klimmek figures it's her, though most folks assume Payne's mother put up the money. Some are fine with that. Some are not. Klimmek is just glad to see Baker wearing an ankle monitor, a condition of his bail.

Klimmek takes the oath. The prosecutor Harris approaches. 'Detective Klimmek,' she says.

Before she can continue, she's interrupted by a woman's scream. Klimmek peers into the gallery and sees the mother of Aaron Diggs collapsing into the arms of her husband. He met the couple once, briefly, the day before. 'Oh God, oh God, oh God,' the woman says, burying her face in her husband's shoulder as she pounds his chest with a fist. Klimmek has seen this before. It's not the murder itself overtaking the poor woman but the banality of it all, the sudden knowledge that a roomful of curious strangers is about to tend not so much to her son's death but to its bureaucratic aftermath. Klimmek can see how it might not feel like justice to someone so aggrieved. But that's what it is.

Klimmek hears Lindon rapping his gavel. Harris steps to the bench and whispers the woman's name. The judge nods and says, 'Mrs Diggs. I understand how painful this must be for you and your family, and I'm deeply sorry that you have to live through it. But I cannot tolerate such outbursts in my courtroom.'

The woman's sobs subside. Harris turns to Klimmek. 'Detective,' she says, 'the defendant, James Robert Baker, brutally ended the life of twenty-nine-year-old Aaron Diggs. Can you tell the court what role you've played in the invest—'

'Objection, your honor. Despite the state's hurry to convict, my client is innocent until proven guilty. And the Bitterfrost Police Department has not proven terribly reliable in its handling of prior murder cases.'

Devyn Payne is on her feet, looking not at the judge or the prosecutor but directly at Klimmek. He returns her stare, thinking, Bring it on, counselor. He may not want to engage the grief of a mother who lost her son, but he's one-hundred-percent ready to take on this lawyer. This time, Klimmek is not going to let his quarry slip away.

THIRTY-FIVE

'Getting in his face from the get-go?'

Devyn hears Jimmy's whisper and leans into him at the defense table. 'You know how sometimes, on the opening face-off, you ignore the puck and jam the heel of your stick down on the other guy's foot?'

Jimmy grins. 'Or maybe step on the guy's stick blade, break it?'

'Yeah.' She points at Klimmek. 'Listen up.'

Devyn collected Jimmy from the jail after he made bail. He was quiet in her car, understandably self-conscious about the contraption on his ankle. As she pulled into the driveway, he looked out over the dashboard and said, 'I remembered something.' It wasn't much. Something vague about headlamps he recalled seeing. She told him to work on remembering more.

Prosecutor Harris begins by walking Klimmek through rudimentary questions about his experience and qualifications. Harris was elected eight months after her predecessor lost the trial of the claw-hammer killer. She is taciturn as an owl and just as fierce a predator. But Harris is merely the vessel for Klimmek. He's the one who matters. He has to be hungry to redeem himself. Devyn doubts he or his colleagues will make the mistakes they made the last time she encountered them in a murder case. The mistakes Devyn used to win an acquittal of the accused double-murderer Sawtell.

Klimmek sits up straight, hands stilled in his lap, a veteran of the witness box, as Harris leads him through questions that establish Jimmy as being at the Lost Loon and encountering Diggs and Hardy. 'Detective,' Harris says. 'You inspected the defendant's house the morning the decedent's body was found, correct?'

'Yes, I did.'

'Why did you decide to do that?'

'Mr Baker's house is within sight of where we found the vehicle referenced in my report. I wanted to ask if maybe he'd heard or seen anything.'

'But he wasn't home when you visited.'

'No.'

'Did anything you saw at the house catch your attention?'

'Yes. I found drops of what looked like blood on a door leading to Mr Baker's kitchen.'

'Were they in fact blood?'

'A lab analysis identified it as such, yes.'

'What blood type was it?'

'AB-negative.'

'And what blood type is the defendant?'

'A-positive.'

'I see, so it's unlikely that that was the defendant's blood?'

'Quite.'

Harris walks to her table and picks up a piece of paper. 'What type of blood,' she says without looking up, 'did Mr Diggs have?'

'AB-negative,' Klimmek says.

Devyn hears sobbing from the gallery but doesn't dare turn around.

'Is that a rare blood type, detective?' Harris says.

Devyn jumps in. 'Unless the detective has a sideline as a hematologist, he isn't qualified to answer.'

'It's not a difficult question, your honor,' Harris says. 'You can Google it.'

'It is the rarest blood type,' Judge Lindon says. 'My wife has it. Objection overruled. Proceed, Ms Harris.'

'Can you say for certain that that AB-negative blood was actually that of the decedent, detective?'

'Not as yet,' Klimmek says. 'We are waiting for the DNA.'

'But it could easily be Mr Diggs's blood, yes?'

'Objection.'

'Overruled. Please answer.'

'Yes,' Klimmek says. 'It's possible.'

'Detective,' the prosecutor says, 'did you execute any search warrants in your initial investigation?'

'Yes,' Klimmek says. 'Mr Baker's home and his workplace.'

'What did you learn?'

'Well, we found a number of things that might bear on this case. For one, we discovered a jacket locked in a cabinet in the shed where Mr Baker works as the Zamboni driver for the local hockey team.'

'Exactly what about this jacket was noteworthy?'

Klimmek steeples his hands beneath his chin. 'One sleeve of the jacket was saturated with what we subsequently determined was blood.'

'What type?'

'AB-negative.'

'Which could also be Mr Diggs's blood?'

'Possibly, yes.'

The sobs from the gallery grow louder. Devyn tries to ignore them. She figured something about the jacket was coming. It's not good for Jimmy, but it's not decisive either; the prosecution hasn't established that the jacket is actually Jimmy's or that he put it where they found it. But she hears Jimmy whisper, 'Shit.'

Harris presses on. 'Were there any other items of clothing that figured in your investigation, detective?'

'Yes. We found a left-handed glove at the scene of Mr Diggs's body and a matching right-handed glove at the scene of the charred vehicle.'

Gloves? Devyn thinks. The prosecution hasn't mentioned this to her and neither has Jimmy. She glances his way. He avoids her gaze.

Harris says, 'The vehicle you mentioned is the one identified as belonging to Mr Hardy, correct?'

'Correct.'

'Do you know if either of those gloves belonged to the defendant?'

'Objection, leading.'

'I'll allow it,' Lindon says.

Klimmek says, 'Mr Baker's credit records indicate he bought a pair of gloves at the hardware store in Bitterfrost that are at least similar to the ones we found.'

'"At least similar?"' Devyn says. 'Please, your honor.'

'If that is an objection, I'll sustain it,' Lindon says.

'Yes, your honor,' Harris says, then to Klimmek, 'Was there blood on either of the gloves?'

'Both.'

'Blood type?'

'AB-negative.'

'Any DNA yet?'

'Not yet.'

Harris picks up some papers from the lectern and places them on the defense table, then turns back to Klimmek. 'One last thing, detective: are you familiar with the defendant's past, particularly with the end of his minor-league professional hockey career?'

'Objection,' Devyn says, leaping from her seat. 'What my client did or didn't do more than a decade ago has no bearing on this case.'

'Ms Harris?' the judge says.

'Your honor, as you'll see, what I'm asking goes to the defendant's capacity for committing such a heinous crime as this.'

'No, your honor, this is an attempt—'

The judge silences Devyn with a palm held high, then considers for a moment. 'I'll allow it,' he says. 'Detective?'

'As a member of the minor-league Erie, Pennsylvania, Rink Rats, Mr Baker initiated a number of on-ice altercations and became relatively famous as what hockey people sometimes refer to as a "goon".'

'Your honor,' Devyn says. 'This is prejudicial and lacking the tiniest scrap of foundation.'

'Prejudicial to whom, counselor?' the judge says. 'Me? Are you saying I can be led around by the nose? You will have your opportunity to cross-examine.'

'Please continue, detective,' Harris says.

'In his last game in the minors, Mr Baker injured an opposing player so badly in a fight that the player was unable to continue playing hockey.'

'Detective, what do you think the defendant's encounter with this opposing player tells us?'

'It tells us he's capable of intense . . .' Klimmek pauses, searching for a word. 'Anger. Intense rage.'

'And in fact, did your investigation of the past record regarding the defendant indicate that this "intense rage," as you put it, was a factor in his psychological makeup?'

'Objection, the detective is not a shrink.'

'Overruled, so long as the detective answers on the basis of the record.'

Klimmek says, 'The record in civil litigation related to his encounter with that player offered evidence that the defendant suffers from "intermittent explosive disorder," a psychological condition in which people lose control of their emotions.'

Jimmy *suffered* from that condition, not *suffers*, Devyn thinks. She could object, but it will do nothing to move Lindon, who obviously has made up his mind.

'One last question,' Harris says. 'Detective Klimmek, you interviewed the defendant the night of his arrest?'

'Yes, briefly.'

'And what did he tell you?'

'Essentially, that he couldn't remember anything after he left the Lost Loon, except that he woke up in bed at home.'

'In bed?'

'That's what he said.'

'Do you believe that the defendant remembers essentially nothing about that night, detective?'

'I do not.'

'Nothing further, your honor.'

Devyn can feel Harris look her way but she stays fixated on Klimmek. She hadn't expected to ask him anything. But she wants to let him know who is boss, as it were. 'Detective,' she says, 'approximately when was the last time you investigated a murder?'

'I think you know the answer, counselor.'

'I'm not on the witness stand, sir.'

Klimmek's face makes it clear that he's mildly amused, or trying to look it. 'Approximately five years ago.'

'Five long years,' Devyn says. 'Did you arrest and charge a suspect?'

'He was your client, Ms Payne.'

The judge interrupts. 'Answer, detective.'

'Yes,' he says. 'We arrested and charged a suspect.'

'Was he convicted at trial, detective?'

'No, he was not.'

'I have no further questions, your honor.'

'All good,' the judge says. 'We will take a five-minute recess and then I will have my ruling.'

Devyn sits. 'Now what?' Jimmy whispers.

'Now the judge will call for a trial,' she says.

'That doesn't mean I'm guilty.'

'No. Now keep your eyes forward.'

Devyn turns slightly sideways in her chair so she can get a view of the gallery. The place hasn't been this packed since that other trial she won, or Klimmek and the prosecution lost. She scans the crowd quickly, trying not to look obvious. Big Henry and his wife. The dry cleaner Figo. The principal of the high school. At least three coaches of kid hockey teams that play against Devyn's youngsters. In a far corner she notices a tall man in a suit with a charcoal topcoat draped over one arm. He's yanking a fedora down low on his eyes and hurrying out of the courtroom. Devyn spies a shock of white hair along the side of his head. He looks like a certain Traverse City lawyer who bills about ten times what Devyn does. He didn't drive more than an hour out of sheer curiosity. He must have a client, even if that client isn't in the courtroom.

Jimmy pokes her in the side and she turns to him. 'You dropped this,' he says, and hands her a business card that must have slipped out of one of her pockets. 'You gonna be a TV star?'

Devyn found the card, from a producer at *Dateline NBC*, slipped beneath her office door that morning. 'No,' Devyn says as Judge Lindon reappears. 'I'll tell you about it later.'

'All rise.'

Lindon gives the gavel a tap and gets right to business. 'The court finds that there is probable cause to believe a crime has been committed and the defendant may have committed it. Whether the crime qualifies as impulsive, with malice aforethought, will be up to twelve of our finest citizens to decide. This matter is hereby bound over to the circuit court for trial.'

Devyn lays a hand gently on Jimmy's shoulder and tells him, 'We'll let the courtroom empty out.'

'Was that bad or good?'

'Neither. It's just procedure.'

'Shouldn't you have called some witnesses or something?'

What witnesses? she thinks. 'Not unless you think you can persuade the judge to throw the case out, which wasn't happening. Like I told you before, we just wanted to get a peek at the other guy's poker hand, not show any cards of our own.'

'So what do I do now?'

'You go live your life—'

'What life? I—'

'—and do not forget rule number one: shut your damn mouth.'

Even as Devyn says it, her semi-conscious mind is churning through the troubling items that came up in Klimmek's testimony – the tire tracks, the blood, the jacket, the gloves – and the potentially problematic ones that remain – the two-jagoffs text, Jimmy's living-room conversation with Klimmek, the toxicology report the cops have yet to share, a vague reference to the Lost Loon security video in the police report. So far the prosecution has offered only the one witness. Are there others? Does it matter? Could the detective suffice?

Half a dozen reporters are waiting when Devyn and Jimmy emerge into the cold. Devyn guides Jimmy past as the journalists shout their inane questions about Jimmy's guilt and how he feels and whether he'll ever drive a Zamboni again. 'We have nothing to say,' Devyn tells them once, twice, three times before bundling Jimmy into her car.

As they pull away, she wishes she had no other cases, no coaching commitments, no men nagging her on Tinder. She wishes she could do nothing at all but find a way to win this case. They're waiting to pull onto Main Street when a reporter outside her window shouts, 'Why did your family bail out Mr Baker but then fire him?' Devyn opens her window a crack. 'You don't have your facts right,' she says. 'And I'll thank you for leaving my family out of this.'

'How the hell is that even possible?' says someone in the middle of the scrum. Devyn sees it's not a reporter, but one of the Dulaney brothers, wearing a smirk. She slams the accelerator and fishtails away.

THIRTY-SIX

The Lost Loon is as well-lit as a 7-Eleven at midnight. A hint of mint-scented cleanser hangs on the air. Jimmy has never seen or smelled the place this spic-and-span. Then again, he's never been inside the Loon on a weekday afternoon. Technically the tavern isn't open yet. A regular named Earl – Jimmy has met him once or twice – smokes in his rusted-out pickup in the parking lot, waiting to go inside and order what probably isn't his first beer of the day. After trying the locked front door, Jimmy found an open side door and walked in. Now he unzips his parka as he strolls to the bar and calls out, 'Hey. Ronnie? You around?'

'One minute,' she shouts from the kitchen behind the horseshoe bar.

Jimmy walks to his nightly stool, the clunky device on his left ankle chafing. He stands with his hands on the bar and looks around, remembering what he can of the night of the incident. He pictures Ronnie fingering her phone, Diggs and Hardy at the shuffleboard table, the woman in the orange hoodie he later saw at Big Henry's, Butch Dulaney and friends playing euchre in a corner.

'Jimmy.'

Ronnie emerges from the kitchen, her hair tied back, big black horn-rimmed glasses on her face. Jimmy doesn't think he's ever seen her in glasses, but he likes it. 'Spectacles, huh?'

'Give me a minute?'

While Jimmy waits, Ronnie fills a pint from the Labatt Blue tap, pours a tumbler full of Canadian Club, and carries them out to a table near the jukebox. Just as she sets them down, the front door opens and in walks Earl, trailed by a huge, unleashed black Labrador. He proceeds to his table, nodding at Ronnie – 'Hello, honeybunch,' he says – and sits down to his liquid lunch, the dog lying beside him.

Ronnie comes around to Jimmy's side of the bar and gives him a hug. 'Jesus, Jimmy,' she says. 'What happened?'

'I was gonna ask you that.'

'I don't know, Jim.'

'You don't know what happened?'

She wraps her arms around herself and looks away, toward the kitchen. 'I don't know if I can talk,' she says. 'You . . . maybe you shouldn't even be in here. The police have been by a bunch. They keep asking me things. They took a bunch of our security video. Of course my boss thinks it's all my fault and he's probably gonna shitcan me. If he saw you here—'

'Don't worry, honey.' It's Earl, across the bar. 'I got your back.'

'Thank you, dear,' Ronnie says.

It dawns on Jimmy that he shouldn't have come. Devyn explicitly warned him not to. But he can't just sit in his house stewing. He could try to drive downstate and see Avery but Noelle told him to stay away. Plus, the Bitterfrost cops might freak if they saw his ankle monitor so far away.

'Ronnie,' Jimmy says, keeping his voice down. 'I'm not here to threaten you. I just want to know what you know. It might help me in – I'm going to be going to trial.' He can feel himself stammering. 'Like what was on the video the cops took? I don't think I caused any trouble that night, did I? I had my highball and had a few words with those guys and I went home, right? Did you see something I didn't?'

Ronnie retreats behind the bar without answering. She grabs a rag and starts wiping the bar. 'I'm sorry, Jimmy,' she says. 'I hate to do this, but I'm going to have to ask you to leave.'

'Leave? Ronnie, come on, this is my place, my, my last refuge. I can't even go to the rink anymore. Big Henry asked me not to come in the diner until this blows over. I saw signs in store windows saying I ought to be stuck in a penalty box for life. Some online wacko is saying I was having an affair with one of those dudes. Are you frigging kidding me?'

'I know.'

'And now *you're* gonna kick me out?'

Ronnie sets the rag down and claps a hand over her mouth. She closes her eyes and shakes her head. 'I'm sorry.'

'I'm sorry, too, bud, but it's time for you to vamoose.'

Jimmy turns to see Earl and his dog standing next to him. 'Excuse me?' he says. 'This is between Ronnie and me.'

'I ain't letting a killer hassle my favorite bartender,' Earl says. He angles his head toward the dog. 'Neither is my partner Kevin here.' The dog, his head leaned back to look up at Jimmy, emits a low growl. Jimmy starts to consider whether he'd have to take the dog out before Earl, then dismisses the thought. He looks back at Ronnie. She's stuck between the cops and her asshole boss, with two kids and no means of support beyond the Loon. She probably has regulars shitting all over Jimmy, too, no-nothing boozers like Earl, jiggling keys in his pocket like that's going to frighten Jimmy.

'Your dog is Kevin?' Jimmy says.

'Yeah. Got a problem with that?'

'Nope. I have a brother named Kevin.' A lie, but maybe it'll back Earl off. 'It's kinda cool.'

'OK, Jimmy,' Ronnie says. 'I gotta go, you gotta go.'

'All right. Let me know when things change. Remember I love you, Ronnie.'

He edges around the dog – really, who the hell names a dog Kevin? – without acknowledging Earl and slides between tables to the front door. He's about to grab the handle when he hears Ronnie call out.

'Jimmy.'

He stops. 'Yeah?'

'Why did you take your truck across the street?'

'What do you mean? I'm parked in the lot.'

'You ain't supposed to be talking to him, Ronnie,' Earl says.

She ignores him. 'No,' she says to Jimmy. 'That night. Why were you parked across the street at the end of the night?'

'I have no . . . I don't know what you're talking about.'

'Think about it,' she says. 'I love you, too.'

Outside, Jimmy starts to turn toward the parking lot, then stops and stares across the two lanes of snow-streaked highway. Beyond the opposing road shoulder, he sees an opening in the thicket of dead brush and stripped trees. It's a two-track dirt road used mostly by snowmobilers. He walks across the empty highway and stands in the middle of the two-track.

He spins to face the Loon. He scans the tavern itself, its parking lot, the woods at the far back edge of the lot, fifty yards beyond the bar itself. The image returns to him, the scrap of memory that flashed in his head when his brother Alex was talking about skating with their father: A pair of vehicle headlamps shining their way out of the dark forest behind the Loon. He's immediately convinced that he saw them from this precise vantage, where he's standing now in the snowy dirt road.

But how did Ronnie know he'd been there, apparently in his pickup? Unless, maybe, the security video? He looks again and, yes, a security camera is mounted on the wall above the Loon entrance, peering down at him. He looks again at the far end of the parking lot. More images begin forming in his head, like ghosts emerging from a crypt. There were two sets of headlamps, not just one. One set followed by the other. It doesn't make sense yet but now he knows he was – if Ronnie is indeed correct – sitting in his truck watching while at least one, maybe two vehicles rumbled slowly around the far reaches of the lot.

But then what did he do?

He sees a police cruiser out of the corner of his right eye, heading his way on the highway. It shouldn't matter. He's not doing anything wrong. But the car slows its pace as it nears, coming almost to a stop in front of the Loon. Jimmy looks away, but he knows the cop at the wheel is staring him down. The cruiser's lights flash three times before it pulls away.

Earl probably called. Asshole.

Jimmy takes his phone out and hits the button to call Devyn. She'll ream him out for going to the Loon. Then she will have to forgive him because he may have something that will help their case.

THIRTY-SEVEN

'Identification?'

The security guard leans out of the narrow window on his hut, his Carhartt coveralls buttoned to the neck.

'How you doing, Charlie?' Klimmek says from his Bronco.

'Fine, sir. I need identification.'

'"Sir?" Are you joking?'

Klimmek worked with the guard's father for fifteen years. The kid almost followed his dad onto the Bitterfrost force but didn't take to the training and opted for private industry. He probably makes a better living, certainly here on the Dulaney spread.

'No, sir. I need some formal ID. Sir.'

Without even the hint of a smile. Klimmek hands his police badge out the window. 'Busting my chops, Charlie?'

The guard hands the badge back and, as he does, Klimmek smells a whiff of alcohol. From last night, he hopes. 'Sorry, sir,' Charlie says, 'it's just been a long day. Seven a.m. comes early. And cold.'

'Gotcha. I hope you have some heat in there.'

Charlie waves him through.

The Dulaney complex sprawls over hundreds of rolling acres anchoring the corner where the southern and eastern city limits of Bitterfrost intersect. Most people would think it looks loveliest during the summer, especially when an evening sun spreads its amber glow across the hills before sinking into Lake Michigan. But Klimmek prefers it now, when the snow makes the swales and peaks resemble the lake itself, and the military-grade fence ringing the grounds seems less menacing for the whiteness flocking its iron bars and grates.

He follows a road cleared of ice and snow past a trio of three-story colonials for the brothers and their families, smoke spooling out of chimneys on each. The pool and tennis court are shut down for winter, but youngsters play shinny on the outdoor hockey rink, fitted with its own scoreboard, twin benches, and NHL goal nets. The Dulaney scrapyard, squatting behind a wall of sleeping trees to Klimmek's distant left, takes up much of the property's western end. The discarded hulks of cars, combines, appliances, trucks, tractors, and trailers encircle a two-story structure housing a forge the Dulaneys use to make buoys, docks, boat hoists, and other necessities of lake life. The upper arm of a steam shovel juts over the forge roof. Neighbors as far as two miles away occasionally gripe about noise and smells emanating from the forge, especially over the past year. City Councilwoman Eleanor Payne has hauled Butch and his brothers before the council more than once to register her complaints, to no avail that Klimmek can see except to annoy the Dulaneys.

The road winds left and up a ridge. From the crest Klimmek sees a low wooden fence surrounding a broad trapezoid of land dotted with roofed hutches and a low-slung building into which a large man in winter garb is corralling hogs. Klimmek parks in a snowless asphalt clearing behind the building, wondering if perhaps the asphalt is heated somehow. He takes his phone out and activates the voice recording app. Klimmek knows that taping Butch without his permission means the recording will be inadmissible in court. The tape is merely for note-taking purposes. There's a text from his wife Kris: **Be careful ok?** He probably shouldn't have let on where he was going. She has heard the stories about the Dulaneys. Klimmek isn't too worried; they have a temper, but they aren't stupid.

'Come on, boys, get your not-fat-enough asses inside,' Butch exhorts the pigs as they grunt past, breath pluming white around their gray snouts. Butch is the middle of the three Dulaney boys and the family's *de facto* patriarch since liver cancer felled the old man. Klimmek has had to deal with Butch, Junior, and DonDon a few times for minor bar skirmishes and, once, when they roughed up a trespasser who unwisely sneaked into the forge. Nothing too serious. They have a reputation for intimidating people who cross them. Klimmek's former chief liked to say the Dulaneys cling to mean like a drunk to a bottle, and the more they drink, the meaner they get.

Klimmek approaches from one side so as not to surprise Butch. Butch must have heard the car, though, because he shouts over his shoulder, 'Hey, mister police man, don't get too close and let one of these animals get a whiff of you. They haven't eaten.' Then he turns and laughs. Klimmek notices Butch's hands are bare in the seven-degree cold.

'Afternoon, Butch. You trying to get frostbite?'

'Hell, I already lost half of two fingers to that. Ain't no biggie. Anyway, I get plenty of heat off these boys.'

'Where do you want to talk?'

'How long's it gonna take?'

'Depends on you.'

Butch chuckles again. 'So lemme get this straight,' he says. The last pig trundles into the shed. 'Basically, my tax dollars are paying for this rich family, the richest in Bitterfrost, for all we know the richest anywhere up north, to get a damn Zamboni driver out of trouble he got his own self into.'

'How so?' Klimmek says.

'Already bailed his butt out of jail, didn't they? If I go to jail, nobody's coming to get my ass out.' Butch stuffs his hands into coat pockets and smiles. 'OK, forget all that. Good to see you, Garth. Come on in where it's a balmy fifty-six degrees.'

Inside they sit facing each other on low wooden stools that have initials scratched into the seats. The ceiling is low enough that Klimmek had to duck coming in, and the place smells of what he assumes to be pig shit and hay and other things Klimmek can't name, as he hasn't spent much time on any sort of farm except while on the job. The only animals he knows anything about are fish and birds and deer, things he hunts. Butch pours himself coffee from a thermos, then plucks a flask from his jacket and adds a couple of swallows of something. Christ, Klimmek thinks, does anybody in this town *not* drink at every single hour of the day? His wife tells him he should be grateful for the constant boozing because it keeps him busy.

Butch offers the flask. 'You?'

'No, thanks. Can we talk about that night at the Loon?'

'Right, right. The night nobody can remember.' Butch's grin spreads his whiskers wide. He takes a healthy swig of his coffee. The guy is big, the stool vanished beneath him. 'Everybody wants to talk about "that night at the Loon." I've had more than a few nights at the Loon, Garth. They all kind of blend together, you know?'

Klimmek came expecting this. His first call to Butch was returned by a Traverse City lawyer named Volk who said his clients the Dulaneys were always eager to assist law enforcement but in this case were skeptical of the city's stomach for taking on the Payne family. Klimmek told the lawyer the Paynes weren't accused of anything illegal, Jimmy

Baker was, and the lawyer clucked that the family might as well be, given their relationship with the defendant. The next day, the lawyer called to say Butch would meet Klimmek at the farm.

'I think you know the night I'm interested in,' Klimmek says.

'Maybe,' Butch says. 'What you got?'

Klimmek zips his jacket halfway down, reaches inside, and produces two photographs he offers Butch. 'Do you remember either of these gentlemen being in the Loon that night?'

Butch takes the pictures and looks at one for a few seconds, then the other, then gives them back to Klimmek.

'"Gentlemen," huh? You play euchre, detective?'

'Occasionally. Why?'

'You think that's an easy game? Like, almost as easy as War?'

'Is this a trick question?'

'Kind of, yeah.'

'I don't know about War, but put it this way, you can drink a lot more beer playing euchre than you can poker.'

'Haha,' Butch says. 'I like that. So, yeah, I saw both those guys in the Loon that night. I guess they were playing War, because they were pretty gooned.'

'Drunk, you mean?'

'Yeah. And giving ol' Ronnie hell.'

'The barmaid.'

'The one and only. You know, we ought to just pass an ordinance or something that says downstaters gotta pay a big damn toll to pass north of Lansing.'

'I'll leave that to our esteemed legislators. Did you see Mr Baker approach these gentlemen?'

'"Approach" is a nice word for it. I "approached" a guy on the rink this morning and about knocked him through the boards.'

'Can you tell me what happened?'

Butch gets off his stool. 'This thing's getting a lot of attention, isn't it? DonDon's wife said she saw something about it this morning on one of those talk shows with all the celebrities and politicians. Hell, maybe it'll make everyone forget about that claw-hammer guy, eh? What do you think?'

Klimmek's not biting. He leans forward on the stool. 'Can you tell me what happened that night?'

'Sorry for the digression. I mean, I don't envy you. You got a tough job. Anyway, these two dudes – I guess they're from Detroit, somewhere around there? – they're making a bunch of noise about paying the bill.'

'They didn't want to pay?'

'No, actually they were arguing about *who* was gonna pay. Like, one guy wanted to pay and the other guy was saying, Fuck you – sorry for my French – I'm paying. Pretty stupid, eh? If somebody else wants to pay, shit, I'll all for it, right?'

'I'm with you on that. Where were you when this was going on?'

'Playing euchre – not War – at my usual table in the corner.'

'Who else was playing?'

'Oh, you know, the usuals, my brothers, some other pals.'

'What other pals?'

Butch squints. 'I'd have to think about that. Don't want to steer you wrong.'

'Maybe one of your brothers remembers.'

'Those two? Mentally deficient. Their testimony wouldn't be worth a damn.'

'I'll be the judge of that.'

'Well, I'm your guy for now, Garth.'

'I guess I could get a subpoena.'

'I'm sure you can and will. But for now, I'm your man.' He grins again. 'Family spokesman.'

'All right, Mr Spokesman. So what happened with Baker?'

'He was sitting over on the other side of the bar. Fact, I didn't see him until I went up to see why these guys were hassling Ronnie. Soon as I get there, he comes over all hot and bothered.'

Klimmek jots that down in capital letters: HOT AND BOTHERED. Then he says, 'You know Jimmy, right? You guys get along OK?'

'I got no beef with him. But he should've just stayed where he was. I mean, you know Jimmy. One minute he's half-asleep, the next he's Mike Tyson. Anyway, soon as he gets over there, these guys get even more uppity, saying they're getting me a drink and Jimmy a drink and one of them even slaps Ronnie on the hand –' Butch demonstrates, clapping his free hand on the one holding the cup – 'and then I can tell sure as shit, Jimmy isn't having any of this.'

'You could tell how?'

Butch refills his cup from the thermos and flask, then stands. 'Follow me,' he says, and strolls toward the back of the shed. Two or three smaller pigs trail along, squealing and snuffling. The

sound, throatier than Klimmek expected, reminds him that he's
never actually heard a pig snort before, not live and up close.
He can hear Kris teasing him, 'What a sheltered life you live.'
Butch opens a metal door that leads into a smaller, darker room.
When Klimmek's eyes adjust, he sees a hog hanging by its hooves
from a brace chained to the ceiling. A fat gash is slashed in the
pig's throat and belly, and the dirt-and-straw floor gleams with what
Klimmek assumes is blood.

'Meet Nicky,' Butch says. 'The Dulaney Christmas hog.'

Klimmek nods. He's trying to be patient with Butch's theatrics.
'Impressive. You're showing me this why?'

'Why else? To make you jealous.' Butch laughs. 'Nicky's gonna
be our guest of honor Christmas Eve. Forty-two of us around the
big table in the big house, Nicky in the middle with an apple in his
mouth. Now that's family, man. Like Norman Rockwell.'

'I'll say. What about Baker?'

'Baker. Right. You ever see him up close in a hockey fight?'

'Not so far.'

'You can find videos on YouTube. You wanna get a good look at
his face and his throat just before he starts throwing bombs. Like
he's gonna explode. The guy's insane, man. He gets this look like
Beelzebub himself possessed him. Damn scary, lemme tell you.'

Klimmek has done some research on Baker's near-fatal assault
on young Cory Richards thirteen years ago but didn't think to look
up videos of other fights. He scribbles a reminder to do so, then
adds a note to double-check the Loon's indoor video for a clear
look at Jimmy's face.

'I have not seen that,' he says.

'Well, you ought to, because that's exactly how Baker looked
when those two dumb-asses started yanking his chain. One of them
was calling him "cowboy." Not too smart, if you ask me. I warned
them they were dealing with a bad ass. I guess they didn't listen.'

'Then what?'

'Then I got the hell out of there. Paid the bill, left a tip, went
home with my bros. Had a little nightcap, went to bed. Skated the
next morning.'

'Skated?'

'Played hockey. Your goombah Devyn was there. You know, you
solve this case the right way, maybe her mommy gets you a pay
raise.'

Klimmek ignores that. 'Your brothers can corroborate your nightcap at home?'

'Hundred percent.'

Butch himself might be a suspect if Klimmek hadn't seen the security video of him leaving the Loon peacefully, then the video of Jimmy Baker's pickup trailing Jerome Hardy's Silverado out of the Loon parking lot. Not to mention the bloody doorknob and jacket and gloves and Jimmy bullshitting him about slipping on his porch. Plus, Ronnie has essentially confirmed Butch's version of events inside the Loon, though she told Klimmek she didn't think Jimmy would have harmed Hardy and Diggs. She's a friend of Jimmy's, though, and as most people know, more than just a friend in the past.

'And you never saw those Detroit gentlemen again?' Klimmek says.

Butch nudges the dangling hog so it swings gently to and fro. 'You pulling my chain with this "gentlemen" bullshit?'

'Just showing some respect for the victim.'

'Shit, man, you should've seen how those guys were dressed, like they stopped at a Cabela's. But, have it your way: "gentlemen." The Zam driver, though, not so gentle.' Butch steadied the swinging hog. 'Ever since he came back to town, you knew he was gonna pop eventually.'

Klimmek says nothing about that, just stands and tucks his notebook into a back pocket.

'I'm no lone wolf like Baker,' Butch adds, as if Klimmek asked. 'We're a family here. We gotta get back to that in the US of A, you know?'

'Uncle Butch.'

Klimmek turns to see a woman, late twenties, maybe early thirties, standing in the door to the room. The detective considers his wife a true beauty, so he rarely dwells on other women's looks, but this one, with her eyes of blue glass and thick red hair tied back behind her ears, gets his attention. She's wearing her parka in a way that makes Klimmek think she might be pregnant. She gives him a dismissing glance then addresses Butch.

'Who is this?'

'Dear, this here is Detective Garth Klimmek. He's working on that big case in town. Detective, this is my niece Catriona. We call her Cat.'

'Hello, Cat,' Klimmek says.

Cat turns to him, assessing, then pastes on a smile that strikes Klimmek as a bit too knowing for her age. 'I hope,' she says, 'you put the bastard away for good.'

'Respect now, dear,' Butch says.

Holding her flat smile on Klimmek, Cat says, 'Lunch is ready.'

'What is today's delicacy, if I may ask?'

'Grits with ham and jam.'

'Oh, boy. I'll be in shortly.'

Catriona leaves without another word.

Well, OK, Klimmek thinks. 'I'll let you get your lunch,' he tells Butch. 'What you've told me so far, you'll testify to it in court?'

'You really gonna put Baker away?'

'We're going to try. Just gathering facts now.'

'The Paynes are probably all over the chief's ass, eh? Hell, two down and whatshername pays to put a cold-blooded killer back on the street. Just like when the Covid was here, they were collecting Uncle Sam's money while the rest of us had to make do on our own.'

'The Paynes aren't Bitterfrost's only wealthy family, Butch.'

Like most Bitterfrosters, Klimmek has heard the story of how the Dulaney brothers' parents and grandparents scraped to piece together their small-town real estate empire – virtually every piece of land south of the river except for the sole plot where the Paynes' hockey arena stands. The truth was, old Hamish Dulaney, a brawler who worshipped Jesus Christ almost as much as Irish whiskey, married into the Fisher Body fortune in the thirties. Despite his obvious faults, he finagled a handsome settlement in the divorce from his philandering wife. He plowed almost every penny he had into every piece of land he could find near Bitterfrost, where he'd gone to hunt and drink booze and find bars to fight in. His son and grandsons take after old Hamish, especially in their disdain of the Paynes. There are stories of Hamish and Calvin Payne coming to blows at that long-ago zoning board meeting where Calvin wound up claiming the rink land.

Butch chortles at Klimmek's little dig and slaps his hog's hairy side. 'Hell, we Dulaneys truck in parts and pigs, the Paynes got their money in stocks and bonds and politicians. You know that. You see whatever the hell they're digging up now over by the rink? You remember the city council giving them any OK to do that? Shit, they don't need permission to do any damn thing they want, do they now? You know that nice chunk of land they own used to be where the boats picked up the timber to haul down to Chicago. Now it's a damn hockey rink. Like a bunch of punks who ain't all that much better than me can support a whole town. And the Paynes get all kinds of tax breaks and this and that so they don't take their team anywhere else. Like they could.'

'Not my jurisdiction, Butch.'

'Lemme tell you, Garth, we got plans for Bitterfrost. We want to be the biggest taxpayers in town. I know that sounds crazy, but it's the truth, swear on my momma's grave.'

'No reason to doubt you, sir. I'll be in touch.'

'Happy to help. Just ring my lawyer.'

A hazy finger of sunlight pokes through the low ceiling of clouds as Klimmek drives the three miles back to town. He didn't expect to extract much from Butch, but he got what he needed, for now. Butch's testimony about Jimmy Baker's attitude toward the two inebriates at the Loon will help convince a jury that Jimmy was preparing to act.

Klimmek's phone buzzes. It's a call from the 734 area code – suburban Detroit. He puts the phone on speaker and lets the call go to voicemail. A few seconds later, a vaguely familiar voice says, 'Detective Klimmek, this is Philip Hardy. I wanted to say I appreciate your expeditious work in getting the killer arrested and charged. But I have to say I'm gravely concerned about him being freed on bail. How in the world could bail be allowed? Does this Payne family I've been hearing about really have that kind of clout? And how do we know this person isn't out there right now looking for Jerome, hoping to eliminate an eyewitness? It was painful to see Baker in court this morning, then just walking free like he was you or me. Please call me at your earliest convenience?'

They're reasonable questions. Bail is unusual in a murder trial in Michigan, but recent court rulings have allowed it in some cases. Yes, the Paynes have plenty of influence in Bitterfrost, though Klimmek doesn't expect prosecutors, judges, and certainly a jury to kowtow to it. Hardy's concern about Baker posing a continuing threat is logical, but Klimmek isn't all that worried about that, either. Baker is wearing that monitor, and he looked plenty scared in the courtroom. His crime was one of passion – rage, as Klimmek and the prosecutor see it – and he expects Baker's attorney will be vigilant about keeping her client in check. He can't imagine a

Zamboni driver being quite clever enough to track down the young Hardy, if in fact he's still afoot.

But . . .

Klimmek pulls the car over and parks alongside a five-foot-tall wall of plowed snow. He climbs out and stands in the middle of the road facing a tunnel of white stretching for a quarter of a mile before it hooks to the right, toward town. Inside the car, his phone starts to buzz. He doesn't move. When the buzzing stops, he stands still, drinking in the afternoon silence, the cold holding the silence, the silence holding the cold.

This is why he has remained in Bitterfrost his entire adult life; not for the lake, or for the glorious summers, or for the beaches and boats and fishing and snowmobiling. He has stayed for the silence of winter afternoons, bereft even of a crow's squawk. And every now and then, even in the middle of a mission such as the one he's on now, he forces himself to stop and listen, knowing the only thing he's likely to hear is his own breathing. All the noise distracting him from what he needs to see disappears.

Search parties of more than one hundred men and woman have fanned out in concentric circles from the spot where Jerome Hardy's charred SUV wound up. That spot sits just north of the river near Bitterfrost's eastern limit. Not far from the Payne family's many acres on that side of the Jako River, nor from the Dulaney spread butting up against the opposite bank. Klimmek takes a step to his right and turns to face the approximate point where he'd first seen the SUV a week ago, about two miles from where he's standing now.

Why there, in that woody clearing, within distant sight of Jimmy Baker's house? What made Jerome Hardy decide to take his car there? Or did Baker make that choice for him? Where had Baker had the time and capacity to hide Hardy's body so well that the posse couldn't find him? They had scoured the woods north to Good Hart and south almost to Harbor Springs. Could young Hardy really still be alive somewhere?

Klimmek's gut tells him no, despite his father's hopes.

He turns to his left, in the direction of town and Lake Michigan. He reaches into a coat pocket and squeezes his Rosary beads. In his mind he recollects the scene outside the Payne hockey arena the night before: the fans hustling inside; the TV reporter rehearsing with her cameraman; the words scrolling on the rink marquee about that night's game; and beyond it all, near the edge of the parking lot, a front-end loader and a bulldozer slumbering in the dark by the defunct shipping docks on the lakeshore. The digging Butch mentioned. He ponders this for a moment, scanning it back and forth in his mind.

'Yes,' he says aloud.

He gets back in his car and picks up his phone. It rings only once on the other end. 'Chief,' Klimmek says. 'If I tell you something, will you promise not to call a press conference?'

Quarton says, 'What exactly do you have, detective?'

Klimmek sighs. 'I hope you can sit on this a little bit. I think I know where the Hardy kid might be.'

THIRTY-EIGHT

'Thomsen,' comes the gruff male voice. 'Do not hang up on me.'

'Who is this, please?'

'Devyn Payne. Defense attorney in Bitterfrost.'

She's standing in the street outside Big Henry's and finally has lucked into the Mackinaw City Police chief, one Jim Thomsen. His voice sounds like he gargles with broken glass.

'Heard of you,' he says. 'Working that homicide down there?'

'Alleged homicide.'

'Aren't they all? I don't know much about it but what I've seen on the tube, so not really sure how I can help.'

'I'm interested in what you know about Jordan Fawcett. She was a client of mine. It's possible she was connected to the murder here.'

'Pretty simple. She came here, picked the wrong bar, drank too much of the wrong drink, and probably left with the wrong people. Which I'm guessing is no surprise to you. But that's really all I can say about an ongoing investigation.'

'Can you tell me who these "wrong people" were that Jordan supposedly was with?'

'No. That's part of our—'

'Any suspects in custody?'

'We – I'm sorry. I need to go. But I can give you someone who might be able to help.'

'Please.'

She hears papers riffling, then he says, 'You might try this detective at the Bitterfrost Police Department. Garth—'

'Klimmek. I know him.'

'Well then, there you go. I wish you well.'

'Hold on,' Devyn says. 'What about the bar Jordan went to?'

'Again, I can't say much in the middle—'

'Come on, chief, a man's future is at stake here.'

The phone goes silent for a three-count. 'Another man's life is over. Maybe two. What about them?'

'If my client is guilty, he'll pay the price. But anything we do to figure out what happened furthers justice for the two guys.'

Again he goes quiet, then says, 'There's no name.'

'What? Who doesn't have a name?'

'The bar. No name.'

'Where is it?'

'You'll figure it out if you're so committed to justice.'

Thomsen hangs up.

So, no-future Jordan spent the last night of her life in a no-name bar with a no-name someone who may have killed her. Makes perfect sense. The Mackinaw City chief was fairly useless. Her client a few minutes ago left her a voicemail suggesting he'd paid a visit to the Loon for a bit of witness tampering. She texted him: **Don't go near that place again!!** And, while she was talking with Thomsen, a text came in with some disturbing news about a TV interview airing tonight. Everything is going so well that she decides she needs to make a trip to Mackinaw City. But first, she needs a word with Big Henry.

Henry's diner closed two hours ago, but Devyn finds him in a food-smeared apron tossing trash into a dumpster in the back lot. Better to speak with him alone than in front of a full restaurant. He notices her waiting by her car and it seems to make him happy. Devyn always imagines him with a halo over his head, because he was named for Finland's patron saint, Henry of Uppsala, also the namesake of the Catholic Church that sits on the Jako across from the rink.

'Where've you been? Huh? Huh?' he says, smiling. 'I've missed you.'

'You suggested we stay away, Henry.'

'Oh, damn, forgot about that. Sorry.'

'Been missing your Swedish pancakes.'

'Those old Finns would kill me if they knew.'

'You got a minute?'

'Inside. Freezing out here.'

Instead of bacon and butter, the empty restaurant smells of lemon and soap. Henry heaves his bulk onto a snack bar stool. Devyn sits next to him, her knees bumping up against his. 'So,' she says, 'what are you hearing?'

'I'd make you something but I'm kinda shut down. Sorry.'

'I'm not hungry,' she fibs. 'What's the chatter?'

'About?'

'Come on, Henry.'

He folds his arms over the top of his gut. 'What do you think?' he says. 'Jimmy. That's all anyone wants to talk about.'

'What are they saying?'

'Depends who "they" is. Maybe you've heard this before, but I think there are basically two kinds of people in the world: people who order eggs and people who go for pancakes.'

'I don't think I've heard that.'

'Well, my unscientific analysis suggests that egg people think Jimmy ought to be fried and pancake people do not.'

'You can't be serious.'

'I'm not. Which is my point. Why do you care what people say in here? Huh? Huh? Your jury's in the courtroom, not my restaurant.'

'I just thought, you know, you hear a lot of things, maybe you've heard something that could help Jimmy.'

He considers, then says, 'It's five o'clock by now, isn't it? Cocktail?'

'You have a liquor license?'

'No. But I'm closed. Brown or clear?'

She says vodka tonic. 'Lime?' he says. Of course. He steps behind the snack bar and pulls two bottles out of a cabinet next to the griddle. He sets her drink on the bar then pours three fingers of Weller into an ice cream soda glass. 'I don't take sides around customers, but between us – here's to Jimmy.' They clink glasses and drink. Henry sets his bourbon down and says, 'I don't get it, Dev.'

'Get what?'

'These people. Jimmy's one of them. One of us. He's on the trophy wall over there, a hero. He had a rough go but he came back home because he trusted us to take care of him. And now people are just – I can't believe some of the crap I hear in here. I almost told Wilkins to leave the other day.'

Wilkins runs charter fishing boats in the summer and fall and spends the rest of the year spewing in Henry's. 'Blowhard,' Devyn says.

'Yeah, he's peddling this dime-store psychology, saying he knew this was gonna happen all along, Jimmy was bound to go off on somebody because that's what he is, he has to beat people up to feel, you know, like a man, and he can't control himself blah blah blah.'

There's a bit of truth to that, Devyn thinks. 'Did you kick him out?'

'I told him this isn't the kind of place for that kind of talk, and he left on his own. Stiffed me on the bill. Good riddance, though.'

'Sorry about that.' Devyn shakes the ice in her drink. 'Does anybody ever talk about Sawtell?'

'You mean the hammer guy from a few years ago?'

'That guy.'

'They used to, of course, but then that kinda quieted down.'

'But they're talking about it again, aren't they?'

'Not much,' Henry says. 'I mean, he wasn't from around here, the people he killed weren't from around here. But, hey, change of subject: You know Anya?'

'I don't think so.'

'Anya Paluk. About yay tall. You've probably seen her on the street. Wears a long green jacket over a hoodie, usually orange. Like she's a deer hunter, but she's not.'

'Homeless?'

'She's not homeless. She has a place outside of town.'

'So what?'

'She usually comes in every morning, right when I open. Gets a coffee and takes off. Heavy cream, three sugars. She was in here the morning after the murder. Later in the morning than usual. So was Jimmy. They talked for a minute. Then she ran out of here like she'd seen a frigging ghost.'

'And you're telling me this because?'

'I'm not positive, but I'm pretty sure she was talking to Jimmy about that night. Something spooked her.'

'You don't know what?'

'Nope.' He sips the Weller. 'She hasn't been in since that morning.'

'You think she might know something?'

'I hear about eighty thousand conversations a day. Most of them go poof in the time it takes me to crack an egg. This one, I keep thinking about. She had this look on her face. Like she was scared.'

'Scared of Jimmy?'

'No. Maybe scared *for* Jimmy.' He peers into his glass. 'To be honest, I'm scared for Jimmy. Do you think he's guilty, Dev? Please say no.'

Devyn plucks the lime wedge from her drink and squeezes it as hard as she can over the glass. 'You know I can't answer that.'

'You can't answer? Or you can't answer honestly?'

'We pleaded not guilty, Henry.'

'I'm aware.'

She picks up the drink and takes a gulp. 'My client,' she says, 'is innocent.'

'I'm glad to hear that.'

'Got a pen?'

Henry snatches one out of a plastic cup while Devyn grabs a napkin from a dispenser. 'What's that homeless woman's name again?'

'She's not homeless.'

'Right.'

'Her name is Anya. Anya Paluk.'

'Spelling?'

'Hang on. I have her credit card on file.' He rummages in a drawer beneath the cash register. 'Paluk. P-A-L-U-K.'

'And where's her place?'

Henry takes the pen and another napkin and draws a rough map.

'Thanks, Henry,' Devyn says. 'Now I gotta get to Mack City.'

'Dark out there. Keep an eye out for deer.'

'Roger that.'

'One for the road?'

Devyn laughs for what feels like the first time in a week. 'No thanks,' she says, then raises her glass, takes a last swig, and says, 'Tell your customers: Order the pancakes. The pancakes are awesome.'

THIRTY-NINE

J immy leaves his pickup in a far corner of the IceKings' overflow parking lot and wends his way through the woods that hug the main lot, trying to stay out of sight before emerging fifty yards from the rear entrance to the rink. He climbs a short stairway to a concrete platform for truck deliveries and, at a door on the arena wall, pulls out a key.

He stops and peers through the late-day twilight at the scene around him that he largely took for granted until his boss barred him – via text – from the rink. Evan's sister, as Jimmy's attorney, ordered him to comply. He can't even do his monthly Zaturdays with Zelda with the youngsters.

Not far from where he's standing flows the Jako River, the dark water eddying out from under patches of pebbly white ice and opening into Lake Michigan. Jimmy listens for the faint burbling. The sparse lights of downtown Bitterfrost glow a few blocks away. To his left, beyond the northern wall of the arena, the lake lies silent in the gloom, slabs of shorn ice butting up against the beach and, along the shoreline, a pair of iron docks jutting into the lake like the arms of a drowned giant. Still sturdy, they haven't been used in decades except as unofficial attractions for tourists curious about the long dead Finnish timber trade. Not far away, stilled construction vehicles wait for dawn to resume work on a new building that will be an IceKings museum, chock-full with photos, trophies, statues, old gear, and other mementoes of the team's history, including a few recalling Jimmy himself.

Many a real estate developer has approached the Paynes with plans to purchase and develop the ten-acre corner, only to be rebuffed by Eleanor Payne, who has insisted that no price is high enough for her 'third child.' Jimmy loves her for that. The corner directly across the river, occupied by 152-year-old St Henry's Catholic Church, is just as unavailable. Which to Jimmy is only appropriate, hockey being religion to IceKings fans.

He slides inside and locks the door behind him. Rather than flick a light on, he lets his eyes adjust so he doesn't attract the attention of office staff working late. The place is quiet but for the low hum of half-illuminated fluorescent lamps. Jimmy gazes down the length of the ice and up into the stands where Zelda's Zealots congregate. The signs that mark their section appear to have been removed. He's read mentions of that online, but actually seeing it gives him a jolt.

He creeps down a corridor that opens into the southeast concourse, a hundred feet from the tunnel where Zelda makes her entrance. He stoops low and scuttles beneath the bleachers, feeling the monitor pinch his ankle. Overhead a scrap of yellow police tape dangles from the steel scaffolding. He jumps up, snaps it away, and stuffs it in a pocket.

He moves beneath the COLD BEER'S sign, the thing bugging him even at this moment. At the Zamboni shed, he's dismayed to find the door unlocked. He doesn't know if that's the fault of his replacement – a twenty-two-year-old girl who recently dropped out of college – or whoever's been snooping in Zelda's sanctuary, certainly the police and probably Evan. Devyn would kill Jimmy if she knew he was there. The cops, if they knew, might usher him back to jail.

Inside the shed, he inhales the oil and refrigerant as he looks out at the ice surface through the window over his workbench. He'd love to go out and run a hand across the surface, see how Zelda is performing for her new driver. It's too light out there to risk it. From his coat he produces a headlamp fitted with an elastic band. He pulls it on and sees that his tools, usually lined up across the back of his bench, are haphazardly scattered about. He resists the urge to rearrange them and crouches in front of the bench. Two of the cupboard doors have been removed – the doors he locked when he hid the bloody jacket. Staring into the cabinet, he wonders how the hell he could have imagined that no one would find the jacket there.

He stands and walks over to Zelda, who, at least to the IceKings public, is no longer Zelda. The big Z on her nose has been painted over. 'Hey, girl,' he says. She could use a washing. He wants to check her oil and tire pressure but there isn't time. He pats her side and whispers, 'I hope to come back soon, Z. But in case I don't, thanks for everything.'

He hears a noise and ducks down, holding his breath. He can't tell whether the sound came from inside the rink or out. He waits a few seconds. Hearing nothing more, he climbs up into Zelda's seat. He looks for the key fob that has dangled from the steering wheel since Avery gave it to her father for his fortieth birthday, a miniature replica of his favorite player, retired Red Wing Steve Yzerman. It's not there. Maybe the new driver, unfamiliar with the greatness of Stevie Y, threw it away.

He gets down and goes to a freestanding metal closet on the wall behind Zelda. The padlock is gone. The twin doors stick anyway. Jimmy pries them open, trying not to make any noise. The bottles of lubricants he used to keep Zelda humming are still on the top shelf. The floor is crowded with boxes of hand cleaner and concession napkins. The rest of the closet is empty. He had gradually filled the closet's back wall with photos of Avery, birthday cards she sent, sticky notes she left him. All that remains are the outlines of old tape strips, the shrine to his daughter eradicated. He scans the entire wall again and at one edge sees part of a photo left behind. It's a picture of Avery at her eighth-grade graduation, her hair done up like a bride's, her face lit with laughter. Jimmy leans into the closet on one knee and peels the piece of photo away. He looks at it for a moment, smiling, before sliding it into his wallet.

OK, he thinks. Outta here.

Outside, he blinks at the sudden brightness of headlights on vehicles parked at the museum construction site. They must have arrived while he was in the Zam shed. Maybe that was the noise he heard. He steps back into the doorway, shielding his eyes with one hand. The vehicles, two cars and an SUV, are painted with the black-and-gold of the Bitterfrost Police. Silhouettes of people Jimmy assumes are officers move around in the shadows, pointing and calling out to each other. Some of them appear to be carrying shovels.

He crab-walks down a slope to the river's edge, follows the river toward town for fifty yards, then dodges into the forest surrounding the main parking lot. Where the woods end, he scampers across the street to the overflow lot. His truck waits beneath a streetlamp that happens to be dark; if Jimmy was still working, it would be fixed, along with the screwed-up parking lot security cameras that Evan hasn't paid to have repaired. Jimmy ducks back into the pines ringing that lot and waits forty feet from his truck.

His phone buzzes. He answers.

'Where are you?' Devyn says.

'Just driving around,' he says softly, 'clearing my head.'

'Better get home to your TV. That *Dateline* show I told you about is airing tonight.'

'With Richards?'

'Yes.'

She had told him *Dateline* might have an interview with Cory Richards, the young player Jimmy almost destroyed the night he left professional hockey for good. 'He can't talk,' Jimmy says. 'That's part of the settlement.'

'He talked.'

Jimmy squats and closes his eyes. 'You gotta stop him, Dev.'

'I can't. Even if I tried, it would make things worse because it would look like you're trying to muzzle him. As I told you, we're better off sitting it out. The Richards thing is past. We need to focus on the present.'

Jimmy opens his eyes. The cops have rearranged their vehicles into a circle on the museum site, their headlamps on high, light seeming to pulse up from the cavity in the earth. At the sight of it, the pinging sound in his brain that punished Jimmy the night of the incident reasserts itself. His head begins to throb.

'Avery,' he says, gritting his teeth.

'What about her?' Devyn says.

'Sonofabitch. Avery. She can't watch this thing.'

'Let's hope she doesn't. But she must know about Richards, right?'

'Of course but – no, this can't be good for her.'

'Sorry.'

'I want to see my daughter again, Devyn.'

'You will. Promise.'

The only cop not in uniform is lowering himself into the hole.

'I'll try to watch,' Jimmy says.

'Call me later.'

None of the officers arrayed around the hole are looking Jimmy's way. He lowers his head and runs to his truck. He pulls out of the lot with the lights off, then flicks them on a few hundred yards down the road. He squints at the gas gauge. Half a tank probably won't be enough.

FORTY

'Easy there, detective. Here, gimme your hand.'

Klimmek reaches up and grabs Officer Sylvester's gloved hand, steadying himself on the side of the gash in the earth the front-end loader opened near the hockey arena. He finds it hard to believe that anyone would want a museum to celebrate a bunch of amateurs who for the most part will never see a big-league rink without a ticket. But rich folks do what rich folks do, and his wife the IceKings fan can't wait for the place to open so she can visit. He supposes she'll make him come along.

He should have thought to check this hole a week ago, when he and other cops were searching the arena. But he's here now. Braced against Sylvester's arm, Klimmek lowers himself to the bottom of the pit, about six feet down through old snow and frozen mud. He steadies himself before letting go. 'Thanks, officer,' he says. He touches his pocket to make sure he didn't drop his Rosary. He feels that sweet tinge of expectation that comes before an investigative discovery, especially one deriving from a semi-crazy hunch. He props his hands on his knees and peers into the bowels of the hole two feet beneath him. A puddle at the bottom has just barely frozen over. Klimmek looks over his shoulder and asks Sylvester, 'You got a baton?' Sylvester hands him his black plastic nightstick.

Klimmek eases down until he can reach the frozen puddle with the baton. He taps the surface once. It cracks, no thicker than an inch. Then Klimmek pounds the blunt end of the baton around the edges of the puddle, the ice giving way. He sees what he suspected he'd see. Or part of it.

Three fingers, a bluish, chalky white, extend out of the water under the ice. Of course the detective can't say for sure who or what lies beneath, but he'd bet his paycheck that the frozen fingers are attached to the body of Jerome Hardy.

FORTY-ONE

The drive to Mackinaw City usually takes forty-five minutes, but the roads are slick so Devyn takes it slow. She googled 'unnamed bar Mackinaw City' about a dozen different ways, without success. Then she remembered her lawyer pal Varga, whose far-north clients have him frequenting dives that make the Loon look swanky. 'I know the place,' he told her. 'Not many people do, but criminal lawyers, you know.'

She's beginning to understand why when she departs US 31 a few miles south of Mackinaw, then follows an eastward bend that empties onto a snowy two-track marked by a sign nailed to a utility pole. All the sign says, in fading red paint, is DONNNT, no apostrophe. Varga explained it was an acronym for De Old Nasty No-Name Tavern. The bastardized form of 'don't' was the proprietor's way of warning strangers away.

Jordan, of course, would have paid it no heed.

The two-track winds through a tunnel of elm and birch, emptying out into a tight clearing barely lit by a lightbulb strung from the branch of a dead oak. Three pickup trucks and a pair of snowmobiles are parked outside a one-story house that looks like it's growing out of the woods surrounding it. Windows on either side of the entrance are boarded up. Devyn pulls up next to the snowmobiles. Before she can put her car into park, a man the size of a grizzly bear bursts out of the entrance and starts yelling, 'Kill the goddamn brights, will you? This ain't a goddamn laundromat.'

Devyn snaps her high beams off and eases out of the car, smelling woodsmoke. The man is standing in the cold in a sleeveless Detroit Lions T-shirt, baggy gym shorts hanging past his knees, and a camo baseball cap perched on ears as big as hands. He is large in every way, side-to-side and from the ground up. His left hand grips some sort of pistol.

'Sorry,' Devyn says. 'I'm new here.'

'No shit,' the man replies. 'What do you want?'

'A beer? Maybe watch some of the Wings game?'

'Sheeeeit.' He slides the gun into the waistband at his back. 'Nobody but my sister, brother, and a few other shitbags I know come around for just a beer and a goddamn game. What are you really here for, little lady? Not that we couldn't use a pretty face for a change.'

Devyn figures if she tells him straight out, he'll probably tell her to hit the road. But bullshitting this refrigerator of a man with a pistol in his shorts doesn't seem wise, either. 'Have you heard about that murder down in Bitterfrost?' she says.

'Oh, man, the one where that guy beat another guy to death? Shit, I don't wanna run into that dude.'

'He's my client. I'm his defense lawyer.'

This seems to briefly dumbfound the man. He slowly nods. Devyn waits. Finally he chortles and says, 'Damn. What's that got to do with us?'

It doesn't sound like a rhetorical question. He's genuinely curious. 'There's something on TV in –' she makes a show of looking at her phone – 'about ten minutes. It's about my client. I was driving up to see a friend in Manistique and got a late start. I didn't want to miss this show.'

'What's it about?'

'It's about another guy my client got into it with.'

'Oh, wait – I think I saw that on my phone. Some hockey player, a while back?'

'Right.'

'Why didn't you just tell me that in the first place?'

'I said I wanted to watch hockey. You got any beer?'

He reaches behind himself and pulls the gun out of his pants. He opens the door and waves the gun toward the inside. 'Name's Chuck,' he says. 'People call me Chuckles. We got lots of beer.'

Chuckles holds the door. Devyn walks in. DONNNT is not much bigger than a two-car garage. The floor is covered with old newspapers and shucked peanut shells. There's a hint of piss on the air, maybe from the Rottweiler that's rising from a blanket against the wall to Devyn's left. A nearly naked blow-up doll wearing a medical mask as her bikini bottom dangles from a corner ceiling. Six stools that look as though they were purchased at six different yard sales stand at a bar topped with plywood. One stool is occupied by a bearded man wearing a wool Shepler's Ferry toque, the other by a red-headed woman sporting a black patch over one eye. 'Deck the Halls,' Nat King Cole's version, plays from somewhere.

'Whatdya like?' Chuckles says, circling behind the bar.

'Bud bottle,' Devyn says. She takes the stool furthest from the redhead and the man with the toque. 'Evening,' she says, and the two smile and nod and lift their bottles. Chuckles sets Devyn's longneck down. 'First one's on the house,' he says. 'You gotta do your business, there's a porta-potty out back.'

'Thanks.'

He snatches a TV remote off the back bar. 'What channel's this show on? Hope it's on the dish.'

'NBC.'

The redhead gets up and moves to the stool next to Devyn. She's drinking something without ice from a Mason jar. 'You mind?' she says. 'I'm tired of that asshole over there.'

Devyn smiles. 'Not at all. Thanks for having me.'

'Oh, I'm not, honey,' the woman says. She takes a long swig of her drink without taking her unpatched eye off Devyn. 'If Chuckles wants to bring in strays, it's his dump, not mine.'

'Watch it,' Chuckles says, then to Devyn, '*Dateline*?'

'Yes, thanks.'

'What the shit?' the man in the toque says. 'Thought we were gonna watch the Pistons.'

'Don't worry, dumb ass,' Chuckles says, 'we'll put the Pistons on after the first boring two hours. Our guest asked and I'm curious.'

'*Our* guest?' the toque guy says. 'She ain't my guest.'

'She's up from Bitterfrost, lawyer down there. Now clam up and maybe you'll learn something.'

Another patron, seemingly younger, comes up to the bar and orders a Diet Coke. A ponytail hangs down the back of his puffy winter jacket. He's wearing aviator shades and a scarf that obscures his face. 'Thanks,' he mumbles, leaving two dollars on the bar before proceeding to the Golden Tee golf game in a corner beneath an unplugged mosquito buzzer. Behind Chuckles's head, the TV screen fills with the image of a man in a wheelchair rolling down a hallway into a kitchen. The man cruises to the fridge, opens it, and takes out a pie that he says he made. 'I've taken up baking,' he says. 'It's a little challenging but fun.'

Cory Richards, Devyn thinks. A center from Norwell, Massachusetts. Played triple-A kid hockey then for a Canadian junior squad in Nova Scotia, where he was drafted in the first round by the Tampa Bay Lightning. Quick for a sizable man, a playmaker known for his slick stickhandling and game vision. Richie, as team-mates called him, saw plays taking shape before they actually did. But he didn't see what was coming on that night in Erie when Jimmy Baker was dispatched to intimidate him. Richards was barely twenty years old and would never play hockey again.

'How bad were your injuries?' asks the host, a woman named Serena who herself looks barely twenty.

Richards takes a forkful of the blackberry pie he made, chews, and answers. 'Injuries were pretty bad. Three vertebrae essentially destroyed. Clavicle shattered. Severe concussion. Dislocated elbow. I couldn't have sliced this pie.'

'The pie is absolutely delicious,' Serena says. 'And you still have headaches related to the incident?'

'Every day. They usually start about five in the afternoon.'

'Occasional lapses in memory?'

Richards hesitates, as if he wasn't expecting the question, then says, 'Not too bad anymore. But yeah, not so good there for a while.'

The segment doubles back to clips of Richards playing as an eight-year-old, then in juniors, the minor league. The Lightning were preparing to call him up to the NHL when Jimmy ended his career.

'Jesus,' toque guy says, 'what happened to that Baker guy? He go to jail?'

'Nope,' the redhead says. 'He just went back to his life. But now he's gonna go to prison for beating the hell out of someone down in Bitterfrost, isn't that right, honey?'

She's looking at Devyn. The whirring of the golf game noise seems to halt; maybe the player is listening in. *Dateline* has gone to commercials. 'Jimmy Baker's been accused,' Devyn says. 'But he still has a jury to face.'

Chuckles jerks a thumb toward Devyn. 'She's the guy's lawyer.'

'Oh, for fuck's sake,' the toque man says. 'This is our guest? A damn lawyer for a killer? Wait . . .' His face lights up and he stands halfway off of his stool. 'Aren't you one of those rich fuckers from down there?'

'Not sure what you mean,' Devyn says.

'Don't bullshit me. What's your name again?'

'Devyn. Payne.'

'Like I said. You own the hockey team. That guy works for the hockey team. So I guess it's all right with you if he kills someone?'

The redhead fixes her uncovered eye on Devyn and says, 'I'm from down that way myself and I still have family there. They're all betting it'll be swept under the rug, like always.'

'My mother owns the hockey team, I don't,' Devyn says. 'And it is not all right for whoever killed that man in Bitterfrost. But just because the police say someone killed someone doesn't mean that particular someone did. That's why we have trials.'

'Did he?' the redhead says.

'Did he what?'

'Did he kill the guy in Bitterfrost?'

Devyn picks up her Bud and chugs a good half of it. The cold burns going down. 'I wouldn't be here if he did,' she says.

Cory Richards is back on the screen, talking about Jimmy.

'Then why the hell *are* you here?' the toque says. 'They ain't got TVs down in Bitterfrost? I never liked that town, you know—'

'Settle down, Sherm,' Chuckles says.

'No, no, it's OK,' Devyn says. 'I did want to see this show. But, I'll be honest, there's something else.'

Chuckles points the remote at the TV and mutes the sound just as Richards is saying, 'I definitely believe he has the capacity—' Chuckles slaps the remote down. 'What's the something else now?'

Trying not to look as nervous as she feels, Devyn takes another sip of beer before answering. 'I have – had – another client who apparently was in this establishment last week. Police in Mackinaw City found her dead the next morning.'

'Her,' the redhead says, her face alive with recognition. 'That wacked-out chick. No surprise there.'

'I'll say,' Chuckles says. 'Read about her. She was trouble, all right. In here late one afternoon, just after dark. What was her name?'

'Jody?' the toque says.

'Jordan,' Devyn says. 'Fawcett.' She pulls up a photo on her phone and shows it to Chuckles. 'This her?'

He doesn't bother to look. 'You a cop?' he says.

'Nope. Lawyer, like I said.'

'Uh-huh.'

She steals a glance at the TV. Richards appears to be choking up as he speaks. But what catches her eye is a news bulletin streaming across the bottom of the screen. All she sees before it gets swallowed by the right border is: **Bitterfrost police have found—**

That can't be good.

'I never seen a woman that skinny and that young drink so much so fast,' the toque says. 'Even the guy with her couldn't keep up.'

What guy? Devyn thinks. 'Jordan definitely led a disorganized life,' she says. 'Do you remember what she was drinking? How long was she here?'

The man playing the golf game sets his empty Diet Coke can on the bar and strolls out. Devyn glances at the mirror behind the bar for another look at his face. The angle isn't right, but she notices the Rottweiler rise to its feet as golf guy goes out the door.

'Your friend drank anything her boy put in front of her,' Chuckles says. 'And she wasn't here very long.'

'An hour maybe?' the toque says.

'You know,' the redhead says, 'she was also quite interested in the news. Like you.'

'She had a guy with her?' Devyn says.

'Never seen him before,' Chuckles says. 'Never want to again.'

'You remember anything about him? He wasn't like, a boyfriend?'

'He seemed a little, I don't know, dyspeptic. And he didn't drink anything but Mountain Dew.'

'Do you remember—?'

'What's with all the questions?' Chuckles flattens his girth against the bar. 'I thought you just wanted to watch the show. If that Jordan woman's dead, she's dead, nobody here laid a finger on her.'

'Maybe that guy's dead, too,' the toque says.

Devyn doubts that. 'I didn't mean to suggest anyone here hurt Jordan. But maybe whoever was with her, you know.'

The redhead starts to say something but Chuckles cuts her off. 'I told you we never seen that guy before, OK? You done with your beer? I don't take to people asking about my customers. Time to hit the road, little lady.'

The *Dateline* segment is wrapping up. Jimmy's arrest mugshot now takes up half the screen, with Richards talking and gesturing on the other half. 'So,' Devyn says, figuring she can risk one last question, 'sounds like you think the guy *did* have something to do with it. Could you just tell me what he looked like? And I'll get out of here.'

'Short. Forty-ish. Goatee. Tattoo sleeve,' the redhead spits out before Chuckles reaches across the bar and slaps a hand against her mouth. She doesn't look pleased but Devyn guesses it's not the first time this happened. The redhead then flips up her eye patch and tries to wink her phlegmy left eye. Devyn doesn't know what, if anything, that's supposed to mean.

Chuckles sets his gun on the bar. 'Good night, Ms Payne,' he says. 'Don't be coming back in these woods again, hear me?'

'Loud and clear,' Devyn says. 'Thanks for the beer.'

Outside she stops a few feet from the door to let her eyes adjust to the dark, trying to think of someone she knows who fits the description of the man who might have been the last person to see Jordan alive. Short, forty-ish and tattooed with a goatee describes about half the guys in northern Michigan, certainly a good number of those on her Tinder feed. She peers into the darkness, looking left, then right, then left and right again. 'What the . . . where the hell is my car?'

'Your car is fine,' comes a rasp from behind her.

Startled, she turns, expecting Chuckles. But it's the guy who was playing Golden Tee, in that puffy coat, dark hair pulled back behind his ears. The scarf is gone, the sunglasses remain, and his coat collar is hiked high enough to obscure the lower part of his face. Devyn scuttles backward into a crouch and pushes the heels of her hands out in front of her like her brother the high school wrestler taught her. 'Who the hell are you?' she says.

'The trackball on that game has seen better days,' golf guy says, his voice barely above a whisper. He eases his coat up to reveal a holster and the glint of what appears to be a badge. 'We need to have a chat.'

FORTY-TWO

Cory Richards is lying. What Richards is telling the *Dateline* interviewer isn't true, Richards knows it isn't true, and he has never made such an assertion before, not even in the litigation.

Jimmy is sitting up in bed, watching the small TV vying for space atop his dresser with laundry piled there for three days, waiting to be folded. He made himself a highball that's puddling untouched on his nightstand.

According to the confidential terms of the civil settlement that Jimmy, the Erie Rink Rats, and the league reached with Richards, he isn't supposed to be giving interviews. But here he is on a program watched by millions, discussing what happened as freely as if he was in his own kitchen – which he is – telling his children why he's confined to a wheelchair.

And he's lying.

The young *Dateline* reporter, Serena something, sits close to Richards, almost touching the arms of his wheelchair with her knees. She's asking about the fight, how it started, how Jimmy got the upper hand, whether Richards ever became afraid.

'You bet I did,' Richards says in his slight Boston accent. 'I had an actual career ahead of me, a real chance at playing in the show. And this guy was going to kill me.'

'Kill you? It was just a hockey fight,' Serena says.

'No. He was insane. I mean, not legally insane, just . . . angry. Like I'd done something to him personally and he was going to make me pay for it.'

'But kill you?'

Richards lowers his eyes. 'That's what he told me.'

'He told you? What do you mean?'

'When we were first down on the ice, he told me, "I'm going to f– I'm going to effing kill you."'

'But don't hockey players in fights always say things like that?'

'Sometimes. But no. Not like Baker did.' Richards keeps staring into his lap. 'I mean, I heard it, the tone of his voice, and I did everything I could to get out from under him. I believed him. He was going to kill me.'

No, Jimmy is thinking as he watches. I never said that. I never said anything like it to anyone I fought. I never even talked. Talking wasted energy. I just did what I was supposed to do, what I was told to do, and headed for the penalty box. Richards never said a word about this in sworn testimony, never brought it up, never had one of his lawyers ask Jimmy about it. But now, after collecting three million-some dollars from the team and the league and Jimmy, he's saying it. Why? Did *Dateline* pay him? Is he suddenly hungry for fame? Or does Jimmy's trial offer him a chance at final retribution too tempting to ignore, the chance to put Jimmy in a prison more literal than the one in which Richards lives?

'Would you testify to this at Mr Baker's trial?' the reporter asks.

Richards raises his eyes. 'I would.'

Jimmy grabs his phone off the nightstand and hits speed-dial number three. His brother answers.

'Are you watching this?' Jimmy says.

'Watching what?' Alex says.

'*Dateline*. I'm on it.'

'I don't watch that true crime crap. What do you mean you're on it?'

'They're interviewing Richards. Because of what's going on.'

'Oh. What's he saying?'

'He's lying through his teeth. He's saying I said things I didn't say, and he's going to testify at my trial.'

'Have you talked with your lawyer?'

'Not yet.'

'Relax, Jim. It's just a TV show. Call your lawyer. Go to bed.'

'Goddamn, Alex, Avery's going to see this.'

'She's a smart kid. She'll understand this is just part of the process.'

'Maybe. Or maybe Noelle will tell her something else.'

'Forget Noelle, man. Think good thoughts. Think about Avery. She loves you.' Alex pauses. 'I do, too, brother.'

As Alex speaks, a red ribbon appears at the bottom of the TV screen: **Bitterfrost police have found a body believed to be Detroiter Jerome Hardy**, it says. **Details at 11.**

'I love you, too, man,' Jimmy says.

He ends the call, turns off the TV, picks the highball off the nightstand, and takes a sip. The drink is lukewarm and watery. He sets it back down, takes up his phone again, and calls Devyn. Her phone rings five times before going to voicemail. So her phone is on but she's not answering, even after telling him to call.

Avery, he thinks. Think good thoughts. He recalls last February, down in Detroit, the two of them taking in a Red Wings game. They went to Lafayette Coney Island before the game for dogs, cheese fries, and Cokes in those frosty little bottles. He got tickets down low in a corner so she could appreciate the ridiculous speed of the game. Avery doesn't play hockey, but she loves it live, the blasting music, the pulsing lights, the players flying past as they flip pucks high over their heads and catch them on their stick blades like jugglers on wheels. Jimmy likes to watch her watch the game, how her eyes widen, how she flinches, laughing, when a player or the puck slams into the glass in front of her. She used to love the goal-tenders best because they, more than anyone else on the ice, mimic the crazy grace of the strikers who soar above the volleyball net in the game Avery plays so well. Then she dated a goaltender and, for reasons Jimmy didn't specifically know but could guess, she didn't like goalies so much.

Between the second and third periods, they watched the Zamboni make its rounds, the driver swinging an octopus over his head as he steered, a crowd-pleasing Wings tradition that Jimmy considered a tired gimmick. But what the hell, Avery liked it. He thought she was going to ask him about it when she turned to him as the Zamboni passed. But what she said was, 'Do you miss it, Dad?'

'Miss what?'

'The game. Playing.'

'I still play.'

The Wings and their opponents were spilling onto the ice.

'No,' she said. 'You ref.'

'Honey, I'm too old for it now anyway.'

'But do you miss it? Don't lie.'

'No.'

She looked away, knowing he was fibbing. 'Look at Seider,' she said, pointing to a young Wings defender. 'What a skater, huh?'

He smiled then at her youthful wisdom, at her patience and forgiveness, her blessed innocence. And he smiles again now, remembering. He looks at his phone and almost calls her, but reconsiders, cautious about putting too much pressure on her. Instead he texts: Thinking of you, Ave.

He sets the phone aside and waits. The phone plinks. He picks it up: NO more texts unless you want police involved

Noelle. 'Goddammit,' Jimmy says, gripping the phone as if he might crush it. He sits stewing, staring at the TV screen while a string of commercials plays out: A treatment for Type II diabetes. An in-house security system that will defeat any would-be intruder. A new kind of taco stuffed with cheese curls.

Fuck it, he thinks. On his phone he brings up YouTube.com, then types in the search window: **How do you remove an ankle monitor?**

FORTY-THREE

The detective purposely stands off to one side, out of the TV lights, while Chief Quarton tells the TV cameras what the police, thanks to Klimmek's hunch, have uncovered: the semi-frozen corpse of Jerome Hardy, son of billionaire Philip Hardy, who is standing alongside Klimmek. Hardy has one hand on the detective's shoulder. Klimmek can feel it trembling.

'We have a lot of work to do yet,' Quarton tells the reporters, 'but we will not rest until the killer of these two beloved young men is convicted of his crime – his crimes, plural – and sentenced to a rightful punishment. We know who that killer is, we need only now to assemble the evidence, piece by piece, item by item, that will convince a jury that he must pay the price. And we will. Today we made another significant step in that direction.'

They're standing in the parking lot outside the IceKings arena, surrounded by half a dozen reporters and camera operators and a few onlookers. As Quarton speaks, two Bitterfrost police vehicles are on their way to Jimmy Baker's house to re-arrest him. Klimmek stares at the slush at his feet, not wanting to glory at all in this moment. All we have, he silently tells himself, is a dead body – OK, two dead bodies – in the woods and in the ground. Inside his head he's running through the evidence he has – the blood, the jacket, the fingerprints, the gloves, the testimonies of Ronnie and Butch – and the evidence he does not yet possess – such as a motive beyond sheer rage. And an eyewitness. He has no one who can say she or he saw or heard what Jimmy Baker did. An eyewitness isn't an absolute must unless, of course, one of the twelve jurors believes it is.

It gnaws at Klimmek as the chief goes on about the evening's discovery. As much evidence as he has, it doesn't all add up as neatly as the detective would like. Yet three months remain before the trial begins to collect more and align it in a way to give the jury a clear, well-lit path to a guilty verdict. If pushed, he'd admit he isn't one-hundred-percent certain. He could never be again after Barrett Sawtell.

Sawtell had no criminal record. He graduated *cum laude* with a degree in economics from Western Michigan University and took a job in the accounting department of a Zeeland furniture company. Soon he was engaged to a woman from Ohio named Ashley. He bought a small getaway cottage on a creek near Bitterfrost, a town he'd frequented as a boy on deer and quail hunts with his father. Ashley would tell reporters at Sawtell's trial that she knew nothing about that cottage, didn't even know he owned it.

No one except bloviating true-crime bloggers professed to understand what consumed Sawtell on the sleety Thursday night he encountered a younger couple on the Division Street Bridge. He charmed them into drinks at Schmatta's, then invited them back to his house on the creek. His fiancé was in Zeeland, thinking Sawtell was on a business trip in Indiana. The couple was from the Detroit area, enjoying an overnight on their way to Mackinac Island. They were quite drunk on screwdrivers when Sawtell duct-taped them into beds and made them sing Elton John songs as loud as they could until he tired of it, put one bullet through each of their throats, then tore them to pieces with the hammer his father bought years before at an Ace Hardware right there in Bitterfrost.

Klimmek knew all of this to be true. But the jury was not persuaded. Mistakes were made in the rush to put Sawtell in prison for life. Sawtell's young attorney, Devyn Payne, took advantage, giving two jurors sufficient pause to acquit. It gave Klimmek no consolation – quite the contrary, in fact – when two weeks after Sawtell went free, he was found late one evening – by a tourist from Ohio, of course – hanging from that oak in the Tunnel of Trees south of Bitterfrost. Police found a single piece of paper pinned to Sawtell's shirt. He'd handwritten a note confessing to killing the 'pretty as pie' couple from downstate. 'Awful singers,' he also wrote. In a postscript, he listed the names of five other women and three men he claimed to have murdered in Michigan, Wisconsin, and Ohio.

'We won't be taking questions tonight,' Chief Quarton is saying. 'We have more than enough of our own. But Jerome Hardy's father is here and would like to offer a few words.'

No, Klimmek thinks. The less said now, the better. But Hardy steps to the microphone. He's sixty-six, clean-shaven with short, squared-off sideburns flecked with gray and the build of someone who works out daily. 'Thank you,' he says, a slight tremor in his voice, 'for taking the time to come out on this unseasonable evening. I would just like to—'

A reporter from Channel 8 in Traverse City steps out from the clutch of journalists and interrupts. 'Mr Hardy,' she says, her camera-man hovering, 'are you confident the police can convict the suspect in this case? As you may know, this town has been disappointed on this count before, in rather dramatic fashion.'

Her question, actually more of a statement, is less for Hardy than for viewers who are probably having their hockey games and nightly dramas disrupted by a news bulletin. But Klimmek can't let poor Hardy answer. He jumps to the man's side, takes his forearm, pulls him gently back, and leans into the mic. 'As the chief said, we're not taking any questions, Ms Reese,' he says. 'Certainly not about past cases.'

The night that state troopers confirmed it was Sawtell dangling, Klimmek himself was watching football with Kris in their living room. He almost didn't pick up the cellphone whirring on an end table. Klimmek asked the officer on the call to read the suicide note aloud. When he finished, Klimmek hung up without saying another word.

'Garth?' his wife said.

He hung his head and sighed. 'We so fucked up,' he said, using the vulgarity he abhorred. 'I fucking knew it.'

The reporter Reese persists. 'Then how about the present case, detective? Why would your suspect dump one body in an easy-to-find place in the woods and the other in a place so close to where he worked? Does that really make any sense?'

Klimmek shrugs. 'Perfect sense to a killer,' he says, knowing he's exaggerating. 'It will all come out at trial.' He turns back to Hardy, who's staring at the ground. 'Mr Hardy, did you still . . .?'

'No,' he whispers. 'Let's just go, shall we?'

Hardy insists that Klimmek join him and Chief Quarton in the police car returning to the station. Sylvester follows in Klimmek's Bronco. Klimmek takes a seat behind Hardy. As they're pulling out of the rink lot, the reporters shouting questions behind them, Hardy turns to address the detective. 'I thought that lady asked a fair question, detective,' he says. 'Can you explain to me how the kill-er's placement of Jerome and Aaron makes perfect sense?'

'With all due respect, Mr Hardy,' Klimmek says, 'what I tell the media and what we'll do at trial are usually quite a bit different.

Between us, I give them stuff they like for their audience. When they get an answer they can use, they stop asking the question. At least most do. The answer keeps them happy, and when they're happy, they're off our backs.'

'Hm,' Hardy says. 'Maybe I should hire you. The folks in the media aren't always my friends. But, tell me, in fact, does what the killer did make any sense?'

Klimmek leans forward in his seat so Hardy can hear him clearly. 'Jimmy Baker,' he says, 'isn't Hannibal Lecter or Ted Bundy or John Norman Collins, and—'

'Who is John Norman Collins?'

'He killed a bunch of coeds in Ann Arbor in the late sixties.'

'I see. I grew up in Fort Wayne. Another world, back then.'

'A better one. Anyway, what I mean is, Baker didn't plan this out. It was, as the cop shows like to say, a "crime of passion," the passion in this case being rage, which everyone around here knows is this guy's fatal addiction. I don't know why he is that way, but it's not for us to say, only to show that he did what he did, and that he had motive.'

'Which is, I'm assuming, that my son and his buddy pissed him off.'

'I'm sorry, sir,' Klimmek says. 'But yes. Probably.'

'God help us all.'

Amen, Klimmek thinks as he sinks back into his seat.

FORTY-FOUR

Devyn leans back against a plywood wall in a dank darkness reeking of mildew and shingle rot, waiting for the Golden Tee player to tell her what is going on. 'Sorry about this,' he rasps. She can just barely make out his shape, about fifteen feet away, the insipid glow of a cellphone casting a halo around his head. 'Couldn't find anything better on short notice. So we're borrowing this. Not exactly a Marriott, but we won't be here long.'

'Good.'

'You're curious as hell, admit it.'

She'd considered bolting for the woods when he surprised her outside the bar. The badge and gun dissuaded her. Maybe the wrong decision, in retrospect, but she wanted her car back. And yes, she was curious. Golf guy had her tie on a blindfold and they drove in silence to this shed or barn or whatever it is. The vehicle, which felt like an SUV, smelled of what she suspected was vape smoke. He removed the blindfold after she sat down.

'You followed me up here?' she says.

He emerges from the shadows, his coat unbuttoned. His dim silhouette etches someone slim and athletic. 'Only way I could get you alone to talk.'

'Maybe next time, try my cell, huh?'

'There's no next time.'

'Who are you?'

'A messenger.'

'For—?'

'Listen up.'

'Why should I? Who the hell are you?'

He rests a hand on his waist where Devyn earlier spied the gun. So he's going to shoot her if she doesn't listen? He moves two steps closer and squats. Devyn sees his grayish-green eyes and a black beard shaved tight to his narrow face, the skin a muted brown. 'I like your tattoo,' he says. 'My old man was a Wings fan. And I heard about that little lace-cutting trick you pulled on the guy at the rink. Nifty.'

'Exactly why am I here?'

'You're here because you have an opportunity to be of help to your government.'

'Oh, so that's what the badge is about? You're FBI or ATF or something? What's your name?'

'I have no name.' His face is as blank as a snowdrift.

'What do you want?'

'You need to step away, Devyn Payne.'

'From what?'

'From your boy Baker. From this case. From that courtroom.'

'Not gonna happen.'

'Look. You don't know what you've gotten yourself into. You need to step away. Just in that shithole bar tonight, you almost got your ass kicked. And those assholes are nothing compared to the people who have an interest in what's going on in your little Bitterfrost. I mean, why are you even bothering any more with that Fawcett woman? She was a piece of shit and now she's dead. Move on. And your client and his convenient loss of memory, that's not gonna wash with these people. Whether he goes to prison or the cops fuck up his conviction – entirely possible, as you know – his days are numbered. What happened to that Fawcett chick will happen to him. And maybe you.'

'What "people"?'

'You don't want to know. But we need you and Baker to get out of our way and let us take care of the real bad guys. People won't talk to us because they're afraid they'll get dragged into that court-room in front of their family and friends and neighbors. Or worse.'

Her phone is blowing up in her pocket. 'Who are these "bad guys"? Are they local? Or from somewhere else? What about . . .' She blurts it out, without thinking, 'What about that drug guy from Detroit? Rooney? Manny Rooney or something?'

Golf guy's expression doesn't change a bit. He picks a splinter of ice off the ground and holds it up in front of his face, examining it. 'You have no idea,' he says. He tosses the splinter away. 'You probably can't save your client, but maybe you can save your brother.'

Devyn feels his words like a stick blade to the solar plexus. 'My brother?'

He lets her think about it for a few seconds, then says, 'He's messing around with some of these people. He has no clue what he's getting into, and by the time he does, it'll be too late. But if you help us, maybe we help Evan.'

Hearing her twin's name takes her breath away again. Calm, she tells herself. She shifts her weight off the wall. She remembers her mother asking her barely twelve hours ago about Evan's recent behavior with IceKings money. And Evan badgering her to walk away from Jimmy earlier, saying it was 'not a good look' for the 'franchise.'

'What is it I can do for you?' she says. 'In theory.'

'I told you. Walk away. Withdraw as Baker's lawyer. Good chance the judge will call a mistrial. That'll give us time.'

Withdraw? No. She can't justify it legally, ethically, morally. But. In a courtroom, there's always a but.

'Time for what?' she says.

'The longer you wait, the less likely we can help you.'

'Time for fucking what?'

'Look. Baker's in a shitload of trouble, and I don't know, maybe you can get him out of it. I have my doubts. The cops got him on video, caught him lying, got blood splashed all over his truck, et cetera. But what's really gonna screw him isn't his present but his past. The jury will look at all that circumstantial evidence and then the prosecutor will explain how he almost killed that guy on TV tonight and the jury will say, holy shit, yeah, the Zamboni driver could have done this. Guilty.'

'That was thirteen years ago. Jimmy walked away and has lived an exemplary life. Everyone in Bitterfrost knows that. I'll make sure the jury knows it.'

'When he goes down, the real bad guys walk.'

'What real bad guys?'

'In closing – no pun intended – if you tell anyone about this, about me, about what I said, be prepared to hire your own lawyer to defend you against charges of obstruction of justice.'

'Please.'

'I should add, and don't take this the wrong way, it's not because of me, but if Evan is in trouble with these people, then others close to him might be, too.'

'So you're threatening me too? My mother?'

'What it is.'

Fuck you, she thinks. 'I assume you'll know if I do what you want,' she says, 'and I assume you'll follow through.'

The trace of a smile flits across golf guy's face. 'I can hear my old man about now: "That's one tough broad."'

'How do I reach you?'

'You don't.'

'I guess you know where to find me. I need my car.'

He stands and tosses her the bandanna. She ties it on. He guides her to his vehicle. They rumble away from the shed, dead tree limbs cracking under the tires. He stops the vehicle and, leaving it running, walks her about seventy paces. 'Sit, please,' he says. He helps lower her to the ground where she props her back against a tree. He rests what feels like his gun butt on her shoulder and says, 'Count to one hundred. Do not get up or take off that blindfold until then.' Then he leans close and says, 'One last thing: Why is your brother so interested in selling the family jewel?'

'What?' Devyn says, wanting to rip the blindfold off. 'The rink? No.'

'The whole shebang.'

'Bullshit. I'd know about that.'

'Every man has his price, right? Oh, and by the way, watch out for Bigfoot.'

She hears him laugh as he trots away. She counts to thirty, forty, fifty, then hears his vehicle starting. She's shivering now, from cold or fear or both. She strips off the bandanna and leans around the tree to look. He pulls away in the dark without lights on. She sees her Toyota parked twenty yards from where she sits, and the yellow glow of the lamp over the bar entrance another forty yards past it.

She waits, watching the shadow that is his vehicle trundling along the two-track back to the highway. She makes a guess and gets up and starts running through the woods. Is this where she's supposed to be careful about Bigfoot? She pulls up short of the highway and squats as low as she can behind a pine. She can just see the road from beneath the lowest fronds. Sure enough, here come the head-lamps of an SUV. Maybe she guessed right. As it comes closer, she sees the interlocking circles of an Audi logo on the front of the hood. Pretty nice ride for a government employee. She raises her phone and, making sure the flash is off, waits until the Audi is close enough that she thinks she can make out the license plate. She snaps half a dozen photos. One will do the trick; an old law school class-mate works for the state and can run the plate. She holds her breath. The Audi passes without slowing down.

Back in her car, she scrolls through texts and missed calls. Jimmy texted: It appears that I am screwed, then called five times. Probably during the *Dateline* interview. Or maybe because of that news bulletin about the cops finding young Hardy's body. If Jimmy saw that, he might panic and . . . she texts: Answer your phone. She counts to ten and calls him again. Again, voicemail. 'Jimmy,' she shouts. 'Where in God's name are you?'

FORTY-FIVE

The cuff is easy enough to snip with garden shears. But Jimmy knows from watching YouTube tutorials that any meddling with his ankle monitor will send an immediate alert to the police. So now he's trying to crush the little black box encasing the electronic gadgetry that could point his pursuers to where he is. He sets the thing on the flat side of a rock he dug out of the creek bank and starts slamming it with a hammer.

He's huddled in a circle of pines along a brook off an unmarked road that curls south of Bitterfrost before reconnecting with 901 and heading directly for Old 27 southbound to Detroit. Jimmy has watched enough cop shows to know what's next. Now that the police have unearthed a second victim they're certain to link to him, his bail is effectively void. They'll be coming for him.

Not for a second does Jimmy think he's going to get away. But he's determined to try to get to Avery before the authorities catch up with him. Even if it's just so Avery knows he tried. He kept calling Devyn, but she was AWOL, so he cut the monitor cuff and got the hell away from his house as fast as he could, nosing along two-tracks used by almost nobody but poachers shining white-tail deer out of season. He can't tell whether he has pounded the tracking device enough to do him any good, but the thing doesn't look like it did twenty or thirty whacks ago. He tosses it and the cuff into the slow-running creek and scrambles through the dark to his idling Bronco.

He keeps his lights off except when he sees the rare oncoming vehicle, taking a roundabout route to Old 27 where he hopes to slowly, quietly make his way downstate, hugging the right lane, exiting if he suspects a roadblock ahead, while the cops are setting traps on I-75 and the highways it intersects. His father favored Old 27 on trips south for kid hockey tournaments because he thought he could go as fast as he wanted between the occasional little towns and their thirty-five-mile-per-hour speed traps. The radio is on low, Jimmy hoping for news but getting little but opinionated sports and opinionated politics.

Now Devyn is calling. Too late, Jimmy thinks as his phone buzzes for the fourth time in the last twenty miles. He knows she's going to tell him to turn around and come back to Bitterfrost. He's not going to do that. The cops eventually will get him, and they'll be pissed off, and he'll go back to jail until the trial and, according to the YouTube lessons he watched, he might even have to pay for damage he inflicted on that black box. All of which changes nothing. Nobody can seriously accuse him of trying to escape. He just wants to see his daughter, maybe for the last time before they send him to prison.

He's south of Grayling, skirting Higgins Lake. His parents once rented a cottage there when he and Alex were still tykes. He remembers Alex forgetting to actually hang onto his fishing rod as he was casting and the pole catapulting into the lake while he and his parents watched, astonished until they started laughing. The memory brings Jimmy a fleeting smile. Alex would howl in protest if he knew what Jimmy is doing now, but he would also understand.

Whenever he sees headlights, he recalls the pair he remembered emerging from the woods behind the Loon that night as he waited across the road. He keeps trying to recollect more but nothing comes. Devyn says she's trying to obtain Loon security video that might help them both understand what he thinks he remembers, but the cops are putting her off. Then there's that inexplicable pinging sound in his head, growing louder now the farther south he goes.

Jimmy sees the first of the snowplows as he nears the northern end of Houghton Lake. A snippet on the radio suggested a snow squall was bearing down. He assumes he's near a county garage because beyond the first plow he sees at least two more lined up on the shoulder. The short wall they form on a westward bend initially blocks him from seeing the phalanx of police vehicles waiting a quarter mile up the road.

All at once, their lights flash on. Shit, Jimmy thinks, hammering the brakes. The Bronco fishtails, leaking into the left lane, and Jimmy swings the steering wheel back, overcorrecting. As he swerves toward the snowbank along the shoulder, Jimmy blinks against the cop lights growing larger as they bear down. He brings the Bronco to a lurching stop, its rear end half in the roadside ditch. He opens his door and hops down, shielding his eyes against the glare. The pinging in his head keeps getting worse. Two state troopers are running toward him down the middle of the road, guns drawn, one yelling, 'Get down, get fucking down now.' Jimmy closes his eyes and lowers himself to the snowy asphalt.

FORTY-SIX

'What do you think? Does Hardy have a point?'

'About what?' Klimmek says. He's crammed behind his L-shaped desk, surrounded by unruly towers of file folders. Quarton sits facing him in an angle-iron chair.

'About the bodies,' Quarton says. 'Why Baker would've put them so far apart in the middle of the night.'

Klimmek finds it annoying that the chief would ask him this now, as state police are zeroing in on a fleeing Jimmy Baker a couple of hours south of Bitterfrost. Quarton could have asked a few other, more pertinent questions before ordering Klimmek to arrest Baker in front of hundreds of his fans. But the big shot from Detroit has spoken, and now Klimmek, not Quarton, is on the hook to explain how and why Baker didn't dump both bodies in the same place. The question was legit, for sure, the timing not so much. For Christ's sake, they just had a press conference.

'I don't know yet, and neither do you,' Klimmek says. 'As you told your media pals, we have work to do. I was under the impression that Hardy wanted a suspect. We have one.'

'He wants the right suspect.'

'Well, shit. Now you tell me.' Klimmek's chair squawks as he swivels it to face his desktop computer. 'Call off the state guys and let Baker go. We can start over, nice and clean. More press conferences. That woman from Channel Eight will be your best friend.'

'Don't even, Garth.'

'Go hold Hardy's hand, chief. I have a job to do.'

Quarton grunts and leaves.

Klimmek asks himself what he was doing when Quarton knocked on his door a few minutes ago. He should have told the chief to just go away. Quarton has never been a detective and hasn't even spent much time as a street cop, instead creeping up the ranks by hopscotching departments, from Ishpeming to Escanaba to Marquette to Gaylord and, finally, after Klimmek's old boss died, to Bitterfrost. It was a bit of a step down as far as places went, but it was Quarton's first full chief job. Klimmek wouldn't be surprised if Quarton is already plotting his next move. Unless, of course, he screws up this case. Then he could be stuck in Bitterfrost forever.

The audiotapes, Klimmek thinks. He was re-listening to the tapes of what the dispatcher heard from the anonymous caller who saw the burning pickup and the nameless dog walker who spied Diggs's devastated body in the woods. There was a third anonymous caller, hours later, who tipped the police to Diggs and Hardy being in the Loon. Klimmek's not interested in that now. He puts listening buds in each of his ears and hits 'play' on his audio app.

He wishes the dispatcher had the slightest luck in cajoling either caller into disclosing a name or some other information that might point Klimmek to a potential witness. But she didn't, or couldn't, so he's left with the raw tape, which isn't all that revealing. The first anonymous caller sounds at first like a woman, although the voice has just enough timbre that Klimmek thinks it might be a man trying to sound like a woman. Still, all she or he says is, 'You got a truck burning pretty bad in the woods out here by Gallesero Road, not far from the old Pearson farm. Fugly scene.' The dispatcher starts to ask something as the caller hangs up. Klimmek recalls the truck and wonders if it was ever really burning. It was barely smoldering when he arrived, and the charring on the truck – or lack thereof – suggested to Klimmek it might never have caught.

He picks the toxicology screen off his desk as the tape proceeds to the second call, which came in one hour and eighteen minutes after the first. The dog walker, voice clearly male, says, 'I'm out walking the dog and I'm seeing a pretty nasty scene down a hill off 901 about four miles out of town.' The dog makes a noise, then the walker continues, 'On the north side of the road. Looks like somebody got thrown out of a car or something. You probably want to send an ambulance.' The dog speaks again, louder this time, and again the caller disappears before the dispatcher can say anything. Klimmek pauses the tape and sits back in his chair, lacing his fingers across the top of his belly. He ponders for the first time the possibility that the two callers were the same person. His gut was telling him they were both male. Plus, both used a similar expression – *pretty* bad' and *pretty* nasty' – to describe what they saw. That could be coincidence. But something else is bothering Klimmek.

He queues up the dog walker audio again. The guy talks, the dog barks, the guy talks again, the dog barks again, the call ends. Klimmek listens to it four times, then fiddles with the app to speed up the playback. The second time through, he sits up in his chair. He turns up the volume. He listens again, then again, then turns the playback speed back to slower than normal. He's listening for the second time at the slower speed when Quarton pokes his head in.

'They got Baker,' he says. 'We'll get him back here, you can wring a confession out of him.'

If he's the right guy, Klimmek thinks.

The chief leaves again, shaking his head. The detective returns the playback to the normal speed and listens to it twice. He plays the tape once more. 'I'll be goddammed,' he says. He can't be certain, but he'd bet twenty bucks that that's not what he thought he was hearing. He and his fellow cops fell for the caller saying he was walking his dog. But it's not a dog. It's some kind of animal, but not a dog, definitely not a dog.

FORTY-SEVEN

The name RONNIE blinks on Devyn's phone. That's good but unexpected, because her old friend has been avoiding her.

'Hey, stranger,' Devyn answers.

'I know, I know, I'm sorry, but—'

'I get it. But you're calling now. What's up?'

'They're saying Jimmy's a fugitive.'

'Who's – what? What's happening?'

'It's on the news. Jimmy tried to escape.'

Devyn was afraid of that, which is why she's speeding down a dark highway back to Bitterfrost. After seeing Jimmy's text about being screwed, she was hoping he wouldn't really do something stupid, hoping he would know that by running he would hand the prosecution a compelling bit of evidence that he's guilty. Not that innocent people, if frightened enough, didn't run.

'Where is he?' Devyn says.

'Don't know, but the news is saying the police are probably gonna bring him in soon.'

Jesus, Jimmy, what are you doing to yourself? Devyn thinks. Even if you are guilty – she banishes the thought before finishing it. Ronnie continues, half-whispering into the phone, 'I have assholes in the bar here saying the cops should just beat him up and leave him in a ditch like the Diggs boy.'

Assholes, all right, Devyn thinks. 'OK,' she says. 'Thanks for letting me know. I'm driving from the sticks and all I can get on the radio is country music and Bible thumpers.'

There's a pause. Devyn hears a man in the background yelling, 'Where the hell's my beers, Ronnie? Parched over here.'

Ronnie says, 'I don't know. I just – we haven't talked, and I thought – I just wanted to reach out. I hope you're doing all right. I gotta get back to work.'

Devyn hangs up, knowing the next time they talk, Ronnie might be sitting in a witness box. Now she needs to find Jimmy. If only he would have agreed to let her install a find-my-phone app on her phone. But he assured her she didn't need that. Now he's officially a fugitive and she has no way to find him.

Except.

She hesitates before making the call. She knows it won't be pleasant. But she's out of options. Her brother picks up on the first ring and starts talking before she can say anything.

'Didn't I tell you this would happen?' Evan says. 'Dammit, Devyn. If he's innocent, why would he run? Tell me that. Why?'

'There are lots of reasons, Evan.'

'Enlighten me.'

'I don't have time. I need you to tell me where Jimmy is.'

'How would I know?'

'Don't play games. I know you're glued to your police scanners.'

He doesn't respond immediately, probably relishing this small moment of small triumph. 'Grayling,' he finally says. 'I think. I can't be sure. Lots of cops talking across different channels. But it sounds like Grayling, or thereabouts.'

Jimmy has spoken fondly about trips his family made to a lake not far from Grayling when he was a boy. 'Thanks,' she tells her brother. 'I'll let you know what happens.' She considers asking him about selling the rink, but this isn't the time, and it's probably just bullshit golf guy told her to get her to do his bidding.

'Don't go getting killed now.'

As she's stuffing her phone in the cupholder, she sees an email alert from the office of the Bitterfrost prosecutor. Jimmy's tox report is in. She shouldn't be looking at it with seventy-some miles to Grayling, but she opens it anyway for a quick glance. She clicks on the attached report while trying to keep her speed at just under seventy-four. Scrolling through, she sees, or thinks she sees, that Jimmy had a trace amount of alcohol in his blood, barely a tenth of a percent. That highball he had at the Loon. Something else catches her attention. She checks her mirrors and, seeing nobody trailing her, pulls onto the shoulder and stops.

The report shows the presence in Jimmy's blood of gamma-hydroxybutyric acid, or GHB, a party drug beloved mostly by people much younger than Jimmy. Liquid ecstasy, some called it. Cherry meth. Devyn had a client once who'd swallowed a bunch and pushed an ex-boyfriend off a second-floor condo balcony. The ex was lucky – he only broke a leg, an ankle, and both wrists – and the client went to prison for five years for aggravated assault. Besides lowered inhibitions, GHB symptoms included feelings of euphoria, agitation, hallucinations, and memory loss, even blackouts.

But Jimmy doing GHB? Devyn finds that hard to believe. He's a one-drink-a-day guy who's painfully aware of his vulnerability to anything addictive. Could someone have spiked that highball? Ronnie? That's almost as unbelievable. But, however the drug wound up in Jimmy's system, it could help to explain his lack of any memory of that night. What if it also reduced his inhibitions? Even made him violent?

Devyn tosses the phone on the passenger seat and guns the car back onto the highway.

First she sees the cop lights, red and blue sabers fracturing the night sky. Then the police cruisers blocking the two-lane highway a few hundred yards ahead. She parks and gets out and walks toward the blockade. She sees no evidence of Jimmy, but it's hard to get a clear look past the officers and vehicles to whatever's going on beyond them. The scene is suffused in a luminous glow from head-lights and magnesium lamps, as if the cops are worried Jimmy could suddenly disappear into the dark.

She's too late. Jimmy's going back to jail and there's nothing Devyn can do about it. He just wouldn't listen. The whole thing pisses her off. *If he's innocent, why would he run?* Good question her brother asked. Her mother will probably be asking too. Devyn has no good answer. Does Jimmy?

As Devyn approaches, a woman in the navy-and-gold uniform of the Michigan State Police, right hand on her hip holster, steps up. 'Sorry, ma'am,' she says, 'but I suggest you turn around and go home.'

'Thank you, trooper,' Devyn says, 'but I'm the attorney for the gentleman I believe you're taking into custody. I should be allowed to see him and speak to the arresting officer.'

'Your car is parked illegally, ma'am.'

Enough with the ma'am, Devyn thinks. She takes a step sideways and squints into the glare. She thinks she spies Jimmy on his knees, his back to her, but then the trooper moves into her line of sight.

'I'm going to need you to leave now, ma'am.'

'Where's Detective Klimmek? He knows me.'

'I don't know who that is, but it's time for you to go.'

'You're not going to help me, are you, Trooper' – she finds the trooper's nameplate – 'Pinkston?'

'Go to your car and drive away, ma'am. Now.'

The trooper steps hard toward Devyn and Devyn head-fakes to her right and scuttles left, peering down the road. She sees Jimmy then. He's kneeling in the middle of the road, a silhouette with his hands behind his head. 'There,' she says. 'Jimmy Baker. That's my client.'

A loud crack pierces the night air. Devyn makes a move and tries to rush past the trooper, who grabs her sleeve in two hands and yanks her sideways. 'What the hell's the shooting for?' Devyn yells. 'Jimmy!'

'Get down, ma'am.'

Devyn pushes back to keep from falling. The trooper doesn't seem too strong; if Devyn was on skates, she'd have no trouble tossing her aside. But she's not on skates and she knows if she persists, she'll wind up somewhere she can be of no use to Jimmy.

The trooper has the heel of her gloved left hand stuck in Devyn's upper torso, just below her neck, forcing her backwards and down. Devyn collapses onto the asphalt and the trooper straddles her midsection, pinning her. Devyn tries to wriggle free, wrenching her head up to where she can see Jimmy. He's face down on the road now, a cop with a knee in his back. 'Did you idiots frigging shoot him?'

'Calm down,' the trooper says.

'Jimmy!' Devyn screams. 'They're gonna try to make you—'

The trooper claps a hand under Devyn's jaw to try to close it but Devyn twists away. 'Don't say anything! Jimmy! Get off me, goddammit. Jimmy! Jimmy!'

PART THREE

FORTY-EIGHT

The rink is dark. Five thirty-seven in the morning.

Outside, Devyn stands on the high south bank of the Jako, eyes closed, listening to the river's whisper and burble. She does this every so often to clear her head and remind herself of how she got here.

Across the river, where St Henry's Catholic Church stands, is where her Finnish ancestors landed more than a century ago, where they stacked boats with timber bound for Chicago, where they made their first livings in this foreign land. Her family were Panaanens then, before her great-grandfather, Pekka, changed the surname to Payne in 1924. She had great-uncles, Jay and Markus, who retired as co-owners of a shipping dock in Chicago. When she visited as a girl, Uncle Jay took her to Wrigley Field to watch his beloved Cubs, Uncle Mark to the southside stadium to cheer for the White Sox. She never told Uncle Mark she liked the Cubs better. As a young Edward Jones broker, the only one then within one hundred miles of Traverse City, young Calvin Payne took a stake in his uncles' business that would yield the wherewithal to build the rink, buy the IceKings, and encourage his daughter to play the game that was today the true love of her life.

She opens her eyes and walks into the rink, navigating the shadows of a corridor she has walked ten thousand times. She couldn't sleep on the fifth day of the trial of Jimmy Baker for the murder of Aaron Diggs. Just like the four days before. She tried the living-room sofa, but that didn't work. She threw on some clothes and went for what she hoped would calm her. A predawn skate.

Calvin brought her to the rink for early-morning skates when she was little. They'd venture onto the unlit ice with sticks and skates and a single puck. Devyn asked why they didn't turn the lights on, and her father said the dark was good for practice. 'You learn to play without looking down,' he said. 'You feel the puck with your hands and wrists so you can keep looking up, where all your team-mates and opponents are. And when your head is up, you won't get it knocked off by someone's shoulder or elbow.'

The door to the referee's room where Devyn dresses is open. That's not right. Inside, her locker, which she never locks, also is open, her equipment scattered across the floor. One of her skates is missing a blade. The cracked plastic halves of her helmet lie on opposite sides of the room. Parts of the palms in her gloves have been ripped out. Across the back of her white practice jersey someone has scrawled in red: WHORE.

No predawn skate today. Devyn starts putting things back in her locker. She'll have to take her broken skate to Traverse City for repair and pay someone to stitch the gloves with new palms. She has extras at home, so she'll be back on the ice soon enough. But whoever did this had to know it wouldn't keep her from playing. The message has nothing to do with hockey.

That's how it is now in Bitterfrost. Three months after Jimmy Baker's arrest, the town that fancies itself a quiet, friendly, anonymous respite from the world is suddenly famous for two vicious killings, a living true-crime stereotype of the rural burg riven by violence. There are people who stand by Jimmy and there are people who think the Paynes are using their money and influence to defy justice. You can see it in the graffiti painted on river bridges, hear it in the paranoid whispers at Big Henry's and Schmatta's, divine it in the boos of fans watching the IceKings, who've lost twelve of their last fourteen games. Devyn's father would be heartbroken.

She goes to her car, turns the ignition, blasts the heat. It's early March and Bitterfrost is just as frozen and gray as it was when the police last took Jimmy into custody. They must be feeling pretty good because Devyn has yet to do much to undermine the testimony of the prosecution witnesses. State trooper Schmidt and Bitterfrost officer Sylvester described the horrific scene where Diggs's body was found. The prosecutor Harris brandished documents from the Cory Richards litigation suggesting Jimmy suffers from intermittent explosive disorder. A hematologist discussed blood found at the scenes and Jimmy's house. DNA in the blood and on the gloves the cops found was positively identified as matching that of Diggs.

A toxicologist told the jury how that GHB, detected in Diggs as well as Jimmy, could have impaired them; Devyn couldn't get her to even speculate as to how the drug could have gotten into Jimmy. A spiked drink maybe? The so-called expert witness wouldn't bite. From the defense table, Devyn imagined she could feel the jurors lean slightly forward when the prosecutor was up, then feel them lean slightly back when it was Devyn's turn. Jimmy sat next to her, quiet and sullen, his 'Every day is a penance' mantra admirable but useless. At least, she thought, he didn't actually confess to the cops. He kept his mouth shut.

Still, she knows she's losing.

Butch Dulaney took the stand yesterday afternoon. In dark suit and royal blue tie, his beard freshly trimmed, Butch recited for the prosecution his view of Jimmy's encounter with Diggs and Hardy at the Loon, describing the 'wild' and 'pissed off' look on Jimmy's face. The prosecutor didn't keep him long. Maybe twenty minutes. Then Devyn peppered him with questions about the Loon on the night in question, where he was, why he stepped up to the bar, how he interacted with the men from Detroit, why he might have carried some animus toward Jimmy after that evening's incident on the ice. Butch answered so calmly and quietly that at one point Circuit Judge Darlene Esper had to ask him to speak up. He didn't smirk. He looked earnestly into the jury box. The only quirk of his testimony was that he repeatedly called Devyn 'Ms Payne,' as if to suggest to everyone in the courtroom that the Payne family, not the Dulaneys, was on trial.

Klimmek took the stand after Butch. With Harris's prodding, he mesmerized the jury for two hours as Devyn watched, feeling helpless. She will start her cross-examination at nine thirty sharp. If she doesn't get Klimmek squirming at least a little on the stand, if she doesn't get the jurors leaning forward for her questions, then Jimmy is probably going to prison for a long time. The detective told the truth the last time he was answering Devyn's questions about a murderer. That didn't work out for him. Which might not bode well for today. She speaks to the windshield: 'Do not lie to me, Garth.'

Her eyelids flutter in the heat washing over her. She grabs a lever beneath the seat and kicks it back. She drowses. A pinprick of light blinks at the edge of the rink parking lot in front of her. 'Who's there?' she hears herself shout. Then a man is laughing. It's familiar but she's not sure of the source until he strolls out of the trees sucking on a vape pen. Golf guy. In his puffy jacket. He exhales a plume of wispy smoke. 'You're four days in,' he says, 'and I see no sign that you're going to do what I asked.'

She says nothing in response.

'Do you have some secret witness stashed away who's going to save Baker's ass at the last minute? If you don't – and you don't

– he's going away, where he won't last, and you're stuck in this shit town for the rest of your life. Is that what you want? Get your ass handed to you in your biggest case ever so you can keep scratching by on white trash and mommy's dole?'

No, she thinks, but she cannot speak.

'And your blessed little cathedral, your rink, that will be gone too. And that will be your fault. Nobody else's.'

She glances at the rink, a barely visible hulk that seems to vibrate in the shadows. She thinks of the blades. Every day, Jimmy asks whether Evan ordered the new Zamboni blades. Are you kidding, Jimmy? she tells him every day, you're in the middle of a murder trial. But finally she promised to ask Evan, and she kept her word, and Evan said, Holy shit, Dev, the blades are good enough and I have more important things to worry about with a team on a losing streak. But she knows he's lying. She doesn't know exactly what he's lying about, but he's lying. He has his own plan.

'Leave me alone,' she tells golf guy, suddenly able to speak.

'Walk away,' he says, vape smoke enveloping his head. 'The longer you wait, the worse—'

She jolts forward in the driver's seat, eyes wide. There is no golf guy out in front of her car. She was dreaming. Her phone is ringing. She looks. It's Varga again, her attorney pal from Petoskey.

'Hey,' she croaks, still half-asleep. 'Why are you up so early?'

'Just got off the Peloton,' he says.

'What's up?'

'I thought you should know. A cop friend texted me overnight. They found a guy in Mackinaw City, beat to death. He was in the same dumpster they found your friend in.'

'No shit. Who's the guy?'

'They don't know yet. Couldn't find any ID. But they—'

'Found a badge.'

Varga hesitates. 'How'd you know?'

'Long story. What was the badge for?'

'Looked like Coast Guard.'

'No way.'

'That's what my guy said.'

'All right.'

'You OK? Trial going OK?'

Devyn looks over at the rink again. 'Not really.'

'That'll change. Promise.'

'Listen, can you do me a favor? Wait a day or so then hit up your cop pal again, see if they have a name?'

'You got it.'

If that really was golf guy in the same Mackinaw City dumpster where Jordan was found, then he wasn't bullshitting about the bad people with an interest in Jimmy's trial. Devyn had thought his license plate would help identify him, but it was attached to a lease car owned by some vaguely named Detroit company. She still doesn't know who he is – or was.

She looks over at the rink again. Is Evan in danger? Is it time for her to seriously consider walking away from the case? And what about the rink? She hasn't had the gumption or a real reason yet to ask her brother about what golf guy said about him selling, maybe because she doesn't want to believe it. 'What the hell,' she says aloud, calling up the weeks-old text from the real estate agent on Tinder. She'd thought at the time that his offer to help sell the property was off-the-wall. Now she thumbs him a reply: **Drink tonight? You come to me. Schmatta's in bfrost. 6ish.**

FORTY-NINE

K limmek clears his bowl of the last soggy Cheerios and sets it in the kitchen sink. 'No banana today, Garth?' Kris says. She's at the table finishing her yogurt and green tea. 'It's good for your blood pressure.'

He hates bananas. 'Not today. Bad luck.'

'That's silly. Will it be bad luck if I come to watch you today?'

'Never, sweetie.'

He hopes that's true.

He'll be taking the stand for cross-examination by Devyn Payne. Years before, she goaded him into admitting to mistakes in the department. And of course, last night, Klimmek again had the dream – or nightmare. In it, he again went to the evidence room two days before the trial and located the hammer, marked as Exhibit 1, and confirmed for the twentieth time that the fingerprints found on the handle were the defendant's. Then, again, he was in the courtroom, stammering before the judge and jury and gallery, unable to produce the hammer or the prints.

The mistake wasn't quite as stark as his nightmare portrayed it, but it might as well have been. Somehow, in the real world, the evidence chain was broken. The defense, in the person of Devyn Payne, sniffed it out after tracking down an officer who'd been fired a few weeks before the trial for beating a drunk driver into unconsciousness. He took the stand over the objections of the prosecution and testified that there had been internal 'issues' related to budget cuts. Two jurors had issues with those issues. The claw-hammer killer Sawtell went free.

Not this time. This time Devyn Payne has nothing. Klimmek came into the trial thinking she must have some surprise to spring in court, something that would turn jurors' heads. But she doesn't even have a list of witnesses, except, perhaps, Jimmy Baker himself. Which Klimmek expects wouldn't go well for the defense. 'When we're all done and we've sent this guy off to prison, I'll eat a whole bowl of bananas,' he tells his wife.

'Don't be perjuring yourself now,' she says. 'What about the other young man? Will you get Baker for him too?'

The prosecution chose to try Baker first for the Diggs murder, leaving Hardy for later. That didn't sit well with Hardy's father, but the Diggs case was cleaner, and if they did their job and convicted Baker, he might plead to the other murder and they would be done.

'Yes, we will.'

Klimmek's phone buzzes. Chief Quarton. Klimmek lets the call go and pulls on his coat and a watch cap. 'Better get going.'

'One whole bowl,' Kris says.

He parks behind the courthouse one hour and fifteen minutes before Judge Esper is to call the trial back to order. Three antenna-topped TV vans already have set up shop in the lot. Instead of going in through the back door, Klimmek walks around to the front. The grand old structure was built long before he was born. During a big case, he likes to be reminded of the majesty of the place.

He takes the sidewalk that borders the snow-carpeted courthouse lawn. The morning is overcast but dry, silent but for a snowmobile's distant growl. Pairs of uniformed officers are posted at each end of the walkway to the main courthouse entrance and either side of the entrance's double doors. As Klimmek turns up the walkway, he sees the black SUV limousine pull up to the curb.

Philip Hardy jumps out of the front passenger seat and circles the limo in his topcoat, opening doors for his wife, the parents of Aaron Diggs, and other family. They're all dressed in black, as if they're attending a funeral. Hardy comes around the front of the vehicle and spies Klimmek. The detective gives him a perfunctory nod. Hardy waves and points up toward the courthouse clock tower. Klimmek looks. Hanging over most of the clock face is a sign painted in silver on a black bedsheet: **DIE ZELDA**

Klimmek shrugs at Hardy, then feigns looking at his phone. He can't imagine how that sign got up there, but however it happened, it can't be good luck. He hurries forward, head bowed. Quarton left him a voicemail. He puts the phone to his ear and hears the chief say, 'Garth, we have a problem.'

FIFTY

The bailiff ushering Jimmy to the defense table has to catch him so he doesn't fall. 'Holy crap, sir, are you all right?' the deputy says.

'I'm fine.'

Jimmy just saw someone he'd hoped not to see. A few rows behind the prosecution table, Cory Richards sits in a wheelchair in the aisle along the gallery, his hands curled grotesquely over the armrests, his back ramrod straight in a spinal brace. As Jimmy gawks, Richards angles his head slowly in Jimmy's direction. He wears the blank expression of someone who doesn't want his true feelings known. Without thinking, Jimmy takes a step, then another, toward that side of the room before the deputy grabs his arm above the elbow, pulling him back. Devyn appears.

'Jimmy,' she says. 'Sit. Eyes to the front.'

'I thought Richards wasn't on the witness list.'

'He's not.'

'But he's here anyway? To witness my crucifixion?'

'I told you, they could still ask to call him. And I would object. But—'

'But what about his NDA? He agreed—'

'Give it up, Jimmy.'

'Yes, ma'am.'

'That ship has sailed. And don't "ma'am" me again or I'm outta here.'

Jimmy cranes his neck to look at her. He thinks she's joking but something in her tone makes him wonder.

FIFTY-ONE

'**M**s Payne?' Judge Esper says.

'Thank you, your honor.'

The gallery behind her is packed with the families of the dead, curious townspeople, reporters, and Cory Richards in a wheelchair. Police officers and bailiffs line the walls. Next to Devyn, Jimmy sits up straight, as she instructed, hands folded one on the other, gazing toward the witness box without the hint of a smile or grimace, also as instructed. He's wearing a navy suit, white dress shirt, and red-and-blue striped tie that Devyn found in his bedroom closet. Detective Klimmek has taken the stand in his own gray jacket, light blue shirt, solid dark blue tie. He looks relaxed, no surprise because the trial has gone well for his team. Devyn hopes Klimmek can help her slow their momentum.

She stands up from the defense table and goes to a lectern set in front of the judge's bench, feeling the eyes of the jurors upon her. She glances their way. Seven men, five women, all of them white, four over the age of sixty, all from the surrounding county, three from Bitterfrost proper. Devyn tries to make brief eye contact with one woman. At forty-one, the divorced mother of two adolescent girls is the juror closest to Jimmy in age. By Devyn's reckoning, she is her client's best hope. Maybe his only one. But that's all he needs. One juror who harbors a reasonable doubt.

'Detective Klimmek,' she says, just as Judge Esper interrupts.

'Forgive me, counselor, but . . .' She stands from her brown leather seat, leans out over the bench, and points a finger at the gallery. Everyone turns to see. The judge is gesturing at Chief Quarton, who's leaning against a wall in a rear corner. 'Chief,' Judge Esper says, almost shouting. 'Stand up straight, this is a court of law, not a speakeasy.' Quarton comes off the wall and as he does, Devyn notices Jordan's mother, Shirlee, sitting on the aisle near him.

'Sorry, your honor,' the chief says.

'Please tell me,' Esper continues, 'exactly what you are doing slouching around in here when you and your so-called department allowed some reprobates to deface this sacred property as they did with apparent impunity overnight? Can you answer me that, sir?'

Devyn isn't sure what the judge is talking about, but she overhears someone behind her whisper, 'My God, that sign on the clock.' Devyn didn't see any sign; she came in the rear entrance. The chief starts to reply but Esper, her onyx eyes hot with disdain, cuts him off.

'You call yourself an officer of the law? Shall we invite the defendant to move for a dismissal?'

'Your honor, I—'

'Get out of here now.' Esper sits. 'And do not come back until that desecration is removed from our courthouse.'

'But, your honor, I need—'

'You need to remove that defilement. I can have one of your officers usher you out if that would be helpful.'

The chief purses his lips and stalks out of the courtroom.

Esper sits. She's a former sheriff's deputy from Starvation Lake who moved to Bitterfrost with her husband eight years ago and ran for election as a tough-on-crime judge. Her auburn hair, streaked with gray and snugged into a plump ponytail, reminds Devyn of the red fox that keeps her mother's yard clear of mice and chipmunks. She wonders if maybe Esper was cutting Quarton down to size a bit. He's been on the news almost daily, including *Good Morning America* and the *NBC Nightly News*, and there are rumors he's a candidate for a job at state police headquarters.

'My apologies, Ms Payne,' the judge says. 'Proceed.'

Devyn straightens her navy suit jacket. Her scarlet silk scarf pairs nicely with Jimmy's tie. She's been trying to match her outfits to his as a way of getting into his head, his eyes, his ears, his limited memories of the night in question. There is so much she doesn't know. Because Jimmy doesn't know. It's frustrating and frightening but she also knows there is much that Klimmek and his colleagues don't know, however much they want to portray it as otherwise. There's an unwritten rule to lawyering, canonized in popular culture by the Paul Newman movie *The Verdict*, that says an attorney should never ask a question to which she doesn't know the answer. But what if said lawyer essentially doesn't know the answer to any of the multitude of questions surrounding a double murder?

If she's where I am, Devyn thinks, I'm gonna ask anyway.

'Detective Klimmek,' she says. 'Good to see you again.'

'How can I help?' he says.

She turns to the jury, half smiling, and addresses Klimmek without facing him. 'That was a colorful yarn you and the prosecutor spun, wouldn't you agree, detective?'

'I would not agree that it was a yarn,' Klimmek says. 'A yarn, to me, is something made up. It's fiction. What we're talking about here today is, unfortunately, not fiction.'

Devyn still doesn't turn to Klimmek. She's talking at once to him and the jury. 'Fiction,' she says. 'Like one of those crime dramas you see on Netflix or Hulu? Are you familiar with those shows, detective?'

'I don't watch much television.'

'I only ask because, as entertaining as those programs can be, I find – and maybe this is because I'm, you know, more persnickety as a courtroom lawyer than the average person – that some of them can feel, I guess, unsatisfactory.' Devyn turns fully to Klimmek, then steps out from behind the lectern and approaches him. 'Like the writers left out a thing or two that was too difficult or incon-venient to explain and hoped the rest of the narrative would keep the viewers from noticing, if you know what I mean.'

'Objection, your honor,' Harris says. 'I don't hear a question in defense counsel's little TV critique. Can we move on?'

'Ms Payne?' Judge Esper says.

'Yes, your honor.' Devyn takes another step toward the witness box. 'A question, detective, on something I must have missed in your nicely scripted colloquy with the prosecutor about the night that supposedly was. Where exactly did this killing happen?'

She's in direct violation of the know-the-answer-to-the-question rule. But Klimmek can't lie about this because it's easy enough to check or challenge. Devyn would love to know the answer, so long as she doesn't hear it from Klimmek. He cants his head to his left.

'Where did . . . can you be more specific?' he says.

'The murder. Where exactly did it happen? Where did Mr Baker supposedly attack Mr Diggs?'

Devyn knows the prosecution doesn't necessarily need to prove precisely where the murder occurred if it presents enough other undisputed evidence – blood, DNA, fingerprints, lies, videotape – to show that Jimmy was culpable. But anything that introduced the slightest doubt into the mind of even a single juror – that woman, for instance – could help him.

'As I testified,' Klimmek says, 'we found Mr Diggs's body—'

'That's not what I asked, detective. I'm aware of what you testified about where the body was found. I asked where the murder actually occurred. As a lifelong resident of Bitterfrost, I personally would like to know.'

'Your honor,' Harris says. 'Can counsel please stop lecturing the witness and let him answer?'

Before the judge can reply, Devyn says, 'Sorry, your honor. Detective Klimmek? Where did this happen?'

Klimmek folds his hands on his chest and ponders the front edge of the witness box. 'We have a number of places where we think the defendant could have committed the actual murders.'

'"*Could* have committed." I didn't see that phrasing in the formal charges against my client. Does that mean it's possible that he didn't commit any murder?'

'I believe you are twisting my words, counselor.'

'Am I?' She turns to face the jury. 'Am I?' she repeats. 'What do you think? The detective said "could have," did he not?'

'Objection, your honor. The detective answered counsel's question and now she's speechifying again.'

'Ms Payne,' Judge Esper says. 'Direct your questions to the witness, please. The melodramatics are starting to get on my nerves.'

'Apologies, your honor. Detective, just so I can get this straight on the record, you and your colleagues in the Bitterfrost Police Department do not know where this murder occurred, is that correct?'

'We have a number of—'

'Did it occur where you found the body?'

'It could have, yes.'

'But it could have happened somewhere else, too, is that correct?'

He hesitates, then says, 'Yes.'

'So you don't know where the murder occurred, do you?'

'We have several options that—'

'It's a simple question, sir. Do you know or do you not?'

He looks directly at Devyn, almost daring her. 'No. I do not.'

'The prosecution has offered evidence that Mr Baker crossed paths with Mr Diggs at the Loon bar and that Mr Diggs was found dead many hours later. But you don't really know what happened in between, do you, detective?'

'We believe, as I testified earlier, based on all the evidence we've offered, that the defendant killed Mr Diggs within that time span.'

'You *believe*, but you do not know, do you, detective?'

'We're playing word games, Ms Payne.'

'I'll let that go for now, sir,' Devyn says. 'You also do not have any murder weapon, do you, detective?'

'We believe the defendant used some type of blunt object.'

'Again, you *believe*. But you have no such object in your possession, correct?'

'We do not at this time.'

'Sounds like another case I – that is, we – tried in this courtroom. So, in your conversation with Ms Harris, you seemed to imply that Mr Baker's lack of memory of that night suggested he was hiding something. Do I have that essentially correct?'

'His faulty memory seemed rather convenient. And he obviously had reason to be hiding something.'

'Not if he's innocent, detective,' Devyn says. 'The toxicology report shows he had the drug gamma-hydroxybutyric acid, or GHB, in his system. Couldn't that have contributed to his memory problems?'

'Objection,' Harris says. 'The detective is not a pharmacological expert.'

'You've got to be kidding me,' Devyn says.

'Overruled,' Esper says. 'Detective?'

Klimmek doesn't look concerned. 'It's possible that it contributed, but we can't know for certain.'

'Do you have a theory about how the drug found its way into Mr Baker's system?'

'We assume he ingested it himself.'

'You assume. But you have no evidence of Mr Baker having a history of taking such drugs, for medical purposes or for pleasure, do you?'

'Not that I know of.'

'What about Mr Baker's history of taking severe blows to the head in hockey fights? Could that also have contributed?'

'Again, your honor. Objection.'

'I'll sustain this one.'

'Your honor,' Devyn protests, 'the detective was allowed to testify about Mr Baker's supposed state of mind, I should at least—'

'Move on.'

Bitch, Devyn thinks. She steps to within a foot of the witness box, her body angled toward the jury, hoping to nudge Klimmek to look directly at the jurors when he answers her next question. 'Detective,' she says, 'how confident are you that Jimmy Baker committed this murder?'

As coached, Klimmek looks toward the jury box. 'I'm confident, Ms Payne, or I wouldn't be up here.'

'Of course, detective, nobody is questioning your integrity. But how confident? One-hundred-percent confident? Ninety-nine? Mr Baker is facing—'

'Objection,' Harris says.

'Sustained.'

'Let me ask this way,' Devyn says. 'Michigan has no death penalty, of course, but if it did, would you feel as confident, detective, knowing that—'

'Objection,' Harris all but shouts. 'Immaterial, irrelevant, and prejudicial.'

'—you'd be sending Jimmy Baker to his death?'

'Sustained,' Esper says. 'Jurors, you will disregard this line of questioning. Ms Payne, you are hereby warned.'

'I withdraw the question, your honor,' Devyn says, keeping an eye on Klimmek, who sighs and turns away from the jury. Good. She walks back to the defense table and gives Jimmy a look that she hopes suggests at least a wisp of confidence. 'I have nothing further for the detective at this time, though I'd like to reserve time for one or two questions later.'

'Fair enough,' Esper says, banging her gavel. 'Fifteen-minute break.'

The room fills with the clatter of onlookers getting up to pee and stretch legs. Devyn surveys the room. She sees Shirlee Fawcett heading for the courthouse exit. Devyn's about to follow her when she spies a Dulaney she doesn't know well sitting in the back row. 'Jimmy,' she says. 'You know that guy? The one with the thing on his neck?'

FIFTY-TWO

The white legal pad in front of Jimmy is blank except for what he etched in block letters at the top of the first page: **TRIAL DAY 4**.

He hasn't quite absorbed what he just witnessed. The detective, so sure and calm when the prosecutor was walking him through the evidence, actually seemed to become flustered by Devyn's blunt queries. Jimmy wanted to check the jurors to see how they were responding, but Devyn had ordered him not to look their way.

He's been mesmerized anyway by Devyn herself. Jimmy usually thinks of her as being much younger than him, even though, in her mid-thirties, she really isn't. In this moment, though, it's as if she has matured into someone wiser, someone shrewder and less naïve, more willing to confront as well as compromise, depending on what is necessary. She drove him nuts with her endless questions about things he thought were irrelevant to the matter at hand – the Richards litigation, his long-ago affair with Ronnie, even his sleep habits – but no matter how much he resisted, she wouldn't relent, she made him answer as best he could. As she pressed Klimmek about the actual location of the murder, and he watched the detective fumble the reply, Jimmy felt his heart speed up a little, a grin in his mind if not on his face.

Devyn gave him a secret look that she probably intended to reassure. He appreciated it. And yet. He doesn't think he can count on an awkward moment or two for the prosecution's star witness to blind the jury to the seeming evidence against him, especially his hapless, pitiless lack of memory. He's been wondering of late, lying awake in his cell, what if he'd simply told the detective what he knew and didn't know that afternoon in his living room? What if he'd come clean about what little he did remember? Maybe he wouldn't be sitting here now, waiting to return to the jail and climb back into his baggy orange clown suit.

But maybe, he's also been thinking, this is where he is supposed to be, how things are supposed to play out. Maybe this is the penance he is destined to pay for his past, for what he did to the wrecked man sitting on the other side of the courtroom.

'Jimmy.'

It's Devyn, standing at his shoulder, asking something he didn't quite hear. He says, 'Could you get me something to drink?'

'More water?'

'I was thinking a highball.'

'Whoa. Who pulled your string?'

'You did good up there.'

'You mean I did *well*.'

'Just testing you. Now what were you asking me?'

Devyn leans down. 'See that guy sitting in the back row on the prosecution side?' she says. 'Got a brush cut? Wearing something like a military jacket?'

'I thought I wasn't supposed to look back there.'

'I'm giving you dispensation. Look over my shoulder.'

Jimmy glances and says, 'DonDon.'

'He's a Dulaney?'

'Yeah. You don't know him?'

'I've heard of him. Don't think I've met him.'

'He doesn't play hockey. Just Butch. Why do you ask?'

'Can you see that tattoo on his neck?'

'Not from here, but I know it. It's like a big eye. Creepy as hell.'

'Like a human eye?'

'Yeah. Like the ones in paintings that follow you around no matter where you move. Why?'

He's watching Devyn's gaze shift from DonDon to something or someone else in the gallery.

'I'm gonna go get some water,' she says. 'You want some?'

'Why?' he repeats. 'Why do you care about DonDon?'

'Nothing. Just curious.'

She's lying, Jimmy thinks.

FIFTY-THREE

'That was absolute unmitigated bullshit,' Chief Quarton says.
'What?' Harris says. 'The stuff about the sign?'
Quarton and the prosecutor are sitting at a small table in a conference room off the courtroom. Klimmek just walked in after using the restroom. 'Well, yes,' Quarton says, 'that stupid sign – it's gone now – but really the questions the defense attorney was asking. Jesus. I can't believe the judge let that go on for more than a second. We don't have a goddamn death penalty in this state.'
'I wouldn't worry too much,' Harris says. 'The judge told the jury to disregard it. They might even view it as a sign of desperation by the defense. It could work for us.'
Klimmek doubts that but doesn't bother saying so. He's still thinking about the look on Payne's face when she was asking him about the exact location of the murder. He'd seen that look before, unbowed and assured, from that very witness box. 'You said we have a problem?' he says.
'So,' Quarton says, folding his hands on the table. 'Our crack technical team, i.e. two part-time geeks with a lot of metal in their faces, has come up with something that, well, I don't want to say screws us, but—'
'Please, chief, allow me,' Harris says.
She explains. The prosecution has shown the jury several videos from the Loon, most prominently one that shows Jimmy Baker's truck pulling out of the woods across the road behind Diggs and Hardy. But the digit-heads, as Klimmek refers to them, have continued to work on enhancing the videos with whatever computer magic they can muster. Their latest sorcery appears to show something that until now has gone undetected.
'Are we sure?' Klimmek says.
'Pretty sure,' Quarton says. 'We've asked them to ratchet the focus a little closer.'
'But we really think they're headlights? From another vehicle?'
'Yes,' Harris says.
'Fuck,' Quarton says.

Klimmek ignores him. 'And they're coming out of the woods behind the Loon. How can you tell?'

'Apparently they're reflected in Baker's windshield.'

'Really?'

'Really.'

'Can I see it now?'

Harris shakes her head. 'We're not bringing that into this courtroom.'

Klimmek leans into the table toward Harris. 'So it's possible that someone else – not just Baker – followed Hardy and Diggs.'

'Possible.'

'But we don't know because—'

'Because Baker turned onto the road and we lost the reflection of the headlights in his windshield. If that's what it was.'

'Uh-huh. And we don't know whose headlights they were? No license plate visible in the reflection, right?'

'No. No clue.'

'Why didn't we notice this before?'

Quarton shrugs. 'We couldn't see what we couldn't see until the techs zeroed in. Besides, we had what we needed.'

Klimmek sits back. They all go quiet for a moment. Then he says, 'So what do we do? Don't we have to—?'

'Nothing,' Quarton says. 'We finish the case. We solve the crime. We put Baker in prison. We tell the world Bitterfrost is safe again. Hasn't this town been through enough hell?'

Klimmek stares across the table at his boss, but his boss keeps staring at his folded hands. Maybe he's thinking about that state police job he's supposedly up for.

Harris breaks the silence. 'I want you to hear me very clearly on this.' She looks first at Quarton, then at Klimmek. 'Do I have your attention?'

They nod.

'Good. I am extremely reluctant to go into court with a we-don't-really-know theory concocted by some youngster who couldn't investigate a shoplift. So we won't.'

'Agreed,' Quarton says.

'Neither of you will ever speak about this issue with our technical people. The conversation we're having now is protected by attorney-client privilege. But any discussions with those tech folks are not protected, and you and they would be required to discuss them in court, if asked.'

'If asked,' Klimmek says. This might be the most bizarre exchange he's ever had with a prosecutor and a police chief. He wishes he hadn't gone to the restroom because it's clear that Quarton and Harris decided how this meeting was going to go before he arrived. 'So,' he says, 'we're not going to tell the defense about this?'

'That's courtroom strategy, which is my purview, detective,' Harris says. She stands and flicks at an Apple watch on her left wrist. 'We need to get back in there. And by the way, detective, don't let Payne rattle you. She doesn't have a clue what Baker did that night.'

Klimmek stays in his chair as Quarton follows Harris out. He touches the Rosary beads in his pocket and starts to run through the possible implications of the reflection the digit-heads think they saw in Baker's windshield. There are too many to properly consider at this moment. He gets up and returns to the courtroom thinking, yet again, all we know is we have a dead body in the woods.

FIFTY-FOUR

Devyn scrambles down the wall of dead judges, squirming past folks rising for a break, blurting, 'Excuse me. Pardon me. Coming through.' All the while she watches the other side of the courtroom as her quarry exits through the double doors. Devyn hopes Shirlee Fawcett hasn't forgotten about their rendezvous.

She reaches the back of the gallery and slides to her right behind a cluster of people crowding into the corridor to the restrooms. Shirlee just slipped out through the double doors. People are giving Devyn looks, some sympathetic, some not. Wait for me, Shirlee, she thinks as she twists sideways to squeeze between the dry cleaner Figo and a woman she thinks is a cashier at Glen's.

'Miss Devyn,' Figo says in his Turkish accent, 'you are doing so beautifully.' She shoots him a smile while scanning the last row of the gallery.

She finds DonDon, coughing into one hand. The tattoo on the right side of his neck is indeed an open eye, no eyelashes, in flat blue ink, as unsettling as Jimmy described. DonDon coughs again and the eye swells for an instant on his leathery skin. Devyn has to look away. But she saw what she needed to see. Now she understands what the redhead at the dive near Mackinaw City was trying to tell her. It's not much, but it's something. She thinks of golf guy and wishes she could tell him there's no way she's giving up on Jimmy.

Outside she hurries down the courthouse steps as fast as she can without slipping and looks for the live oak near the public parking lot. The gigantic tree has stood for more than 120 years, defying the normal lifespan of its kin, and inspiring a nickname, the Sapling. That's where Shirlee proposed to meet when she and Devyn spoke on the phone last night. Devyn can't see her at first, but then she notices a head leaning out from behind the Sapling's five-foot-wide trunk. It's Shirlee, who said she hoped not to be seen with Devyn. 'I don't want nobody thinking I'm taking sides,' she said. 'I already get more than enough grief from these people.'

Half-running, Devyn makes a show of pulling out her keys as if she's going to her car. Shirlee slides back behind the oak. Devyn wonders if she's already been drinking. Probably, she decides. Maybe it's part of her mourning for Jordan. Maybe it's breakfast. Devyn slips around the tree and steps to where the trunk obscures the view from the courthouse.

'Shirlee,' she says. 'Thanks for coming.'

'Hello, honey.'

Shirlee wears a red woolen coat that reaches past her knees. It reminds Devyn of her mother going to Sunday Mass at St Henry's. It was a weekly ritual until her father died and Eleanor never returned. Devyn still attends now and then, solely because she likes the readings.

'That was a good show you put on there, yanking old Klimmek's chain pretty good,' Shirlee says. 'I used to work with his wife, you know, and old Kris, I can tell you, she would not appreciate it. She thinks Garth walks on water.'

'Thanks,' Devyn says. 'I don't want to keep you long.'

'No, you don't. Let me see here.'

She hefts a purse the size of an anvil off her shoulder and begins digging through it. She pulls out a chrome-colored booze flask as if it was nothing more than a tube of lipstick and plows into the bottom of the purse. After a few seconds, she comes out with a sheaf of papers she shoves at Devyn. 'Put 'em away fast, honey,' she says.

Devyn stuffs the papers in her suit jacket. She failed to grab her winter coat in her hurry to get out, and she's beginning to feel it. 'OK,' she says. 'These are Jordan's phone records?'

'It's what the company gave me after I badgered 'em for like two weeks. Calls and emails and everything. Finally had to sign some sheets of paper about ten times. It's like they don't want to help a customer, you know? Wait – hang on, I need to take this.'

Shirlee puts her phone to her ear and turns halfway away from Devyn. 'How are you, dear?' she says to her caller. She listens for half a minute, then says, 'Well, things wasn't looking too good for Mr Baker until his lawyer got hold of that detective and it seemed to turn around a little.' Shirlee listens again. Then, 'That's fine, honey, I got it. You call and I'll tell you what I can. I don't always understand all the legal mumbo-jumbo but . . . what's that? Anya, honey, you gotta speak up, my hearing's not so great.'

Anya? Devyn thinks. Could that be the woman Big Henry told her about? How many Anyas can there be in Bitterfrost? An Anya was in the Loon the night of the murders. Jimmy remembered her as the woman in the orange hood who seemed to get upset when he saw her the next morning at Big Henry's. Devyn tried to contact her, without luck, even cruised past the dilapidated house Henry directed her to.

'OK,' Shirlee is telling Anya, 'but I ain't gonna be in court no more today. Got chores at home, so maybe you ought to check in with somebody else . . . Yeah . . . OK . . . take care, honey.'

She turns back to Devyn. 'Piece of work there.'

'Name's Anya? She from around here?'

'Yeah, Anya, and yeah, she's got a house here, but she's holed up somewhere downstate so I been giving her updates.'

'Why is she interested?'

'I don't really know, though she was pretty shook up about Jordan. You'd have to ask her.'

'Were they friends?'

'She was Jordan's AA sponsor.'

Say what? 'Jordan was in recovery?'

Shirlee chuckles. 'Well, she was until she wasn't. Didn't take, if you know what I mean. Then Anya fell off the wagon too. One minute AA, next minute drinking buddies.'

'You don't know exactly where she is?'

'I kinda do. Why?'

'I'm still trying to figure out what happened to Jordan. Cops in Mackinaw don't really give a damn. Maybe this Anya could help.'

Shirlee shrugs. 'I don't know, but wait, lemme see.' She goes into her phone, scrolling with a forefinger. 'Here. Hamtramck. Smack in the middle of Detroit. Know it?'

'Not really.' As a girl playing for a Bitterfrost boys' squad, Devyn played in plenty of tournaments in and around Detroit. She's heard of Hamtramck, but never visited that she can recall. 'Do you mind giving me her number? I could text her copies of these phone records, maybe she could make some connections for us.'

Shirlee considers this. 'Probably I shouldn't be giving out her number, but I got an address. Had to forward some mail. You want that? You could write her, maybe she'll give you her number.'

Devyn's not about to write, but she says, 'Sure.'

Shirlee dives into her purse again and comes out with a scrap of napkin she hands to Devyn. 'I think that's it. Can you just put it in your phone?'

'Thanks,' Devyn says. She taps the address in and hands the napkin back to Shirlee. 'And thanks for the phone records, too.'

'You think this'll help figure out what happened to Jordan?'

'I hope so,' Devyn says. 'Again, I'm sorry about what happened.'

'No surprise, really. Except maybe that it didn't happen even quicker. OK, I'm gonna get lost.'

Devyn pinches her suitcoat shut and moves onto the nearby sidewalk, following it to the lot behind the courthouse. As she rounds a corner of the building, she feels the presence of someone behind her and turns to see. Standing half a dozen steps away is a woman with eyes so pale in their blueness that Devyn imagines she could see right through to the back of her brain.

'Excuse me?' Devyn says. She knows this woman but can't place her yet.

'Why were you looking at my father?' the woman says.

'Your father? Who's your father?'

Then it dawns on Devyn. Cat Dulaney. They had a few run-ins back in the day, on the rink and off. Her father, Devyn thinks, is DonDon, to whom she bears a passing resemblance.

'You were looking at him. In the courtroom.'

'I'm sorry,' Devyn says, not wanting to get into it with any Dulaney, let alone this one. 'I don't know what you mean.'

'You're lying.' Cat smiles blandly and gives her head a barely discernible shake. 'Why does your family want to destroy our family?'

'I don't want to destroy anyone.'

'Yes, you do.'

'I'm sorry, but I have to get back to work.'

Devyn turns and walks quickly to her car, where she glances over a shoulder and sees that Cat Dulaney appears to have gone.

In her car she turns the ignition, fires up the heat, and pulls out the papers Shirlee gave her. The upper right-hand corner of each page is marked with the Verizon logo. Jordan Fawcett's phone records for the last three days of her life show when calls and texts were sent and received, to and from which numbers. Devyn trails a forefinger down the side of the page displaying calls and texts to and from Jordan on the day she wound up in Mackinaw City. One number, area code 231, shows up again and again.

She starts to call the number but stops herself because she doesn't want her number showing up on the other end. She turns the car off and goes inside the courthouse, keeping an eye out for that odd Dulaney woman. She finds an unoccupied desk in a clerk's office and punches the 231 digits into a landline phone. The call goes directly to voicemail. 'Triple D here,' the gruff male voice says. 'Try later or go to hell.'

She doesn't recognize the voice but doesn't need to. She places the receiver in the cradle, her head spinning with questions. Why would Jordan be texting with this guy when, if Devyn's hunch is correct, she wanted to get away from him? Did she harbor a secret death wish, as an addict might? Or did she imagine she could convince him she wasn't the threat he thought she was? Foolish girl.

Devyn recalls the text Shirlee showed her when she first visited Jordan's mother three months ago. **If something bad happens, check my phone. Don't let them feed—** The rest was jibberish. Jibberish that made Devyn feel hopeless for Jordan. But Devyn now has taken Jordan's advice and discovered a disturbing possibility: Sometime on the last night of her life, Jordan found herself in that decrepit bar with somebody who calls himself Triple D. Hours later, she was dead in a dumpster. Triple D, with the tattoo of an eye on his neck, has to be DonDon Dulaney.

But why would DonDon Dulaney pursue Jordan to Mackinaw City on a winter night? To get drunk and laid? No. Jordan was Butch's squeeze, not DonDon's. Besides, the Dulaney boys never had to chase what they wanted. Then again, if they were under duress, if somebody knew something the Dulaneys didn't want them to know, or didn't want them to spread, they would act accordingly. Did whatever Jordan knew have anything to do with Diggs and Hardy? Devyn planned to find out. That was probably going to involve a quick trip downstate, to Hamtramck.

FIFTY-FIVE

'Kris,' Klimmek says.

'Yes,' his wife replies. 'Is chicken fine for dinner?'

Nothing is fine right now, Klimmek thinks, but he says, 'Sure.'

'Thighs OK?'

Klimmek doesn't hear her. From the office off the courtroom, he's listening to the clamor of people returning. 'I wish you were here.'

'I thought I was bad luck so I stayed away. Did things not go well? It's almost the weekend. You can forget the trial for two days.'

'I wish.'

'You have to work? I thought this was a done deal.'

'So did I.'

'What happened?'

Klimmek sighs. He doesn't really know, just like he didn't really know the last time a big case like this got away from him. At least that time, he was certain he was going after a bona fide murderer.

'How long till I can retire?' he says.

'You can retire tomorrow if you like,' Kris says. 'What happened?'

'Can't talk about it here. Tonight. Over chicken thighs.'

'I'm gonna come for the afternoon. Anyone good on the stand?'

'The Loon person. Ronnie Bergeron.'

'I'll be there.'

'Good.'

He recalls Quarton looking away when Klimmek suggested they might need to tell the defense lawyer about the reflection in Baker's windshield, how Harris bigfooted him with her courtroom strategy crap. He's back where he was with the claw-hammer case, except in reverse. Failing to convict a murderer isn't nearly as tragic as jailing an innocent man.

'We'll talk tonight,' Kris says. 'Whatever happened, it will pass.'

'You know,' he says, 'the thighs do have more flavor.'

The call over, Klimmek types a fresh text: Talk? But his fingers hover unmoving over the recipient window. He can't quite bring himself to fill it in with a name and hit send. Not yet.

FIFTY-SIX

Ronnie looks nice all dressed up. Jimmy always thought she did, even though in their short time together, she rarely wore anything fancier than jeans and a T-shirt. Once they went to her cousin's wedding in Bellaire and Ronnie wore a frost-white cotton dress with a wide sash of royal blue that showed off her curves. For a minute or two, Jimmy thought maybe this thing would work out better than he'd expected.

Now, sitting up straight in the witness box, she smooths her white button-down blouse as Harris plies her with questions about that night at the Loon. What did you serve the defendant? A single highball, Sprite with a shot-and-a-half of whiskey. Did you see anyone attempt to put anything in his drink? No. Did the defendant appear to grow angry with the behavior of Diggs and Hardy? Not at first. But eventually? Eventually he became perturbed, yes. But he was defending me.

She's answering too quickly, more hurried than the cadence Jimmy knows. She doesn't always look directly at the prosecutor as she answers. To Jimmy, she seems uncomfortable, which may not be surprising for someone testifying in the murder trial of a former lover and current friend. Jimmy tries to catch her gaze, but she either won't or can't acknowledge.

The defendant left the Loon before Diggs and Hardy, yes? Yes. And he was 'perturbed,' as you put it? Ronnie glances past Harris toward the gallery. I think so, she says, yes. Do you recognize the defendant's truck in the video we just showed you? Yes, that appears to be Jimmy's. Can you please, for the benefit of the jury, read aloud the text you received from the defendant at approximately two forty-two a.m. that night? Yes: **those two jagoff's won't be bothering you again.**

'Objection,' Devyn says. 'The prosecution hasn't established for a certainty that the text was sent by Mr Baker.'

'It came from his phone, your honor,' Harris says. 'His phone records, introduced as Exhibit 8B, indicate that.'

'I'll let it go for now,' Esper says. 'Proceed, Ms Harris.'

'Nothing further, your honor.'

Devyn slides Jimmy her legal pad, where she has scribbled a question about that two forty-two a.m. text: *Remember writing that?* She has asked him this many times already, and the answer remains the same: He can't recall writing it, but he can't be one-hundred-percent sure he didn't. Devyn knows there's something about it that bothers him, but he can't testify to it unless he wants to risk cross-examination. He shrugs. Devyn pulls her legal pad back.

'This is going to be fun,' she says.

She rises and walks to the lectern facing Judge Esper. 'Ms Bergeron,' she says. 'You and Mr Baker once had a relationship, is that so?'

'We still have a relationship. Jimmy and I are friends.'

'Still.'

'Yes.'

'I guess I meant a romantic relationship.'

'That was a while back.'

'How long a while?'

Ronnie fiddles with a bracelet on her left wrist. Stalling. 'I'd say at least five years ago. Maybe six or seven. Something like that.'

'And by "romantic," you mean you were seeing each other on a regular basis?'

'Pretty regular, yes.'

'And you were sleeping together?'

'Objection, irrelevant,' Harris says.

Devyn looks to the judge. 'I'm heading somewhere, your honor.'

'Hurry up,' Esper says.

'Thank you, your honor. Ms Bergeron, about how long did that romantic relationship last?'

Jimmy sees Ronnie's eyes dart toward him then flit away. 'Not all that long. Maybe six months. Maybe a little longer.'

'I see. But you got to know him pretty well, I imagine.'

'As much as anyone can know another person in six months.'

'Relationships can be complicated.' Devyn turns and looks past Jimmy toward the jury box. 'Ms Bergeron, were there things that, for lack of a better phrase, drove you crazy about Mr Baker?'

Jimmy stirs in his seat, wondering what Ronnie might say, how it might influence the people sitting in judgment of him. 'Maybe a couple of issues,' she says. 'Nothing too bad.'

'For example.'

'Sometimes,' she says, and stops, closes her eyes. 'Sometimes he had nightmares.' Devyn waits. Jimmy can tell Ronnie's trying not to cry. 'And he'd . . . he'd kinda strike out in the middle of the night, thrash around. One night I woke up and he was sitting up in bed, throwing punches in the air.'

'Ms Bergeron,' Devyn says, 'I'm sorry I have to ask you this, but did Mr Baker ever strike you, unintentionally or not?'

Ronnie blows out a sigh and pinches her eyes shut again. Jimmy swallows hard, remembering. Devyn slips a tissue from her pocket, walks to the witness box, and hands Ronnie the tissue. Harris is on her feet. 'This seems highly unnecessary, your honor. Counsel is upsetting the witness to no apparent purpose.'

'Ms Payne,' Judge Esper says. 'Get to it.'

'Ms Bergeron?'

'It's all right,' Ronnie says. She looks at Jimmy now, and he holds her gaze for a second, willing her a bit of courage. It's OK, he wants to say, even if it isn't. 'He almost hit me once. By accident. He didn't mean to, I don't think. It was like he was sleepwalking. He said he was sorry.'

'But he *almost* hit you, he didn't *actually* hit you, yes?'

Ronnie hesitates, looking into the gallery again. 'That's right.'

Jimmy recalls the dull bruise his punch left on her shoulder. Ronnie asked him to go sleep on the living-room sofa. It was the last night he ever spent at her apartment.

'Why do you think he had those nightmares?' Devyn says.

'Objection,' Harris says. 'Speculative.'

'Overruled.'

Ronnie says, 'I don't know. Probably just a side effect or something of, you know, all those hockey fights he was in.'

'Please tell the jury, Ms Bergeron, was Jimmy proud of those fights?'

'Again, your honor,' Harris says. 'Speculation. Hearsay.'

'The witness will answer.'

Jimmy resists the urge to see how Richards is responding. Ronnie shakes her head. 'No. He wasn't proud. Not at all. If anything, he was sad about them. Maybe even, like, embarrassed.'

Again Harris stands. 'What does any of this have to do with anything?'

'Your honor, the prosecution brought up my client's hockey fighting past at the prelim and has alluded to it at trial.'

'Proceed, counselor, though you are testing my patience.'

Devyn reaches into the lectern and produces a remote that controls a digital screen facing the jury. She points it and hits a button. The screen fills with a picture of the text Harris asked Ronnie about earlier. 'This is where I'm going, your honor,' Devyn says. 'Prosecution Exhibit 2C.'

She's walking a tightrope with the judge, and Jimmy loves her for it, although he isn't sure where this is going either. Devyn turns to Ronnie. 'Might another thing that drove you a little crazy be the fact that Mr Baker was quite picky about grammar?'

A hint of a smile tugs at one corner of Ronnie's mouth. 'Jimmy – Mr Baker – was definitely a grammar Nazi.'

'How so?'

'Oh, he had – still has – a million little, I called them, obsessions.'

'For instance.'

'Let's see. He hated – hates – the word "ain't." And the word "got," even though he uses it once in a while. He was always telling me to say "fewer" when I said "less." And punctuation – he'd get worked up about apostrophes. One time he pulled the car over to point out an apostrophe on a billboard that bugged him. He called it "offensive."'

Jimmy hears a titter ripple through the gallery. 'Ms Bergeron,' Devyn says, 'could you direct your attention to the screen to your left?' Ronnie turns. 'This is the text that the prosecution maintains Mr Baker sent to you at two forty-two a.m. the night Mr Diggs died. Please take a moment to review it.'

Ronnie looks. Jimmy rereads it again. 'Please tell the jury, Ms Bergeron, if there's anything about that text that gives you the slightest doubt that Mr Baker wrote it.'

Ronnie looks past Harris to the gallery for a third time. What, Devyn thinks, is so interesting back there? 'I haven't thought about this for a while,' she says. 'But . . .' She stops, clearly uncomfortable.

'But what?' Devyn says.

'There's no way Jimmy wrote that.'

'Why do you say that?'

'For one thing, he was an absolute maniac about using capital letters to start sentences. He's got –' she glances at Jimmy – 'I mean he *has* pretty big thumbs, though, and sometimes his phone didn't do what he wanted. And he'd tell the phone, as if it could hear him, "Do what I want to do, dammit, not what you want to do."'

'I see,' Devyn says. 'Anything else?'

'Oh, yeah,' she says, pointing at the screen. 'That apostrophe. The one on the word – can I say that word in here?'

'Go ahead.'

'The one on the word "jagoffs." As Jimmy lectured me a million times, that's –' she waggles her fingers in the air to signify quotation marks – 'incorrect use of an apostrophe to index – I mean indicate – a plural. People do it all the time, and it drove Jimmy bananas.'

'And he never, at least in your experience of his texts or emails or letters, ever used an apostrophe to signify a plural?'

'Never. Because I would've shoved it up – I would've thrown it in his face. He knew that.'

'Did you throw this apostrophe in his face?'

Ronnie takes a breath. 'I guess not. We didn't talk right away. And the text came so late, I actually was worried about Jimmy. He doesn't stay up that late. I thought maybe something was wrong.'

'Is it possible, though, that this improperly used apostrophe was due to the auto-correct function? Or auto-*in*correct? Could the phone have mistakenly inserted the apostrophe?'

'No.'

'Why do you say that?'

'Because Jimmy didn't trust auto-correct. He turned it off.'

Devyn walks back to the table and shuffles some papers, letting the jury digest that last string of testimony. She picks up a file, puts it back down, and addresses Ronnie. 'Thank you, Ms Bergeron.' Then to the judge. 'No further questions, your honor.'

'That last exchange took me back to Catholic school, diagramming sentences,' Esper says. 'Ms Harris, re-direct?'

To Jimmy, the prosecutor looks like she's doing her best not to scream. Harris stands but remains at her table, glaring at Ronnie. 'Ms Bergeron, you just testified that, in your opinion – I'd actually call it conjecture – the defendant couldn't have written that text about Mr Diggs and Mr Hardy not bothering you again, is that correct?'

'Yes.'

'But when we interviewed you about that night back in December, you did not tell us that the defendant couldn't have written that text, did you, Ms Bergeron?' Ronnie looks into her lap. Harris repeats, 'Did you?'

'No,' Ronnie says softly.

Harris says, 'Can you speak up, Ms Bergeron?'

'No,' Ronnie says, louder.

'On the contrary,' Harris says, 'you told us you had no reason to believe that anyone but the defendant had sent you that text, isn't that correct?' She holds up a sheaf of papers. 'I have a transcript here I can show you if that will refresh your memory.'

'You don't need to,' Ronnie says. 'I did say that. Back then.'

Jimmy looks back and forth between Ronnie and the prosecutor, thinking, what changed between then and now? He wants Harris to ask, but she apparently has accomplished what she wanted to accomplish, because she asks Judge Esper, 'Would this be a good time to break for the weekend?'

'One second,' Esper says. 'Ms Bergeron, are you saying you told the police one thing and now you're telling this court the exact opposite?'

Again, Ronnie balks before saying, 'Things change, Darlene.'

'Judge Esper in this room, Ms Bergeron. Sounds to me like you bull-shitted someone. Exactly what changed?'

Ronnie peers yet again into the gallery. Jimmy can't resist looking himself. He sees neighbors and Zelda Zealots and complete strangers. And DonDon Dulaney, glowering from the back row again.

'I guess I was afraid,' Ronnie says.

'Afraid of what?' Esper says. 'Afraid of the police?'

'Maybe. I'm not sure.'

'You're not sure. All right. You're excused, Ms Bergeron, at least for now. And Ms Harris, if you were attempting to impeach the witness, I believe you succeeded. The jury is duly advised.'

'Your honor,' Devyn says, standing.

'Sit down, Ms Payne. You had your chance. Are you agreeable to breaking for the weekend?'

'Fine.'

Esper lifts her gavel as Harris stands and interrupts.

'Your honor, may I approach?'

Esper waves the lawyers up. 'Your honor,' Harris says, 'the prosecution would like to add a witness who will testify first thing Monday.'

'Who *would* testify if I allow it, Ms Harris. Who is this surprise witness?'

'I wouldn't call it a surprise, your honor. We just weren't sure he would have the capacity to do it.'

'And?'

Devyn jumps in before Harris can speak. 'It has to be Cory Richards, right? I mean, he's been sitting here all week chomping at the bit.'

'He's the gentleman in the wheelchair?' Esper says.

'Yes, your honor. He had an encounter with the defendant some years ago that put him in that chair.'

'Objection, Ms Payne?'

'Absolutely. I fail to see what this witness can tell us about what did or didn't happen on the night of the alleged murder.'

Harris leans into the bench. 'We believe the witness can illuminate for the jury the defendant's capacity for extreme violence.'

'Ms Payne, you did bring up hockey fights. On the other hand, it is a bit late for this, don't you think?'

'Perhaps, but as I said, Mr Richards—'

'Are you confident he can handle testimony? And cross?'

'I am.'

'Please,' Devyn says, 'your honor—'

'Overruled. I'm inclined to hear what the witness has to say. If I think it's immaterial or beyond the pale, I will so instruct the jury.'

'Your honor, I can't help but wonder if the presence of such a witness in this case might prompt an appellate court to toss out the verdict.'

Esper lets her reading glasses drop from her nose, her eyes lit with pique. 'Are you anticipating a guilty verdict then, Ms Payne? Or more to the point, are you threatening me?'

'No on both, your honor.'

'Glad to hear that.' She slams her gavel down, the crack reverberating in Devyn's ears. 'Ten a.m. Monday.'

The jury files out. Devyn gathers papers and legal pads into her briefcase. Two uniformed deputies approach. Jimmy leans close to Devyn and whispers, 'You can't stop Richards?'

'Apparently not.'

'All right,' Jimmy says. 'But can I just ask?'

'Ask what?'

'Why did you *have* to ask about me hitting Ronnie?'

'Why?'

'What if she said yes?'

'She didn't. The jury needed to hear that.'

'Why?'

'You're a damaged person, Jimmy. That doesn't mean you're a murderer. It means you're human.'

'What in the hell does that even mean?'

She clicks her briefcase shut. 'It means you're lucky to have me as your lawyer. Which reminds me: your brother left me a message. He couldn't make the trial because of work. But he requested a visit this weekend. So you might see him at the jail. That would be good, yes?'

'That would be good.'

'OK. I will try to stop over this weekend, if they'll let me.'

'All right,' Jimmy says. But he has that gnawing feeling, again, that Devyn isn't telling him the whole truth.

FIFTY-SEVEN

Klimmek locks the door on the office where he's been watching the trial on closed-circuit TV. He doesn't want Quarton or Harris barging in. He doesn't want to see or hear from either of them.

He sits on the desk. Court has adjourned until Monday. Klimmek knows he's in for three sleepless nights. Yes, barmaid Ronnie told the cops what they wanted to hear back when. He didn't doubt her then – he had no reason to – but what she said today has the sickening ring of truth. And if Jimmy didn't write that text, who did? Presumably, someone with access to his phone. Hardy? Diggs? No. Someone else. Maybe someone whose headlamps were reflected in Baker's windshield.

He picks up his phone. His wife, who was in the courtroom, answers immediately. 'Kris,' he says. 'Can you talk?'

'Just got to my car.'

'Do you think she lied to us?'

'The bartender?'

'Yes. Ronnie Bergeron. You made it in time to see her?'

'For the last part of it. I didn't see you.'

'I was watching on TV in the back.'

'Well, on balance, I'd say yes, the bartender lied to you.'

'Why would she do that?'

'She said she was afraid of something.'

'I was listening too, Kris.'

'You know what happens, Garth. People will lie to cops. They don't expect to get called on it. It's different in court. The judge, the gallery. Perjury and all that.'

This is precisely why Klimmek locked the door and called his wife of thirty-two years. She has an acute sense of what is right and what is wrong, and she isn't afraid to say so.

'OK,' he says. 'I'll be home by six.'

He starts the same text he abandoned earlier that day, then thinks better of it. No need for a digital record. What the heck did he do with that business card? He thinks. Remembers. Back in December, he forgot the card was in his pants pocket and it went through the wash. Somehow it survived and Klimmek folded the tattered remainder into his bulging wallet.

Now he digs it out and dials the 616 number. He hears three rings, then a series of clicks and a long high-pitched beep. He pictures a boxy gadget sitting on her kitchen counter, plugged into the wall along with a toaster oven. A recording of her voice comes on: 'This is Devyn's home line. Leave a message.'

Klimmek waits. After another beep, he says, 'Find me. Don't forget the doughnuts with sprinkles.'

FIFTY-EIGHT

The real estate agent Devyn met on Tinder wolfs the Salisbury steak with mashed potatoes and peas. 'Classic,' he tells Devyn. 'My dad used to get this at a place called Redford Inn when we lived near Detroit. Just six ninety-nine back in the day, can you believe it?'

The potatoes and peas are gone and the steak nearly so by the time Devyn manages her way through all the small talk to what she came for. She has barely touched her chicken Caesar salad. She's feeling the two vodka-tonics she shouldn't have had. Schmatta makes a heavy cocktail, like just about everything in Schmatta's Fine Dining. The heavy wooden doors. The heavy wooden chairs and tables. The curtains that inexplicably block the view of the Jako flowing past outside. Even the host herself.

Schmatta isn't her name, first or last, but a nickname she insists she doesn't know the origin of. It's what people have called her since she opened the place thirty years ago. Tinder guy – his name is Kurt – really does look like his online photo, forties, lean and angular, soft green eyes, with neatly coiffed salt-and-pepper hair and matching stubble. He's wearing the up-north-business-dude quarter-zip with a Grandview Golf Club logo stitched over the left breast. Like most guys Devyn has dated, Kurt is happy to talk about himself. Which, on this evening, is fine, because of what she wants. They've discussed winter and snowmobiling and summer and water skiing and the best places to eat in Traverse City. Devyn wants to get down to business when he asks what she does with her hair.

'You don't think that's a little intrusive?' she says.

Kurt, half-smiling, says, 'Point taken. Whatever you do, I like it. Makes you look mature.'

'Mature? Seriously?'

'It's a compliment. Come on. Honest.'

He owes her one now. 'Actually, I don't do anything with my hair,' Devyn says. 'But what about you? Do you just buy and sell, or do you also develop?'

'All of the above,' Kurt says. He's separating a last scrap of meat from a blob of fat. 'Developing is the most fun because, you know, you feel like you're creating something, maybe growing something that'll be good for the community at large.'

'Like that strip club in Alden somebody tried to expand?'

Kurt laughs. 'Wasn't me, promise.'

'You can make more money developing, right?'

'Generally, yeah. You take more risk if you're putting your own money into a project, but the risk-reward is higher. What about you?'

'What about me?'

He shoves his plate aside and pulls his glass of red closer. The way his head tilts toward the glass makes Devyn wonder if he ever wears a baseball cap backwards. She hopes not.

'I don't know much about lawyers,' he says, 'except the ones who handle real estate, but from afar it looks like you're in a high risk-reward situation yourself with that Zamboni guy.'

'Certainly high risk. Not sure about the reward.'

'Zamboni drivers probably aren't millionaires.'

'Barely hundred-aires. But, speaking of hockey, I wanted to ask about a text you sent a while back about the Bitterfrost rink. I didn't know if you were joking, but you mentioned something about it being sold?'

'Do they have a go-to dessert here?'

Dammit, she thinks. 'The coconut cream pie.'

'Done.'

'What about the rink?'

Now Schmatta appears at Devyn's side. 'Everything OK here?'

'Everything is excellent,' Kurt says. He stands. 'May I have a slice of the coconut cream?'

'Yessir.'

Kurt excuses himself. Schmatta waits as he walks to the men's room. Then she leans down to Devyn. 'Heads up,' she says. 'There's a couple that's gonna be here –' she glances at her watch – 'any minute. You'll recognize them. Just didn't want you to be surprised.'

'What couple?'

Schmatta whispers in Devyn's ear.

'Great,' Devyn says. 'You want me outta here?'

'No. I'll pick 'em off at the door and shuffle 'em to the back.'

'Appreciate it.'

Schmatta leaves as Kurt returns. 'Sorry,' he says. 'Where were we?'

'The rink,' Devyn says. 'You said something about it being for sale?'

'Wait one second. What the hell is up with the IceKings? What is it, eight losses in a row? Nine? I mean, after the Red Wings, they're my team. Is all this drama with the Zamboni dude messing with their heads?'

She tells herself not to be annoyed. 'Hockey players don't give much thought to the Zam driver,' she says. 'They're just not playing well.'

'I was just thinking—'

'Have you ever played hockey?'

'When I was like six, yeah. But—'

'Then shut up, OK?'

She smiles her best smile to let him know she's kidding, a little. Kurt leans back and puts on his own semi-embarrassed smile as Schmatta sets his pie down. 'Jeez, sorry,' he says. 'I was just going to—'

'No, that was a little harsh. It's true that most players don't think about the Zam driver, unless he screws up the ice.' Devyn shows him another smile. Kurt is actually OK. She might even see him again. 'How's your pie?'

'Fabulous.'

'Good. So, the rink. Did you say somebody wants to sell it? Or buy it? I didn't quite understand.'

'That text. Forgot about that. One of my partners got a call out of nowhere from some lawyer inquiring about the property.'

'The rink property.'

'Yeah.' He scoops up a forkful of pie. 'Where the river meets the lake. Sweetest property in Bitterfrost, along with the church across the creek. And like I said, I'm a fan of the team, so I knew your family owned it.'

'Is something going on with it? Why did he call you guys?'

'I don't really know. Somebody must be taking a look. Sometimes people call us because we're one of the only groups that branches out much beyond TC.'

'Uh-huh.'

'It doesn't seem like a property anyone would be eager to unload. But then, you know, it's a matter of how much money does it take to turn someone's head?'

Evan's head, in this case. It would also have to be enough to get their mother's attention, because she controls the trust that oversees the IceKings and the real estate. Could she be swayed by a monster offer? Only if she could find another site that would suit the team's needs. Devyn can't imagine her parting with the team. Evan knows that, though, so what is he doing?

'Do you happen to know who's inquiring?' she says.

'About the property? Not off the top of my head.' He smiles while swiping whipped cream from a corner of his mouth. 'Why are you so interested?'

'It's been my second home for most of my life.'

'Right. I'll text my guy after dinner.'

'I won't be offended if you text him right now.'

'Well, I don't like to monkey with the phone when I'm with someone nice, but with your permission . . .'

While he taps on his phone, Devyn sees Schmatta ushering a woman and a man past the bar. She averts her eyes. Too late. The couple stops and the man peels away toward Devyn. He's chubby, in his sixties, wiry gray hair askew, winter coat unbuttoned. Devyn saw him outside the courthouse earlier, gesturing vigorously as he spoke with Philip Hardy. She thought maybe the two were arguing.

'Melvin,' the man's wife calls out from where she's standing with Schmatta.

He arrives at the table and says, 'Ms Payne.'

Kurt looks up from his phone.

'Evening, Mr Diggs,' Devyn tells the father of Aaron Diggs. She doesn't know what else to say. The less the better.

'Are you not enjoying your salad?' he says. 'You haven't eaten much. Our friend Miss Schmatta will be disappointed.'

'The salad's fine. I guess I'm just not that hungry.'

'You save your hunger for the courtroom, don't you, Ms Payne? Or perhaps you're having trouble eating these days. Sleeping, too, I'd wager.'

Kurt starts to get out of his chair but Devyn waves him down. 'I'm sorry, Mr Diggs,' she says. 'I don't think this is the time or the place.'

Diggs's lower lip is trembling now, his cheeks flushing red. 'What exactly is the time or the place for you to tell me – tell us – why you would defend the murderer of our son? Please let me know, Ms Payne, so we can be there when it's convenient for you.'

Schmatta takes him gently by a shoulder. 'Please, Mr Diggs,' she says. Diggs glares at Devyn as he turns to go. Schmatta has her arm around him, apologizing, telling him dinner is on the house.

'Boy,' Kurt says. 'I don't envy you.'

'Occupational hazard. Guess we shouldn't have come here.'

'Next time, Petoskey. Or Charlevoix.'

'I'd like that. After the trial maybe.'

'For sure.' He holds up his phone. 'My guy got back to me.'

'Good. What'd he say?'

He turns the phone back to himself and squints. 'Says he got an informal query from an attorney for a company called something like Bad Boys.'

'Bad Boys?'

'He's double-checking.' Kurt takes another bite of pie. 'You want some of this?'

'No, thanks.'

'Ah, here we are. The attorney is a TC guy named Volk. Can't say as I know him.'

'I've seen him,' Devyn says, without saying where. She asked around; Volk may well have been the tall man with the topcoat hurrying out of the courthouse at Jimmy's prelim. She guessed then that he had a client with an interest in the case. She's more sure now.

'He's repping this – Bad Company – wait, it's actually, B-A-A-D with two As – actually, three – plus an "ass."'

'Plus an "ass?"'

Kurt chuckles. 'Sorry. To be precise, it's BAADAss Boys LLC.'

'I don't know it.'

'They're probably in the state database. I have the app. Want me to check?'

Devyn wonders if maybe she's given Kurt a more interesting night than he expected. 'If you don't mind,' she says.

'Not at all.'

As he returns to his phone, she reaches for his fork and scoops up some pie, smiling. 'All right,' he says. 'BAADAss Boys, all right. The attorney is one Erik Volk of Volk & Castellini in Traverse. I actually know Castellini a little from the golf course. Kind of a clown but the guy gets a lot of business.'

'What about Volk?'

'Don't know much except he'll represent just about anybody with a pulse and a checkbook. Conscience not a requirement.'

'Hang on a sec,' Devyn says, going to her own phone. She searches 'Erik Volk' and a picture pops up on LinkedIn. It is indeed the topcoat guy from the prelim. 'And what's that say about the company?'

'Let's see. They do list a principal here in lovely Bitterfrost.' He stretches the phone across to Devyn. 'Know him?'

She looks.

'You OK?' he says.

'Yeah. Fine. Thanks.'

'Sure?'

'Yes,' she says, 'but, you know, I just remembered something. I really should get the bill and, you know, get going.'

'I hope it wasn't something I said.'

'No, not at all. It's been a fun night.'

'It's been a night, for sure. Next time, not Bitterfrost.'

Outside, he gives her half a hug and a peck on the cheek. She tells him to stay in touch, meaning it, but she can't get to her car fast enough. She's pulling out of Schmatta's lot when she notices something stuck in one of her wiper blades. She stops the car and snatches an envelope from the windshield. Inside is a birthday card for an eight-year-old. The numeral is embossed on the trunk of a blue elephant dancing in a pink tutu. Whoever left the card used a green felt pen to add a three to the eight, for thirty-eight, the birthday Devyn will mark in four days. She opens the card. The canned message inside is written over in the same green:

have a good one

IF YOU MAKE IT

FIFTY-NINE

Klimmek's coffee is cold. He hasn't picked up the foam cup since bringing it into the evidence room an hour ago. He's alone with a video tape and an audio recording. Watching and listening, again and again.

He concluded half an hour ago that, yes, those are headlamps reflected in Jimmy Baker's windshield, and yes, those headlamps could be on a vehicle that trailed Baker as he followed Diggs and Hardy in their SUV. That settled in Klimmek's mind, he's now focused on the security video from inside the Lost Loon.

He'd made a note to check, as Butch Dulaney suggested, the expression on Baker's face while dealing with Hardy and Diggs. Frontal views are few but, as Butch suggested, Baker's face indeed takes on a distinct tension as his encounter with the two appears to escalate. He's clearly unhappy with the younger men, as is Ronnie. But Klimmek has also watched a dozen or so YouTube videos of Baker's minor-league hockey fights, and the look on his face in those conflagrations seems, at least to Klimmek, less inhibited – almost numb, in a way – than the one he sees on the Loon video. Maybe he's missing something. It's possible Baker hadn't yet reached peak rage while he was still in the bar. There's no way to know. But it doesn't really matter because Klimmek's focus now is not on Jimmy but Butch Dulaney.

It's just a brief shot, no more than a second or two. Klimmek didn't notice it before, probably because he was so invested in proving the Baker charges. As Butch walks away from Baker and Ronnie and Hardy and Diggs, he glances over his shoulder. Directly at the camera. The more Klimmek studies it, the more he becomes convinced that Butch's peek wasn't on a whim, like he wanted to check the Red Wings score. Butch knew the camera was there. He knew where all the cameras at the Loon were. He wanted to know what they might be collecting.

Klimmek's cell chimes. It's a text from his wife: **D left Schmatta two mins ago.**

Klimmek responds: **Thanks. Airtag in place?**

Kris: **Guess so**
Klimmek: **I'll follow from here.**

He grins. Kris learned how to attach tracking devices to cars when their son was in his goofball years. As today's court session was coming to a close, Klimmek texted her to please leave early and tag Devyn Payne's car – a Toyota Camry, license plate PAYNER – in the courthouse lot. Luckily, she didn't ask whether she really ought to be part of whatever he was doing. She just did it.

He'll have to leave soon. But one more thing.

He slides his headphones onto his ears and queues the audio from the chat he had on Butch's pig farm three months ago. He has narrowed it to a fifteen-second patch near the end. Butch is griping about the Payne family's influence in Bitterfrost. Klimmek let that little rant distract him and he missed something he dearly wishes he hadn't.

He listens again as Butch asks if the police are really going to put Jimmy Baker in prison. An animal grumbles in the background – a pig, definitely a pig, not a dog. 'We're going to try,' Klimmek tells Butch. Butch then suggests that the Paynes are probably pressuring the chief to let Baker go. 'Hell,' Butch says, 'two down and whatshername pays to put a cold-blooded killer back on the street.'

Klimmek replays that sentence again. Then again. Then once more. He wants to be sure he's hearing now what slipped past him before. He shuts the audio off, removes his headphones, and heads out to the parking lot. He has an appointment with Devyn Payne she doesn't know about yet.

SIXTY

A*very,* Jimmy writes in pencil on a yellow pad.

Nothing else comes. He doesn't know what to write anymore. He has asked in each of his previous eleven letters about her volleyball season, her cello classes, her dates (if any), her thinking about possible college destinations. He knows nothing new because Avery hasn't responded. Jimmy can't even be sure his letters reached her. He can imagine Noelle intercepting them and stuffing them into a drawer. Or a shredder. He would like to blame his ex-wife, would like to hate her for keeping him from Avery, but he can't. She lived with his violence for too long. Not physical violence. He never came close to that. But the violence that clung to him like a shadow, the anger that helped him do his job and followed him around as he and Noelle confronted the whirl of fallout – legal, financial, emotional – from the Richards incident.

'Bakes.' The deputy on night duty is at Jimmy's cell door. He was once Jimmy's teammate on the IceKings. Not the smoothest skater but always game to scrap for the puck in the corners. 'Lights out.'

'Got it,' Jimmy says. 'Kings don't play till Sunday, right?'

'Monday.'

'I lose track of time in here.'

'You and me both.'

'They've lost what, eight in a row?'

'Eight of nine. Lost tonight to those Waterloo scrubs. Doubt they're making the play-offs.'

'That would be the first time in, jeez, more than a decade.'

'Yeah. Bums have cost me a pile of cash.' His grin is sheepish. 'But I'm hoping you're gonna bail me out.'

'What's that supposed to mean?'

The jailer's name is Johnson but everyone calls him Hoover, a nickname he'd rather not have earned. He lost his shit once during an IceKings game and invited the entire opposing bench to fight. 'I'll fight you all,' he yelled as two refs tried to restrain him. Someone on the bench shouted, 'Blow me,' and Johnson exploded, 'I'll blow you all.' Not his smartest moment. One ref laughed so hard that he slipped and fell, breaking a wrist. Johnson, aka Hoover, took an early shower.

'You think the trial's gonna be over Monday?'

'Ask my lawyer. Why?'

'I'm in an over-under pool. Took the under. Need the thing to be over by three p.m. Monday.'

'Why'd you take the under?'

Hoover folds his hands behind his back. 'I don't know. Guess I figured your lawyer ain't got much to say.'

Perhaps true, Jimmy thinks. 'Doesn't *have* too much to say, Hoove.'

'Huh?'

'Who's running the pool?'

'You know Charlie J? Works security at the pig farm.'

'For the Dulaneys?'

'Yep. He's got – I mean, he *has* – about six hundred bucks in the pot.'

'The Dulaneys are betting on my trial?'

'Just how long it lasts. They were gonna do a wager on whether you're guilty or not but nobody would take . . . uh, you know.'

'Thanks, Hoove. I'll do what I can to move things along.'

'Appreciate that. And by the way, you got a visitor coming tomorrow. Nine thirty.'

'I know.' Brother Alex. 'But I thought it was Sunday.'

Hoover considers this, then smiles like he knows something Jimmy does not. 'Nope,' he says. 'A little surprise.'

'Wait. What?'

The cell goes dark. Jimmy listens to Hoover's receding footsteps, a door opening then slamming shut. He waits for his eyes to adjust. Then he sits down and finishes his letter to Avery: *I love you, honey.*

SIXTY-ONE

The map Big Henry drew is smudged. Devyn snaps on the overhead light and squints, then lifts her eyes to look out the windshield.

The house is tiny. Probably not even a two-bedroom. Had to have been built in the 1950s, maybe earlier. Plankboard walls and a crumbling concrete porch. Cardboard covers a window next to the front door. The roof sags on one side, as if it might slide off at any minute. A satellite dish barely clings to the roof, wires dangling. A swing set sits next to the house, chains swaying and clicking in the night breeze. A pickup truck leans back on its bare rear axle in the backyard, where dead weeds poke up through the snow.

The house sits in a tight clearing ringed with pine and brush dusted with snow. Devyn would prefer not to go inside. She steps onto the porch. A board creaks, the only sound besides a low whistle of wind. Three miles south-east of Bitterfrost proper, without another building in sight, the place strikes Devyn as lonely, even desperate, like so many post-World-War-II homes crouching outside little northern Michigan towns, battered remnants of families battered by petty scraps and jealousies and too much of everything bad for you. She expects that if she did go in, she would smell cigarette smoke and alcohol and see emptied milk cartons and barbecue potato chip bags scattered on the floor.

She circles the property once, snapping photos. As she's circling through the back yard, she notices a pair of headlights on the road in front of the house. She leans into a shadow along the house and peers around a corner. A Bronco. Klimmek? The vehicle putters along for a hundred yards or so, then speeds on.

Back on the front porch, she grasps the knob of the outer door. It swings open. The inner door, a slab of dark wood peeling white paint, is locked. She shoves first, then tugs. It doesn't budge. She tries to peek around the yellowed newspapers duct-taped inside the window box, but it's too dark inside to see anything. She knocks four times and hears nothing but the wind. She didn't expect anyone to be there; she just wanted to see the place and size up the surrounding area.

Her phone dings in her pocket. She wants to look, in case it's what she's been waiting for, but she bobbles the phone and it bounces on the porch just as a wash of light spills across her feet. She turns and sees auto headlamps blink off. An image of that threatening birthday card flashes in her head. She snatches up her phone, feeling an urge to run.

The Bronco door opens and Klimmek steps out. Devyn starts to relax, then stops herself. Is the detective here to arrest her for something? Like maybe trespassing? Maybe not, she decides, recalling the message he left on her answering machine. She picked it up when she stopped to change before dinner with Kurt. The detective said he wanted to talk. About what, Devyn can't quite imagine. He walks to the bottom of the porch steps. Devyn says, 'You scared the shit out of me.'

'If I were sneaking up on you, I wouldn't have left my lights on. Anyway, you were supposed to find me. And bring doughnuts.'

Devyn isn't accustomed to Klimmek joking around. 'Sorry, no doughnuts tonight. I've been busy.'

'Looks like.'

'How did you find me?'

'I'm a cop.'

Bullshit, Devyn thinks. She'll need to check for a tracking device on her car. 'Why did you bother?' she says.

'I want to get it right this time. I suspect you do too.'

She looks past him to a thin stand of skeletal trees, a field spreading beyond it. 'Not sure what you're talking about,' she says, lying only a little.

He points at the porch steps. 'Do you mind?'

'Fine.'

He comes up. 'Obviously,' he says, 'we were never here.'

'Obviously.'

'You need to know something.'

He tells her straight out about the reflection of the headlamps in Jimmy's windshield that night outside the Loon, how it might be nothing, maybe the techs have it wrong, but he thinks it could be important. He doesn't say out loud that the prosecutor wants to keep it to herself, but Devyn understands. 'Why are you telling me this?' she says.

'Let's just leave it as is.'

'As it happens, one of the only things Jimmy remembers from that night – or thinks he remembers – is that other set of headlights.'

'News to me.'

'I didn't know how to get it into evidence without Jimmy testifying, and Jimmy testifying would probably be a disaster. Might as well just plead it out and hope he gets a shot at parole in twenty years.'

'Why would you drive out to this dump at this hour?'

'Not going there.'

'Come on. I could lose my badge for telling you what I just told you.'

'And I could be disbarred.'

That might not be true, technically, but Devyn needs the leverage. She has somewhere to get before Klimmek figures it out.

'Then I have to assume you're here to find someone who might know something that would help your man. I, too, would be interested in talking to that person. I guess I can look up the address easily enough.'

'And you'll learn the landlord is some faraway real estate company that isn't gonna tell you squat.'

'Why don't you want to deal?' Klimmek says. 'What do you have to lose? Monday morning we're gonna put that gentleman in the wheelchair on the stand and he's gonna tell the jury your client was one-hundred-percent capable of killing those young men. And the jury's going to agree.'

She stares past the trees to the field. It appears there's an opening at the far end, big enough for a vehicle. A shiver runs through her, and she marks the place on the map in her mind. 'Do what you have to do, detective. If you can live with it.'

'You'll have to live with it, too, counselor.'

'I'm not the one who screwed up with Sawtell, detective. That was you and your people.'

'Congratulations. You put a vicious killer back on the street. And your fellow barristers gave you a prize. Did you put it on your mantle?'

'I don't have a mantle. But while we're talking about prizes, let me ask you, do you know anything about what happened to Jordan Fawcett?'

'I know she met an ugly end, but that's pretty far out of my jurisdiction.'

'I think I know what happened.'

'Have you told the police in Mackinaw?'

'They don't care.'

'Why does Jordan Fawcett matter all of a sudden?'

'It's not all of a sudden to me. How about the guy who was just found dead in the same dumpster where the Mackinaw mopes found Jordan?'

'I'm not aware.'

'Jesus, detective. You can't see past your own headlights, can you?' She reaches into her jacket for the birthday card she found on her windshield. She hands it to Klimmek. 'This wasn't you, was it?'

He takes a look, reads the inside, shakes his head. 'I'm sorry to see that.' He hands the card back. 'We can get you some protection if you like.'

'Jordan needed protection,' Devyn says. 'I don't need protection. I need you to stop tailing me.'

'Are we going to talk again?'

She nods. 'Chance of that.'

SIXTY-TWO

Klimmek is pulling into his driveway when the return call comes.

'Garth,' the caller says. 'Been a while.'

'Tommy,' Klimmek says. 'How 'bout those Spartans?'

Klimmek and 'Tommy' – Mackinaw City Police Chief James Thomsen – studied criminal justice together and quaffed many pitchers of beer at Michigan State. 'Like clockwork, Izzo's got 'em going just in time for the hoops tournament,' Thomsen says.

'Let's hope. Sorry to bother you so late.'

'No problem, brother. Whatdya got?'

Klimmek tells his old friend he's interested in two possibly unrelated Mackinaw City murders that bear one eerie similarity. He wishes he'd pushed his own chief to look harder at the Fawcett killing, but Quarton wanted the 'big fish.' He felt a little naked earlier when Devyn Payne brought up Fawcett and then the unnamed man who wound up in the same dumpster. Payne knows more than she's telling. It's starting to make Klimmek nervous.

'We've gotten pretty much nowhere on Fawcett,' Thomsen says. 'We know she was last seen at a dive in the woods near here, but everyone who was there that night suddenly got amnesia. Seems like she was headed for a nasty end regardless.'

'What about the other? Is there a connection?'

'Same damn dumpster. Not sure yet about a connection, but something's not right. The guy had no wallet, no ID, no phone. But he was wearing a Coast Guard badge.'

'He was Coast Guard?'

'Maybe, maybe not.' Klimmek hears a door close in the background. Thomsen says, 'Between us, for now?'

'Sure.'

'For some reason, the feds are interested.'

'FBI?'

'DEA. And the actual Coast Guard.'

'Why?'

'They won't say.'

'You have a name of the victim?'

'They might but they haven't shared it with us.'

'The guy have a car?'

Klimmek's wife steps out of the front door of their house and folds her arms in the porch light. He waves and points at his phone. 'Possibly,' Thomsen says. 'State Police found an Audi abandoned off Wendell Road. Traced it to a leasing company downstate.'

'That road's not too far from where I am.'

'Maybe he was headed there.'

'Bitterfrost?'

'You got a hockey rink, right?'

'Yep.'

'The lieutenant I talked with said the rink address was in the car's navigation system.'

'Maybe the guy was a hockey fan.'

'If so, he missed the game.'

'How did he die?'

'Serious head trauma,' Thomsen says. 'Looked like maybe a baseball bat, or something like it.'

Klimmek recalls Aaron Diggs splayed in that clearing, the cavernous dents in his head. 'Good to know,' he says. 'Did these agents ask about Jordan Fawcett?'

'They don't care about her.'

Nobody cares about her, Klimmek thinks. Except Devyn.

'What about Jimmy Baker? They ask about him?'

'The guy on trial? Nah.'

'OK. Listen, Tommy, thanks. We gotta get a beer one of these days.'

'Anytime. Go Green.'

'Go White.'

Klimmek sits in the darkness, thinking. He's investigating a double murder upon which he and his superiors have already rendered a definitive judgment that could send a man to prison for most if not all of his life. But what he's doing now could shred his own case. He's toiling for the opposition, spying for the enemy, clerking for Devyn Payne. The last thought almost makes him laugh. She knows more than he does, including things he probably should have known – no, *definitely* should have known. He's trying to catch up. He could be disciplined, he could be fired, he could be humiliated. If Quarton was peeking over his shoulder, Klimmek would no longer have a badge. But Quarton is sleeping somewhere, probably dreaming of state police headquarters. And Klimmek is doing what he set out to do when he was attending his first classes at the academy: put bad guys in jail. He has accomplished that many, many times. He failed with Sawtell. And he will fail again if he doesn't keep doing what he's doing now, as bizarre as it seems.

He gets out of the Bronco. Kris calls to him from the porch, 'You've been out here a while. Everything all right?'

'No,' he says. 'Everything is totally messed up.'

SIXTY-THREE

Devyn parks behind the rink where nobody following her can see unless she sees them first. She feels around in the usual places for air tags: bumpers, grilles, wheel wells. She finds the one Klimmek or his flunkie left inside the right rear wheel well. She decides to leave it so Klimmek doesn't know she's the wiser. At least not yet.

Evan is in his office, a boot propped against his desk. He's watching videotape of the IceKings' latest loss, 4–1 to a bottom-feeder squad from Iowa. Devyn heard about it on the car radio. The announcer actually said the team 'looked like dogshit,' with the S-word bleeped out. It made Devyn laugh. Evan is probably not in a laughing mood.

'Can you believe this fucking target?' Evan says without turning. He's talking about the IceKings' starting goaltender. 'Stick's off the ice, legs open as a sorority chick, and he comes off the pipe, lets in a shot that wouldn't register on a sundial.' Devyn watches the replay of a fluttering shot that wobbles between the goalie's legs as the goal light flashes behind the net. 'But this hotshot fully expects – fully fucking *expects* – to be drafted this year by an actual National Hockey League team.' Evan swings his foot off the desk and points at a chair across from his desk. 'He sat right there the other day and asked me if I thought he might sneak into an early round.'

'What'd you tell him?'

'I told him he ought to take up fucking pickleball.'

'No, you didn't.'

'I should have.'

'Or maybe you should have told him you're trying to sell the rink.'

Evan's jaw momentarily goes slack, then he straightens in his swivel chair and smooths his pullover before answering. Smoothing is one of his tells. 'I don't . . . what exactly are you talking about?'

'Leave the pullover alone and tell me that.'

'Have we been drinking tonight, Dev? Fun-and-tonics? Or just beers? Sneak some into the jail for Jimbo?'

'In fact, I had two vodka-tonics with a real estate guy who said you're sneaking around trying to sell the property.'

'What real estate guy?'

'You wouldn't know him.' She sits on Evan's desk, peering down at her brother. 'Tell me this, Ev: why did you kill off Zelda?'

'What real estate guy?'

'Do you think it's a coincidence that the team has played like shit since Zelda and Jimmy disappeared?'

'Jimmy was Zelda, Zelda was Jimmy,' Evan says. 'We can't be celebrating a murderer.'

'Alleged murderer.'

'We can't be celebrating an alleged murderer.'

'Especially if you're trying to pump up the value of the – what do you call it? – the *franchise* for a sale, right?'

Evan says nothing for a good three seconds. Confirmation enough for Devyn. 'No,' he finally says. 'You have it all wrong.'

'Ever hear of BAADAss Boys LLC? As in –' she spells it out loud – 'that ring a bell?'

Evan gets out of his chair. 'I've heard of a lot of companies, Dev. And, by the way, just because someone expresses interest in a property doesn't mean the property is for sale. Maybe you oughta stick to babysitting killers.'

'That's kind of an odd name, don't you think? BAADAss Boys? What do you think that stands for?'

'You want me to leave you tickets for Monday's game? You can bring that real estate douche. And by all means, wear your Zelda's Zealots gear.' He gathers some papers from his desk, nudging her aside with a shoulder. 'OK, I'm outta here,' he says. 'I have a hockey team to get back on track, and a business to run.'

'B: Brandon,' she says.

'Time to go, Devyn.' He's stuffing the papers into a beat-up leather satchel embossed with the initials of their father. 'I'm going home to work.'

'A: Alasdair.'

'Now.'

'A: Aidan.'

He slings the satchel over a shoulder, grabs an IceKings parka off his chair, and hurries past Devyn toward the door. 'Good night, sis. I love you. Have a fine weekend.'

'D: Dulaney.'

He pulls up short in the doorway. Without turning around, he says, 'Like I said, just because someone expresses interest—'

'Butch Dulaney? Are you frigging kidding me?'

He's just standing there now, head bowed, holding his satchel to his chest. 'I didn't – you don't understand.'

'You're right, I don't understand. Please tell me how I have it all wrong.' She remembers what Butch told her in the locker room when she almost planted a skate blade in his nuts. 'They don't wanna put up a damn Walmart, do they?'

'Nobody's putting up a Walmart. Jesus.'

'Why are you even talking with the Dulaneys?'

Her phone is ringing. She can't hazard a look now.

He tosses his satchel on a sofa. 'Even if I was seriously considering an offer from anyone, what business would that be of yours?'

'This is part of our family. It's part of—'

'No. No. No. You chose to be a lawyer. And while you were going to keggers in Ann Arbor, I was here slaving away, Dad's bitch. And I'm not talking about working on the finances or marketing or selling tickets, I'm talking about sharpening skates and sweeping up locker rooms and racing out for coffee with three creams and two-and-a-half sugars because some D-bag winger who was never going to make the show had a superstition when really –' Evan's scanner is squawking now – 'he was mostly superstitious about being hit by guys on the other team. You wanted nothing to do with it. You were gonna make a shitload of money for some big Detroit firm, so you left me here to take care of the team and the arena and the property and, God help me, Eleanor. Who's now paying your rent. I don't know exactly what happened with your big law firm but that was the bed you made.'

Lousy metaphor, Devyn thinks. 'OK,' she says. 'But I want to know why you're doing this. The Dulaneys have coveted this place forever. I don't really know why, except it might make them a little bit bigger fish in this little shit pond. But we've told them a thousand times to go away. Why now, Evan?'

'I don't know. The price is right? If we don't take it now, we might not get the chance again?'

'No. Never.'

'For Christ's sake.' He picks his father's satchel off the sofa. 'I will handle it. Now just go.'

'Evan.'

'Just fucking go.'

He actually goes first, leaving her standing alone in his office. She looks across his desk at a framed photo on his credenza. Eleanor, Calvin, Evan, Devyn. Twenty or so years ago. They're smiling at center ice, all done up in IceKings gear. Calvin is hefting the league championship trophy.

Her phone is buzzing. She pulls up the voicemail from Varga. 'Hey, Dev,' he says. 'The name of the dead man is Nikola Grbic. G-R-B-I-C. Serbian, I think, though he grew up in Detroit. Rap sheet half a mile long, though mostly little stuff, nothing violent. One other thing. My guy overheard one of the federales refer to whatever they're doing as Operation Bigfoot. Not sure what that means. Feel free to call.'

Devyn listens a second time to make sure she heard it right: *Bigfoot?*

SIXTY-FOUR

One step into the visitors' room, Jimmy stops and tells the jailer, 'You can't bring him in here.'

'Already did,' Hoover says.

'Take me back to my cell.'

'It'll be fine.' Hoover nudges Jimmy forward.

'Does my lawyer know? You need to call her now.'

The man in the wheelchair, his neck held erect by a steel brace, spins around to face them. He's not Jimmy's brother, who was supposed to visit this morning. 'Hello, Jim,' Cory Richards says.

'You can't just do this,' Jimmy tells Hoover. 'Get Devyn. Now.'

'Why do you need your lawyer?' Richards says. He's puttering toward Jimmy, who finds the hum of the wheelchair's electric motor unsettling. 'What good have lawyers done you over the years?'

Jimmy looks helplessly at Richards, back at Hoover, then back at Richards again. He's just two feet away now, staring into the manacled hands Jimmy holds just as helplessly before him.

'What are you doing here?' Jimmy says.

'I came to speak with you, *mano a mano*. Totally off the record.'

'Bullshit. You came to get me to hang myself for your testimony on Monday. This is just . . . it can't be legal.' He looks at Hoover. 'Get me out of here, Hoover.'

Hoover doesn't move.

'If you want to hang yourself, that's your business,' Richards says. 'It will not leave this room. Although –' he cranes his neck against one side of the brace, the metal depressing his cheek skin – 'we'll need the officer to leave.'

'Are you kidding me? Hoover!'

'Calm down, Bakes,' Hoover says. 'I don't think the guy's gonna beat you up.'

'Bad joke, officer,' Richards says, grinning.

'Seriously, Bakes, I can call Payne-in-the-butt, and she can tell me to clear you and Cory—'

'Cory? What the fuck, Hoover?'

'That's his *name*, Bakes. I can clear you both the hell out of here, or you can listen to what he has to say, and he can listen to what you have to say. I mean, have you two ever actually talked?' So Hoover made this happen? Or helped it along? Did he ask the chief or the prosecutor or the detective or Devyn? Or even so much as mention it to them? Sounds like not. Which is weird. Hoover never struck Jimmy as a peacemaker. He once cross-checked an opponent so hard into the half-wall that the guy dislocated *and* separated both shoulders. Hoover snickered while the guy squirmed on the ice, screaming. Jimmy doubts Hoover ever had a sit-down with that victim.

'Never have, Hoove, for good reason,' Jimmy says.

Hoover looks at him, then Richards, then abruptly turns and leaves the room. Jimmy spins to Richards, who's nodding as best he can in the metal neck sleeve that gives him the look of a praying mantis. Seeing the brace gives Jimmy a funny feeling on his own neck, as if someone was pressing hard just beneath his right ear.

'I get it,' Richards says. 'You're on the spot. But really, Jimmy, if you think about it, *I'm* the one who's on the spot now. *I'm* the one taking the stand Monday. *I'm* the one in position to condemn someone – you – to virtual death. I didn't plan this. I was just going on with my life and the next—'

'Oh, for fuck's sake, Richie. What are you really doing here?'

Richards smiles, maybe because Jimmy used his nickname. 'As I said, whatever is said here remains here. I will never repeat it.'

'Come on,' Jimmy says. 'We signed a non-disclosure agreement as part of the settlement. I haven't said a thing. But there you are on TV, telling millions of people what a violent bastard I am. And I'm supposed to believe you when you say you'll keep your mouth shut?'

'You probably shouldn't. But I'm here. Partly because I was – mandated is too strong a word, maybe compelled, something like that – to do that *Dateline* thing.'

'And there was money involved.'

'Technically, no, but yes, there was talk of a series.'

'Great.'

'Not gonna happen. Anyway, on one hand, I wish I hadn't done the thing. When I watched the show and heard myself say what I said' – he pauses, considering – 'I knew I only said it because I had a TV camera in my face. On the other hand, when I watched – and I actually couldn't bring myself to watch the entirety of it – I knew I had to speak with you.'

'You lied about me saying I wanted to kill you. I never said that.'

'No, you didn't. Let's just say I had some less-than-fortuitous coaching.'

'From?'

'My agent.'

Of course Richards has an agent. 'So why, exactly, do you want to talk to me now?' Jimmy says.

Richards idly taps a forefinger on the joystick attached to his right armrest. The motion looks almost involuntary. Although Jimmy hadn't ever thought of Richards as one of the lunkheads who tend to populate the lower reaches of the hockey world, he's impressed by how level-headed and – what's the word? – *articulate* Richards is. The guy went straight from Massachusetts kid leagues to Canadian juniors to the minor pro leagues. Didn't attend college, didn't grad-uate from high school. But here he is properly using words like 'fortuitous' and 'mandated.' Maybe he's clever enough to trap Jimmy into saying something that can be used against him. Or maybe he's past that. Jimmy doesn't think he can begrudge him either.

'You know, Jim,' Richards says, 'there are lots of people who've talked about what happened thirteen years ago. But the two people affected most have not. At least not to each other.'

'Do you want me to tell you I'm sorry? I've said it enough in court papers, in interviews, on—'

'I didn't come for that.'

'Then what?'

Richards closes his eyes for a few seconds, then says, 'Do you miss it?'

'Miss what?'

'The game.'

'Which game?'

'What other game is there? Hockey.'

'I mean which hockey game. The one where you pass and stick-handle and look for odd-man chances and shoot the puck at the other goalie? Or the one where you just pound the shit out of each other?' When Richards doesn't reply right away, Jimmy says, 'Sorry.'

'No, that's fair,' Richards says. 'Me, I prefer the first version. And I miss it. I miss the pregame skates. I miss taping my sticks in the bathroom before games. I miss hearing the horn go off when I scored, especially if it was a tip-in. God, I loved tip-ins. And the room. More than anything, I miss the locker room. The guys, the chirping.'

'Wait. You went into the shitter to tape your sticks?'

'True story. When I played juniors in Halifax – the Mooseheads, baby – we had this coach who was superstitious about guys taping sticks less than an hour before puck drop. Who knows why. One time I didn't get to it till like half an hour before the game, so I had to sneak out and do the taping in a bathroom stall. Scored a hat trick that night, plus a helper. So after that, I had to tape 'em in the bathroom every night.'

Yes, he did, Jimmy thinks. He motions at the table. 'You wanna?'

Richards maneuvers to the table and bumps a hardback chair aside. Jimmy sits facing him, dropping his cuffed hands on the tabletop. Richards looks almost nothing like Jimmy remembers him. He's thin and frail, his two legs, bundled together, barely the thickness of one. But his face is alive, his gray eyes surprisingly, almost disturbingly, bright.

'My lawyer is going to kill me,' Jimmy says.

'She's good,' Richards says. 'I'm not sure she's gonna get you off, but she's doing her best. In my uneducated opinion.'

'How did you get here anyway?'

'My brother drove me. With great reluctance. Refused to come inside.'

'Didn't he play in the Q?'

'Yeah. Moncton. Goaltender. Tore up a knee pretty bad, had to retire.'

Jimmy now recalls the brother glowering from the courtroom gallery. 'That's too bad,' he says.

'Yeah. So let me ask you something slightly off topic. You know that lawsuit all those players with concussions filed against the hockey powers that be?'

'I've read about it.'

'You were not a party to it, were you?'

'No.'

'But they must have asked you to join.'

'About twenty times.'

'Why didn't you?'

Jimmy stares at his knuckles. They look like a bulldozer rolled over them. 'Every day is a penance.'

'Pardon me?'

'Nothing. I just – I didn't think I should benefit from misery I inflicted on others, even if I was also a . . .' Not 'victim;' he hates that word. 'Even if I was also the prey.'

'I wondered. So here's something else, a little more on point. I don't know how much you remember of our . . . encounter . . .'

'Not much. I kinda just blacked out that stuff.'

'. . . but I have to ask. When we first got to dancing, I took a pretty big swing and it seemed like you let me hit you.'

'Part of my plan.'

'Really?'

'Yeah. Get hit once, it really pissed – got me going.' An image of his father reaching over the car seat to smack Alex flashes in Jimmy's head; he feels the car swerve, the tires chewing shoulder gravel. 'And when I got going, well, you know. I'm sorry about that.'

'Just leave it alone, man.'

'No. I wish I hadn't, for a lot of reasons.'

'Jimmy. Listen to me. I welcomed it.'

'You welcomed having your spine cracked?'

Richards leans his head back an inch and gazes briefly at the ceiling. 'If you recall, I had all the skills. But there were questions.'

'Were you tough enough? Did you have the grit?'

Richards chuckles. 'They were saying I'd be the next Bruce Boudreau, breaking all the scoring records in the minors but never making the big league.'

'You could definitely play, Richie.'

'I know. And I'm not trying to exonerate you here, Jim, or even forgive you. What you did to me was, I don't know, all those terrible things people said it was. But I knew what a beast you were going in, and I asked for it anyway. I looked for it. And I got it. And here we are, two hockey guys who totally fucked up their lives.'

Jimmy doesn't know what to say. He's thinking back to the actual fight, something he hasn't done since his lawyers in the civil litigation demanded it. He sees Richards's head snapping back, the spray of blood across the glass behind him, the jubilant faces of the fans sitting close. He sees Richards fall to the ice, feels himself leap onto the semi-conscious player's back and grab his jersey by the collar. The refs pull at Jimmy but he's too strong for them. He lifts Richards off the ice and slams him back down, then does it again, then again before he feels himself finally being dragged away, seeing the motionless numeral fourteen in royal blue on the back of Richards's white jersey and . . .

Something shifts in Jimmy's head.

'You still with me?' Richards says.

'Yeah.'

But he's not, really. He's suddenly in a field, a dark field cut with shafts of light, on his knees in snow almost to his waist, and he's trying to lift a man off the ground and slam him back down but there are hands all over him and something cold against his cheek and he feels himself being dragged backward through the biting dry snow, hears voices telling him they'll fucking kill him right here, right now.

'Fucked up, all right,' Jimmy tells Richards. 'But at least I can still walk.'

'In a prison yard? I'd rather tool around in my chair out here. Sorry about that, Jim. And sorry I have to testify on Monday.'

The voices swirl around Jimmy back in that field. Voices of men, loud and vulgar. Something punctures the right side of his neck. He feels a stab of pain before everything goes black. Then it all vanishes into some void in the back of his brain and he returns fully to the visitors' room in the jail. In a blink he understands why the neck brace bothered him earlier.

'Jim,' Richards says. 'Are you all right?'

A sob, unbidden, forces its way out of Jimmy's throat. He tries and fails to hold the next one back. He lets his head fall awkwardly into the steel securing his hands, trying to cover his face. He's weeping now, without knowing exactly why. Except he's remembering things he didn't remember ten seconds ago. He hears the wheelchair rounding the table. He raises his head and swabs at the hot tears on his cheeks with a wrist. He sets his hands back on the table as the old buzzing starts behind his eyeballs, spreading heat into his throat, his belly, his arms, and his hands, balling into fists.

'My God,' Richards says. He's at Jimmy's side. 'What's wrong?'

Jimmy closes his eyes. He takes a deep breath, then another. He silently repeats the words to himself: *intermittent explosive disorder.* He steadies his breathing. His hands slowly unclench.

'What are you going to say, Richie?'

'In court?'

'In court.'

'You might find this hard to believe, but I honestly don't know. That's kind of why I came here. What would you have me say?'

'No. Stop right there. Not another word.' It's Devyn, who just barreled into the room ahead of Hoover. 'Do not answer that question, Jimmy. We don't need to be accused of witness tampering.'

Jimmy glances at her then turns back to Richards. 'Do what you have to do.'

'I will.'

'I wish you the best.'

'And you, Jim. Really.'

Richards rolls back from the table. Hoover holds the door and follows him out. Jimmy watches, wishing he could have said something more, something clearer, though he isn't sure what it would be.

'Jimmy,' Devyn says, 'what the hell are you thinking?'

He lifts his hands, then sets them back down. 'Take a seat,' he says. 'We need to talk.'

SIXTY-FIVE

F our hours later, Devyn is glancing back and forth at her rear- and side-view mirrors, scouring southbound I-75 behind her for any sign of a tail. Earlier, before leaving Bitterfrost, she plucked the air tag out of her wheel well and slapped it onto a FedEx truck parked behind the post office. Still, Klimmek by now may have figured out why Devyn was at that house in the woods. Or someone much more dangerous could be watching.

She reamed out Hoover for letting Cory Richards see Jimmy without consulting her. Hoover said he thought it would be good for Jimmy. She reprised her rant for Quarton, who apparently had no clue the meeting took place. She hopes Jimmy did himself no harm. They'll find out Monday in the courtroom. The encounter did seem to excavate some buried memories from the night of the murders, memories that might be helpful if Devyn can complete the mission she's on now.

The thunderstorm descends just after she passes the exit for US 23 south of Flint, about sixty miles from her destination, Hamtramck. Devyn has loved storms, the more violent the better, ever since the one she witnessed crossing the Minnesota prairie. She was ten years old. She and her father were returning to Bitterfrost after a spring hockey tournament. They had to drive through Sunday night because she'd played in the championship final that afternoon – a 5–4 double-overtime loss to Little Falls – and Dad had to be back in Bitterfrost Monday morning.

Thunder began crashing through the darkness just after eight. Lightning followed, with nary a drop of rain. Searing white bolts as wide as the interstate smashed into the earth like fists thrown from heaven. The table-flat expanse stretching out from the roadsides lit up as if it was instantly summer noon, the scrub brush and pin oaks flashing in silhouette then vanishing into the night.

'Pretty darn horrifying, isn't it?' Calvin Payne said. 'But you don't have to be afraid, that's what's so great about it.'

'Couldn't the lightning hit the car?'

Her dad laughed. 'No. Just watch. But leave the window closed, eh?'

They drove another half mile. Devyn said, 'You never want me to be afraid, do you, Pop?'

Calvin kept his eyes on the road. 'No, Devvy,' he said. 'If you're careful, there's never any need to be afraid.'

The storm she's driving through now isn't much by comparison. A scattering of bolts, mostly to the east, probably crossing from Lake Huron. An occasional rumble of thunder. Raindrops the size of silver dollars. Devyn has her windshield wipers going at top speed. Her father wasn't always careful, but he never seemed afraid. Devyn, though, is definitely afraid now. And she's aware she isn't being terribly careful.

She knows – or thinks she knows – a few things today that she didn't know twenty-four hours ago. She knows 'Bigfoot' describes a mythical creature that stalks the forests of the Upper Midwest and Canada, a fetish of conspiracy theorists and other wackos; what it has to do with Jimmy Baker, she doesn't yet know. She suspects that Aaron Diggs traveled to Bitterfrost not to hunt or fish but at the behest of Detroit people he worked for – 'extracurriculars,' as his parole officer put it – whom she hopes she'll never have the misfortune to meet. People like maybe that Mario Rooney. And she knows that Anya Paluk, the tenant of that shabby house in the woods, is hiding in Hamtramck, probably fearing for her life. Devyn must get to Anya before anyone else does and persuade her to take the witness stand in Jimmy's trial.

Three miles north of the exit for Clarkston, Devyn notices a pair of too-bright headlights maybe a quarter of a mile behind her. The lights are set high above a rail of yellow lights that seem to be blinking, although that could be a rainy illusion. Looks like a pickup. So not Klimmek? She thinks she noticed the same pattern of lights in her mirror when she veered off I-75 earlier to pee. Why didn't the vehicle get miles ahead of her while she was at the rest stop?

The map on her phone says she's forty-one miles from Hamtramck. She could pull off at Clarkston and try to lose this tail, if that's what it is, on off-highway roads. Or the follower could feel emboldened at being free of the interstate, track her down, and then who knows what? Devyn doesn't want to end up like golf guy Grbic. She keeps an eye on the rear-view while she picks up her phone and dials Varga. He answers right away.

'Bigfoot?' she says. 'A sasquatch killed those guys?'

Varga laughs. 'The hunt for the mysterious beast goes on.' Watch out for Bigfoot, golf guy Grbic told her as he left her in the woods near Mackinaw City. She thought then he was just messing with her. Not anymore. 'Seriously,' Varga says, 'my guy said he thought the Coast Guard got involved because whatever's going on has something to do with submarines. And Chicago.'

'Submarines? In Chicago?'

'I know.'

'Is Grbic really Coast Guard?'

'Doubt it.'

Devyn lets Varga go. She's really lost now. Chicago? She thinks of her Chicago uncles, both long gone; she doubts their shipping business deployed submarines. She checks her side-view mirror. 'Holy shit,' she says. The white and yellow lights are bearing down on her left, barely a hundred yards away, with no vehicles visible behind it. She shifts into the far right lane in case she wants to exit and feels the wheels shimmy on the wet road. She grabs her phone again, thinking she'll call 9-1-1, then fumbles it to the floor at her feet as light fills her car interior. 'Dammit,' she shouts, pounding the accelerator and edging left, hoping to cut the pickup off.

The truck swings past her left taillight and pulls alongside. She glances sideways and sees the passenger window is down and a thin male face is leering at her from inside a hood. She can't see his mouth but his eyes, perched above cheekbones that seem to glow in the dark, are dead black holes. She looks away, shivering with fright, gripping the steering wheel so hard that her knuckles hurt. The truck darts ahead and swerves right, barely missing her front end. Whoever they are, they're trying to run her off the road.

'God fucking help me.'

One second later, a dark shadow bounces off her windshield. She hammers the brakes as the thing flies past and something else smacks her in the face, slapping her head backward into the seat. She hears glass shattering, metal cracking, men cursing. Her nostrils fill with the smell of smoke. The airbag went off. The Toyota swings back and forth from one side of the road to the other but Devyn finally gets it under control and veers onto the exit ramp for Clarkston.

In the rear-view mirror she sees two men scrambling around the pickup truck, which is leaning nose first into the median, a dead animal, probably a deer, stuffed into the windshield. She hopes the truck is disabled but she can't count on it. At the top of the exit ramp, she turns left and drives at the speed limit until she sees lights blazing from the windows of a party store. She pulls around to the back and parks with the car running.

'Jesus,' she says, exhaling with her eyes closed. She sits still for a moment, trying to quiet the trembling in her hands and forearms. She opens her eyes and flicks on the overhead light. The airbag is deflated on the steering wheel. A quarter-inch-wide crack snakes down the windshield from the rear-view mirror to the lower left corner. As long as it doesn't spread too much, she should be OK. A tuft of hairs is stuck to one of her windshield wiper blades. Deer hairs, she supposes.

She leans into the rear-view and inspects her face. A purplish bruise is forming around the outer socket of her right eye, and the eye itself is starting to close. She gets out of the car and limps to a pile of dirty snow at the edge of the lot. Her left ankle is killing her; she must have twisted it when she hit the brakes. She scoops up a handful of snow and presses it to her eye as she hobbles back to the Toyota.

She wants to be on her way but she's hesitating. She knows she can no longer keep everything she knows to herself. If these people chasing her, whoever they are, finally catch up, the truth about what happened to Jerome Hardy and Aaron Diggs might never be known.

She can't take that chance.

'Where are you?' Devyn says when Klimmek answers.

'Going into a meeting I'm not going to enjoy,' he says.

'You got a minute?'

Devyn tells him almost everything she knows. About Aaron Diggs and his extracurriculars, about Operation Bigfoot, about Chicago, about golf guy Grbic and his plea for her to abandon Jimmy, about Anya Paluk. She withholds Anya's exact whereabouts because she doesn't want Klimmek getting some pal downstate to look for her. But now he knows more, a lot more, than he knew a few minutes ago.

'Why are you helping me?' Klimmek says.

'I'm helping my client,' Devyn says. She puts her car in gear and rolls out to the road in front of the party store. No headlights in either direction.

'Does Baker know what you're doing?'

'Talk later.' She pulls onto the road, ankle throbbing and eye stinging, headed again for Hamtramck.

SIXTY-SIX

Clouds like battleships hover over Lake Michigan in front of Philip Hardy's rental home on a bluff south of Bitterfrost. Klimmek regards them from the vast picture windows in Hardy's living room. Far below, jagged slabs of ice bob in the shoreline water. They look harmless from a distance but Klimmek knows they can turn a dock into toothpicks in seconds.

'Detective,' Hardy says, 'shall we sit?'

Klimmek turns to see Chief Quarton standing with the man whose son Jerome was killed along with his brother-in-law after their evening at the Lost Loon. He recalls how Philip Hardy described his son when the detective and Quarton first met him: Jerome Hardy was 'a well-meaning young man' who had 'a knack for being in the wrong place at the wrong time.' So true, Klimmek thinks. That's why he asked the elder Hardy to meet.

Quarton whispers something to Hardy. 'Of course. I'll get the refreshments,' Hardy says, and goes to the kitchen. Quarton joins Klimmek at the windows. The chief's face is pinched with distress, his graying eyebrows knitted at the bridge of his nose.

'This is highly irregular, Garth,' he says, speaking softly. 'Calling a meeting like this without consulting me first? Would you care to indulge me with a headline or two before Mr Hardy returns?'

'I'm not in the headline business, chief.'

'Humor me.'

'I have some questions about Mr Hardy's son.'

'Haven't we put this man through enough already?'

'We're not funeral directors, chief. If we're going to put the right people in prison, we need – or at least *I* need – to know more than we do now.'

'Are you serious? Garth, the trial is about to wrap up. The jury is going to convict. We are this close to putting the right guy in prison. You're gonna have a crisis of conscience? Now?'

Klimmek steps away from Quarton and calls toward the kitchen. 'Mr Hardy, ready when you are.' Then he turns back to Quarton.

'What if we don't have the right guy? Are you OK with that? Can you live with that?'

They gather at a circular table in the middle of a glass-walled turret off the living room. Hardy sets out coffee and bottles of water and a bowl of mixed nuts. He's alone here, his wife having returned downstate for the weekend. Not for the first time, Klimmek marvels at Hardy's hair, oddly as silver as Devyn's. From their first meeting in Quarton's office to the press conference at the rink to the trial, Hardy's hair always seemed exactly the same, never shorter, never longer, the same subtle waves in precisely the same place, as if it never grew, as if Hardy got a haircut every morning, which Klimmek supposes is possible. It reminds him of that werewolf song: 'His hair was perfect.'

'How do you think the trial is going?' Hardy says as he sits between Klimmek, on his left, and Quarton. The windows behind him show nothing but darkness.

'The trial seems to be going as trials do,' Klimmek says. 'It's not like a football game, where there's a running score that tells you who's ahead from one minute to the next. Especially when the other team hasn't even put its offense on the field.'

'Does Baker's attorney even have an offense?' Quarton says. He chuckles then. Nervously, Klimmek thinks. Hardy doesn't crack a smile. Quarton plows ahead. 'Please, Mr Hardy,' he says, holding up an open hand. 'Don't confuse Detective Klimmek's circumspection for negativity. Detectives are a skeptical bunch. We are confident in our case.'

'Detective,' Hardy says, leaning into the table, 'the night of that press conference out by the hockey arena, I asked you if the placement of Jerome's body –' he pauses, gathering himself – 'made sense, and you essentially told me it was irrelevant, because Baker is no Hannibal Lecter, rather he was a captive of his passions, his rage. Do you remember that?'

'Sounds about right.'

'You seemed fairly sure of yourself then. Are you no longer so sure? Is that why you're here?'

Klimmek had been aware of Diggs's criminal record since early in the proceedings. He'd spoken briefly with Diggs's parole officer, who seemed to be in a hurry and didn't tell him much that he didn't already know. Now, minutes before Klimmek arrived at Hardy's rental, Devyn told the detective about Diggs's possible ties to the Rooney character in Detroit. Klimmek felt blind-sided. A quick Google search confirmed that the so-called Black Mario was not a man to be trifled with.

'I'm here because, as occasionally happens as a trial is proceeding, we've come upon some new information. I need to ask you a few questions.'

Hardy sits back. 'Go ahead.'

Klimmek holds up a digital tape recorder. 'Do you mind?'

'If you're going to record, I'll need my lawyer here.'

'Never mind.' Klimmek pockets the device. 'Can you tell me again why your son was in Bitterfrost?'

Hardy gives Quarton a glance, then turns back to Klimmek. 'As I think I said before, he and Aaron were on their way to the UP for this silly outhouse race. They stopped here for the night. Unfortunately.'

'Bitterfrost is quite a detour off the route from Detroit to the UP, Mr Hardy. Your son didn't perhaps say something about his brother-in-law having business here, did he?'

Quarton bows his head and claps one hand over the other on the tabletop. He might not appreciate Klimmek asking a question he's never heard before. 'No. Jerome never said anything like that to me.'

'Are you – or were you – aware that Aaron, perhaps before he befriended Jerome, had some run-ins with the law? Specifically over the possession and sale of illegal drugs?'

Quarton speaks up. 'Where are you going with this, Garth?'

Hardy is shaking his head. 'I knew – well, suspected – Jerome shouldn't be palling around with Diggs. I didn't know the particulars, but I just had a feeling. I had some of my people check him out, and yes, he had some hiccups in the past, but he seemed to have cleaned up his act. Either way, once Jerome fell in love with Raina – Diggs's sister – we were stuck with him.'

'Were you happy about that?'

'It's family, detective. You understand. But I do want to say this: My son does not – did not – do drugs. He didn't do them, he didn't possess them, and he certainly didn't sell them.'

How would you know? Klimmek thinks. 'Mr Hardy,' he says, 'are you familiar with the name Mario Rooney?'

Hardy goes silent, as if he's weighing whether to answer or not. 'The Black Mario?' he finally says. 'That's what the Detroit papers

call him. Even though he's not black. He's some kind of Eastern
European.'

'Rooney's a funny name for an Eastern European,' Quarton says.

'Mother's maiden name,' Klimmek says.

'A drug dealer?'

'If you look up the definition of "kingpin" in a dictionary,'
Klimmek says, 'there's a picture of this Rooney guy.'

Hardy is eerily quiet. Quarton asks, 'Violent?'

'You know those heads the Detroit cops found in a sewer by
Comerica Park a few years ago? Three of them skewered together
like a shish kebab?'

'That was Rooney?'

'Greeks who crossed him. Their bodies showed evidence of
torture.'

'My gosh. Were the bodies right there?'

'No. They were in a meat freezer in a Greektown restaurant.'

'Why in God's name are you asking *me* about this person?'

'I don't know anything for sure yet,' Klimmek says. 'But I have
reason to believe Diggs was working for Rooney.' The reason being
Devyn Payne. 'Rooney may have had his eye on certain property
here, and he may have sent Diggs to scope it out, maybe make an
inquiry.'

'What property?'

'The hockey rink.'

'Isn't that owned by the defense lawyer?'

'By her mother, effectively.'

'What does any of this have to do with my son? A drug dealer
is interested in some land up north and . . . and . . .'

He throws up his hands, unable to finish.

'We're going to stop right there,' Quarton says, slapping his hand
on the table. 'We're badgering a bereaved father.'

Klimmek stands. 'Please let me know if you figure anything out.'

'Wait,' Hardy says. 'Are you saying this Rooney person had
something to do with . . . oh, God.' Hardy covers his face with a
trembling hand. Quarton rushes over to him, glaring at Klimmek.
'I'm sorry about this, Mr Hardy, you've been so good about helping
us. I didn't know—'

'No, no, no,' Hardy says, dropping his hand from his face. 'I
want to know the truth.'

'I'm afraid I don't know the truth yet,' Klimmek says.

'You don't know the truth? Then what are we doing in that courtroom?'

'We're doing what you urged us to do when you got on that conference call in December. Isn't that right, chief?'

Quarton doesn't respond. Hardy says, 'So it's my fault.'

'No, sir, it's not.' Klimmek sits back down. He wasn't sure he was going to do what he's about to do, but he pulls the recorder back out and holds it up. 'May I play something for you?'

Hardy nods. Quarton says, 'Do I need to call the prosecutor?' Klimmek ignores him, setting the device on the table. 'Be very careful,' Quarton says, 'with what you're sharing, detective.'

'Shortly after the incidents, I had a conversation with a local named Butch Dulaney who was in the bar the night your son was there.'

'He wasn't a suspect?'

'He had an alibi, corroborated by his brothers, and according to security cameras at the establishment, he left quietly before Jerome and Diggs did. But I want to play you a snippet of our conversation. Incidentally, he wouldn't let me record, but I did anyway. That makes it inadmissible in court.'

'Please play it.'

'Again, detective, careful.'

'Here's the set-up,' Klimmek says. 'Butch and the Payne family, who as you know employed Baker, don't get along. Haven't for a long time. Butch was bitching to me about how we were handling the case, supposedly letting the Paynes have their way.'

'The Paynes being a pretty powerful clan up here.'

'Correct.'

'Let's hear it.'

Klimmek pushes a button on the device. On comes Butch's voice. 'The Paynes are probably all over the chief's ass, eh? Hell, two down and whatshername pays to put a cold-blooded killer back on the street.'

Klimmek waits for Hardy's response. Quarton says, 'And?'

'Can you play it again, please?'

Klimmek does. Hardy says, 'Dulaney obviously doesn't appreciate the lawyer's mother posting bail. Otherwise, I'm not quite getting it.'

'I interviewed Butch Dulaney a few days after the murders. At that point, your son was still missing. We hadn't found his body yet. Until that night, several hours *after* I spoke with Dulaney.'

Recognition spreads a shadow across Hardy's face. 'My lord,' he says. 'Can you play it once more?' Klimmek does. Hardy listens, then says, 'Dulaney said *two* down. Did I hear that correctly?'

'Mr Hardy,' Quarton says, 'this is evidence that has not been entered into the public record. You should not be listening to this.'

Hardy says, 'But you should be, chief, shouldn't you? Is it possible you have the wrong man in jail?'

'No. We know Dulaney saw your son with Diggs at the Loon that night. He probably assumed they were both dead.'

'That's your position?'

'Yes. But I can assure you we'll look into this. And I'll be asking Detective Klimmek why we haven't heard about this piece of evidence until now. *Inadmissible* evidence.'

'You will, huh?' Hardy stands. He's not a large man, Klimmek thinks, but he has a certain presence. He supposes that's probably true of most people who've accumulated more than a billion dollars. 'Please get out of my house, chief.'

'Mr Hardy, I'm deeply sorry that you—'

'Get out now, and do not contact me unless you hear from me or my lawyers first.' Hardy turns to Klimmek. 'Detective, you weren't recording me just now, were you?'

'I was not.'

'Good. May I have one more moment of your time?'

Outside, Quarton waits by Klimmek's car.

'What was that, detective? You made me look like an idiot.'

Klimmek's key fob blurps. 'Couldn't afford not to.'

'What's that supposed to mean? That you couldn't trust me with your earth-shaking discoveries? All of which could be bullshit? That you had to tell Hardy so he could go on TV any minute and blow up our case?'

'Close enough.'

'You think it's funny?'

'Tragic is more like it.'

'You'll need to give me that recorder.'

Klimmek flips it to Quarton.

'It's worthless in court anyway,' the chief says.

'Then I'm sure it won't keep you up tonight.'

'No, it won't. And while you're at it, you can give me your badge, too. As of this minute, you are suspended.'

Klimmek almost laughs. 'Serious? Who do you think is going to do the real work around the shop? That kid Sylvester?'

'Not your concern anymore, Garth. If I see you anywhere near the courtroom Monday, I will have you arrested. Meanwhile, you might want to check the fine print on your pension before you do anything too stupid.'

Klimmek watches the chief drive away. He takes out his personal phone and, just for fun, checks the app supposedly tracing Payne. It shows her stopped at a FedEx warehouse in Traverse City. He shakes his head and taps out a text to her: **Meeting went better than expected.**

SIXTY-SEVEN

Devyn pulls onto Joseph Campau Avenue in Hamtramck. She has never seen a street quite like it.

Tattooed twenty-somethings bounce along the Saturday night sidewalks, trailing vape smoke past clothing stores adorned with enormous flowing-script signs sent from the last century. There are pawn shops and Polish bakeries, hookah joints and halal delis, a discount outlet hung with twin signs announcing both a Grand Opening and a Liquidation Sale. The spire of a Catholic church against the sky a few blocks away, not far from the dome of a mosque. Eggs-and-gyro diners, party stores, taco stops, fried-fish-and-chicken emporiums. Devyn would love to get a beer at the bar with the blood-red shark's head jutting from the brick above the front door.

But she has somewhere else to be.

Why? She knows the immediate reason, but what's the bigger picture here, as her father might ask her. She's almost three hundred miles from Bitterfrost on a hunch. And even if her hunch is correct, she doesn't know if she can make happen what she wants to happen, what she needs to make happen if she is to have a chance – if Jimmy is to have a chance – in court on Monday. But that's the rub, isn't it, she can hear her father asking. Are you here for Jimmy? Or are you here for yourself? Are you here to try to save an innocent man? Or are you here to redeem yourself for defending a guilty one?

Maybe all of the above.

She opens her window and breathes in scrumptious aromas she wishes she could name. Pulaski Street is coming up on her left. She almost turns onto it before she notices it's a one-way going against her. She proceeds another block to a side street framed by bungalows of clapboard and brick. Parked cars and pickups crowd the curbs. When Devyn reaches Mackay, she turns again, circling back toward Pulaski, pulls over, and kills her lights. Muddy alleys run behind one-car garages. Televisions glow from a few windows, but the neighborhood has mostly gone to bed. Devyn can see the house she needs to get to, a two-story red-brick on the corner of Pulaski and Mackay, half a block away. She picks up her phone and chooses Harris, Genevieve.

'This is important,' Devyn says. As she speaks, she keeps glancing between her side- and rear-view mirrors. 'I need your help.'

'That isn't how these things usually work.'

'I have a witness who needs protecting.'

'That's interesting. Last I looked, you had no witnesses.'

'I have one now. We'll deal with it with Esper tomorrow or Monday.'

'How do you know I won't object?'

'I expect you will, but the judge will side with me.'

'Confident, are we? So who exactly is this witness?' Harris enunciates 'witness' as if to put quote marks around it.

'I can't tell you yet,' Devyn says. 'Suffice to say she knows what happened the night of the murders.' Devyn isn't absolutely sure of that, but Harris doesn't need to know.

'The law requires me to protect witnesses who may be in danger.'

'She's in danger as I speak.'

'I'll assume she did not witness your client committing murder.'

'Correct. Which is why she needs protection.'

'Are you nearby?'

'No. Downstate. She's in hiding.'

'Where, exactly?'

'Can't say yet.'

'How then do you expect me to help?'

Before she can answer, Devyn hears the rumble of an approaching vehicle. White and yellow light floods the corners of the intersection in front of her. A black pickup speeds through it from the left, against the one-way. She sees a gaping hole where the truck's windshield should be.

'Shit,' Devyn says. 'I have to go.'

'Go where?'

'I'll get back to you.'

Devyn eases out of her car and locks it. Then she scrabbles around to the back and squats, peering over the trunk. How the hell did they find her? Did she miss a second air tag on her car when she was looking for Klimmek's? Was she that sloppy? Or did the people in the truck have an idea where she was going?

Doesn't matter now, she thinks. She detects something to her right. A man in a window on the house there is looking at her through pulled-apart curtains. She waves and smiles and gestures toward her tire, as if it might be flat. The curtains fall shut. Time to leave.

She scampers out from behind her car, crosses Mackay, and ducks into an alley just as white and yellow light again spills into the intersection. She squeezes herself between the side of a wooden garage and a buckled cyclone fence. She takes out her phone and dials 9-1-1.

'Hamtramck police,' a woman says.

Devyn whispers, 'I need to report an abandoned vehicle.'

'How long has it been abandoned, ma'am?'

'Oh, at least a week.'

'Address?'

Devyn tells her the intersection. The woman says, 'Can I get your name?'

'Sure, it's Veronica—' She ends the call before finishing.

In a gap between houses, she sees the pickup truck pass, the face of a driver she can't make out scanning through his opened window. She presses harder into the garage. The truck keeps going. But then she hears its engine modulate, sees the red glow of brake lights.

She starts to move away from the garage but her coat sleeve catches on the fence. She tries to yank it free as she sees the silhouette of someone walking through the reddish light behind the truck. She wrestles her way out of the coat and leaves it hanging on the fence. She runs into the alley, favoring her right leg because of her twisted ankle, back in the direction of her car. She should feel cold but sweat leaks down her back, her heart hammering. She shambles across Mackay and swerves onto a concrete pathway that opens onto Pulaski. Lowering her head, she minces forward, tripping once on a walkway crack and almost pitching onto her face. Fuck, fuck, fuck, she whispers to herself. At the opening, she stops, afraid her gasping will give her away.

She hears the truck move closer, then stop again on Mackay. Where her car is parked. So they're going to check it out, but they must not know Devyn's precise destination or they would have descended on her by now. This is her chance. She edges a solid wooden gate open, then half-hops, half-runs onto Pulaski into the narrow space between two houses across the street. She guesses she won't be returning to her car anytime soon. Her boots squish in puddles as she sidles between two garages. She leans half her head around one of them and sees the pickup parked next to her car, two men circling in the shadows. They look surprised by the police cruiser that rounds the corner behind them. The men start to hustle back to their truck then stop and turn to the cruiser, their backs to Devyn, as the flashers come on. That missing windshield may require some explaining.

Devyn walks across Mackay into yet another alley and veers into the yard on her left. She crouches in a shadow and takes out her phone. She gets Ronnie's voicemail. 'Hey,' she tells it. 'Would you be OK to drive after work? I mean, like, a long way? Like a really long way. Sorry, but . . . call when you can.'

She walks through the yard and climbs three concrete steps to a planked porch lit with a bare bulb. The porch is cluttered with kids' bicycles and plastic bags bulging with Diet Coke empties. The pink Schwinn with its rusted chain guard reminds Devyn of a bike her parents gave her when she was seven. She was always stealing Evan's identical blue bike because it annoyed her that a girl had to have pink.

There's a doorbell. She pushes it. She hears a melody of three chimes inside. She leans into the outer screen door, listening. The voices are muffled, the words in another language, Devyn assumes Polish. She pushes the doorbell again, hoping she's close enough to the door that she can't be seen through the kitchen window beside it. The heavy inner door sucks open. The tang of sauerkraut floats past. A woman she doesn't recognize stands with one hand on the doorknob. Devyn tries to stand a little outside the circle of light so her scary-looking eye isn't as noticeable.

'What do you want?' the woman says. She's older, perhaps in her sixties, wearing a housecoat of faded flower print. Anya's mother? An older sister? A cousin? She looks back into the kitchen and shakes her head at someone or something Devyn can't see. She turns back to Devyn.

'We are not interested.'

'Please.' Devyn holds up a business card that reads, 'Devyn Payne, Counselor at Law, Bitterfrost, Michigan.' She says, 'I need to see Anya.'

The woman glances over her shoulder again, then says, 'What's with the eye? Looks like shit.'

'I slipped on some black ice.'

The woman slowly shakes her head. 'No,' she says. 'There is no one here. No Anya. Nobody. Go home now.'

'Shirlee sent me. Jordan Fawcett's mother.'

'We don't know no Shirlee. Why do you have no coat?'

'Anya knows Shirlee. If I could just speak with Anya. She will know why I'm here. Please just—'

The woman pushes the door closed. The porch light goes dark.

'Shit,' Devyn says. She wraps herself in her arms, feeling a shiver spread through her neck and shoulders. She thinks for a few seconds then begins to pound her fist on the screen door window, not caring whether she breaks it. 'Please,' she says.

She hears more talking inside. The porch light comes back on. The inner door opens. A different woman, younger, stands there in jeans, fluffy slippers, and an orange hoodie.

'Anya Paluk?' Devyn says.

The woman pushes the screen door open. Her face is pale and round and weary. 'You are going to get me killed.'

PART FOUR

SIXTY-EIGHT

The security gate is shut, the guard house dark when Klimmek drives past the Dulaney brothers' property at six-thirteen a.m. He drives another mile-and-a-half and pulls into a turnoff shrouded by a copse of elm. He turns his Bronco to face the road, shuts off the lights, and waits. He brought along a scanner in case another cop happens to head his way.

He unwraps a sandwich Kris made. Scrambled egg on wheat with cheddar and tomato. 'Just eat it because, the way it sounds, you might not get another chance today,' she told him. 'And the hell with Quarton.' The sandwich is still warm, the cheese melty, the eggs peppered the way he likes. He eats it slowly with a go-cup of black coffee, thinking there's no way he'd be on a predawn stakeout if Quarton hadn't suspended him.

He's wiping his fingers on a napkin when he sees the soft glow of car lights whiten the sky to his right. Security guard Charlie is on his way to work. Back when Charlie let Klimmek into the Dulaney compound for that chat with Butch, he mentioned starting his day at seven. There was something else, too, the detective noticed.

He aims his speed gun at a ridge two hundred yards to his right. Charlie's SUV clocks in at seventy-eight miles per hourr as it crests the rise. Too fast, although nobody drives near the limit in these parts. Klimmek flips his headlamps on. The SUV slows. Charlie doesn't hazard a glance as he passes. Klimmek pulls out behind him and speeds to within ten feet of the rear bumper, flashing his brights. Before he gets out, he reaches into a pocket and touches his Rosary.

Charlie stares straight ahead, handing over his license and registration as Klimmek shines a flashlight into the vehicle. 'What's the hurry?' he says.

Charlie shrugs. 'Work.'

Klimmek glances at the license and registration, then says, 'Drinking this early, Charlie?'

Charlie chuckles unconvincingly. 'No, sir,' he says. 'I did have a couple of beers last night.'

Klimmek isn't positive he's smelling alcohol now, but he's certain he did the last time he saw Charlie.

'Can you step out of the car, please?'

Charlie steps out and lays a hand atop the SUV door. He's a smidge taller than Klimmek, his chin stubble a scalded orange.

'What's this about, officer?'

'You know, your dad used to have a nip or two some mornings. Said it cleared his head for the day.'

'I didn't know that.'

'I liked him. Good cop, most of the time.'

'I'm sorry, what do you mean by that?'

'Nothing,' Klimmek says, satisfied he's rattled the younger man.

'Sorry if I was speeding, officer. There's no one out and—'

'Detective. You were twenty-three over.'

'Detective. Maybe you could cut me a break? For the old man's sake?'

'One second.'

Klimmek walks back to his Bronco, taking his wife's phone out of his coat pocket. As she was preparing that sandwich, he was checking the Facebook app on her phone for the person he just pulled over. He finds the page again. Then he leans into the Bronco and grabs a breathalyzer out of the center console. With Kris's phone in one hand and the breathalyzer in the other, he saunters back to Charlie.

'Maybe I can help you out a little,' Klimmek says. Charlie is looking straight at the breathalyzer. He may or may not have had a wake-up drink, but he knows a cop can do pretty much anything he wants. 'I don't imagine a drunk-driving citation at six thirty-two in the morning would look good on your job review.'

'Appreciate it.'

'But I need a little help, too.'

'How so?'

'That forge the Dulaney boys have,' Klimmek says, nodding in the direction of the property. 'Looks like it's gotten larger.'

'They're doing a little renovation. No biggie.'

'Have you noticed anything unusual? Something new they're going to start making?'

Charlie swallows hard. He might prefer jail to talking about the Dulaneys with a cop. 'What do you mean, offi–detective? Far as I know, they're doing what they always do, docks and buoys, stuff like that.'

'I'm thinking about seagoing vessels,' Klimmek tells Charlie. 'You know, boats. Big boats. Big boats that can go underwater.'

'Like submarines?'

Yeah, Klimmek thinks, like what Devyn told him about last night. The Google search he did from his living-room recliner at four that morning turned up an odd story about Mexican cartels using 'semi-submersibles' to ferry drugs. 'Like submarines, yeah, but smaller. Some people – criminals, mostly – call them Bigfoot. Because they're not supposed to be real.'

The glimmer of recognition in Charlie's eyes is unmistakable. 'I don't get into the forge much. But I've heard they're trying to expand.'

'Good. So what I need from you is a photograph or two.'

Charlie glances toward the property. 'Of what?'

'Of one of those boats. A Bigfoot.'

'Why?'

'Between you and me? The department is thinking of getting one. But I doubt your bosses are going to help.' He holds up the breathalyzer, waggles it. 'I'm confident you can.'

Charlie starts shaking his head before Klimmek is even finished speaking. 'I – I can't, detective. I really can't. They don't like me going anywhere but my little booth. Can't you find a picture online?'

'Wouldn't be as authentic as one from a local business.' Klimmek sticks Kris's phone in front of Charlie's face. 'But here's an online picture for you. You know this guy?'

Charlie looks. The Facebook post shows a man embracing Charlie with one arm while brandishing a red Solo cup with the other. The corners of the man's smile reach almost to his sharp cheekbones. The two pose in front of a barn on a sunny day. Dozens of people are gathered around in shorts and T-shirts, smiling and drinking. Charlie posted the photo the previous July with the notation, 'Annual Dulaney Hog Fest. Good times!!'

'I guess that's me,' Charlie says.

'I meant the other guy.'

'Um. Jeez. Not sure. There were a lot of people there. It's a big party.'

'I hope you didn't drive that night.'

'Nope.'

'So who's the guy?'

'I really can't be sure. Sorry.'

Klimmek pockets the phone and sidles in close to Charlie. 'Maybe I can refresh your memory. Does the name Rooney ring a bell?'

'I don't—'

Klimmek pronounces it slowly: 'Mario Rooney.' Charlie looks at his boots again. 'Isn't that guy who's giving you that big hug one Mario Rooney of Detroit? You know, the "Black Mario?" Drug dealer? Murderer? Gangster? That's your buddy, Charlie?'

'No.'

'You look pretty cuddly in this picture. What would your daddy think, Charlie?'

The sound of metal clanking rises from the direction of the Dulaney property. People down there are going to work. Charlie's going to be late. 'I don't *know* him know him. Honest. He was just there. I guess he knows B—.' He stops himself. 'I don't know. Honestly, I have no idea.'

Klimmek recalls what Butch said in the pig shed about boats hauling timber to Chicago from the land where the rink now stands. 'Uh-huh,' he says. 'Butchie doing some business with that guy?'

Charlie looks at the ground. 'Not that I know of.'

'Tell you what. I'm gonna write you a warning for speeding. It won't cost you anything, and that way, if anyone down at the farm asks why you're late, you can say you got pulled over.'

'All right.'

'I'm gonna need those pictures by noon today or I'll be paying a visit to your little booth. Now give me your phone.'

'Detective, please—'

'The phone, kid.'

Charlie complies. Klimmek punches in his personal cell number and hands the phone back. 'Are we done?' Charlie says.

'Not until those pictures show up in my phone.'

'Yeah. My dad– well, never mind. You set me up, detective.'

Klimmek smiles. 'Next time, drive the limit. And feel free to tell the Dulaney boys I said hello.'

He makes a U-turn, relieved that no other cars happened by, and starts back toward town. He promised Kris he'd return her phone by seven thirty. On his own phone, he sees a text from Devyn asking him to run a criminal check on one Anya Paluk, forty-seven years old, of Bitterfrost.

SIXTY-NINE

Devyn has her keys out, but her office door is unlocked and open a couple of inches. Maybe the cleaning people came early this morning. After last night, Devyn isn't taking chances. She uses her right foot to nudge the door enough that she can see inside.

'Good morning, dear,' Eleanor Payne says. 'Constance let me in.'

Devyn's mother sits in Devyn's Costco swivel chair, legs crossed on Devyn's Costco desk. Boxes of files are stacked halfway up two walls, not unlike Costco. Eleanor says, 'You're too young to know what a phone booth is, but this office is barely bigger than one.'

'It's all I need,' Devyn says. And all she can afford. 'I hardly ever come here anyway. I just gotta grab a couple of pens and batteries. What are you doing here? Aren't you supposed to be in bed?'

'What happened to your eye?'

'Slipped on ice.'

Eleanor considers that, then uncrosses her legs and leans into the desk. 'I wanted to make sure I saw you. You spoke with your brother. Now I suppose you think you know everything.'

'Evan told you?'

'Of course he did.'

Devyn wants to feel more betrayed than she actually does. After all, she never swore Evan to secrecy. 'Whatever,' she says. 'I don't think I know much at all, except that he's talking to someone about selling the rink.'

'No, dear. *We* are talking about it.'

'We? Meaning you're in on it?'

'How could I not be, Devyn?'

'Since when?'

'Since, I don't know, since the prospective buyers got serious. A few weeks ago? Ask Evan.'

'What does "serious" mean?'

'It means they're offering serious money they apparently actually have.'

Devyn drops her coat on one of the two chairs facing the desk and plops in the other. 'The Dulaneys, Mother?'

Eleanor sits back while avoiding Devyn's eyes. 'I don't want to talk in particulars, but more than one party has expressed interest.'

'Really? You don't want to talk in particulars? Am I not part of this family anymore?'

'Save the melodrama for the courtroom, Devyn. Although you personally stand to benefit greatly from a sale of the property, the trust controls it, and I am effectively the trust.'

'But Evan knew. He knows.'

'Evan runs the place, Devyn. You just play in it. And the interested parties initially approached him, not me.'

'He didn't approach them? What about that museum you're building?'

'You mean where that boy was found? It's cursed now. I'm not building anything on top of that.' She sighs. 'Look, Devyn, we didn't tell you because you're preoccupied with the trial and—'

'Horsepucky, as you like to say. That rink's been part of my life since I learned to skate, and I deserve to know if you're going to sell it out from under me. Especially if you're going to sell it to the Dulaneys.'

Eleanor puckers her lips, as she always does when she's losing patience with her children. 'Nothing at all might happen. Which would be too bad for you because this is real money, and you would have a real share. You could get a real office with real furniture from a real store. You could actually pay your own living expenses. You could move the hell out of Bitterfrost if you like and go somewhere where you could be a real lawyer.'

Devyn stands. 'Jesus, Mother. Now? Now you're telling me this? Do you know how much shit I have on my plate right now?'

'That's precisely why we – I – didn't tell you. But you had to go snooping around like you do and cornering your brother and—'

Devyn sputters a laugh. '"Cornering" him? Are you fucking joking?'

'Language, young lady.'

'This would not be happening if Dad was still here. No way. He'd tell the Dulaneys to go pound sand at their pig farm.'

'You think you know so much, Devyn. Listen to me. You need to get this trial behind you and then we will sit down with a glass of wine and have a nice, calm chat about the rink and the property and our family.'

As her mother speaks, Devyn's past twelve hours unspool in her head like a movie trailer. Sitting with Anya in her aunt's kitchen, eating cold potato-and-mushroom pierogi. Watching a tow truck haul her car away. Teasing pieces of Anya's story out of her, one ugly detail at a time. Keeping Anya from telling what she knew on the ride home with Ronnie, blessed Ronnie, who never once asked why she had to collect them. Renting a car at eight a.m. in Traverse City, then delivering Anya into protective custody at the jail where Jimmy was asleep. Icing her eye and ankle before sleeping herself for an hour before stopping here on her way to the courthouse.

She walks around the desk – 'Excuse me' – and yanks the handle of a drawer next to her mother. The drawer flies out of the desk and clatters to the floor. Devyn reaches down and grabs a pack of AAA batteries, a legal pad, and two black felt-tip pens, then picks up the drawer and tosses it on the desk. 'You know what, Mother?' she says.

'What, dear?'

'Do you even give a shit whether Jimmy goes to prison?'

'Devyn. I put up his bail.'

'No, Dad put up the bail. His money, not yours. I have to go now. Please do us both a favor and do not show your face in court or I will ask to have you removed.'

'You can't do that.'

'You're right,' Devyn says, 'I probably can't have you dragged out, but I certainly can ask for it in front of about half the town. How about that?'

'How about bullshit, you didn't slip on any ice?'

At the jail, Devyn is glad to hear Anya is still asleep. The woman had a long night and, if the judge lets her testify, she's going to have a longer day. Devyn grabs a coffee and walks out to her rental car. She sits in the passenger seat and turns on the radio. A local newscaster is talking about today's court session. '. . . Richards, the hockey opponent Baker almost killed in a fight some thirteen years ago, is expected to take the stand in what . . .'

Devyn turns it off. From a pocket she pulls out a scrap of paper where she scribbled a few notes for her cross-examination of Richards: *Threw first punch. Violated NDA. Negotiating book deal.* Followed by a string of frustrated question marks: *???????*

How do you attack a man in a wheelchair?

And how will the prosecutor attack Anya if she testifies?

Devyn leans back, shuts her eyes. She's dozing off when she hears a noise outside. She opens her eyes to see someone standing over the front of her car, staring at her through hideous white-framed sunglasses. She blinks twice before recognizing Butch Dulaney. He has his arms folded across his broad chest and he's nodding as if he knows something she'd rather not know. She opens the door and steps out. He raises a meaty fist and brings it down on the rental's hood with a whump.

'Whoa, what are you doing?' Devyn says.

'Rental? Serves you right for driving a fucking foreign car.'

'Do I need to call an officer?'

'You know,' Butch says, 'pigs gotta eat too.' He grins again as he turns for the courthouse. Devyn yells after him, 'Thanks for the birthday card.'

SEVENTY

'I don't see him,' Jimmy whispers. 'Shouldn't he be here already?'

'Eyes front, Jimmy.'

'Speaking of eyes, did you get hit by a puck?'

'Stick,' Devyn says.

'Yeah? Is that also why you're limping?'

Devyn gives him a smart-assed smile. 'I slipped on my porch.'

'You don't have a porch.'

She swings around in her defense table chair toward the gallery. Jimmy saw it was full, as usual, when he was ushered in. But one person who has attended every session is conspicuously absent. Also, it's now ten-twenty and there's been no sign of Judge Esper, who has started the proceedings promptly at ten sharp each morning.

Devyn turns back to Jimmy. 'You're right,' she says. 'He should be here by now. Maybe he had some medical issue. Did he say anything to you?'

Jimmy pictures Cory Richards at the table in the jail. 'He said he'd be here.'

A bailiff bends down and whispers something to Devyn. She stands. 'I'll be back. Eyes front.'

The whole morning feels strange. Jimmy thought he noticed more police officers than usual guarding the entrances. Do they expect he'll be convicted today and will try to escape? That's almost funny. Klimmek, too, is missing from his usual seat behind the prosecution table. Even Devyn seems uncharacteristically distracted, never mind her black eye and limp.

He feels a tap on his shoulder and half-turns to see another bailiff standing along the gallery rail with Jimmy's brother, Alex. 'No touching allowed,' the bailiff says, stepping back.

Alex smiles. 'How you doing, Jimbo?'

Jimmy nods. 'Absolutely perfect. Beer after court?'

'Hell, yes. Hey, I'm sorry I didn't make it this weekend. Jamie got some bug and started throwing up and, you know.'

'You're a good dad. Anyway, it turns out I had a pretty interesting surprise visitor. Tell you later.'

'Good. I'm rooting for you, big guy. No way you did this. No way.'

'I hope you're right.'

'I know you feel responsible, because you always do, because you're always the responsible one. But you didn't do this. Those days are long behind you, Jimmy. I know.'

'We'll talk about it over that beer.'

'Or two.'

'That's enough now,' the bailiff says. 'Take your seat. The judge will be out shortly.'

SEVENTY-ONE

'First things first,' Judge Esper says. She's sitting against the front edge of the giant mahogany desk in her chambers, wearing a blue-and-gold fleece stitched with the logo of a hockey club from Starvation Lake. Devyn is in a chair to her left, Harris to her right.

Esper turns to the prosecutor. 'So he's a no-show?'

The look on Harris's face tells Devyn she either doesn't know the answer to Esper's question or doesn't want to admit it. 'I'm sorry, your honor, but we have not been able to reach him.'

'He has an attorney, right?'

'We haven't been able to reach her, either.'

'So, Mr Richards is a scratch for today and, I'm guessing, forever.' She nods to herself. 'When I was in your shoes, Ms Harris, I had a pivotal witness who decided the night before his testimony was perfect for getting drunk, stealing a car, and driving it into our pristine river. Through the ice, mind you. He was lucky not to drown, but I wound up having to prosecute him after dropping the case against the first guy. Justice, after all.'

'Sorry, your honor.'

'Don't be. Are you happy, Ms Payne?'

Devyn is relieved that Richards might not testify, but instead of copping to it, she says, 'Actually, I was noticing all the photos of hockey players on your credenza. I coached one and think I coached against another.'

Esper glances over her shoulder. 'We have almost enough for a full shift now. Two in midgets, one at college, one in a beer league in Kalamazoo. No goalies, thank heaven. All smarter than their father.'

'It's a great game.'

'Usually. What happened to your eye?'

'Caught a stick.'

Esper looks skeptical. But she says, 'What about this mystery witness? I'd like to – or, hold on – does the prosecution wish to formally object to Ms Paluk testifying?'

'Yes, your honor,' Harris says. 'She was sprung on us literally in the past thirty-six hours. We complied with defense counsel's request for protection, and we've taken good care of her. But we have no real idea who this woman is or what she plans to testify or, critically, whether she's even remotely germane to the case. At the very least, we should be granted time for some of our own investigating. Whatever Ms Paluk's testimony is, it's not about to go stale over the next few days.'

'Ms Payne?'

'Your honor, it was a struggle to get Ms Paluk to agree to testify at all. She's desperately afraid that those threatened by what she says will do harm to her or her family. If we wait, she could change her mind and—'

'You could subpoena her.'

'That won't guarantee her cooperation, your honor. She has worked up the nerve to take the stand now. We should respect that. Ms Harris will have every opportunity to impeach her on cross.'

'You say she witnessed the murder of Mr Diggs?'

'And Mr Hardy, your honor, although that is not at issue now.'

'Give me a hint as to how, please.'

Devyn reaches into her briefcase and produces a sheet torn from a yellow legal pad. She hands it to Esper.

'This is a map?' the judge says.

'Yes. Sorry, I'm not exactly a cartographer.'

'I can see that. So, locate this for me?'

Harris gets out of her chair. 'Your honor, may I?'

She motions Harris closer. 'Where is this, exactly?'

Devyn tells her how to drive from Bitterfrost to the house crudely etched on the map. Esper nods. 'I've probably driven past there a thousand times.'

'That's where Ms Paluk lives.'

'How do we know that?' Harris says.

Devyn goes back to her briefcase. She hands Harris some official-looking sheets stapled together. 'That is Anya – Ms Paluk's – lease.' Devyn's Tinder buddy Kurt helped with that. Harris takes it without a word.

Now Devyn gets up and, standing next to the judge, points to a place on the map. 'This is where Ms Paluk saw what she saw.' She moves her finger half an inch. 'She laid in the snow watching.'

'So she says,' Harris says.

Devyn retrieves another sheet from her briefcase and lays it in front of Esper and Harris. 'Ms Paluk was treated for frostbite the next day. Her fingers and her cheeks. This is her doctor bill.'

'For all I know, that could be for a Covid shot,' Harris says.

'M-hm,' Esper says, handing the map back to Devyn. 'This is not on point, Ms Payne, but I'm curious.' She pauses for a long moment. 'Several years on, what do you think about your handling of the Sawtell case? You don't have to answer, just don't bullshit me if you do.'

Now there's a question out of left field. It would be inappropriate in the courtroom, but here, in chambers, Esper can ask whatever she wants because none of it is on the record. Devyn sits back down. 'To be honest, your honor,' she says, 'I try not to think about it. It's in the past, and I did the job I was supposed to do. The jury acquitted him, I didn't.'

'But you've thought about it plenty these last many weeks, haven't you, Ms Payne? Again, no bullshit.'

'Yes, your honor, I have.'

'And what have you concluded?'

Even though the question doesn't bear directly on Jimmy's trial, Devyn knows she can't screw up the answer. She looks past Esper to the credenza and a picture of a teenage boy taking a slapshot. Devyn coached him on the Little Kings two or three years ago, and he had a hell of a shot for a skinny kid. His name is – Devyn strains to recall – Alden. She's grateful for the focus. She returns her gaze to the judge.

'Sawtell tried to tell me he was guilty,' she says.

'He did?'

'Yes. I stopped him.'

'My God,' Harris says. 'Your honor—'

'Quiet, Ms Harris, this doesn't concern you. You stopped him because you didn't want to know?'

'Correct. It's not my job to know.'

'But maybe you could've entered a plea. He might still be alive.'

'Perhaps. He never asked me to enter a plea, and the case was too hot for the prosecution to offer one. But I do wish they'd done a better job.'

'I've had a few murder cases in recent years, but I don't recall you participating,' Esper says. 'You didn't turn down clients because you thought they were guilty, did you?'

'I probably shouldn't comment on that, your honor.'

'Fair enough. Did you consider a plea for Mr Baker?'

The judge's inquiry now is bordering on inappropriate, but there's nothing Devyn can do about it. She wants Anya to testify. She did consider seeking a plea deal for Jimmy, for about the time it takes to tie a skate. 'No,' she tells Esper. 'Jimmy is innocent. Ms Paluk's testimony will prove that, and if she isn't allowed to speak, justice will not be served.'

'Well, well,' Esper says, then turns to Harris. 'Ms Harris, I've been in Bitterfrost now for more than fifteen years. I have to wonder if I've ever seen this Paluk woman. Have I?'

'Your honor, I couldn't—'

'Yes, your honor,' Devyn interrupts. 'You have. In the video.'

Esper turns to her. 'Which video?'

'The one from inside the Lost Loon on the night of the murders. She's sitting at the top of the horseshoe, around the corner from Diggs and Hardy.'

'That's the mystery witness?'

'The woman in the hoodie.'

Esper eases off her desk and directs herself to Harris. 'Did you or any of your people talk to this woman?'

Harris cannot bring herself to look at the judge. 'I'm afraid not, your honor.'

'Why not?'

'We tried but couldn't locate her. And we didn't think she'd add much anyway, given that what happened to Diggs and Hardy happened somewhere other than the Loon.'

'But Ms Payne located her. And I assume the woman's going to add something, is that right, Ms Payne?'

'Yes, your honor,' Devyn says.

'So,' Esper says, 'let me get this straight, Ms Harris: you want extra time to check out a witness you could have checked out months ago, is that right?'

'Your honor, we were focused on the best possible evidence, not some lush who happened to be in the same bar as the victims. We could have talked to every single—'

'A lush? Maybe you know more about Ms Paluk than you're letting on.' Before Harris can reply, Esper stops her with a raised hand. She walks behind her desk and sweeps her black robe off the back of a leather chair. 'Objection overruled,' she says. 'We will hear from Ms Paluk.'

SEVENTY-TWO

The three photos from the Dulaney forge are a shade dark and one is blurred in a way that suggests Charlie rushed. Klimmek responds to his text with a thumbs-up emoji, then shifts the phone so wife Kris can see. They're at their kitchen table with cups of tea with lemon. She's sugar. He's honey.

'Look at this thing,' Klimmek says. 'Reminds me of my old Sunfish.'

'I don't think your Sunfish could go underwater, though.'

'Nope. But I did, plenty.'

These semi-submersible boats nicknamed Bigfoot really do look more like the sorts of trainers Klimmek and his friends sailed as kids: nearly flat ovals, shaped almost like surfboards, about twenty feet long, with shallow, streamlined hulls made of what looks to be plastic or fiberglass.

'They call this a narco-sub?' Kris says.

'My half-assed online research suggests what the Dulaneys are making is much smaller than the submersibles used by the Mexican cartels to move product. But these smaller semis ride lower on the water and can travel almost entirely submerged. Very hard to detect.'

'By "product," you mean drugs?'

'Coke, heroin, fentanyl, and this new thing, really bad stuff, xylazine. Horse tranquilizer. All big sellers, of course. You can stow many millions of dollars' worth even in one of these littler subs.'

'I didn't know the Dulaneys were into drugs.'

'They might not be, yet.'

'Should you really be telling me these things, Garth?'

'Probably not,' he says. He picks up his tea then sets it back down without drinking. 'In fact, no. But I have to tell someone, and the people I'm supposed to tell don't want to hear it.'

'But should you even be *doing* these things? Are you sure the chief is going to reinstate you?'

'I'm not sure of anything, honey.'

'Except that Baker didn't do it.' She stands and picks up her tea. 'I think I've heard enough. I'm going to go finish my book.'

What Klimmek doesn't tell his wife is the bigger picture he's gleaned from Devyn Payne's digging, a couple of calls to Detroit cop buddies, and his own educated guesses. This Mario Rooney appears to be interested in establishing underwater smuggling routes along the Great Lakes linking Chicago's Mexican gangs to Canada and the Saint Lawrence Seaway. His associates the Dulaneys can build him the Bigfoot boats and Bitterfrost can provide the perfect unassuming landing spot, where the rink now stands. He doesn't doubt that Butch would be happy to have it restored to its former shipping glory, especially if he profited.

Somehow – hard to say why, with all the money to be made – Rooney and the Dulaneys got crosswise. At least that's what Klimmek and Devyn figure. Maybe Rooney sent Diggs to check out the scene. And then, perhaps, he sent Grbic, unless he really was with the Coast Guard, which Klimmek wouldn't bet a dollar on. All of them sacrificial lambs, along with the unlucky Jerome Hardy. Klimmek wonders if Diggs even recognized the Dulaney brothers that drunken night at the Loon. Maybe not. Maybe that's why he's dead.

Klimmek checks his watch. Ten thirty-eight. The trial should have resumed by now. Devyn texted ten minutes ago to say Judge Esper had yet to appear. But he can't expect her to keep him posted. He dials Philip Hardy's cell. It goes to voicemail. He's probably in court, but Klimmek tries his rental house anyway.

A woman answers. 'Mr Hardy's office.'

Klimmek isn't sure whether he should identify himself. Does this woman know her boss is talking to a suspended cop who is surreptitiously interfering with a murder trial? 'Good morning,' he says. 'Could you tell Mr Hardy his visitor from the other night is on the phone?'

'Excuse me?'

'He'll understand.'

Before Klimmek left the rental two nights ago, Hardy asked him for advice on how he could help 'spread the truth.' It surprised Klimmek, who assumed Hardy had an entire floor of media experts who could offer counsel. Yesterday afternoon, Klimmek scoured his email and texts for the many messages he'd received from newspaper reporters and TV producers and prepared a list of contacts that now rests next to his tea.

The woman comes back on the line. 'Mr Hardy is going to be tied up most of the day' – of course, Klimmek thinks, at the trial – 'but he'll try to return your call in the next few days.'

'The next few days? No. This is urgent. Can you please ask him again? Tell him it's Garth.'

She puts him on hold again, this time for closer to a minute. 'I'm sorry, Mr Garth,' she tells Klimmek. 'But Mr Hardy—'

'That's all right, Emmy, I'll handle it.' Hardy has jumped onto the call. 'Detective Klimmek?'

'You're not in the courtroom?'

'I have an attorney there. He said there's been a delay.'

Hardy's voice doesn't sound right. 'OK, well, I have the information I promised and can—'

'I'm sorry you went to the trouble, detective. I won't be needing it after all. I've had, I guess, a bit of a change of heart.'

What? Klimmek thinks. For a second, he doesn't know what to say. Then, 'How so, sir? You seemed pretty gung-ho the other night. You said you wanted to know the truth.'

'Yes, of course.' Hardy pauses. Klimmek pictures him standing at his massive windows, looking out toward the lake. Or who knows, he could be back in Detroit. 'I've reluctantly decided I'm going to step back and let the system do its work. I believe in our system of justice. I don't want to be out there criticizing it because I have a personal ax to grind.'

Our system of justice? That can't possibly be it. The savage murder of his son is an ax to grind? No. Someone got to Hardy. Maybe Quarton? Harris? Rooney? Is he afraid of his son being publicly connected to Diggs's doings? Klimmek walks out onto the back porch and closes the kitchen door. 'Forgive me for saying, Mr Hardy, but what about justice for Jerome?'

Another pause follows. Klimmek supposes the silence is supposed to underscore Hardy's moral advantage in this conversation. His kid died, therefore he can do no wrong. Klimmek has met a parent or two who've taken the same sad and perilous stance.

'First of all, detective,' Hardy says, a serration on his voice, 'I cannot bring my son back. Second, the wheels of justice are turning in Judge Esper's courtroom. I trust her and the police to bring this matter to a' – he hesitates – 'an acceptable resolution. An equitable one. For that matter, I trust you, detective. Didn't you spearhead this investigation? Aren't you the one who marshaled the considerable evidence against Baker?'

A text from Sylvester pops up. Anya Paluk, the woman he checked on for Payne, is taking the stand. Devyn is impressive,

Klimmek thinks. He says, 'I am no longer part of the investigation, sir.'

'I heard something like that. It's true?'

'It is. So, tell me, Mr Hardy, who got to you?'

'Pardon me?'

'You came to us in December demanding a culprit. Just like that, we gave you one. Then we get close to putting him in the stocks and you decide maybe we don't have it right – or at least that's what I heard the other night. Now you've had a "change of heart," to which I say, with all due respect, bullshit.' Klimmek knows he should stop now, for his own sake if not Baker's. But he can't. 'Guys like you don't have changes of heart. You'd have to have a heart for that. But you apparently don't. Not even for your son. Or Jimmy Baker. Isn't that right, Mr Hardy?'

Hardy clears his throat. Klimmek knows what's coming. He considers hanging up but doesn't do so fast enough. In the calm and measured voice of a rich and powerful man who rarely if ever gets dressed down, Hardy says, 'I'm sorry you feel that way, detective, but let me assure you that you don't really know what you're talking about. Anyway, given your current status, we shouldn't even be having this conversation. Thank you for calling. I wish you the best in your future endeavors.'

Klimmek finds Kris in a recliner in the family room. She lets the book she's reading, *Dead Man Running*, fall into her lap.

'Garth,' she says. She sounds alarmed. 'What happened?'

'I'm sorry, honey. I'm on my own.'

He explains. Kris gets out of her chair. 'You are never on your own, Garth,' she says. 'I'm going.'

'Going where?'

'To the courthouse. Keep your phone close. I'll have mine on with the volume as high as it'll go.'

SEVENTY-THREE

Devyn sits down next to Jimmy at the defense table. 'What happened in there?' he asks.

'We're good. Eyes front.'

He watches Harris take her seat across the well as Judge Esper hurries to her bench, robe fluttering behind her. 'All rise,' the bailiff calls out even as Esper waves for everyone to sit. 'Sorry I'm late,' she says. 'Ms Harris, you have no further witnesses?'

'No, your honor.'

'Ms Payne?'

'Your honor, the defense calls Anya Brygida Paluk.'

Harris stands. 'Your honor, we will object—'

'Overruled. Ms Paluk?'

Devyn leans over to Jimmy. 'You can look.'

Jimmy turns in his chair to see a slight, hunched-over woman, flanked by two uniformed officers, walking from the back of the courtroom. She's not in the orange hoodie she wore that night in the Loon or the next morning in Big Henry's, but he recognizes the face, round as a pie plate, eyes downcast, her lank hair pulled back in a single braid. She's in a simple blue dress Jimmy has seen Devyn wear at one IceKings gathering or another.

As Anya situates herself in the witness box, she lifts her eyes to Jimmy. They focus on his face for a full second, then flick away, betraying no emotion he can detect. He remembers leaving the Loon and how she ducked her head out from beneath her hood and said Diggs and Hardy deserved to get their asses kicked. Seeing this woman now, as vulnerable and seemingly helpless as him, Jimmy feels the desire to reassure her with the smallest of smiles. But such gestures, Devyn has warned him, can make jurors suspicious. Instead, he steeples his hands and sets his chin on his gnarled knuckles, giving Anya a nod that he hopes no juror perceives. If she notices, she doesn't show it.

'Ms Payne, the last-minute nature of this is a bit irregular,' the judge says. 'So before you proceed, let me make it crystal clear that if I sense or hear or think I sense or hear the witness say anything that sounds like a blatant untruth, I will halt the testimony immediately and have it stricken from the record. Am I clear?'

'You are, your honor.'

'Proceed.'

Devyn shuffles to the lectern in the well, favoring one leg. She opens the laptop she set there earlier, then walks to the witness box, hobbling a little. Jimmy rivets his gaze on Anya, who three times now has tried to settle her hands into her lap. He imagines Devyn coaching her in how to comport herself on the stand, where to look, where not, when to smile (if ever), where to put her hands. He's fidgety himself because he doesn't know exactly what Anya is going to say. Devyn told him only that she saw things. Important things. Devyn said she didn't want him to know so the jury would see him respond to Anya's testimony with genuine emotion. 'You might not like some of it,' she told him earlier.

'Anya,' Devyn says. 'I'm going to ask you some questions about the murder of a young man named Aaron Diggs.'

'I understand,' Anya says. She has a slight accent that reminds Jimmy of a Polish defenseman who once played for the IceKings.

'Did you know Mr Diggs?' Devyn says.

'No. Did not know.'

'But you're familiar with him?'

Jimmy recalls Diggs, in his clownish jacket stitched with all the fishing and hunting patches, drunkenly insisting that he pay the tab.

Anya nods. 'I saw him and his friend in the bar.'

'On that night?'

'Yes. That night.'

'Which bar was that?'

'Loon. Lost Loon.'

'Did you – do you – go there often?'

'Not too often.'

Probably true, Jimmy thinks. He can't recall another time he'd seen her in the Loon, although he wasn't there every night himself. He figures Devyn is seeking to pre-empt the prosecutor portraying Anya as a boozer with an unreliable memory.

'What time did you leave the bar that night?' Devyn asks.

Anya closes her eyes, then opens them. 'Almost the last hour.'

'Midnight?'

'Tak. I'm sorry, my Polish. Yes.'

'Thank you. And you went straight home from the Loon?'

'Yes. Home.'

'Where is home, Anya?'

She hesitates. Jimmy wonders if she's not as versed in the local geography as the lifelong Bitterfrosters in the room. He doesn't know how long she has lived here. Devyn told him only that she moved here to be with a man she'd met online. Nothing more.

'Five minutes one way, then right – no, wait, yes, right – ten minutes. On Gallesero Road. A house. Small house.'

Devyn returns to the lectern and taps on her laptop. An image of a digital diagram appears on a screen that stands on a table between Anya and the jury. The diagram displays the shape of a house to the north of Gallesero Road crossing west to east. Digital trees ring the house tightly on the east, west, and north. A narrow path between the trees directly north of the house leads to a clearing that is labeled MURDER SCENE. A small digital arrow points to a thicket facing the clearing, accompanied by another arrow-shaped label that reads ANYA.

The jurors shift in their seats to see the screen better. This is the first time they or almost anyone, Jimmy included, is seeing where the murders may have actually taken place. Jimmy glances over a shoulder at the gallery behind the prosecution, where Klimmek usually sits. He's not there.

'Do you understand this map, Anya?' Devyn asks.

'Yes. Good.'

Devyn points to the arrow indicating Anya. 'And is this approximately where you were on that night?'

'Looks OK.'

'What did you do when you arrived home from the Loon that night, Anya?'

'Make a cup of tea. Have something to eat.'

'What did you have?'

'Pierogi. Polish dumpling.'

'After that, did you finally go to bed?'

'No. I mean, I was going to sleep but there was noise.'

'There was noise where?'

'Outside.'

'Did the noise keep you from going to sleep?'

'Yes.' She closes her eyes for a few seconds. Then, 'Very noisy. Very loud. And lights. Bright lights.'

'So what did you do?'

'I went to look.'

'You went outside?'

'Yes.'

Anya is staring into her lap. Jimmy thinks he sees her shoulders shaking. He leans into the table and clasps his hands together. The courtroom is silent except for Anya's stifled whimpers. She lifts her head.

'Was not good,' she says.

Devyn gestures toward the jury. 'Please tell us.'

SEVENTY-FOUR

Devyn listens as Anya sets the scene. The vehicles – a sedan, two SUVs, two pickup trucks – formed a semicircle in the middle of the clearing, their criss-crossed headlight beams illuminating the silhouettes of six men. Jimmy was one. Two others knelt facing each other at the center of the pooled light, their hands behind their backs, one shaking with what Anya thinks were sobs. A woman stood off to one side, smoking. She turned away when the beatings began. An animal Anya believed to be a pig wandered among them, nosing the snow.

'Did you recognize any of those men? Or the woman?' Devyn asks.

Anya nods. 'Some. Yes. From the bar.'

'The Lost Loon. Earlier that night?'

'Yes.'

'Do you see any of them in the courtroom?' Devyn asks.

Anya points to Jimmy at the defense table.

'Was the defendant Mr Baker in the Loon?' Devyn says.

'Yes. And at the restaurant the next day.'

This surprises Devyn. Anya didn't mention the restaurant before. 'The restaurant?'

'The café. I spoke with Mr Baker. A little.'

'And did you tell him what you saw the night before?'

'No. I was . . .' She balks. 'No.'

'I see. Do you see anyone else from that night here?'

Anya surveys the gallery. She lifts an arm and her finger trembles as she indicates a man with a shaved head glowering in the back of the room. 'Maybe him, there.' Junior Dulaney, thin with a gaunt face spotted with scraggle, doesn't flinch. Devyn turns and sees Junior's brother DonDon sitting in the row immediately in front of him. She does not see Butch.

'"Maybe?"' Devyn says. Whatever weaknesses reside in Anya's testimony, Devyn seems determined that the prosecutor not be the one to bring them to light.

'I – I was not close to see so clearly.'

'Objection, your honor,' Harris says.

'Sustained. The jury will disregard.'

'And where were you at this time, Anya?'

Anya describes how she lay at the base of an oak, peering across the crest of a drift as the scene unfolded fifty yards away. Leaving her house, she'd pulled on a coat but hadn't thought to bring a hat or gloves. Once she saw the two young men from the Loon on their knees, she was too afraid to retreat home, lest she be dragged into the light herself. Lying in the ice-crusted snow, she tells the jury, she wished she'd stayed in bed.

'You could not see perfectly, is that correct, Anya?'

'Not. No.'

'Could you see this man?' Devyn points to Jimmy.

'Yes. He was there.'

'I'll come back to that. What about the woman? Did you recognize her?'

'Yes. It was my friend, Jordan.'

'Jordan Fawcett?'

'Yes.'

Devyn takes a thin sheaf of paper from a folder on the lectern. 'Your honor, if I may offer Exhibit 6A, which is a Mackinaw City Police report about an investigation into the apparent murder of Jordan Fawcett approximately four days after the murder of Mr Diggs.'

'Any objection, Ms Harris?'

'I don't see what connection this woman's death has to the case at hand.'

'Your honor, Ms Paluk just testified that Jordan Fawcett was at the crime scene that the prosecution never could identify. Then she was murdered herself.'

'The witness will answer.'

'Thank you.' Devyn is glad Harris didn't press on Jordan's identity, because it wouldn't serve Anya to delve into her and Jordan's apparently failed efforts to stop drinking. 'Now, Anya – I know this won't be easy – I need you to describe as clearly as you can what happened on that night in the field behind your house.'

Anya narrates the tale in the halting voice of someone who doesn't want to even remember what she saw and heard, let alone talk about it. Devyn stands close to the witness box so, Jimmy assumes, she can at least give Anya a reassuring look if she falters.

Two of the men on their feet began slapping and punching the bound men. One man pitched face forward into the snow and his assailant yanked him up by his hair and kicked him in the ribs, eliciting a strangled howl that Anya says she felt in her sternum. 'Please, God,' one cried out, 'someone help us,' and Anya feared her own whimpering would reveal her hiding spot. One of the attackers kept saying, 'Here's a message for your friend Mario, fuckhead.' And then he whacked the bound man in front of him across the face with the heel of his hand.

'Mario?' Devyn says. 'Who is Mario? Do you happen to know, Anya, who they were talking about?'

'No.'

'How could you even hear them?'

'They were yelling, quite loud.'

Devyn sneaks a peek at the jury box. The jurors are leaning toward Anya. Good. The woman she's been counting on is swiping her cheeks with a tissue. Better. 'You said there were two men who did the beating. Did this man –' again she points at Jimmy – 'participate in any of the violence?'

'Objection, speculation,' Harris says. 'It was dark, the witness was quite a ways away, and by her own admission, she was distraught.'

'You made your point,' Esper says. 'The witness will answer.'

'Again, Anya,' Devyn says, 'did the defendant Mr Baker commit any of the brutal violence you witnessed that night?'

'No. But they tried.'

'They tried? What do you mean they tried?'

SEVENTY-FIVE

They tried.

Anya is speaking, and as Jimmy listens, he's feeling the gloved hand at the scruff of his jacket, squeezing hard enough that the collar choked. He feels the nub of something hard poking his right ribcage. Maybe a gun?

When the young man in the jacket with the patches – Diggs – starts begging for mercy, Jimmy sees from the corner of one eye the woman bolt, screaming like she was the one being beaten. He feels himself being forced down into the snow, but then he looks up and sees Butch Dulaney chasing her and shouting something angry but inaudible. Before Butch reaches her, her car pulls away spraying snow.

Butch comes back, pulls Jimmy to his feet, and shoves him forward. 'Wanna join the fun?' he says. 'You wanted to fuck with these asshats? Be my guest.'

'What happened then, Anya?' Devyn says.

Jimmy winces.

'The man pushed Mr Baker toward the men on their knees.'

'Did Mr Baker cooperate with the man?'

'He dragged his feet, he tried to get away. But other men came.'

'And then what?'

'He – Mr Baker – he was on his knees. And the man had a gun.'

'Objection,' Harris says. 'How could she see in the dark from so far away.'

'I could see the headlights reflected,' Anya says.

'I'll allow it for now,' Esper says.

'What did the man want Jimmy to do, Anya?'

She takes a breath and brushes a stray hair from her face. 'He told Mr Baker to do it.'

'Do what?'

'I didn't know.'

'Did he threaten Mr Baker?'

'He said he would shoot him.'

'Shoot him where?'

'In the head.'

'Is that exactly what he said, Anya?'

She shakes her head. 'He said he would blow Mr Baker's head off. He used a swear word.'

'And what did Mr Baker do?'

'He tried to stop. He dragged his feet.'

'You mean he literally dragged his feet.'

'Yes. To try to stop them. But they took him to the man on his knees.'

Jimmy recalls scraps as Anya narrates. He knew the men who were yelling and pushing at him. The three Dulaney brothers. Butch had something in his hand that he kept pushing into Jimmy's neck. He was shouting and gesturing so wildly that he slipped in the snow and Jimmy leapt up and grabbed Butch and flung him to the ground, then again, and again, as Butch screamed for his brothers to get this motherfucker off him.

'Mr Baker threw him down like doll,' Anya is saying.

At the defense table Jimmy grits his teeth, pressing the fingernails of his right hand into his left palm.

'And that man who was throwing the other man down,' Devyn says, 'you're sure that was Mr Baker, the defendant you see sitting here today, yes?'

'Yes,' Anya says. 'I saw his face many times in the light. He was the same man who sat near me at the bar.'

'Thank you. Then what happened?'

'The other men, they pulled him off. Then he fell down. He stayed.'

'He didn't move?'

'No.'

'Like he was unconscious?'

'Objection. Speculative.'

'Sustained.'

Devyn presses on. 'Did you ever see him get up?'

'No. He laid there. Did nothing.'

Devyn sets a hand on the edge of the witness box. 'Then what, Anya?'

One of the men dug in a pickup flatbed and returned with what appeared to Anya to be a baseball bat. She saw it glint in the light as the man swung it over his head, laughing. Hearing this, Jimmy grits his teeth and presses his hands together until his knuckles turn white.

'Did you hear him say anything, Anya?'

'Something about tigers.'

'Tigers? Like animal tigers? Or maybe our Detroit baseball team?'

'Objection. Leading.'

'The witness will answer.'

'Yes,' Anya says. 'Baseball team.'

'Did he say anything else?'

The sound begins to echo in Jimmy's head.

'He said, "Time for batting practice."'

The sound of a baseball bat against a human skull.

'"Batting practice." Are you certain?'

'Yes. Because I raised up without thinking, and thought they would see.'

'What did you see then?'

'Put my head back. Down. Could not watch. Only hear.'

'And what did you hear?'

'I heard one, the sound of something –' she stops, closes her eyes, opens them again – 'something cracking. Like an egg. A big egg.'

'Anything else?'

She's shaking her head again, almost as if in disbelief. She says something Jimmy can't make out. 'Excuse me, Anya,' Devyn says. 'Can you say that again, a little louder?'

'The pig,' she says, blurting it, almost too loud. 'The pig. The snorts. The . . . the slurping. So . . . disgusting.'

'Objection, your honor, this—'

'Overruled.'

'Did you actually see what the pig was doing?'

'No.'

'Where did it even come from, Anya?'

'I don't know.'

Devyn returns to the lectern and picks up a sheet of paper. 'Anya, I need to ask you something you may find uncomfortable.' Devyn holds up the paper. 'You have a criminal record, correct?'

Shit, Jimmy thinks. That can't be good. But Devyn must assume the prosecutor knows and she's getting ahead of it. Anya stares into her lap again. 'That was long time ago. I was young. Stupid.'

'It was seventeen years ago, but you were convicted of aggravated assault on the man who was your husband at the time, is that right?'

'He was a bad man.'

'Noted,' Devyn says. 'You also perjured yourself in court. You lied.'

Anya shrugs. Jimmy wishes she didn't. Perjury is not the charge this jury needs to hear. 'I had to,' she says. 'But I am not lying now.'

Devyn turns back toward the jury box. 'Batting practice,' she says. 'Pigs slurping. A man unconscious—'

'Objection,' Harris says. 'This isn't time for closing arguments.'

'Sustained.'

'Nothing further,' Devyn says.

As she sits, Jimmy covers his face with his hands, not caring what she or the jurors or anyone might think, the pinging resounding again and again and again in his brain. Now he understands what that sound is about.

SEVENTY-SIX

Harris steps to the lectern. 'Ms Paluk,' she says, 'you've offered us a rather detailed description of what you supposedly saw from your little snowdrift. I'd like to review the circumstances of your experience.'

Devyn fully expects this. But it shouldn't be damaging. Devyn herself sought to bring out anything that could hurt her testimony in the jurors' eyes.

Anya nods.

'It was dark, yes?' Harris says.

'Except for the cars.'

'Of course, the headlights. Correct me if I'm wrong, Ms Paluk, but wouldn't those bright beams also have created shadows?'

'Some.'

'Some. And these various men you described were moving around in these shadows, yes?'

'Yes.'

'Is it possible, Ms Paluk, that you mistakenly thought one man was doing something when actually it was one of the others? Could you have confused who was who?'

'I don't think so.'

'Hm. And you are one-hundred-percent certain of that?'

'No.'

'Thank you. You testified that at one point you ducked your head down for fear of being seen, and you couldn't see, you could only hear. Is it possible you ducked in this way more than the one time?'

'I don't know.'

'You don't know?'

'I don't remember.'

'But it's possible that there were things you did not see?'

'Possible. Yes.'

'You were in the Lost Loon bar earlier that night. How much did you have to drink in the Lost Loon, Ms Paluk?'

'I believe' – she thinks about this – 'two beers and one whiskey.'

'You believe. Would your credit card bill for that evening reflect what you just said? Or would it show that you actually had a lot more to drink?'

'Paid cash.'

'Convenient,' Harris says, glancing toward the jury as she steps from behind the lectern, approaching Anya. 'So, Ms Paluk, where have you been?'

'I don't understand this question.'

'Three months have passed since Aaron Diggs was murdered. You say you witnessed his murder. And yet, for three months, you said nothing to the police, nothing to the prosecutor's office, nothing to this court. Why? Where were you? What were you – what *are* you – hiding?'

'I was not here.'

Devyn stands. 'Objection, your honor. What difference does it make where she was? She's here now, testifying. Under oath.'

'Sustained.'

'I was afraid,' Anya shouts. Devyn sees tears in her eyes. 'I know what happened to my friend Jordan. They would have killed me.'

Devyn sees Butch Dulaney again pounding on her car hood and asserting that pigs have to eat. Now she thinks she comprehends the meaning of the garbled text Jordan sent her mother: Don't let them feed mxjsfi!2s((.

Harris takes another step toward Anya and gestures toward the jury. 'You lied to good people like these before, didn't you, Anya?'

'I am not lying now.'

Harris turns to the jury, shaking her head. 'No more questions.'

Devyn stands. 'Re-direct?'

'Make it quick,' Esper says.

'Two questions.' Devyn remains at the defense table and puts a hand on Jimmy's shoulder. 'Were you afraid of this man, Anya?'

She shakes her head, dabbing at her eyes. 'No.'

'Who were you afraid of, Anya?'

Anya's gaze shifts again to the gallery. But her eyes can't find what they're looking for. 'Those men,' she says. 'From before.' Every head in the courtroom turns. The two Dulaneys are gone. 'They killed my friend Jordan.'

'Objection,' Harris says.

'Sustained. The jury will disregard. Are you about through, Ms Payne?'

'Yes and no, your honor. I have nothing further for Ms Paluk.' She looks across the well at Harris. 'But I would like to bring one witness back.'

'Which?'

'Detective Garth Klimmek.'

'No,' Harris says. She's on her feet, avoiding Devyn's glare. 'The defense had ample opportunity to cross-examine the detective.'

'Counsel approach, please,' Esper says.

Devyn and Harris proceed to the bench. Esper leans down. 'Ms Harris,' she says, 'I don't believe you objected when defense counsel asked to reserve another question or two with the detective.'

'Your honor,' Harris begins, but the judge cuts her off.

'Where is the detective anyway? I don't see him.'

'I don't know, your honor.'

'But I see his wife here. She's in my ceramics class.'

'Your honor,' Devyn says. 'If I may?'

'You may.'

'It is my understanding that the detective has been suspended.'

Esper turns to Harris, eyes wide. 'Is that true?'

'I believe it is.'

'Why?'

'I shouldn't say, your honor. I'm not his supervisor.'

'Really? OK. So we'd have to find the detective. Which shouldn't be too hard. How long would you need with him, Ms Payne?'

'One question, your honor.'

'One question.'

'I would ask if the detective still believes Mr Baker is guilty.'

Esper closes her eyes and lets loose a long sigh. She puts her reading glasses on, then takes them back off and lets them swing below her chin. 'What the hell are we doing here?' she says.

Part of Devyn – a big part, she has to admit – wants badly to have the case go to the jury, so at least one of Jimmy's peers can publicly pronounce him not guilty. She knows it's a selfish desire; she wants to think her defense and not the prosecution's screw-ups will free Jimmy. Like her mother told her over lunch in Petoskey, Devyn has the need to *win*. But she can't be one-hundred-percent sure of an acquittal.

'Your honor,' she says, 'I think you have grounds to call a mistrial and release my client.'

'Please,' Harris says, 'I think—'

'What you ought to be thinking about, Ms Harris, is why *you* didn't call Ms Paluk.' She bangs her gavel once and tells the courtroom, 'We will take a ten-minute recess.'

Devyn looks into the gallery. Her mother, sitting in the back row, offers her a smile. Devyn can't tell if the smile carries pride or defiance. Possibly both. She remembers something else her mother said at that lunch: 'If you lose, you might as well move somewhere else.' Devyn turns away, knowing that, win or lose, she can't stay in Bitterfrost.

SEVENTY-SEVEN

Three miles from the Dulaney property, Klimmek sees the smoke swirling black and gray into the sky. He dials Sylvester. He didn't wait to hear the cross-examination of Anya Paluk over Kris's phone. Listening earlier to Devyn's questioning, he realized Anya was the third anonymous call the morning Diggs was found. Alas.

He considers the night before that morning. The particulars of what happened – the body dumps, the half-assed attempt at torching Hardy's SUV, the disposing of the unconscious Baker – shouldn't be all that hard to pin down. But they embody a wholly different investigation that Quarton and Harris cannot now ignore. And with all that Klimmek now knows about the Dulaneys and Bigfoot and Rooney, motives shouldn't be difficult to divine.

He's dying to know some of the still-unknown details of that night. He has imagined some: One or two or all three of the Dulaneys choosing to deposit young Hardy's SUV within sight of Jimmy Baker's house, to help frame him. Junior and DonDon arguing over the perverse decision to bury Hardy in the excavation site near the rink; maybe one of them thought it was funny. One of them stuffing Jimmy's cellphone in the car seat so the cops might find it. Two or maybe all of them dragging unconscious Jimmy through the snow in his backyard to his kitchen. Their vehicles leaving the criss-cross of tracks in Jimmy's snowy drive. Klimmek also has pictured himself tracking down Anya Paluk before Devyn and heading off the disaster of Baker's trial. Instead he was chasing Baker, and Quarton, and Harris, and Hardy.

But at least?

The plumes of smoke rising from the Dulaney place give him a sour feeling. He knows, deep down, that it's his fault, his failing, his blindness, that led to this terrible result. Yes, Quarton and Harris rushed and bullied him, but he didn't have to let them. He blew it. Again. Like his friend Big Henry says, we see what we want to see, then we stop seeing.

His phone clicks. Before Sylvester can speak, Klimmek says, 'Got a hell of a fire at the Dulaney place. You need to send people.

A lot of them. Call the state boys in Gaylord and Traverse. And warn them all the Dulaneys may be – will be – armed.'

'Hold on. What?'

'Just do it. I'll be at the Dulaneys' in a minute.'

'Got it.'

'Reminds me. You grew up on a farm, right?'

'Yeah. Near Mio, other side of seventy-five.'

'Remember what you said the morning we found the bodies? Something about animal smells.'

'Yeah.'

'Pig,' Klimmek says. 'It was pig.'

He hangs up. He's only a mile away and can see spires of orange and red and yellow leaping beyond the stands of pine guarding the Dulaney property. 'Dammit,' he says. 'Dammit all to hell.'

SEVENTY-EIGHT

Ten days later

Devyn is boxing up the last of her summer clothes when her phone buzzes. The words BITTERFROST POLICE appear on the screen.

'Devyn Payne.'

'Sylvester here, counselor. Detective Klimmek wanted me to call.'

Devyn made out with Sylvester once under the bleachers at a high school football game. Things didn't progress from there.

'Now what?' she says.

'One of the Dulaneys is dead.'

'Which?'

'DonDon.'

DonDon's brother Junior is in custody. He found an Oscoda fishing captain who agreed to ferry him across Lake Huron to Canada, but the skipper's wife recognized Junior from the news and alerted the cops. Butch, always the smartest of the three, remains at large, probably in another country. On the last day of Jimmy's trial, the brothers disappeared by the time Klimmek and other cops surrounded the family compound, where they rounded up two wives, four children under the age of fifteen, and two older siblings. They were released after refusing to answer any questions.

'Poor DonDon,' Devyn says. 'How'd he die?'

'Gunshot.'

'Self-inflicted?'

'Doesn't look like it.'

'When?'

'Late this morning, early afternoon.'

'Where?'

'Uh, sorry,' Sylvester says. 'Confidential for now.'

'Where, goddammit?'

SEVENTY-NINE

The Hill-Top Motel sprawls in a semicircle on a gravel lot along US 131 between Mancelona and Kalkaska, a bit more than an hour's drive from Bitterfrost. Across the road, police have cordoned off a swath of forest with yellow tape. Klimmek doubts they'll find anything useful.

'He wasn't no trouble,' the proprietor, a seventy-ish woman named Carole, tells the detective and Devyn. Devyn rolled up five minutes ago, wedging her Toyota among the state and county cop cars parked at various angles around the lot. Klimmek didn't seem surprised to see her.

They're standing a few feet from an ice machine between rooms 210 and 211. Devyn wonders why a motel with only one floor would number rooms with the numeral 2. Pure Michigan, she thinks.

'I only seen him once a day,' Carole says, 'when he came to the office to pay his bill.'

'How long was he here?' Klimmek says.

'Let's see, uh, today would've been . . . four days.'

Too long in one place if someone is committed to finding you, Devyn thinks. But DonDon wasn't known for his smarts.

'Did you hear the shot?'

'I'm sorry to say I did not,' Carole says. 'And I was sitting right there.' She motions toward the office a few doors away.

'The shooter probably used a suppressor. Do you figure Dulaney was coming to pay his bill?'

'Dulaney?' Carole says.

'Sorry,' Devyn says. 'That's the dead man's real name. He probably used something else with you.'

'Yeah. He was Wendzinski or Wendowski or something like that. I'd have to look. Was he a wanted guy?'

'Wanted for murder in Bitterfrost,' Klimmek says.

'Well, I'll be,' Carole says, clapping a hand to the side of her face. 'I was harboring a fugitive? Am I in trouble?'

'No, ma'am. Could you give us a minute?'

Blood stains the wall next to the ice machine and a patch of concrete where DonDon fell. Local police already removed the body. Klimmek waits for Carole to close the office door behind her before he says, 'I don't like it.'

'It's bullshit, right? We're supposed to think Rooney did this.'

'Exactly. But Rooney's a butcher.' Klimmek motions toward the wall. The stain there is barely bigger than the palm of a hand. The bullet did its damage with minimal mess. 'This is the work of a paid professional.'

'Did the locals get a bullet?' Devyn says.

A Channel 8 TV van rolls into the lot and, even before it stops, out bounces the same reporter who was asking questions at the museum site when Jerome Hardy's body was found.

'They found one bullet,' Klimmek tells Devyn. 'A .338 Lapua Magnum. Popular with snipers.'

Devyn looks across the road, into the woods. She guesses the shooter would have posted up there and fired a single shot through DonDon's right temple. He was dead before he hit the ground.

'What are you gonna do?' she asks Klimmek.

'Did you ever notice Philip Hardy's hair?' he says. 'How it always looked exactly the same?'

The question catches Devyn by surprise, especially coming from Klimmek. Maybe he's jealous. 'You mean perfect?' she says.

'Yeah. I gotta make a call.'

'Detective Klimmek,' says the TV reporter as she trots up with her cameraman. 'Does this have anything to do—?'

'Go away, Tawny Jane,' he says, and starts walking toward his Bronco, Devyn in step. When the reporter follows, Devyn spins around and, backpedaling, says, 'Back off.'

The reporter stops. 'Maybe we could talk later? Off the record?'

Klimmek ignores her. 'So,' he asks Devyn, 'you're really going to leave us?'

'Looks that way.'

'Good for me, I guess. Maybe not for our fair town.'

'You mind if I listen in on your call?'

Klimmek steps up into the Bronco. 'What the hell,' he says. 'Follow me to Kalkaska.'

As Devyn waits for traffic to clear on US 131, a woman appears out of nowhere outside her window. It's Cat Dulaney, daughter of the dead man, who accosted Devyn outside the courthouse during the trial. Devyn considers pulling away but decides that would be cruel and rolls her window down. Cat steps closer, and Devyn notes that she looks quite pregnant. If she's been crying about her father, Devyn can't tell. 'I'm sorry about your dad,' she says.

'No, you're not,' Cat says. 'We know you and that detective did it. Or had it done.'

'That is not true,' Devyn says, but Cat scoffs. 'You were always a bitch, thought you were hot shit,' she says. 'Goddamn Paynes. Never got enough, do you?'

'Cat.'

'Go fuck yourself.'

She starts to walk away, then stops and turns and shouts at Devyn, 'We ain't done yet, bitch. You wait.'

EIGHTY

Klimmek sets his phone face-up on the Bronco's center console. Devyn's in the passenger seat. They're parked on the main drag outside the Kal-Ho Lounge. On the other side of the street, the plaque on a trout sculpture the size of an elephant boasts that Hemingway fished there.

'Five minutes till he calls back,' Klimmek says. He looks at Devyn. 'Your eye looks better. How's the ankle?'

'Not bad,' she says. 'I skated this morning.'

'Good. So, I've been thinking. There's a couple of things I don't quite get.'

'Yeah?'

'Like that pig.'

'What pig?'

'The one at the scene Anya testified about. How did it get there? I mean, the Dulaneys didn't carry it around with them all night.'

Devyn thinks for a second, then says, 'One of them must've gone to get it.'

'Holy Jesus,' Klimmek says.

'Twisted, all right. What else?'

'Why'd those guys downstate try to run you off the road? I mean, do you even know who they were?'

'Short answer is no. Could've been someone working for the Dulaneys, trying to keep me from my appointed rounds. Or could've been someone working for Rooney, trying to get me off the trial, like their guy Grbic, who was definitely not Coast Guard. Either way, serves their purpose. The Dulaneys wanted Jimmy convicted, for obvious reasons. Rooney wanted him out of the way so you guys would go after the Dulaneys. Or they could use whatever they knew as leverage to get a deal on the drug smuggling.'

'Makes some kind of sense, I guess. To a criminal.'

'At least the rink property is off the table, for now.'

'How'd they track you down in Hamtramck?'

'You got me. Another air tag?'

'Do you think that face you saw in the truck was Rooney himself?'

She shudders at the memory of those eyes. 'No idea. Maybe.'

'Why would the boss get personally involved in something like that?'

'Seems unnecessary, maybe even stupid. But as you know, "criminal mastermind" is an oxymoron.'

'Ah, there he is.'

Klimmek hits the button to answer the call. The voice of Philip Hardy's executive assistant comes over the speaker.

'Mr Klimmek?'

'Detective,' Klimmek says.

'Please hold for Mr Hardy.'

Half a minute passes. 'Detective, good to hear from you,' Hardy says. 'Glad to hear you're back on the beat.'

'Thanks.' Devyn watches Klimmek. He's staring at a hole in the windshield. She's not one-hundred-percent sure what's coming, but she feels oddly excited about witnessing it. 'Thanks for taking my call.'

'Why wouldn't I?' Hardy says, lightly, as if he's joking.

'Right. You have nothing to hide.'

Hardy goes briefly quiet. 'No, I do not.'

'Mr Hardy, I thought you'd like to know that one of the Dulaney brothers, the one they called DonDon, was shot and killed sometime in the past several hours outside a motel near Kalkaska.'

'That's terrible.'

'Do you know Kalkaska, sir?'

'Um, no, I can't say I do.'

'You might pass it on the way to your summer place in Harbor Springs. But I doubt you'd like Kalkaska much, sir.'

'I guess I'll take your word for that.'

'I never got a chance to ask what you thought about the outcome of the case against Mr Baker.'

'Are you asking me now?'

Judge Esper's ten-minute recess turned into an hour with Devyn and Harris in her chambers. The judge didn't have to bother calling a mistrial because Harris reluctantly agreed to drop all charges against Jimmy and restart the murder investigation.

'Yes, sir,' Klimmek says.

'What's with all the "sir" stuff, detective?'

'I'm asking your opinion, sir.'

'The case was all right, considering,' Hardy says. 'I thought, as I'd hoped, that justice was served.'

'"Justice was served,"' Klimmek says. 'Are you talking about the trial of Jimmy Baker, sir? Or this morning's news about DonDon Dulaney?'

'I don't follow.'

'It's today's killing, isn't it? Because this Dulaney or one of the others, or all of them, murdered your son, isn't that right? Justice is served because you got your revenge and you sent your message, right?' Klimmek is still gazing at some distant point down the street. Devyn loves what she's hearing even as she can't believe it. The detective is accusing Michigan's most powerful private citizen of murder.

'I don't know what you're talking about, detective,' Hardy says, as Devyn has heard from many a cornered culprit. 'But I will say this.' He pauses for effect. 'This case was too big for you. It was too big for Bitterfrost. And you all let it get away from you.'

'Did we?'

'Do you remember how I asked you at one point if this was just a local matter, or was there something bigger at play? You had no answer. Now you have a dead man on your hands and, who knows, perhaps more coming. Rooney was the something bigger, right? As I understand it, the Dulaneys and Rooney didn't get along any better than your Paynes and Dulaneys.'

Your Paynes? Devyn thinks, resisting the urge to jump in.

'Sir,' Klimmek says, 'there better not be "more coming."'

'Is that a threat, detective?'

'When we first met, you told us you had money and planes and anything we needed to, as you put it – I wrote it down – "get this matter resolved." You said, "Whatever is necessary."'

'I wanted to know what happened to my son. And you and your inept chief and prosecutor couldn't figure it out. Defense counsel did a better job than you did, detective.'

'You're dead wrong about that, Hardy,' Devyn says.

There's a pause on the speaker, then, 'Ah, Ms Payne. What a surprise to hear you eavesdropping on what I thought was a confidential conversation. My mistake. But it was your mistake not to reach out to me, Ms Payne. We could have avoided so much mess. But now I'm afraid I have to get back to my life without my son.'

The call ends with a click.

'Sorry, Garth,' Devyn says. 'I just—'

'It's fine,' he says, still staring.

'What are you going to do?'

He turns to her. 'I'm gonna buy you a farewell beer.'

EIGHTY-ONE

Devyn packs her gear bag the same methodical way she has for years: Skates first, terrycloth jackets on each blade, each skate in its own compartment. Between the skates she tucks her waterproof sack filled with tape, scissors, stick wax, Aleve. Next the gloves go in, palms up. Helmet, its plastic bubble shield wrapped in cotton. Shin guards, side by side, elbow pads snuggled into each. Shoulder pads draped across everything, her bulky pants on top of those.

She zips the bag shut, heaves it onto a shoulder, and slams her locker door. All that's left inside are a worn-out stick and a leaky water bottle. She could toss them in the trash, but she wants Jimmy to find them and think about her after she's gone.

She finds him in the Zamboni shed, his legs protruding from under Zelda. It's almost midnight on a Thursday. Devyn and Jimmy are the only souls left in the Calvin & Eleanor Payne Memorial Ice Arena.

'Better late than never, eh?' he shouts from under Zelda.

'Ah,' she says. 'Finally got the new blade?'

'Yup.' He slides out on his butt and gets to his feet. He's in safety glasses, grease-stained jeans, and a grimy IceKings sweatshirt. He tosses the glasses on his workbench, which is lit by a lamp hanging overhead. 'Got us a shiny new blade. And a spare, too.'

Devyn sees the second blade leaning unboxed against the bench. She's never seen a Zamboni blade up close. It's an impressive piece of machinery, a thick, gleaming silver wedge that is longer than Devyn is tall.

'A little *too* late for the team, though, huh?' she says.

The IceKings lost their last two regular season games the weekend before, falling short of qualifying for the league play-offs. The players have packed up and dispersed. Evan has vowed to rebuild what was once a perennial league power. Devyn wished him luck when she told him she was leaving Bitterfrost for good.

'Yeah, well, the boys weren't going anywhere anyway.' Jimmy grins. 'Too many distractions.'

Including Jimmy himself. The fans who supported him during the trial cheered his homecoming with Zelda. The ones who'd wished him gone resigned themselves to his return or canceled their season tickets.

Devyn says, 'I didn't see your truck in the lot.'

'Nope. Been walking from the house. Good for clearing the head.'

'Lots to clear.'

'Yep. Any idea where you're gonna be skating next?'

Devyn lets her hockey bag slip to the floor. 'It's gonna be a hike from Hamtramck no matter where I play, but I'm guessing Hazel Park's closest. Or maybe Dearborn.'

'Doesn't that Hardy guy own a rink downtown?'

'Shut up, Jimmy.'

Grinning, Jimmy walks to the workbench and wipes his hands on a rag. 'So I hear Junior's flipping, huh? Ratting Butch out?'

'Shit, Butch is a ghost. But no surprise on Junior. Funny, Hoover told me Junior and DonDon almost got into a fight themselves about where to dump the bodies to best frame you. And where to stash the baseball bat.'

'They never did find that, did they?'

'Not yet. You know, Jimmy, I wish I could be here to see Junior sentenced. Would be good to see Klimmek back in action.'

'Without you there to torture him.'

'Jimmy, he saved your ass.'

'No, Dev, you did.'

Or, she thinks, maybe that deer on I-75 did.

Jimmy drops the rag on the bench. 'I really wish you weren't going.'

'Thanks, Jimmy. I'll miss you.'

'Yeah,' he says, turning back to Zelda.

She thinks Jimmy might actually be choked up. She says, 'Lemme know when they catch up with Butch, eh?'

'Bad guy, Dev. A really bad guy. I should have . . .' His voice trails off.

'I should have worked harder on him.'

'Wait,' Jimmy says. 'Was that "should of" or "should have?"'

'Stop. How's Avery?'

Jimmy turns back to her, looking grateful. 'She's great. Just had a face-thingy with her. She's headed to a volleyball camp in California next month. I'm going.'

'Noelle's fine with that?'

'Avery's fine with it.'

'Cool. Please give her my best.'

'I will. Maybe you can come see her play next season, since you'll be in the area.'

'For sure.' Devyn nudges her hockey bag aside with a foot and steps closer to Jimmy. 'I've been meaning to ask you something.'

'Shoot.'

'When you left the Loon that night, why did you follow those guys?'

Jimmy leans on his bench. He's silhouetted against the window behind him, through which Devyn can see the rink lying still and silent in the dimming overhead lamps. She'll miss that, too.

'You asked me this before,' he says. 'I told you, I don't remember.'

'And I didn't press it because it was useful to your defense. But you were on Diggs and Hardy's trail *before* the Dulaneys got their bright idea and grabbed you and drugged you. This is just us now, Jimmy.'

'Why do you care?'

'I care because I want to know if you thought you were going to take care of Diggs and Hardy yourself.'

He blinks. In disbelief? Shame? 'What do you mean, "take care of?" If you mean kill them, the answer is no. As far as I can recall, I never intended to kill or even hurt them. Although I could have. I want to think I was making sure they'd get out of town.'

He wouldn't have had to intend murder to do serious damage, as Cory Richards could attest. For Devyn now, triumph and regret are both within reach. She chooses the former. 'Not guilty then,' she says. 'I better get to bed. I'm headed downstate at the crack of dawn. I'll come visit, if only to see my girl Zelda.'

Jimmy holds his arms out. 'Hug?'

They embrace, Devyn pressing her cheek against his chest, surprised at how hard his heart is thumping. She gently pushes away.

'Lemme take your bag,' he says.

'Nah, I got it.' She slings it over a shoulder. 'Stay in touch.'

She enters the darkened corridor she has walked so many times. Past the concourse where she sneaked her first beer, a three-dollar-and-fifty-cent Pabst Blue Ribbon, when she was fifteen. Past the double doors where Zelda, and before her, Xavier, rolled onto the ice to the utter delight of so many friends and neighbors. Past the face-off circle where Devyn stood afternoon after afternoon trying to teach the wobbly girls and boys of Bitterfrost how to play the greatest game. She stops there, in a shadow at the south-east corner of the arena, for a last look.

The sandpaper heel of a hand slams into her throat and propels her backwards off her feet, her bag flying from her shoulder. Devyn twists her head just enough that it doesn't bounce off the concrete floor. 'Pig for pigs,' she hears a voice croak. 'That's for my brother.' She tries to scream for Jimmy but her windpipe won't let her do much more than gasp.

Butch climbs on top of her, trying to pin her between his knees as she strains to wriggle free, his beard scratching the sides of her face, her stomach convulsing at the reek of alcohol mixed with tobacco dip slithering past her nostrils. She manages to roll onto one side and blindly throw an elbow that hits something she can't see. 'Bitch,' Butch says, his voice pinched.

She connected somewhere because he loosens his grip and she clambers up and away and runs back toward the Zamboni shed. Butch catches her by a foot and she goes down again. 'Just me and you now, honey,' he says. 'If I'm all done, you're all done.' He must have followed her here and assumed the sole car in the parking lot meant she was alone.

'Jimmy,' she tries to yell, her throat catching again. She looks up. She's lying in front of the door the refs use to enter and exit the ice. If she can get out onto the ice, she thinks, maybe she can get away. She reaches for the door latch as Butch tries to yank her back and she jerks her foot out of her shoe and jumps up, fumbling at the latch. She tries to shout again but can't. She wrenches the door open and flings herself face down on the ice as Butch's hand brushes the back of her coat. 'Bitch,' he says again, his voice a guttural growl. She scrambles away toward the face-off circle to the right of the goal crease. She minces along on a shoe and a stock-inged foot, hearing Butch huffing up behind her. She glances back and her shoeless foot slips out from under her. She tumbles down between the face-off circles and slides onto her back. There's Butch, moving toward her, an aluminum baseball bat in one hand. Devyn looks toward the Zam shed. The lamp over the bench is still on. She tries to shimmy away but in seconds Butch is standing over her, leering, gripping the bat in both hands.

'Butch,' she croaks. 'Don't.'

He laughs. 'You think this is a fucking Batman movie? You're gonna talk me out of it? I'm already dead, so you're dead, too. And by the way, where the fuck are those laces you owe me?'

He raises the bat. Devyn closes her eyes. She hears Butch scream as something wet and warm sprays her face. She hears Butch scream again. She opens her eyes. Butch is in a heap on the ice, howling. Devyn swabs at her face. Her fingers come away bloody. She gets up on an elbow. Butch is squirming a few feet away, blood spurting from the back of one of his legs, steaming as it streams toward her.

Jimmy, in those safety glasses, stands over Butch. He's holding the spare Zamboni blade in both hands like his own baseball bat, slowly raising it as if he's going to swing it again.

'Jimmy,' Devyn rasps, straining to push the words out of her bruised throat. 'Call the police. An ambulance.'

He's not hearing. The look on his face, cold and bloodless and horribly blank, is like none Devyn has ever seen, not on her most wretched clients, certainly not on Jimmy Baker. It frightens her more than Butch's bubbling blood, more than the gurgling sounds he makes beneath his whimpers.

'No, Jimmy,' she pleads. She struggles to her feet. 'Stop. Please. Jimmy. Penance. Every day, Jimmy. Right now. Stop.'

He looks at her, his eyes welling, his chin trembling, the Zamboni blade hovering in the air behind his right ear. He's saying something, or trying to say something, but it's too soft for her to make out. He's standing directly over Butch now, the blade poised to strike.

'Jimmy,' Devyn says. She takes a step toward him. He swallows hard. He shakes his head. The blade clangs to the ice behind him.

Now she can hear him speak.

'Don't go,' he says.

Acknowledgments

Thanks for reading, folks. I hope you liked it.

Part of this work of fiction was inspired by a superb book of non-fiction, *Darker Than Night* by Detroit journalist Tom Henderson. I thank him for his richly detailed reporting and evocative writing.

I'm indebted to the good people at Severn House, especially Victoria Britton, the commissioning editor who committed to publishing this story. Vic has moved on to a new challenge in which I wish her the best while hoping that our paths cross again. Vic's replacement, Laurie Johnson, helped finish this project with grace and intelligence. I'm also grateful for the support of Severn House Publisher Joanne Grant and the work of Rachel Slatter, Martin Brown, Piers Tilsbury, Nick May, Lianne Slavin, and Mary Karayel in bringing *Bitterfrost* to the world.

Many others helped me either by reading *Bitterfrost,* answering questions or offering advice and encouragement. Thanks especially to Jim Thomsen, Anna Quindlen, and Jonathan Eig for their close reads. Also: Ric Bohy, Jim Casurella, Sharon Doering, Joanne Doucette, John Galligan, Keir Graff, Steve Hamilton, Michael Harvey, Mark Hornbeck, David Kocieniewski, Dave Poulin, Joe Reid, Misha Skoric, Simone Stock, Steve Taylor, Dan Tompkins, and Lisa Zupan. Northern Michigan attorney Ron Varga gave me invaluable advice on the world of defending criminals (after a kind introduction from another helpful Michigan lawyer, Jim Harrington). Chicago police detective John Campbell gave me advice as well as his copy of the definitive text on homicide investigation by Vernon J. Geberth. Detective Klimmek paraphrases a classic Geberth line about knowing only that you have a dead body in the woods. My friend Eduardo Perez-Chavez took me for a fun and educational Zamboni ride at Chicago's glorious Johnny's IceHouse. I might never have published a single novel without the help of Trish Grader, Shana Kelly, and Suzanne Gluck many years ago.

My wife Pam has been an early reader of all my novels and is endlessly patient with and supportive of my fiction (alas, she'd also like to see less hockey in my books). Nothing inspires me more than watching our three children and their partners bring up our beautiful grandkids: Asger, Six, Deenie, Miles, and Sawyer. Their laughter is the most delicious music of my existence. I must also thank the many hockey teachers I've been lucky to skate with over the decades, especially the Shamrocks, the YANKS, the Clammers, and every beer-leaguer in Detroit, Chicago, Washington, and Florida. Keep your heads up!